Praise for *The Heart o*
prequel to *Hope lik*

"Pepper Basham weaves a stunning tale of suffering and hope set in the heart of Appalachia. Blending romance, humor, and history, *The Heart of the Mountains* reveals a God who not only heals the broken but redeems hearts in ways no one can imagine."

—Tara Johnson, author of *All Through the Night,*
Where Dandelions Bloom, and *Engraved on the Heart*

"*The Heart of the Mountains* is a world created with exceptional skills by Pepper Basham. It immersed me in the mountain life until I could see the scenery, smell the plants, hear the mountain breeze and the bird calls. All of that was wonderful, but more than that was the way I felt as I read. The hurt, the love, the longing, the loss, the fear, the joy. Basham created a beautiful, emotional work of art. I enjoyed every word."

—Mary Connealy, bestselling author of *The Element of Love*

"Pepper Basham's *The Heart of the Mountains* has a perfect title, as her story reveals the hearts of her characters as they face one challenge after another in their mountain community. You'll hardly have time to catch your breath from one exciting scene to the next. Great characters, great setting, great background history. Great story! You won't want to miss it."

—Ann H. Gabhart, bestselling author of *Along a Storied Trail*

"Exciting. Moving. Humorous. Touching. *The Heart of the Mountains* touches every sense. With characters that are strong and determined and a story that moves like honey dripping from the comb, Pepper Basham has nailed this Appalachian story. Set in 1919, Basham draws the reader in with the strength and sassiness of Cora Taylor. She grasps the era, the mountains, and heart of the people of the mountains. This must read will find you flipping page after page and sad when it ends. Pepper Basham's work is exquisite."

—Cindy K. Sproles, author of Christian Market Book Award,
Novel of the Year, *What Momma Left Behind*

"*The Heart of the Mountains* is a beautiful story of second-chances, redemption, and finding home. Filled with breathtaking scenery, heart-tugging encounters, and tender romance, this latest story by Pepper Basham will leave you feeling as if you've just spent time in the dangerous, yet fascinating, Appalachian Mountains."

–Gabrielle Meyer, author of *When the Day Comes*

HOPE LIKE
Wildflowers

PEPPER BASHAM

BARBOUR
PUBLISHING

OTHER BOOKS BY PEPPER BASHAM

Hope Between the Pages
The Red Ribbon
Laurel's Dream (My Heart Belongs in the Blue Ridge)
The Heart of the Mountains

A Freddie and Grace Mystery:
The Mistletoe Countess
The Cairo Curse
The Juliet Code

Hope Like Wildflowers © 2024 by Pepper Basham

Print ISBN 978-1-63609-951-4
Adobe Digital Edition (.epub) 978-1-63609-952-1

All scripture quotations, unless otherwise noted, are taken from the King James Version of the Bible.

Scripture quotations marked ESV are from The Holy Bible, English Standard Version®. Text Edition: 2016. Copyright © 2001 by Crossway, a publishing ministry of Good News Publishers. The ESV® text has been reproduced in cooperation with and by permission of Good News Publishers. Unauthorized reproduction of this publication is prohibited. All rights reserved.

This book is a work of fiction. Names, characters, places, and incidents are either products of the author's imagination or used fictitiously. Any similarity to actual people, organizations, and/or events is purely coincidental.

Cover Model © Idiko Neer/Trevilion Images

Published by Barbour Publishing, Inc., 1810 Barbour Drive, Uhrichsville, Ohio 44683, www.barbourbooks.com

Our mission is to inspire the world with the life-changing message of the Bible.

Member of the
Evangelical Christian
Publishers Association

Printed in the United States of America.

Dedication

To the amazing women in my family,
past and present, who have been "caught by Jesus"
and passed their love for Him down to the next generation.

Thank you.

Chapter 1

October 1917, Oak Plains, NC

A HIGH-PITCHED HOWL SPLIT THROUGH the shadowed dusk, echoing against the towering pines of the forest. Its haunting refrain incited a chill over Kizzie McAdams' skin.

Her attention shot toward the sound, but the twilit woods gave no visible answer. She didn't have to see the wild glowing eyes to know what followed her in the dark.

Coyotes. Her breath snagged on the very thought.

With a tighter grip to her tattered travel bag, she stumbled forward, her protruding abdomen contracting into a hard ball of needled pains. The spasms had been coming more regularly, but she wasn't sure how seriously to take them. Pain knifed a little deeper as if in answer.

Sunset bowed to nightfall's cloak, lengthening the shadows along her path, its last golden-red hues dying into the gloaming like a foretaste of her immediate future.

Her body shivered from the mixture of her pain and her thoughts.

No. She rubbed her palm over her stomach. She had to keep going. Only a little longer now. A mile? Maybe less?

Charles Morgan's land waited on the other side of the woods. If she could only get to him, he'd take care of her. He'd told her he loved her.

Her hand smoothed against the tightness of her stomach.

And this baby.

After all, if people love you, they take care of you, don't they?

The question echoed back to her in mockery, and the renewed memory of her daddy's unrelenting words barreled through her mind.

You done ruint yourself, girl. And I ain't got no place for ruint young'uns.

Her breath lodged in her throat.

Charles had to help her.

She hobbled a few more steps, her unbalanced weight paired with the uneven terrain slowing her progress. Her attention raised to the thin gold band clinging to the horizon like the finish ribbon in a footrace.

Just a little farther.

She glanced back the way she'd come, the forest leaving no trail of her slow journey. Fresh tears threatened her vision, and she almost laughed at the impossibility of their presence. How did she have any tears left? She'd cried on and off for the last two months, moving from one closed door to another. After leaving her parents' house deep in the Blue Ridge Mountains, her daddy's angry rejection and her mama's pleas replayed over and over in her mind.

"Don't cast her out, Sam," her mama had begged.

The sober faces of her siblings as they watched Kizzie take the long trek down the road from the only home she'd ever known haunted her.

But Daddy had disowned her.

Sent her away forever.

And she'd never see them again.

With what little money Kizzie had, she'd attempted to find a job in various towns over the last two months, but no one wanted to hire a pregnant woman without a husband to claim.

Each place offered the same rejection, the same glances of shame.

So she'd wandered until she used up the last of her money and decided she only had one place left to go.

Her body ached. Dirt caked beneath her fingernails and in her hair. The boys at school had once called her the prettiest girl on the mountain, but no trace of that girl existed now. Leaves knotted in her dark hair, and scratches from the forest left marks along her arms and cheeks. She wasn't sure how bad they looked, but her tears alerted her of their presence on her face.

The last three nights, she'd slept on hard, cold forest ground, dreaming of the warmth of her family's cabin, only to wake up hungrier and more alone than the day before.

Another howl, much nearer than the last one, interrupted her sob.

Kizzie dashed away the tears and pushed her sore feet into a faster pace.

Her stomach roiled from tension and hunger, any satisfaction from the beef jerky and stale biscuit of last night's supper long gone.

Up ahead, a faint light filtered into the darkening forest.

Was that a house through the trees? Her stomach tightened again, slowing her stride.

Leaves rustled in the shadows behind her, a steady rhythm drawing closer.

Something was following her. Running.

More rustled leaves.

Her face chilled.

"Help me," she cried into the night.

The flickering light through a window blinked into view. "Please. Help."

The yip of a coyote warned her of her assailants. Another howl erupted so close it raised the hairs on the back of her neck.

Perhaps she deserved this fate. Her choices. Her mistakes.

What sort of mother could she ever become with such a wretched beginning?

But her little baby didn't deserve it.

A growl rumbled from behind, sending chills skittering over her shoulders and forcing her into a run.

"Help!" she called again as the front porch of the house emerged through the gathering dusk. "Somebody, please. Help me."

A boom of gunfire crippled Kizzie to her knees, and a warm rush of liquid ran down her legs.

Dear heavens. Had she been shot in the stomach? A renewed ache gripped her back.

What on earth?

Another blast thundered from ahead, followed by a yip of pain behind her. At least the gunman aimed for the coyotes, whether he was welcoming to a castaway or not. She pushed past her own hurting and rose from the ground.

Up ahead, the silhouette of a large man marched toward her, fading sunset glowing orange behind him and obscuring his face. A mountain of a man, with shoulders wider than the surrounding pines.

He raised the gun again, firing into the forest, and another coyote's cry responded.

The pain in her middle withered her to the earth, but she shuffled backward in the dry leaves as the massive man drew nearer.

"You 'bout got yourself killed, girl." The deep rumble of his voice percolated with a strange combination of steel and tenderness. "Let's get you outta these woods."

He tossed the rifle over his shoulder and offered a hand. Kizzie reached for it, her legs wobbly. The man caught her up before she wilted back to the ground, his face nearer, skin as brown as walnuts, eyes even darker. "Miss Kizzie?" He released a long sigh and glanced over the forest again. "What are you doing out here in the night?"

Joshua Chappell. Kizzie's bottom lip wobbled. A friend.

"Joshua." She eked out the name on a sob. Of all the people to find her!

She started to say more, but another pain racked through her, inciting a cry.

"You're hurt, young'un." He made a quick turn and increased his pace toward the house. "Let's get you to Nella. She'll know what do."

A sudden sense of safety whooshed over her, like nothing she'd known in months. Strength, calm, protection. Joshua and Nella Chappell were some of Charles' best tenants and had made her feel welcome since the first day she'd walked onto the Morgan land to take a job as a housemaid.

Almost a year ago now.

Kizzie pressed her face into his shoulder, the tears spilling down her cheeks as the pain brought another whimper.

He walked faster.

She'd known such loneliness, so much grief over the past few months, but a sense of safety from Joshua Chappell's arms poured through her, strengthened her. Her shaky sigh breathed out with some of her fear.

Even if they knew the truth, the Chappells wouldn't cast her out, would they?

The glow of lantern light swelled into the darkness as Joshua's boots hit the wood of the porch steps.

"What are you dragging into this house, Joshua Chappell?" came the distinctive voice of Joshua's wife. "We can't take on no more stray critters—"

Joshua turned, the lantern light from the porch glowing fully upon them, halting Nella's words.

"Have mercy! Kizzie McAdams?" Nella stepped aside from the door's threshold. "What on earth was you doin' out in them woods this time of night?"

"I. . .I'm sorry, Nella." Kizzie sniffled a reply.

"I think she's hurt." Joshua moved past his wife to deposit Kizzie on a chair near the small fireplace alight with flames. "Something ain't right."

Firelight gave the small room a cozy feel. She released a deep sigh and pressed back as far into the curved wooden chair as her body allowed. Her feet ached. Her head throbbed. And the unusual twisting in her stomach nearly brought on a bout of nausea.

The Chappells' three children sat at the small table in the next room. Ruth, Elias, and Isaac all stared with wide eyes, Isaac with his spoon still in the air as if in midbite.

Nella replaced her husband at Kizzie's side, her dark eyes scanning over Kizzie's entire body. "What are you doin' lookin' like you ain't seen a washstand in days? When was the last time you ate?" She plucked a leaf from Kizzie's hair and showed it to her. "You know it ain't safe in them woods on your own, girl, especially come nightfall."

Kizzie wasn't sure if Nella really wanted an answer with the sudden onslaught of questions, but she ventured on answering the first. "I ain't had no place."

"Ain't had no place?" Nella repeated, her voice pitched higher. "You mean to tell me, you been sleepin' out in them woods for heaven knows how long?" Her brow puckered. "And why is that?"

Kizzie ran a hand through her dark hair, more loose than pinned up. "I was coming back from my parents' house after. . .after a short visit."

She looked away, tears beginning another rise in her eyes. The last thing she wanted was to share her shame with someone else, especially the good Chappell family. Disappoint someone else.

"You *walked* from up near Maple Springs?" Nella's gaze grew in intensity, more questions in those eyes than Kizzie had any interest in answering. "That's over twenty miles of mountain paths."

Kizzie refused to elaborate that she'd walked much farther than the distance from Maple Springs if she counted all the towns she'd wandered through along the way. And her body felt every bit of it.

Another pain sliced through Kizzie's middle. She pressed her palm over her hardening abdomen and sent Nella a look. Discretion was becoming increasingly difficult, especially at the moment. "I. . .I don't know what's wrong." She lowered her voice, her gaze flickering to Joshua. "I think Joshua's gunshot scared me so bad, I lost my water."

"Lost your. . ." Nella surveyed Kizzie from face to dusty boots, pausing on her middle. With a deep sigh, her eyes drooped closed for only a second, and a renewed wash of heated shame rose from Kizzie's chest into her face.

Did Nella know? Or was she only embarrassed at the fact that Kizzie, at such a growed-up age, had lost her water?

After focusing another second on Kizzie's face, Nella turned to Joshua and some unspoken exchange sent him into motion.

"Boys, get your things. We're havin' an overnight in the barn loft."

The two boys jumped up from the table with happy cries and ran up the narrow steps nearby.

"Ruth." Nella stood and shifted her attention to her daughter. "Get some willow bark from its drying place in the barn and return directly."

Ruth glanced from her mama to Kizzie and then, with a slight nod, left with her daddy and brothers out the front door.

The room fell quiet and Nella lowered back to Kizzie's side. "How far along are you?"

Nella's words brought Kizzie's gaze to hers. "What. . .what do you mean?"

"The baby ain't gonna stay inside forever, girl. And I reckon you didn't lose your water in the sense you're thinkin'." She released a long sigh. "It's likely the beginnings of the baby comin', so there ain't no use pretendin'."

Kizzie's eyes pinched closed. "I've. . .I've tried to hide it."

Another sigh drew Kizzie's attention to Nella. "I had my suspicions a month afore you left. . ." Her gaze dropped to Kizzie's small round stomach, made all the more prominent by the way the dress curved around her in her sitting position. "You can hide a lot behind an apron, but women know. Though you ain't gained near to nothin' with this baby, so I can see how you could keep it a secret for a while." Her gaze flitted to Kizzie's face. "But Mr. Charlie's interest in you ain't been no secret."

Kizzie's smile wavered into place. "He says he loves me."

Nella's brows tipped, her expression saying something she didn't voice, but whatever it was stripped Kizzie's smile right off her face.

"And you ain't sure how far along you are?"

Kizzie shook her head. "No, but I've felt the baby movin' since summer."

"Summer?" Nella rocked back on her heels, studying Kizzie with more intensity. "When did you have your courses last?"

Kizzie looked away. Nobody talked so openly about such a thing.

"Ain't no use in gettin' prudish now, Miss Kizzie, not with your baby on the way." Nella stood. "We need to know how to prepare."

How to prepare?

One of the unfortunate by-products of moving down to the Morgan farm to work as a housemaid meant leaving her mama's gentle instruction behind, but even her mama didn't talk about courses or how babies came to be. Though Kizzie had learned the latter one on her own. "I've never been good at tracking it, since it don't seem to come regular like my sisters' do, but I. . .I ain't had one since early spring." Another pain took her breath, deeper, sharper.

Nella waited for the pain to pass and then took Kizzie by the arm. "We need to get a place ready for you and that baby." She walked Kizzie through a tiny door to a room with a large bed in the center. Likely Nella and Joshua's room. "When Ruth gets back we'll have you chew on some willow bark to help ease the pain, but ain't nothin' gonna take the pain away. Givin' birth is one of the hardest pains God made. Here's hopin' for your sake, it'll be short. But 'twould be wise for you to walk or stand as long as you're able, to move the birthin' on." She took Kizzie by the shoulder, her expression sobering. "And since we don't know how far along you are, then it'd be wise to prepare yourself."

Kizzie looked up from bracing her hand against the iron spindles at the end of the bed. "What do you mean?"

Nella rounded the bed, bringing another blanket from a simple wardrobe on the other side of the room. "The stress of the walk and the chase with the coyotes could have put you into early birthin', and the baby may not be ready to be borned."

Not ready to be borned?

All warmth fled Kizzie's body.

If the baby ain't ready to be borned. . . ?

The baby would die.

Nella stepped close, her lips pinched. "You ain't heard much about bein' with child?"

"Only enough to make me wonder or scared."

Nella's lips twitched. "Those are both good and human feelings, and that's a fact." She frowned, capturing Kizzie's gaze in her own steel one. "You listen to me, girl. Listen to me, and we'll sort this out with the Almighty's help. You hear?"

Kizzie nodded, squeezing the bed spindle tighter as the pain swelled all around her middle now. How she needed God's help. But she dared not ask. If her own father wouldn't offer forgiveness, why would God?

She'd sinned against Him and her family and even this little baby.

Why would He want anything good for her at all?

She leaned forward, holding on to the bed through another pain. *But for the baby, God? Would You help take care of the baby? He ain't done nothin' wrong. Please.*

If the Almighty wouldn't listen to Kizzie's prayer, maybe He'd listen to Nella's. . .and save this baby.

A new cry broke through Kizzie's.

Small, high-pitched, and loud.

Every part of Kizzie's exhausted body froze, the physical relief giving way to a sudden rush of awareness.

Her baby?

"He ain't much for size, but he's got a good caterwaul on him." Nella grinned up at Kizzie as she wrestled a wriggling bundle into a towel, her forehead as damp with perspiration as Kizzie's own. "That's a good sign for sure."

He? Had Nella said 'he'?

"A boy?" Kizzie croaked the words out, her throat dry. "Did you say my baby's a boy?"

"I sure did." Nella tucked the towel around the little one and walked to Kizzie's side. "I'm gonna give you a peek of him and then hand him to Ruth for a quick minute so's we can finish up with you. Then you can hold him to your heart's happiness."

A small red face, wisp of hair plastered to his damp little head, peeked above the towel. His crying began to quiet, and two large blue eyes blinked wide.

"He's. . .he's beautiful." Kizzie reached out and touched the towel, her fingers brushing the baby's cheek. He quieted even more.

"Well now, he knows his mama's voice, don't he?"

His mama? She looked from her son to Nella, the pronouncement sinking deep.

Something changed inside her. Her role shifted. Her identity. She was no longer just Kizzie McAdams. Now she was a mother.

And someone small and fragile relied on *her*.

"We'll get him washed up." Nella slipped the baby into Ruth's arms. "You got the bowl prepared for him, don't you, girl?"

"Yes, ma'am," came Ruth's quiet response as she stared down into Kizzie's son's face. "He sure is little."

"He is that," Nella agreed, returning to the bed. "Which is why I had you set them towels and that washbowl by the hearth. You keep that baby as warm as you can. Only uncover little parts of him to wash, then bring him here once you're done." Nella nodded toward Kizzie, her expression softening into a small smile. "His mama will want him."

And so it was within ten minutes, Kizzie held her little son in her arms.

Nella told Kizzie she'd be back with a biscuit and meat and left her alone in the room with her tiny babe.

Those little eyes stared up at her, his fingers stretching out, so she offered one of hers. He fisted her finger, tightening the indescribable feeling she had for this little person even more.

All the emotions crowding in bordered on overwhelming.

How could she love someone so much when she'd just met him?

Her smile fell. And how would she take care of him?

The magnitude of their current situation hit her afresh, and she tightened her hold on her son.

"I'll protect you, little one," Kizzie whispered. "You're mine."

She looked upward, her throat tightening. Whether God had heard her own prayers or Nella Chappell's, Kizzie whispered a quiet "Thank You." Even if she was a fallen child, undeserving of God's love, perhaps He still appreciated gratitude.

And just maybe, He loved her little baby with a bigger love than Kizzie's shame.

Her son began moving his face toward her chest, a strange grunt-like noise rising from him. His little grunts grew in volume.

He needed something. But what?

Nella reentered the room, plate in hand, and took in the scene. "Well, looks like Mama ain't the only one who's hungry." She set the plate down nearby and approached the bed. "I imagine once he eats, he'll go on to sleep and give you a chance to rest."

"For all of us to rest," Kizzie said, searching Nella's face. "I can't thank you enough for what you've done, Nella. I promise, I'll leave as soon as I'm able."

"Hush now." She pulled a chair closer to the bed. "Ain't nobody gonna make smart choices after sleepin' in the woods for who knows how long then givin' birth to a baby. You're plumb tuckered out, and it's a miracle from heaven you ain't took worse to goin' into birth on such little sleep and food. God must have more work for you to do, Kizzie McAdams."

Kizzie looked up into the woman's eyes. Nella's expression held a deeper knowledge and, maybe, hope?

She couldn't imagine God had much for her to do with the mess she'd made of everything so far.

Running away from home for a "better life."

Becoming pregnant outside of marriage.

Now, penniless and homeless with a little baby in need of much more than she had to give.

Kizzie drew in a breath as her son became more aggressive, his mouth pursing against her blouse.

"Here now." Nella moved closer. "Your boy is lookin' for some food, and I can see by your eyes you ain't got no notion 'bout what to do, so let me give you some learnin'."

Within only a few minutes, the baby quietly drank, his little fingers flexing and opening against Kizzie's blouse in time with the sound of his happy feeding.

Nothing but her son's noises filled the silence for a few seconds. And then a sudden exhaustion swept over Kizzie, tugging at her eyelids. She rested against the pillows.

"I reckon, with you comin' back to the Morgans', your daddy and mama sent you away?"

Nella's words held no judgment or pity. Just fact.

"Mama would have had me stay." Kizzie swallowed through her tightening throat, sliding her fingers over her son's small head. "Daddy was drunk, but I reckon he'd have come to the same decision drunk or sober." Her eyes warmed with a new wave of tears. "I'm an outcast to them."

Nella nodded, her dark hair somewhat loosed from the tight braids she usually wore. There was no telling what Kizzie's hair must look like. "Whiskey makes the best of men fools or villains." She stood and walked to a nearby table where some of the soiled towels waited. "Though, like any mountain man, he's got that pride to nurse, ain't he? Acceptin' you back in after what you done might make him look weak among his other kin, and I reckon he wonders at what sort of future you'd have."

She paused by the bed again, those dark eyes of hers holding Kizzie's attention. "You're gonna need to be strong, girl. The world won't treat you or your young'un kindly. You need to press in to the Lord. He'll give you strength and hope." Nella placed a palm on Kizzie's arm. "He embraces the outcasts. Renews their joy."

"I can't change what I've done."

"No, you can't." Nella shook her head, but the light in her eyes never dimmed. "You'll live with your actions like we all do, but you don't have to live without hope or purpose. You're gonna need Him, Kizzie, 'cause there's a good chance you're gonna be on your own. Few men are keen to marry a woman in your situation."

Kizzie fought against the thought, despite the tremor in her heart. "Charles says he means to marry me."

"But you went to your parents?"

The question gnawed at the back of Kizzie's mind, but she rose to the defense. "He can't marry me just yet, but I know he means to. He loves me, and he's gonna love our baby."

"I ain't sayin' he don't have a preference for you, girl. I seen it with my own eyes." Nella sighed and moved toward the door, her lips pressed tight. "But he's a respectable, rich man, Kizzie, and fit to become richer once his mama dies and he inherits his daddy's land as his own. Rich, respectable men don't marry poor, unwed mamas."

"But he *will* marry me, Nella." Even though Nella had spoken the words gently, they stung like barbs. "Just you wait and see. He's promised. As soon as his mama dies, he means to make me his wife."

Nella took a few more steps toward the door, gaze still fixed on Kizzie. "Press into the Lord for your strength, Kizzie McAdams, 'cause there's a real good chance Charles Morgan's mama is gonna live forever."

Chapter 2

Five days and Charles Morgan hadn't come.

The morning after little Charlie's birth, Joshua had gone to the Morgans' grand home in the center of their three hundred acres to privately deliver the news. From Joshua's report, Charles took the news with a smile, asked after Kizzie and the baby's welfare, and promised to arrive as soon as he could get away.

Of course, as the son of the prominent Morgan matriarch and heir to his father's property, Charles had responsibilities to attend to. So she shouldn't nurse any disappointment that he failed to arrive.

And of course, the action meant nothing as far as Charles' real care. Kizzie couldn't expect him to drop everything to visit her when he'd sent her to stay with her parents for the birthing.

Kizzie stared at the sleeping baby wrapped tightly in a sling against her chest, a sliver of hope still entwined with Charles' last words. Just maybe—she smiled down at her little one—Charles took his time because he was making plans of his own.

Plans for a wedding.

The faintest wish, inspired by the few fairy tales her mama spun to her and her siblings, unraveled within her breast, much like the feeling she'd had the first time she'd seen Charles Morgan.

He'd appeared in the doorway of his grand home, late afternoon sunlight at his back and a laugh in his voice. Every daydream she'd ever conjured about a handsome man settled directly on his head as she peered around the corner from behind a chair where she knelt, cleaning up a broken vase Mrs. Morgan had thrown in a fit of temper.

That woman lived with as much of an unpredictable nature as Kizzie's daddy, and Mrs. Morgan didn't even take whiskey.

It hadn't taken long at all for Charles to notice Kizzie among the servants, finding her in various places throughout the house. First complimenting, then encouraging her to talk, then kissing her...and by slow degrees, she gave herself, heart and all, to him.

The small size of the Chappells' house kept the little family nearly on top of each other when they were all home together, but the love between the five of them came through in their interactions. Joshua held a more quiet, strong presence, teasing Nella and the children in his own way, and Nella fueled the life of the house with her energy and "sass" as she called it.

Kizzie had been known for her own "sass" back home as the fourth young'un of a large family, but somewhere along the last several months, she'd lost her fire. Had it been from her shame? Or the tension circulating under Mrs. Morgan's heavy hand? Or maybe she was afraid if she got too fiery Charles would up and leave her be?

Too much quiet time sent her thoughts in dark places, so once Nella allowed, Kizzie joined in with the chores. As Nella and Ruth washed laundry in the barn, Kizzie cleaned the house. Nothing too taxing, but some simple sweeping or washing dishes, sometimes even helping with the meals, much like back home. And, just like Mama, Nella knew which herbs to use for healing and made up some tea to help with Kizzie's afterpains and aches. She even offered guidance with caring for Charlie, just as Kizzie's mama would have done.

It was a mercy Kizzie didn't deserve after the trouble she'd caused the Chappells, but her options proved incredibly small at the moment.

Kizzie's throat tightened as she scrubbed an iron pan, the renewed ache of her last view of her parents slicing through her chest. When the drink wore off, her daddy would regret his actions, but he'd never go back on them. 'Twasn't the way of mountain men.

Their word hardened like steel, even if their hearts softened.

She couldn't return home.

Her attention lowered to the sleeping babe at her chest, and she firmed her will against the weakening grief. Someone else relied on her now, and she needed to think about him. And the future.

Though she wasn't too sure what that future looked like.

She couldn't stay with the Chappells forever.

If only Charles would arrive, she'd have a better idea. He'd sent her home to be with family during the final stages of her pregnancy, but since home hadn't taken her—her throat tightened at the flicker of another memory—surely, Charles would do right by them.

The front door opened, and a rush of heat rose from her stomach into her face.

Could it finally be Charles?

A stomping sound accompanied the doors creaking, and her pulse slowed.

Not yet.

Isaac Chappell emerged from around the corner, book and papers in hand. With a heavy sigh, he crashed down into a chair at the little kitchen table, his books colliding with the wood. Thankfully, not loud enough to wake Charlie, though, if what Nella said about babies feeding often was true, her little one was due to wake soon.

"What's got you all flustered, Isaac Chappell?"

"Cipherin'." The boy raised dark weary eyes and pushed a book across the table towards her. "It's gonna kill me dead."

Kizzie twisted her lips tight to keep from grinning. "I ain't never heard tell of addition and subtraction leading to someone's demise, but I know it's caused my little brother, Isom, a heap of trouble."

"Ain't nobody can learn it. If we was meant to need more than ten fingers for countin', why didn't God give us more?"

"'Cause I reckon He figured you'd be able to do without them fingers for countin' once you learned how to use your mind for it." Kizzie slid into the chair next to him and drew the book close. "I always liked math in school. Not too bad at it either."

"You like it?" Isaac looked at her as if she'd grown an antler from her head.

"Well enough." She leaned toward him, offering a smile. "We could study on it together, if you want?"

He raised a doubtful brow, his frown deepening before he heaved out a hefty, "All right."

Kizzie moved closer, careful not to squish little Charlie, and asked Isaac to point out his current assignment.

"Ah, division." Kizzie nodded at the place he marked. "It can be a little tricky, and that's a fact."

"Don't make no sense a'tall." His voiced raised in protest. "Numbers cain't just disappear, no matter how you put 'em on the page."

"They ain't disappearing like magic. They're disappearing like when your mama makes some good corn bread and there's nary a piece left at the end."

"That ain't because of math." His nose crinkled with his frown. "That's 'cause we're hungry."

"And your mama cooks real good corn bread." Kizzie nodded and raised a brow. "But there's math happenin' too." She reached over and took a clean sheet of paper from his notebook then ripped it into smaller squares.

"That's what I want to do to my math page every time I see it."

Kizzie pinched her lips against a chuckle, attempting to show appreciation for the boy's struggle. "Well, I'm pretending our paper is corn bread."

He nodded. "Then that would be Granny's corn bread, 'cause it kinda tastes like paper."

Her laugh escaped. "Well, let's pretend it's your mama's corn bread for this example, all right?"

"I ain't gonna eat it." He crossed his arms. "Especially for math."

Her laugh burst out again, and it felt good. How long had it been since she'd laughed? And just within a minute she'd done so twice. Maybe she needed more folks like Isaac in her life. "I wouldn't want to eat paper for math's sake either."

"Good." He nodded, studying the papers on the table. "But I don't see how we're gonna get math from paper corn bread."

"You pretend acorns are grenades." She narrowed her eyes at him. "I think you can dip down in that smart head of yours and pretend paper is corn bread."

A slight twinkle deepened his dark eyes along with a flicker of a dimple at the corner of his right cheek.

"Now, let's say we got five pieces of corn bread here." Kizzie counted out five pieces of paper. "And there's the five of y'all wanting the share equally. How many pieces can each person get?"

"I'm giving Daddy that one." He tapped one of the largest pieces. " 'Cause he been workin' all day long and's gotta keep up his strength."

"That's a fine answer for sure," Kizzie said. "But no matter the size, it's still just one piece. Size smarts'll come in handy when you're learning fractions."

"Small folks is faster than big'uns." He pinched his lips tight at the declaration.

Kizzie's eyes narrowed as she tried to follow the conversational turn. "Usually so."

"Which means I already got some size smarts." The glint resurfaced in his eyes. "And I'm faster than Grandpaw."

Another chuckle bubbled up. "I bet you are, but back to the corn bread. How many pieces does each person get?"

"That's baby math." He smirked. "Five pieces for five people. Each get one."

"And. . ." She placed more pieces with the current papers. "If you have ten pieces of corn bread, how many does each person get?"

"That's baby math too." He rested his chin on his hand. "Two."

She shrugged a shoulder. "Baby math or not, you just did division."

His dark eyes rounded. "I did not."

"You sure did. Division is just how numbers are divided by other numbers like how you divided that corn bread for people." She gestured toward him. "What if your mama made a whole bunch of corn bread. Twenty-five pieces for your family. What then?"

He studied on the idea a minute, murmuring under his breath. "Now four would only get to twenty, wouldn't it?" His face lit. "Five. We'd each get us five."

"That's right. So it's multiplication backwards." She nodded, embracing the warmth of doing something to give back to this family who'd done so much for her. "Five times five is—"

"Twenty-five," he shouted. "Well, I'll be! It *is* like multiplication backwards."

Kizzie grinned and stood as Charlie began to squirm awake against her chest, likely helped on by Isaac's enthusiasm.

"What you say to Miss Kizzie helpin' you out, boy?"

Kizzie glanced up to find Nella leaning against the doorway, her smile soft.

"Thank you kindly, Miss Kizzie." Isaac tagged a grin onto his gratitude, and a gentle warmth swelled into Kizzie's face.

"It's no trouble a'tall, Isaac." She stood, dusting her hands off on her skirt. "I'd be happy to help any time."

Kizzie stepped toward the other room to adjust Charlie against her for a feeding, and Nella followed, tugging off her soiled apron from the washing. "You have a way with young'uns."

Kizzie sent her a smile. "I reckon I ought to be used to 'em. I got five younger siblings." She ran a hand over Charlie's little fuzz of golden hair. "Though brothers and sisters ain't nothin' like caring for your own child."

"But it's a good trainin' ground so you ain't caught off guard quite as often as you would be if you hadn't had those siblings." Nella nodded toward the kitchen. "I'm glad you was here to give him some help."

"It's the least I can do for all y'all have done for me and Charlie." Kizzie patted Charlie's back as he made happy eating sounds. "I don't know where we'd be if not for your family." A chill skittered up her spine. "Food for coyotes, I reckon."

Nella's brows bunched, and she gave her head a shake. "I ain't never had a good mind for figures."

"We all got our different smarts." Kizzie grinned. "I ain't no good at writing letters, plus my penmanship is rotten. But math?" Her smile quivered a little, the recollection softening her response. "Well, I reckon I got it from my daddy. He has a good mind for math and measuring, like no one I've ever seen. He can just see the numbers in his head for a piece of furniture or buildings and. . .make it."

"You any good with working figures for business?" Nella sent Kizzie a measured look. "Like managin' a business or savin' for one?"

Kizzie's thoughts flitted to a conversation she'd overheard between

Joshua and Nella the day before about saving to buy their own land instead of being beholden to the Morgans. And Joshua had plans to start his own mill with skills he'd learned from working in Virginia a few years back.

"Nothing as big as my own business, but I helped manage a little grocery back home and learned a heap about tending a store. Me and my sister Laurel would take turns stayin' with Mrs. Cappy, and she had no trouble giving us as much responsibility as we wanted." Kizzie grinned. "Or didn't want, but she used my love of math a lot with keeping her books and helping with inventory."

Nella studied Kizzie a little longer and then dipped her chin. "You know, we ain't expectin' nothin' in return for you bein' here, Kizzie. Ain't never expected nothin'. But if you've a mind to help us out, I think I know a way."

"You mean about wanting your own place? Opening up a shop of your own too?"

Nella nodded. "But Joshua and me, well, we didn't get school as young'uns. Wasn't no place for us." She gestured to the kitchen. "Not like we're givin' to our own. We could both use some learnin' with numbers and plannin'."

Kizzie's jaw dropped a little. "You want me to teach you math?"

Nella's gaze never wavered. "If you're willin'."

"I ain't no teacher, Nella." Kizzie drew in a breath. "But if there's something I can teach you, I'll be happy to try."

"We'll take whatever you can give us." She waved around the little house. "Workin' your whole life for somebody else's property ain't where we want to stay. The world's a changed place since my parents came out of the war betwixt the states. If we can have our own home and land, and even shop, then we're willin' to work hard for it."

Kizzie had never put much thought into working for another person without having ownership of your own place. People in the mountains valued their land, their homes. But tenants gave part of their hard-earned produce or skills to the landowner in exchange for a place to stay.

Not their own.

"I don't have one doubt about that." Kizzie's lips tipped. "And I'd love to see you have your own place."

"That'd be mighty fine indeed."

The sound of men's voices came from the front of the house, breaking into their conversation. Kizzie's body stilled. Her attention focused on the familiar timbre of one of the voices. Her attention flew to Nella, heat draining from her face.

She should be excited.

Charles had finally come.

She gripped the side of the chair, her breath lodged in her throat.

Why was she so skittish?

Nella's gaze dropped to the sling, and Kizzie turned her back to the door, gently tugging little Charlie from his meal, covering herself, and placing him up on her shoulder.

"You stand tall, girl." Nella touched Kizzie's arm. "You ain't got no reason to hang your head to that man. He's your baby's daddy, and you ain't done no more wrong than him."

The front door opened, and in walked a smiling Charles Morgan, looking as wonderful as the first time Kizzie had seen him with the sunlight behind him and his hair blowing wild about his head. He reminded her of a picture she'd once seen in a book at school of a Greek god. Until she caught sight of Joshua behind him. Kizzie blinked. Next to Joshua, Charles really wasn't so tall and those broad shoulders she'd always admired seemed narrow and small in comparison.

Charles came to a stop in front of her, a look of wonder softening his entire expression as his focus shifted from Kizzie's face to the little bundle wiggling against her shoulder.

Yes. This was what she'd hoped to see. This awe at the sight of his firstborn son. The look any good daddy ought to show in light of such a sweet miracle.

He shifted a step nearer. "This. . .this is. . ."

"Charlie." Kizzie tipped her chin up at the announcement, her palm tightening on the baby's back.

Charles' gaze shot to hers, the faintest tip to one corner of his mouth. "Charlie?"

He stared at the baby like he'd never seen one before as Joshua and

Nella silently slipped from the room.

The warm glow of the hearth cast a soft light on Charles' features, drawing Kizzie closer to him. "He's been sweet so far. Hungry often, but so sweet."

"I'm glad." Charles leaned in, looking down at his son. Charlie stared right back with similar intensity. "My son."

The whispered response squeezed through Kizzie's heart. Yes. His son. And their little family. Kizzie shifted the baby in her arms. "Do you want to hold him?"

Without a word, Charles drew in a deep breath and wiped his palms down the sides of his slacks in answer. Kizzie's smile softened. He proved quite the sight, fumbling around like a schoolboy, when all she'd ever known was the confident landowner or dashing suitor. Perhaps the future wasn't so terrifying after all. All Charles needed was time to adjust to the idea of a wife and child.

Kizzie transferred the baby into his arms, taking in the wonder of Charles' response. "He...he has light hair like me," he said.

Warmth branched through Kizzie's chest. Hope, all the way from Charles' voice to her heart. "He sure does."

"But blue eyes like you." Charles glanced up, holding her gaze, his smile crooking in the way it did when she remembered first falling beneath his spell.

She'd never had a man look at her the way he had.

Speak to her the way he did.

She'd felt every bit like Cinderella in the presence of her handsome prince.

Heat flooded her face, and she lowered her attention to their baby, slowly bringing her palm up to cup little Charlie's soft head. "Nella says he's strong, even though he's small. He eats like he's trying to catch up though."

Charles took hold of one of Charlie's fingers, the connection creasing the man's smile even wider. "He is strong." Charles caught Kizzie's gaze. "Like you, I hear."

She raised a brow.

"Joshua told me about your daddy and the coyotes."

"Yes." Kizzie looked away. "The Chappells have been real good to me and Charlie."

He cleared his throat. "I'm sorry I didn't come sooner."

She searched his eyes for any hint of deception. "Are you?"

"I should have come as soon as I heard." He nodded. "I'd hoped your family would help you for however long necessary, but. . . I spent yesterday making a plan, one I should have thought of from the start."

She held her breath, her smile on the brink of unfurling in anticipation of the one question she'd wanted him to ask since kissing him. "Plan?"

"It's the perfect plan." His eyes sparkled as he reached out to run a thumb down her cheek. "I've already given the Petersons notice."

Kizzie blinked out of the fog his touch started in her head. The Petersons? The family that lived on the far side of the Morgan property? What did they have to do with her future?

"They'll be out of the house by next week, which means you and Charlie can move there as soon as I make some improvements to make it suitable for you and my boy."

The words failed to make sense.

"That house is in the best location for you. Nearer to town, only a few miles from the Chappells'." Charles nodded back toward the way Joshua and Nella disappeared. "I've already asked Joshua to help keep an eye on you."

"You. . .you want me to take Charlie and live in the Petersons' house?" The statement came slowly, still not making sense even when spoken.

"Well, it's not really the Petersons' house. It's mine." Charles urged Charlie back into her arms. "And it will be yours once you move there. It's one of the best pieces of land I have on the property."

"And. . ." Realization began to dawn, a slow, sinking feeling curling in her stomach. "You won't be there with us."

"Of course I'll be there when I can." He ran a hand through his hair and stepped back. "But the land requires me to work from the main house to take care of things."

Her jaw tightened. "Then why can't me and Charlie come stay with you there?"

"Kizzie." He ground out her name, nothing like how he'd said it earlier. "We've talked about this. There's no way I can marry you until my mama dies."

Pain pulsed in her chest, but she stepped forward. His mama was closer to Kizzie's granny's age than her mama's but still, not too old. "I didn't say marry. I said stay with you."

"You know that can't happen, since we're not married. And if I marry you. . ." He waved toward her, and the action stung, dismissive. "Somebody without any money or status, my mama will disinherit me, and then we'll have nothing."

"But. . ." Her desires and expectations wrestled against his offering. Didn't he, at least, offer her something? A home? "When will we get married, Charles? I can't stay unmarried to you and sharing your bed forever."

He rested his hands on her shoulders, his smile resurrecting but not reaching his eyes. "I've wanted to marry you since the first day I saw you, but without my inheritance, I can't offer you anything."

"Your heart is a good start."

His gaze softened. "You have that already. You always have, but to live the life I want to give you, we need money." He squeezed her shoulders. "You and Charlie are mine, and I'll take care of you, but right now, the only way I can do that is to provide you a home."

Home? But without him?

She looked down at the baby in her arms. Her heart swelled with need, hope. What choice did she have, if she wanted to be near Charles and take care of her baby?

"Isn't that enough for now?"

He rushed ahead, giving no time for an answer. "And just wait until you see what I have planned for the house, Kizzie. A new cookstove, a fence around the backyard. And I've already planned to have rugs on the floors to keep you warm through the winter."

His apparent pleasure curbed a little of the ache growing inside her for something she couldn't quite define. She ignored it and embraced his offering. "Sounds mighty nice."

"It is. Just wait and see." He looked over his shoulder toward the door. "Which reminds me that I need to make sure a new bedstead is ordered for you too." His attention dropped to Charlie. "And a cradle."

He pressed a kiss to her forehead and stepped to the door, cramming his hat down on his head as he went. "I'll be back to help you move soon, all right?"

She nodded, breathing in the cold air the open door swept into the room.

"See you then."

Kizzie stood in the quiet of the room, the crackle of the fire the only sound.

The bridge of her nose tingled, and her eyes stung. The strangest sense of. . .what? Lostness? Loneliness? Something ached through her chest. Why? Wasn't she getting so many things she wanted? Time with Charles. A place for her and Charlie?

She looked at the baby in her arms. He returned her stare as he sucked his fist. Kizzie ran a finger down his cheek, the ache branching deeper. "We'll be all right, little one. I'll make sure we are."

But the admission failed to find its way to her trembling heart. She wasn't strong enough to make a promise like that. Hadn't they almost been killed by coyotes only a few days ago? Wasn't she living off the kindness of someone else?

Voices pulled her attention back toward the kitchen, Joshua's boots beating across the floor. He rounded the threshold in front of Nella, his dark eyes zeroing in on Kizzie.

"Mr. Charles just left here, and I don't like what I heard, Miss Kizzie."

Kizzie's body tensed at the edge in Joshua's voice. Would they cast her out too? When they knew she'd soon be living in sin in a house Charles made for her?

"I can't just stay here with y'all." Her words wobbled out, and she looked to Nella for some help.

"You got a place here for as long as you need, girl." Nella stepped forward, her attention moving from Charlie back to Kizzie's face. "But did we hear right by Mr. Charles that you'll be moving to the Peterson place?"

The look in Joshua's eyes paused her immediate response.

"He said he's giving the Petersons notice and moving them elsewhere." Joshua's voice lowered, strained, as if he was making some attempt to keep it low. "Is that what he told you?"

Kizzie swallowed then nodded. "Said it'd be a few weeks till me and Charlie could move in."

"It ain't right." He shot Nella a look. "This ain't good, Nella, and I mean to tell him so."

Joshua cast another glance to Kizzie before turning and marching from the room.

"What. . .what does he mean, Nella? I. . .I gotta go somewhere, me and Charlie. We can't just keep stayin' here."

Nella released a long sigh, taking her time before meeting Kizzie's gaze. "Girl, it ain't got nothin' to do with what you've done, but everything to do with Mr. Charles movin' one of his tenants before the lease is up, especially the Petersons." She pressed her fingers to her temples before meeting Kizzie's eyes again. "There are some folks you can swindle, and they won't do much about it. The Petersons ain't those kind of folks." She stepped forward, placing her hand on Kizzie's arm. "You keep up your guard, girl. Mr. Charles may have just started trouble you and little Charlie weren't meant to fight."

Chapter 3

Kizzie sat beside Charles in his Model T as they moved over the dirt road from the Chappells', the back seat of the car packed with blankets and pots and a few canned goods, courtesy of Nella.

Charles sent her a grin, his enthusiasm transferring to Kizzie a little, despite the lingering concern about the Petersons. Kizzie didn't know much about the family, since they lived as far from the main house as anyone on the Morgan property, but she'd heard enough to steer clear of them. One of the other maids even whispered about how the Peterson father was one of the biggest bootleggers in the area, and despite authorities knowing of his illegal runs, he'd never gotten arrested.

Joshua mentioned something about how Mr. Peterson had things to "hold over" almost everyone, including the police. But, since Kizzie's sins already lay out there for the whole world to see, she couldn't think of any reason the Petersons would bother her.

She pulled Charlie close and looked over at Charles. "You said you gave the Petersons another house?"

"Of course. I wouldn't break their tenant contract. I just set them up at a vacant house nearer the main house."

She studied his profile. Nearer the main house? "But why didn't you send me to the vacant house instead of moving a whole family out of this one?"

His jaw tightened. "The Petersons could use a bigger house."

The answer fell short of the mark.

"And this will give you easier access to town and keep you close to the Chappells."

Why did she get the sense he held something back? Her mind sifted through what little she knew about the situation, and then her thoughts hinged on a possibility.

An achingly painful possibility.

Was Charles moving her and the baby as far away from his home as his land permitted? She shook her head against the notion. Surely not! He said he wanted to be with her.

"You'll have everything you need." He gestured with his chin. "And the fence around the back will keep some of the critters in the woods from getting too close to the house."

Her gaze moved to the forest along one side of the road, and a chill skittered up her spine at the memory of those coyotes. She'd grown up surrounded by woods her whole life, but the forest back home had been familiar to her—patched with people she knew along the path.

And her family had been there. Nearby. Scattered all over the mountain, ready to come at her cry. She squeezed her eyes closed. All her growing up, she'd imagined the world beyond the mountains like some sort of fairy-tale life, a place where she wanted to escape.

How had she failed to see what she'd possessed all along, even back in the mountains? How many immeasurable strengths and loves.

"Don't worry, Kizzie." Charles covered her hand with his. "I've thought this through, and it's going to be a good place for you and Charlie. We can still move forward as a family, even if it's not the conventional kind."

As a family? Didn't the notion sound sweet?

"I'll visit as often as I'm able."

The warmth stilled its movement, and she curbed her disappointment with a smile for him. It had taken three weeks to get the house ready for her, and he'd only visited once.

Once.

Another truth struck through her silly, girlish ideals.

Why had she been so foolish to believe a man like him would marry her? A poor nobody from the mountains? Cinderella was one thing. Real life was another.

Pining for a wish didn't do any good. All she could do was embrace what she had.

Around the turn in the road, a small house came into view. Perhaps a similar size to those up in the mountains, but that was where the similarities ended. Whitewashed wood, a porch lining the front, large windows with dark green shutters, and. . .even a green front door.

It was one of the prettiest houses she'd ever laid eyes on.

After growing up in a ramshackle mountain cabin fit to bust from her large family, Kizzie barely knew what to do about living in a place like this. Of course, she'd lived in the attic rooms of the Morgan house when she'd worked as a maid, but never a whole house just for her. And now Charlie.

"I knew you'd like it," Charles said, bringing the car to a stop in front of the house and waving toward a long road ahead. "Town is thataway."

He rounded the car and opened the door for her to exit, and her gaze traveled back to the house. The entire experience would have been almost storybook if this had been her wedding day with Charles as her groom.

"You get Charlie inside and settled, and I'll start unloading some of these things for you." He nodded to the house, his brown eyes almost glowing. "You're going to love it."

Kizzie moved up the path to the front steps, taking in the clean look of the place. Her brother Jeb had often talked of building a white clapboard house. Would she ever see it if he did?

Her throat closed, so she swallowed, taking the three steps onto the porch. With a little turn of the knob and push to the door, she stepped across the threshold into a front room, through which she could see into a kitchen. All the floors gleamed as if they'd just been laid. The front room boasted one soft chair and a rocking chair, both facing the fire, with a circular rug in between. Against one wall stood a small table with two additional chairs, just near the doorway into the kitchen.

She took timid steps forward, breathing in the scents of fresh paint and floor polish. Her mama would have loved the kitchen. Cabinets with doors to hold food or dishes. A new cookstove. Another type of container similar to something she'd seen in the Morgan house, but she couldn't remember what the box-shaped device held. Another little table waited in here with two chairs and. . .a high chair?

Have mercy! She could have fit two of her mama's kitchens inside this one.

A back door opened into the fenced-in yard, and another door stood at the juncture of the corner of the kitchen and the wall to the sitting room. Stepping closer, she peered into a bedroom, complete with large wrought iron bed, washstand, wardrobe, and. . .a cradle in the corner. Two large rugs lay on the floor, one on each side of the bed, to buffer against the cold of winter.

She'd never had her own room before. Even as a maid, she shared a room.

"Did you see the bathroom?" Charles rounded the threshold into the kitchen, carrying a box of miscellaneous items. "It's on the back of the house. Newly added." He nodded toward the kitchen sink. "And there's running water. Not hot water, like we have at the big house, but at least you can stay warm and dry while getting your water."

The joy radiating off him piqued her own. He placed the box on the floor and left the room for another haul. Simple white curtains hung on each of the windows, fresh and clean. The scent of lye and, perhaps, Sunlight carbolic soap wafted in along with other smells like the scent of pine burning in the fireplace and the fresh scent of rubbing oil, likely used to refresh the furniture. She knew the task well, as one of her own at the Morgan house.

Unlit lanterns waited by the bed, and Kizzie stepped forward, lowering a sleeping Charlie into the cradle. He released a quiet sigh and stretched out his body, his eyes never opening from his slumber. She nudged the cradle, and it moved in gentle rhythm as Charlie stilled back into a deeper sleep. The tiniest of smiles touched his cupid lips, and Kizzie's own responded.

What was it Granny used to say? If a newborn smiles, angels are watching over him?

Kizzie nodded. Well, she'd hold on to the idea. She didn't expect God had any angels left for her, since she'd been so discontent back in the mountains and then made so many wrong choices since coming to the Morgan farm, but. . . Her gaze fastened on little Charlie. At least angels guarded her boy.

She met Charles in the kitchen as he placed two more crates down. Then he guided her to one of the back windows. "If you look out there, you'll see I had the boys build you a washhouse with its own stove. I even got one of those rotary washing machines to take some of the toil out of the process." His grin broadened again. "With a baby, I suppose you'll have lots of washing to do. Cole said the space could be used for canning too, if you need it."

"Thank you." The words came out slow, almost whispered. The past month, her life had turned upside down and started spinning in directions she could barely follow. Cast out by her daddy. A baby. And now, mother in a home by herself being kept up by the father of her child.

But not married.

"And there's a cow in the barn, plus one of my older mares for the buggy. Her name is Daisy."

He marched back through the house toward the front door, leaving her by the window, her thoughts crowding in until her eyes stung. *No.* She couldn't be afraid or weak now. This was her life.

She had to accept the consequences of her own choices and move forward. She drew in a breath and turned toward the nearest box, its contents showing cooking utensils.

"And I've told Mrs. Hanes, the owner of Sally's Place in town, that you'll stop in this week to choose a few ready-made dresses." His gaze met hers as he set another box down. "You can alter your own clothes, can't you?"

She'd never owned a ready-made dress in her life. "Yes."

He studied her, stepping close to rest his hands on her shoulders. "Do you like it? Imagine if your family could see you now. Wouldn't they be impressed?"

For something she didn't earn.

Or deserve.

From a man who wouldn't marry her?

Impressed wouldn't be their response.

"I imagine they'd think it was somethin' else, for sure."

His smile deepened the lines at the corners of his eyes, but her heart faltered to respond in kind, an untamed worry taking up residence in her mind. "You...didn't move us here because you're ashamed of us, did you?"

"What?"

"This house is about as far away from you as your property can go. Is that why you chose it?"

He lowered his head and took her hands, led her to one of the kitchen chairs, and then sat down next to her. "I'm not ashamed of you." He breathed out the words, squeezing her hands. "You need a home. It's my responsibility to provide that. This house is one of the newest and best built on the land, it's near town, and far from my mama."

"Your mama." Kizzie released the words like a sigh. Always, his mama.

His palm warmed her cheek, and she looked up at him. "It's not the way I want it, but it's the way things have to be for now." His thumb trailed against her skin. "I'll take care of you and Charlie. Don't worry."

He gave her a quick kiss, said his goodbyes, and then walked out the door, leaving a waft of wintry wind and a slight chill in his wake.

She wrapped her arms around herself and moved to the porch, watching Charles' car disappear in a cloud of dust down the road, the blue late-afternoon sky bending to new hues of orange and red. Forest or field spread in each direction, without another house in view.

She cast a look behind her at the clean floors and lovely furnishings, quiet creeping over her as if it had fingers.

So quiet.

The bite of early December wind stung her cheeks and brought the scent of snow on the air. Two years ago, her heart would have been beating with anticipation for a frosted world of sleigh rides and snowball fights with her siblings. Heat burned her eyes, and she closed them with a sigh.

But now? Alone?

She'd never lived alone.

With a deep breath, she shook away the tug of melancholy and glanced along the front porch to a woodshed just at the edge of the yard. Stacked to the brim, it promised that, despite the cold or weather, she'd at least have ample warmth. She paused on the thought. How often did one tend a fire to keep it alive in winter? Her mother and Laurel always seemed to keep the fire while Kizzie had helped some with cooking but mostly tended the younger children, cared for the animals, and helped with laundry.

With Charlie's frequent night feedings, she'd have ample opportunity to keep watch.

She returned to the house and began unpacking boxes, the thrill of organizing her own kitchen dispelling a little of the daunting idea of keeping house and watching Charlie on her own. After all, she had only one to take care of, and her parents had had nine. Surely, just one and a house couldn't be so difficult.

After finishing up the kitchen, she moved to the bedroom. A dying fire greeted her, so she stirred it back to life and put away the only other dress she had, a simple frock she'd carried in her bag to the Chappells'. The simple blue gingham she currently wore belonged to Nella.

Perhaps she'd venture to town tomorrow.

At the rate Charlie was growing, he could use some new clothes too.

Nestled beneath her minuscule list of personal items lay her mother's Bible, the leather cover creased from use. Kizzie gently tugged it from the small crate, the scent of leather and pine washing over her like a hug from her mama.

She hugged the book against her chest, her eyes closing against another rush of tears. Maybe some of her mama's strength could transfer from this big book into her own heart.

Her attention flitted to the sleeping baby in the cradle.

For Charlie's sake, if nothing else.

With a sigh, she placed the book on the dresser by the bed, her fingers slipping over the familiar leather one last time before she turned back to the kitchen.

Three hours.

It had taken three hours for Kizzie to ready the house, herself, then Charlie, before hitching up the buggy, only to discover Charlie had spit up on her dress and soiled his diaper.

She'd never felt so stupid or unprepared in her life.

Couldn't she even manage to make it to town and visit one dress shop on her own?

The scrubbed milk stain on the shoulder of her borrowed dress only confirmed her need for more clothes.

Finally, with a clean and sleeping baby in a little crate at her side and Daisy, the mare, at the helm, Kizzie steered from the barn onto the road toward the little town of Casper. Underneath the exhaustion, a tiny hint of pride straightened her spine a little. She'd done it. By herself.

Clothed. Fed. Somewhat clean. And riding in her own buggy.

And if she ignored the fact that the sun was almost midway in the sky, she'd feel even better about her progress. The cool air nipped at her face but failed to dim her smile as the sudden awareness of her plans washed over her. She was on her own, going shopping for ready-made dresses at an actual shop! And Charles had given her enough money to purchase things for Charlie as well as the house.

She'd never seen so much money in her life, let alone held it.

She slid her hand into her pocket and clenched the small purse. Her own buggy. Her own house.

She grinned down at Charlie.

Her own little baby.

Maybe this new way of life wouldn't be so bad.

Another waft of snow-scented air and increasing clouds promised a chilly ride back home, but she'd brought plenty of blankets for Charlie and a treat or two for Daisy to keep everyone content, she hoped.

Almost an hour later, Casper came into view. It seemed a decent-sized place, from her little experience with towns. Houses dotted the road, growing more frequent and fancier as Kizzie drove the buggy nearer. She'd only been inside the mercantile a few times, and once into the millinery. Never in the two dress shops and certainly not with the purpose of purchasing something for herself.

The buildings from the main part of town rose into the sky. A few of them even stood five stories high, competing with the two steeples in view for which may be the tallest. There was something exciting about seeing a place so full of life and people and. . .opportunity. Brick-and-white clapboard buildings lined the dirt main street, with a few carriages as well as an automobile paused in various places along the way. The pristine mercantile stood on the left side of the street, tall and white with a long front porch. An older gentleman nodded at her passing, his smile crinkling his already-wrinkled face. Wasn't he the owner of the mercantile?

What was his name? Berry? Oh yes, Mr. Berry.

Kizzie offered the man a small wave, only causing his grin to grow. She'd make sure to stop in there for her other items. She had a feeling that he and his wife would be happy to help her locate things she needed for Charlie and her home, even things she didn't know she needed.

The two dress shops stood across from each other near the end of the street. A bright yellow sign to the left read SALLY'S PLACE. That was the store Charles had said a Mrs. Hanes owned.

Kizzie brought the buggy to a stop and took a few minutes to appease Charlie's fussing before stepping down to the street. The shop boasted several dresses in the front window, much too fancy for anything Kizzie needed. She paused and scanned the street. As a mama working on a little farm on her own, frills and lace weren't practical at all. She stared at a particularly lovely frock with pink flowers poised in the window.

Her gaze trailed down the pretty pattern, complete with delicate lace at the wrists and neckline. Oh, to wear something so nice.

Would Charles like it?

With a deep breath, she tugged the blanket closer around Charlie and stepped through the door into a bright space lit by gaslights and showcasing various types of women's clothing. A whole shop filled with everything from hats to boots to undergarments and some of the finest dresses she'd ever laid eyes on. She'd never imagined stepping inside such a place with the actual intention of purchasing something.

A pair of women stood to one side of the door, looking at the dresses in the window, but Kizzie's attention focused on a beautiful woman behind the nearby counter. She wore a blue day suit with embroidered sleeves, and as Kizzie approached, her expression dissolved from a welcome smile to a frown. Her steely blue gaze measured Kizzie from her dusty black boots all the way up to her hatless head. "I'm not hiring."

Kizzie blinked at the statement. "Hiring?"

"I already have enough seamstresses at present." Her attention filtered down over Kizzie's stained dress once again. "And I'm not looking for a saleswoman either."

Saleswoman? "I'm not seeking either, ma'am. I'm here to buy a few dresses."

"Really?" One of her golden brows arched high. "And you have ready money?"

Heat swelled into Kizzie's cheeks, and she stood a little taller. "I do. I was told to come specifically to your shop, assuming you are Mrs. Hanes."

The woman's other brow rose to match the first, lifting nearer her golden head. "I am." Her gaze took another detour down Kizzie. "And who might I thank for sending you?"

"Charles Morgan." The name slipped out in defense, her gaze holding to the woman's. Kizzie knew all too well how Charles' name held power, even if the son invoked less intimidation than his father had.

The woman's smile stilled on her face as she looked over Kizzie again, pausing for a moment on Charlie. "Ah."

"Charles Morgan?" one of the women by the window whispered too loudly to be ignored.

"I suppose that's the one we've heard about." The other woman responded at the same volume. "His kept woman."

The label spilled like ice over Kizzie's skin, dousing any of the pride she'd felt from making it to town on her own.

Kept woman.

She'd heard of kept women before and never in a good light. The phrase brought a whole host of images Kizzie never imagined matching.

Loose woman. Prostitute.

Her breath caught as the warmth of shame heated her face. *Not good enough to marry.*

"I suppose we can find something. . ." One of her golden brows tipped with her smile. "Suitable for you."

Suitable? The phrasing paired with the women's words hinted at a mocking meaning, which heated Kizzie's face even more.

She slipped back toward the door a step.

"Perhaps I've come to the wrong shop." She cleared her throat from the rising emotions. "I'm actually looking for practical and. . .modest."

"Practical and modest?" Mrs. Hanes did little to hide her smug smile.

"Modest?" one of the ladies by the window scoffed in a false whisper to the other lady. "Too late for that, from what I can see."

"This. . .this ain't the right place for me." Kizzie shook her head. "Thank you kindly."

She backed out the door into the cold, squeezing Charlie close and bracing herself against the burn in her eyes. The label "kept woman" reverberated in her head, piercing like nettles. She barely made it into the buggy before the tears came, with Charlie joining in. Against the cold, she maneuvered to modestly cover herself as she fed him, the buggy providing further protection from the wintry air and curious onlookers.

No one waited back home for her.

No one looked for her return.

No amount of pretty things in the world could fill her heart's ache for a hug from someone who loved her.

She'd never felt so alone.

Wind blew around her, drawing her attention toward the darkening sky, a single ray of sunlight slipping through the clouds like a ribbon of gold to the earth. Was heaven just on the other side of the ribbon? Had she lost her chance to find her way there someday? Kept women didn't make it to heaven, did they?

She opened her mouth to pray but then pinched her lips closed, the echoes of the storekeeper's voice crowding in against more heavenly thoughts.

Her bleary gaze finally fastened on the general store, a simple frock showcased in one of the front windows along with household items and supplies. She sniffled and wiped at her face with her gloved hand.

All she wanted to do was ride back to the house and never leave, but life didn't work with her wants. Charlie needed clothes. She needed to purchase other items.

The needs had to bend to the wants.

A reality that seemed to go hand in hand with being a parent.

She pressed her eyes closed, aching for the comfort, the wisdom, of her mama.

Almost as if the desire nudged a memory, Kizzie heard her mama's voice in her mind.

"Life is hard, Kizzie. You can look for easy in all kinds of places, but more likely than not, that easy turns to its own kind of hard. The real test is what you do when the hard comes. There's bound to be more times in life than not that the hard gets too big for your own shoulders. That's why you need someone bigger, stronger, wiser."

But Mama hadn't been speaking about her own shoulders.

She'd been referring to God's.

Tears burned afresh beneath her lashes.

God? She looked up at the pale afternoon sky. "Protect Charlie?"

The whispered words barely made a sound against the breeze, but stating them aloud somehow helped ease the ache around her heart a little. She finished up with Charlie and then, when he'd fallen asleep, braced herself for a trip to the general store.

But neither Mr. nor Mrs. Berry made any comment about her relationship to Charles Morgan, and Mrs. Berry even held Charlie so Kizzie could try on a few of the ready-made clothes and shoes before purchasing them.

By the time she made it back to the house, the wind had picked up, tossing a few flurries around like autumn leaves. She settled Charlie in his cradle and then took care of the horse and buggy, her movements growing slower by the minute after having used more energy in this one day than she'd done since Charlie's birth. By the time she made it into the house, snow covered the ground, crowding her vision with large, fluffy flakes.

She jerked off her gloves as she stood on the porch steps, and then caught a few flakes in her palm. Snow. White. Clean. Beautiful. Turning the world into a wonderland of crystal and ice.

For some reason, she smiled.

She wasn't sure why.

But the moment reminded her of sweeter times, of roasted chestnuts and music around a fireplace. Of corn-shuck dolls and whispered secrets between sisters. Of piggyback rides and long winter walks.

Of family and love.

And hope.

Her heart squeezed in her chest, and she looked up into the sky, the cool flakes kissing her face.

"I don't know if You still hear me, but if You do. . .well, I'd just like to know. Because it wouldn't feel quite so lonesome if I knew You heard me. Do You even hear the prayers of. . .of. . .kept women?"

Her heart pricked against the name.

A verse she'd heard seemed to whisper to her across the wind. *Thou wilt keep him in perfect peace, whose mind is stayed on thee: because he trusteth in thee.*

She paused on the thought as she turned toward the door. *Keep.*

What would it be like to know God kept her, instead of thinking about the idea of how Charles "kept" her?

The wind swirled the flurries around her, and she breathed in the cool air, the tightening in her chest a little looser. After another look around at the wintry landscape, she slipped inside the house and closed the door.

Chapter 4

THEY SHOULDN'T ALLOW FOLKS LIKE her to own a shop. And allowin' them women to say such things to you?" Nella scrubbed at the pot in her sink as Kizzie helped Isaac with his math homework. "Ain't nobody should go around advertisin' their own meanness."

"But they're right, Nella." Kizzie turned toward the woman, lowering her voice. "If Charles don't have no mind to marry me, but he keeps me nearby, don't that make me what she says I am?"

"I reckon that depends on what you're doin' when he comes to see you," Nella murmured beneath her breath. She gave her head another shake. "Has he paid a visit since you got into the house?"

Nella's answer pinched at Kizzie's conscience, but what else could Kizzie do? Where could she go? She was alone in the world. But. . .but surely, Charles loved her. After getting her the house and clothes and. . .the baby! "Not yet. But he sent a wagonload of firewood by way of the Simpkin boys."

A huff came from the woman. "You've been there a week now." Another round of mutterings followed, and then Nella placed her palm on the counter and turned, her apron dotted with water. "Well, you might as well come on over here for Sunday lunches from this point on. Ain't no cause for you to stay in that house all by yourself when we're only half a mile away."

Maybe Kizzie wasn't so alone after all.

Her smile pricked up a little, embracing the sweetness of Nella's request. "I don't want to intrude on your family."

The woman spun around with one sudsy hand on her hip. "You think I'd ask if it was an intrusion?"

That raised brow of hers forced any argument dead on Kizzie's tongue. "You're in need of company, and I can't thank you enough for being willin' to help the young'uns and me and Joshua with learnin' math. Joshua's already started shortening his time on workin' the books, and we've made a few good decisions on ways we can cut costs to save more money."

"I wish you lived along the main road, 'cause it would be a good location for a shop. And the property where my house sits near the river would be a fine spot for a gristmill. The nearest one is at least five miles up the way."

"Joshua worked for nearly ten years before he came to tenant here." Nella's eyes brimmed with pride. "He learned the work and ain't afraid of startin' from scratch if it will be his own."

Owning land brought its own sense of pride with it too. She knew all too well from back home. A family's land was all they had, and it was prized above almost anything else except family. . .and faith, for those who were churchgoin' folks.

"Kizzie, I can't remember what I'm supposed to do with an extra one." Isaac's voice pulled her attention back to his work. "These two numbers make sixteen, and I put the six down, but now I have a five that's just floatin' around in my head with no place to land."

Kizzie smothered a chuckle. "I got a place for that number to land right here, Isaac." She pointed to the spot on his paper. "Remember, we add that extra number to the one in front, even when we multiply."

"Well, ain't that nice and tidy." His grin split wide. "Stays the same in addition and multiplication. I'm real glad." He sighed. " 'Cause lots else changes."

Kizzie grinned and turned back to Nella. "I'd be happy to look over your recent numbers too if you want." The idea of showing her abilities, in the wake of her visit to town, pushed her forward with more confidence than she perhaps should convey. "I ain't got no big training, but working for Mrs. Cappy on her books really taught me a lot about keeping figures right and budgeting. She told me I had a knack for 'em."

Nella dried her hands and studied Kizzie for a moment. "I'll talk to Joshua to see what he thinks 'bout it, but if you have some good advice to help us, I'd be real grateful."

"I think it'd do me more good just to know I'm being useful to somebody."

One of the woman's hands went to her hip. "Now don't you go listenin' to ugly thoughts like that, Kizzie McAdams." The needling brow poked high again. "Ain't no good comes from puttin' yourself down, and you got a whole lot of good in you. The girl I met at the Morgan House all those months ago was always ready with a smile or a laugh, and it's been a shame to have her missin' these past few weeks."

The statement grounded Kizzie because it was true. She'd changed since meeting Charles. Become more nervous and serious. Her silly daydreams had taken a dark turn into reality, leading to actions that broke her own heart and left behind a great deal of regret, if she was honest.

How silly she'd been! To lose herself in the fairy stories.

Well, real life sure was a fast and tough teacher.

"So you'll come to supper from now on then? Sundays?"

"I'm helping because I'm happy to, Nella." Kizzie's shoulders dropped. "Y'all don't owe me a thing."

"I know that, but we're friends, ain't we? And friends invite friends to supper now and again, don't they?"

The finality in her voice curbed any further argument. "Thank you."

The woman dipped her head and returned to the wash pan to attack another pot. "We got church on Sunday, if you want to come along with us there too. It's not far from your house."

Church? Kizzie's throat closed at the idea. She wasn't likely to attend any church in the state she was in, but *their* church? Kizzie moved her attention back to Isaac's math scrawling. "I. . .I ain't too sure that's the right choice for me. Not with. . .not with all I—"

"You gotta find your people, girl. You ain't meant to live this life alone."

Oh, how she felt the sting of that truth every night when the house creaked and the fire crackled and only the sound of Charlie's and her own breathing softened the silence of the empty house. She shook her head. "I can't go to *your* church."

"Last I heard, church was open to everyone."

Surely, Nella knew. "But I'm...I'm not like you." She waved toward herself. "I wouldn't fit into your church."

"Not fit in my church, girl?" Nella swung around, her hands holding a wet plate. "What on earth do you mean?"

"I'm white."

Nella's eyes shot wide for a second, and then her lips flickered for the briefest moment. "Last I read, God loves *all* His people, so He'll take you too." She shrugged and turned back to the wash pan. "And if anyone at church has something to say agin' it, they ain't been readin' the same Bible as me."

"Nella."

"You sayin' God loves some of his children more than others?"

"No, of course not." Kizzie pinched her eyes closed. "But there's also what I've done. How...how I'm livin', I ain't the sort for church, Nella."

She spun back to face Kizzie so fast, even Isaac flinched along with Kizzie. "Don't you know your Bible a'tall, girl?"

Kizzie refused to answer because the answer wouldn't look favorably on her.

"You're the very kind who ought to be in church."

Kizzie's shoulders slumped a little beneath the weight of that statement. She needed more than church. She needed a way to start over on the right path. To return to the girl she'd been before coming to the Morgans'.

"That can't be so. I've made such a mess of things all around."

Nella slid down in the chair next to Kizzie and took her hand, the action the most affection the woman had ever shown her. "I could tell you everything's gonna be easy, but you know that ain't so. But if you press into the Lord, you'll get through it, and better than you were before, I'd reckon."

How could that be true? If her own daddy didn't want her, why would God help her? "The Lord don't want nothing to do with the likes of me, Nella."

"Well, that just goes to show how little you know about the Lord.

The broken kind's who He's been after from the start." Nella squeezed Kizzie's hand, drawing Kizzie's attention back to the woman's face. "God ain't got no use for them folks who think they're all right. He came for the ones who know they need more than their own wits or hearts or strength to be able to live right." Her brow pitched northward again. "And, the secret is, ain't none of us good enough to live life without Him, so just remember that, Kizzie McAdams. Church ain't for the healthy and well. It's for the sick and helpless."

Kizzie's gaze paused in hers for just a moment before she turned away to meet Isaac's. His big brown eyes asked questions for which Kizzie didn't have answers.

Or didn't want to answer.

"Just think about it." Nella patted Kizzie's hand and stood. "You got an open invitation anytime you want to come."

"Thank you."

"And, girl, the world is gonna call you a whole lot of things." Nella returned to her work, but her words came strong. "*Lots* of things. Believe me, I've heard a whole lot." She peered over her shoulder. "But you get to decide what and who you're gonna believe. What you're gonna stand on. Ain't nobody else can make that decision but you."

Kizzie swallowed through her tightening throat and moved back to help Isaac just as Charlie started making wakeful noises from his place in a small crate in the corner. Kizzie welcomed the distraction, the closeness of cuddling up with her little one.

A shelter against the loneliness.

She sat in the rocking chair by the fire and cooed over Charlie's little fingers and his perfect lips and the way those blue eyes stared at her with such wonder and interest.

She looked back toward the kitchen where Nella sat next to Isaac, teasing him with a cookie and glancing over his work.

Church is for the sick and helpless? The broken?

But what if some people, some situations, were *too* broken?

"Is that one of your new dresses?"

Charles sat at the little table holding Charlie as Kizzie worked to get supper set up for them. Their first meal together in the house, just the three of them.

He'd shown up two hours ago, as the sky started waning into dusk, and announced his plans to stay the night to ensure the house kept warm enough for his liking. His arms were ladened with a crate of hearty options. A readied chicken which just needed piecing and coating to fry, some jams, and a loaf of fresh bread. Kizzie already had potatoes and some canned beans.

Kizzie smiled as she readied the plates with the largest supper she'd eaten in the house yet. Feeding one didn't require as much fanfare. Some eggs or beef jerky, or something from Nella's leftovers.

But Charles had brought a few chickens too and housed them safely in a portion of the barn fitted for that purpose, so now Kizzie wouldn't have to wait on his deliveries but manage more herself, something she was beginning to understand as her future.

She nudged the unsettling thought away and embraced the present.

"It is." She carried their plates to the table, feeling Charles' gaze on her the whole way. Her body warmed from the missed appreciation. "Do you like it?"

He stood and walked over to her, little Charlie perched on his shoulder. The baby's bright eyes surveyed the room, happy noises bubbling from his cupid mouth. Did he like the idea of his parents eating under the same roof too? As a family?

"Blue is always a nice color on you." His gaze trailed over her, heating her skin. "I don't recall seeing such simple dresses in Sally Hanes' window."

The heat died in her face. "I didn't go to Sally's." She plucked Charlie out of Charles' arms, and the baby nuzzled against her neck, rubbing his button nose in a sleepy fashion. "It was easier to just get everything I needed at one place."

Which wasn't a lie.

Charles nodded, taking the seat across from where she stood. "I hadn't thought about trying to manage the shopping while caring for Charlie."

Kizzie smiled, swaying a little as the baby's movements started to calm. "The Berrys were real good to help me with Charlie while I shopped." She looked down at her frock. "And I thank you, kindly, for the clothes. I don't think I've ever had such fine ones before."

"And these are the simple ones." Charles shook his head as if her gratitude didn't make sense. "Sometime you'll have to purchase some of the nicer things at Sally's."

Not as a kept woman, she wouldn't. But as a wife? Maybe.

Charlie calmed even more, his fingers fisting and unfisting the collar of her dress. He'd be asleep soon, and she'd get a chance to actually sit with Charles and share a meal, like they'd never had the chance to do before.

"Where would I wear nicer things, Charles? These clothes are more than fitting for a mama in a little house who goes to town every once in a while." She smoothed a palm down Charlie's back. "I mean to take my two older dresses and use them as work dresses for when I plant a garden this spring so I can keep the newer ones for special times like when I go to town or. . ." Her gaze met his. "When you're here."

Charles slid a palm to her waist, stealing her breath, his hooded look sending her pulse into a skitter.

"Looks like Charlie's asleep," came his low response, the intention in his voice almost mesmerizing.

She'd felt so lonely.

So unloved.

And here he came, sweeping into her little world as if he belonged right there with them, warming the whole house with his laugh and his talk, giving her little touches on the arm or hand, physical connection to another person she'd missed as she spent hours and days alone with just her and the baby.

"I'll take him to his cradle and be back to sup with you."

His smile crooked in such a way that her breath shallowed. She'd barely turned the corner back into the kitchen, when Charles swept her into his arms. Without a word, his mouth covered hers, the sensation sending her into a tactile rush of memories. . . His lips, his caress, the sweet words he promised her over and over again.

And she knew.

She'd give him whatever he wanted if she didn't have to feel the loneliness of his absence or think about the emptiness of being a "kept woman."

No. She was his. A fiancée, of sorts, because he'd promised he'd marry her.

One day.

And even though she knew he'd be gone in the morning, she'd take right now. A night where her world could look almost perfect.

And she could embrace their little family for one night.

That had to be enough for now because it was all she had.

A chill seeped around the heavy quilt as Kizzie forced her eyes open to the view of her dimly lit bedroom. Quiet permeated the air with the same expansiveness as the unusual chill. She released a long breath and rolled on her side, tugging the quilt closer to her chin. The pillow opposite her lay untouched, a reminder of Charles' absence. Only two days before, she'd awakened to the warmth of his arms around her, her cheek against his shoulder. The memory arched a deeper cold, which seeped through to her bones.

He'd left the house emptier than it had been before.

Less cheerful.

How was it possible? She'd managed the silence and emptiness well enough the first week, but now... After experiencing one evening as the family she'd dreamed them to be, everything seemed changed.

Loneliness proved an achingly painful bedfellow.

But here she lay. Again. On her own with little Charlie, with her thoughts and the coos of her baby to span the hours.

Her eyes fluttered closed, her pulse skittering at the memory of his touch. His kiss. The strength of his body wrapped around hers, buffering any cold, any sense of accusation from the outside world.

Charles had been so tender, so affectionate with her. Whispering all the wonderful endearments she'd longed to hear from him.

Words of love. Of desire.

Everything she should want.

And yet, the ache pouring through her chest, in his absence, boasted no comfort from the night they'd shared. Why? Shouldn't she be happy for any of his attention? For his provision?

What sorrow touched some deep place inside with a feeling she couldn't quite name? Questions, longing, pressed through the silence as it had the afternoon before, nagging at the corners of her mind as she went about her chores.

How long was this to be her life? This pretending of a family?

His arrival and departure put her heart through the rise and fall of a seesaw in the school play yard. Now her bleary-eyed gaze landed on her mama's Bible, and she looked away. Shame?

She turned away from the sight, swallowing through a gathering of tears. A prayer waited on her lips, at the very tip of her heart. A dusty hope for a childhood faith long left untouched.

But, no.

She was too far gone now.

With a groan, she sat up, pulling the quilt with her as she rose to stave off a shiver. Winter daylight peeked through the drawn curtains but much brighter than she'd expected.

How late was it?

Her body trembled with another convulsive shiver as the warmth from her bed dissipated into the morning air.

Why was it so cold? Her body stiffened. She'd tended the fire at least once in the night. After grabbing her threadbare robe and pulling on another pair of socks, she peered in the cradle to check on Charlie. His breath puffed through his rosebud lips in contented slumber, but his little cheeks were cold to the touch. Kizzie placed another blanket around him, cocooning him a little around his head before she walked into the dark sitting room.

Faded light strained to push through the white curtains, offering a hazy view of the space. Without the firelight, the chill sank deeper, darker.

Kizzie approached the hearth and froze. Not only was the fire completely out, but a pile of dirt lay over the wood. Her attention shot to the chimney.

Had dirt fallen from the roof somehow? Chimney sweeping had been one of the completed tasks on Charles' list before Kizzie moved into the house. So how could the dirt have gathered so quickly? And after a snow?

Scooping out the surprisingly large amount of dirt would take time, and she needed warmth at once. She rushed to the back porch and gathered an armful of wood, and within a few minutes she started up a little blaze in the kitchen stove.

At least this could knock the chill off.

She'd succeeded in removing half the dirt from the fireplace when noise from the bedroom hinted to Charlie's need, so she fed him, put on her boots, and then made a quick breakfast of bacon, eggs, and leftover biscuits. Her chilled skin welcomed the heat from the stove, the warmth from the tea. And once Charlie had finished his breakfast, she settled him onto his cushion in the little crate she'd moved into the kitchen so he could lie safely near the heat while she finished cleaning the fireplace.

It took another half hour before the sparks of a new fire blinked to life. Her body trembled from the extended cold and exertion, and the thin socks beneath her boots did little to prevent the additional chill.

Did the Berrys carry thick wool socks and robes in their store? On her next trip, she would make sure to find out.

Once the fire took, she cleaned up her breakfast things and poured warm water into her washbasin. The heat of the liquid washed over her skin, removing the dirt and ash caked between her fingernails and smudging her face.

After donning a clean dress, she slipped Charlie into his sling and opened the curtain on the window in the sitting room. Her attention caught on a strange sight in the front yard.

What was it? A scarecrow of sorts? Some wooden semblance of a person, made of sticks and a sack of straw, except wearing a bonnet and dress?

Was this a joke from Charles?

She stepped to the front door and opened it, the chill of the morning air nothing compared to the tremor of her heart. Yes, a scarecrow-like figure stood on a spike in the yard, just by the road for any passerby to see. But its shape and unexpectedness wasn't what cooled her blood.

No.

A wooden sign hanging around the scarecrow's neck proved the darker disturbance.

Etched across the sign in sharp-drawn letters were two words.

Freeze, Whore.

All heat fled her body.

She retreated into the house, her palm going to cover Charlie's back.

Her gaze searched the distance for any sign of the person who'd left the warning, but every direction looked as empty as it had after Charles rode away two days before.

An internal shudder, stronger than any she'd felt from the cold, moved through her body.

Who would do this?

Her attention shot to the fireplace.

Had the same person who left the warning also doused her fire?

The chill grew into a tremor from her toes to her head.

She'd known warnings. Seen them back home in the mountains. And if folks in the flatlands kept to any sort of mountain rules, these warnings were never to be taken lightly.

Ever.

She slammed the door and bolted it shut.

What should she do?

Her first instinct was to take the gig to the Morgan house and tell Charles, but. . .well, he didn't want her to cause trouble with his mother. But surely, when it involved her and Charlie's safety, he'd make an exception?

Doubt crowded out the idea.

Her gaze lifted to the wooden ceiling, the tremble in her body taking on a voice. "Help me? I know I don't deserve it, but. . .please?"

She paused, thinking. Hoping. Praying, even though she doubted God listened to her. Her breaths pulsed shallow. How would her own mama advise her?

Tell somebody you *trust*.

Joshua and Nella. They'd be closer.

No, she needed to tell the one person who was supposed to help her, because he'd know what to do.

She wrapped Charlie in a blanket, rushed for her coat, and ran out the back door toward the barn and her buggy.

And, hopefully, she wasn't riding into a bigger problem than the one she was leaving behind.

Chapter 5

THE MORGAN HOUSE STOOD IN the center of a field, trees lining the drive to the expansive white Victorian. A covered porch wrapped around the front, encompassing a rounded edge where a turret room rose above the rest of the roofing.

The first time Kizzie had walked up to the residence, over a year ago, she'd thought of castles and fair damsels and knighted men, like from the old ballads her mama and granny sang. And still, even now, as the buggy approached, the beauty of the place stirred her mind in a fanciful direction.

She'd only imagined a world like the one within those walls when she lived in her family's cabin in the mountains—dreamed of a place with fresh linen coverlets and delicate china plates of rosebud prints. Of silk gowns and slippers.

Of love.

She frowned as the memories crowded one over the other, reality creeping through the daydreams like a haint of the forest, stealing each sweet dream and twisting it into a type of nightmare.

She looked down at Charlie.

Except her babe. Her smile tempted release as one of her mama's phrases slipped into her heartache like a balm.

Somehow, even in the middle of broken dreams, God touches the raw, painful remnants with a teensy bit of stardust.

Could it be that despite Kizzie's wrong choices, here lay a reminder of how good could still find a way? That hope still persevered?

Her heart shivered beneath the idea, teasing her thoughts toward a revelation she didn't quite grasp yet. Or maybe one she couldn't truly believe.

She kissed the top of Charlie's fuzzy head and brought Daisy to a stop just within the tree line. The notion of parading her buggy all the way up to the front door, as if she were a welcome guest, didn't sit too well with her.

Charles probably wouldn't like it at all.

Drawing her shawl closer around her shoulders, Kizzie steeled herself against retreat and marched across the open space toward the house. The wind blew an icy wave against her face, perhaps in warning? She faltered at the base of the porch steps. Should she turn around and go to Nella instead?

She firmed her shoulders. It wasn't Joshua and Nella's responsibility to bear her burdens, to always give her help. Charles promised he would.

And, as a respected landowner in the community, he had power and influence Joshua and Nella didn't.

The porch loomed over her with its decorative wooden frame as she took each step nearer the door. Light glimmered from inside through lace curtains behind tall windows.

Kizzie had cleaned those windows and washed those curtains.

She released a breath, causing visible puffs in the frosty air, before knocking on the door. Silence responded to her knock, and then the faint sound of heels on hardwood drew nearer.

Those weren't the sound of a man's shoes.

She shifted a step back as the door swung open to reveal Mrs. Eliza Morgan.

Kizzie hadn't seen her since she'd overheard Mrs. Morgan ordering Charles to "fix" the problem of Kizzie's pregnancy, which led to Charles suggesting Kizzie return home. From the upstairs window, Mrs. Morgan had watched Charles enact her plan and drive Kizzie away from the house toward the train depot, her expression as unwelcoming then as it was now.

One of the woman's pale brows curved skyward. "I wondered how long it would take you to disregard Charles' request. Do you need *more* money?"

Disregard his request? "I'm here seeking guidance, Mrs. Morgan, not money."

Her gaze trailed down Kizzie. "I should have kept to my rule to never hire comely young women, no matter the skill."

Kizzie shivered as much from the cold air outside as the frigid look in Mrs. Morgan's eyes. The porch barely shielded Kizzie from the breeze, but a sliver of humor in her wanted to latch on to the compliment within Mrs. Morgan's response. "I think Charlie and I are in danger."

"Charlie?" She spat out the word, and then her gaze dropped to the baby. Her expression, if only for a second, softened before her gaze rose back to Kizzie. "Another way to emotionally snag my son?"

Kizzie blinked at the accusation. No wonder Charles tried to keep her away from his mother. There wasn't a feeling bone in her body. "I—I don't have any mind to sn—"

"You don't fool me, Miss McAdams. I've known too many young women like you. Opportunists. Only, *this* time I wasn't able to stop Charles before he made a lasting mistake." Her gaze dropped again to the bundle in Kizzie's arms.

Kizzie drew Charlie closer, to protect him from Mrs. Morgan's steely gaze.

Had there been other young women? Servants in the house too? Kizzie had never considered the possibility.

"I'm only here for help. That's all."

"That's all? Not only has he reordered his world to take care of you, but the rumors. . ." Her lip curled. "The talk. People know, and it hurts Charles."

Kizzie stiffened in defense, but the truth pinched. Did Charles feel the sting as acutely as she had from the ladies in the dress shop? "I'd never want to hurt him."

"No?" A light glimmered in the woman's brown eyes. "Because you love him, is that it?"

"Yes, ma'am." She raised her chin. "As much as I know what it is, I do."

Mrs. Morgan's eyes narrowed for the briefest moment. "Then if you do, you should leave him alone. The burden you bring into his life, the stain on his good name? Every day you stay, you hurt him more."

Was that true? Kizzie shifted a step back. "That ain't so."

Mrs. Morgan advanced, leaving the shelter of the door. The glint in her eyes took a predatory turn. "Don't you know? Your reputation automatically sullies his by association. Girls like you have long been dangerous to good, upstanding men."

"I ain't dangerous to nobody, least of all Charles." Kizzie rasped out a weak argument. "I want to take care of him."

"Care?" A dangerous flash lit the woman's eyes, inciting a responsive tremor. "Please don't tell me you have false notions he'll actually marry you." Her lips curved into a humorless grin. "You, with your poverty morals and mountain manners?" Kizzie shrank as the woman's gaze trailed down her again, her expression conveying unsheathed disgust. "Charles knows his place, and it isn't with someone like you."

Without another word, the woman stepped back into the house and closed the door with a resounding thud that Kizzie felt in her chest. Charlie jerked from the noise, a whimper quivering his little chin into a half dozen wrinkles. She ran a gloved hand down his cheek, his eyes searching her face as if to make sure all was well.

All was not well, but she smiled at him anyway and suddenly wondered, how many times had her own mother smiled to her children despite the tremors of her heart? Was that something mothers had to do often?

She walked back to the steps and paused. The accusations replayed in her head. The insults.

The meanness of the woman, with her airs and better-thans. Kizzie had noticed them when she worked for Mrs. Morgan but never considered standing up to her for fear of losing her job.

And then for the woman to glare at Kizzie's little baby with such disgust?

A child who had no hand in any of the decisions or mess between her and Charles?

Heat rose from Kizzie's stomach into her face, dousing any chill from the wind.

She'd made wrong choices, selfish choices, but she wasn't alone in them. She'd lost her way and didn't know how to plan for the future, but she certainly didn't fit Mrs. Morgan's descriptions.

And she'd never tried to trick Charles Morgan into anything.

Kizzie turned from the steps and marched back to the front door, her fist tightening at her side with each step. With all the tension from the past month fueling her, she slammed her fist against the door.

The door flung open, and Mrs. Morgan's eyes flashed wide. "How dare you—"

"You don't know me." Kizzie stepped forward, her height matching Mrs. Morgan's, something she'd never noticed before. "And if high-class values are anything like the self-righteous, cruel airs you're puttin' on, then I'll stick with my poverty morals any day of the week."

"Why, you insignificant—"

"Your son was old enough to know exactly what he was doing, even more so than me, and you can close your eyes to that all you want. No matter how much you excuse his acts or yours, or turn a blind eye to the truth. And your big house and rich clothes don't cover the fact that your heart is full of meanness and pride with just as much need for healing as mine."

The woman raised her chin and narrowed her eyes. "I'm *nothing* like you."

"And this baby?" Kizzie raised Charlie up a little into Mrs. Morgan's view. "He's proof positive that God can make something beautiful out of broken things. I know I don't deserve it. I'll readily admit that, but I'm not losing out on the joy of having him in my life. You're the only one losing out by not embracing this grandson of yours." Kizzie stepped backward onto the porch.

"Are you attempting to blame Charles for your wickedness? Hateful girl!"

"I ain't blamin' Charles for anything more than I blame myself, but here's one of the differences between you and me, Mrs. Morgan." Kizzie held the woman's stare. "I admit my own brokenness and the trouble I've caused, which means there's a chance I can make a difference for good and maybe even *do* good for other folks who need an understanding soul, but you got your nose so high up in the air, you can't see your own steps and you're bound to fall hard."

"Foolish girl. Your arrogance is highly misplaced." She sneered. "Whatever you decide to do, Miss McAdams, it will not be at my expense." Her words were edged with a growl.

Kizzie drew in a deep breath, a sudden sting coming to her eyes. "If I ever wanted anything from you, it was your kindness. Not your money, or even your son."

Kizzie's voice gave out on her, the sudden fury dying with the same speed at which it had come. Her body quivered from the spent effort, and as the door slammed behind her for a second time, she rushed down the stairs to her buggy.

Tears blurred her vision as she set the buggy into motion, pushing Daisy into a canter. She'd barely made it a mile when a horseman drew into her periphery. She turned to see Charles, hat pulled low, waving for her to stop.

She pinched her eyes closed. She felt the slightest urge to encourage Daisy into a full-on gallop, but the mare would never outrun Charles' stallion, especially when attached to a buggy.

She'd barely brought the buggy to a stop when Charles lighted on the step and moved to sit beside her. "What were you thinking, Kizzie? Coming here?"

Perhaps a little of the fire from her confrontation with Mrs. Morgan still hummed beneath her skin, because she didn't so much as flinch at his unfeeling accusation. "I came for help, but I won't make the same mistake again."

"You can't just show up here." Charles' breaths pumped his chest in quick movements. He sighed, his attention falling on Charlie, who stared at him with wide eyes. "It's. . .it's not a good idea."

"Yeah, I got that notion plain and clear."

"It's one of the reasons I tried to keep you away. Her mind will not be altered, and you put both of us at risk to come."

"Both of us?" Her voice pitched to fighting-high. "Last I looked, I'm the only one alone in a house far from the man who promised to help me."

His shoulders sagged, but he met her gaze. "If I don't conform to her wishes, Kizzie, I won't have money to take care of you, no matter where you are. You know this."

"She didn't even know Charlie's name."

"You. . .you told her?"

"Yes. But it wasn't my place to tell her. It was yours." She tugged Charlie closer. "Are you ashamed of him too?"

"I'm not ashamed of either of you." His palm rested on her arm. "But if we don't bide our time wisely, we'll lose everything."

Why did she feel like she was losing everything anyway? "Then tell me, Charles, where am I supposed to go when I need your help?"

"My help?" He searched her face, his breaths slowing. "What do you mean?"

Charlie started nudging toward her, likely hungry, so Kizzie carefully turned to adjust her gown so that she could feed him as she told Charles of the morning's events.

His pale face offered some solace to her. At least he seemed to feel the horror of the situation a little. "I'll find a way to end this."

"How?"

"I'm not sure." He removed his hat and pushed a hand through his hair. "But I'll ask around. See if someone knows anything about who would do this." He took Kizzie's free hand into both of his. "You can trust me to help you when you're scared, Kizzie, but. . ." He halted, looking away as if searching for an answer in the air. "If you need me again, don't come here. Send Joshua to find me."

The flicker of sweetness budding in her chest when he took her hand wilted inside her. "But don't come myself?" The admission gouged at her heart. "Don't sully your pretty little world with your kept woman?"

"Kizzie." He squeezed her fingers as she tried to pull away. "It's not like that at all."

"Your mama's right, Charles. I've got nothin' to bind me to you but this baby, and even with him it's just my word. The word of a fallen woman don't carry a whole lot of weight."

"You have my promise."

"I appreciate your promise." She caught the laugh before it released. "I do. But your promise won't hold water in a court of law or if, God forbid, something happens to you." Her voice trembled. "Don't you see? As much as I'd like to rely on your promise, the truth is it's only as lasting as your life and your mama's patience. I have nothing to protect me or Charlie."

He lowered his eyes, slowly shaking his head.

"And...what if they come back?" She hated how her voice trembled, so she swallowed to clear it. "What if they come tonight and do worse?"

He blew out a long stream of air that puffed into a smoky hue around them. "Then I'll send Cole to keep watch around the place. How about that?"

Cole, his cousin and right-hand man.

And someone Kizzie never felt quite comfortable around. Her chest tightened.

But what choice did she have? She shook her head. "I'll talk to Joshua and Nella. They care about me and Charlie."

Charles' expression tightened for a second before he released a sigh. "Fine, but I'll come by tomorrow afternoon, and we'll sort this out together."

He kissed her cheek and remounted his horse, giving her a long look before he rode back in the direction of his house.

She readjusted Charlie so he could sleep and continued her trek the way she'd come. Hopefully, she'd not worn out her welcome with Joshua and Nella, but at the moment, they seemed the only people in the world she could trust with her situation.

How silly she'd been to trust in fairy tales and storybooks. To believe leaving her mountains would offer her a life of castles and romance. That "perfect" waited somewhere in the flatlands.

All of this was only partially Charles' fault. She'd placed him on a pedestal, charmed and mesmerized that he'd chosen her from among all the other gals. Coming from a place where she'd grown up with the boys in the mountains, his fine clothes, sweet smell, and pleasing words met every hope she had when she'd left home to take the maid's job.

How blind she'd been to think she knew how the world worked!

How shortsighted to doubt her mama's advice!

She didn't know a whole lot about the love betwixt a man and a woman, but she knew enough to know that it had to be more than this uncertainty and wondering and. . .loneliness.

No wonder the idea of knights and princes and gallant men of old were lost to time and childhood. They didn't exist, except in stories, and she'd been a fool to hang her future on the silly notions.

Men were men.

They were going to take care of themselves first, weren't they, with no care for the women in their lives, especially if the women weren't highbrow, rich ones.

She hadn't wanted to believe it of Charles. Not when he'd swooped in with his smile and his lovely words and his warm kisses, but if he'd really loved her, wouldn't he care? Wouldn't he have dropped his plans and come to help her sort out this situation instead of arranging to send someone else?

Her eyes burned with fresh tears. Maybe she and Charlie really were on their own after all.

She frowned. Better to be practical now. Sensible.

Instead of having silly romantic notions.

Her gaze flitted to the horizon, where the sun was pushing through the clouds, tugging her heart heavenward. If only. . .if only God could love her even now.

She turned the buggy toward Joshua and Nella's house, forcing her thoughts away from dreaming about the impossible and her heart away from grieving whatever loss she felt with Charles. Neither did any good.

And then her attention caught on a small tuft of white pushing up through faint remnants of the most recent snow. White as the snow, a few tiny petals of winter pansies nudged skyward, bowing a little in the breeze but continuing to rise back in place between each gust.

The sight of them paused Kizzie's self-flailing and downward spiral.

Winter pansies.

A simple little wildflower and yet, the way it rose toward the light despite the snow and wind captured a part of her doubts and wouldn't let go.

Like. . .hope.

But was there any reason to hope?

Her gaze moved back to the sky as sunbeams filtered through the clouds and bathed the earth in a dance of gold.

She shouldn't hope. She'd only fail again. Or someone else would fail her.

But her heart refused to release the tethered scraps of it.

She breathed out a long breath. "I know I ain't got no right to talk to You. And by all accounts, You may not want to listen to someone like me, but if there's anything I can do to make You love me, Lord, I want to try. I. . .I ain't got nobody else. And I need You. Even if it's just the leftovers of Your love, I reckon they're better than a feast anywhere else. I'll take the scraps."

The sunrays moved toward her approaching buggy, bathing her face in warmth for a moment, offering a teensy bit more hope than she'd had a moment before.

Maybe, just maybe, she wasn't too lost after all.

Chapter 6

Joshua wasn't at home, but Nella took the information with a tightened jaw and nod. "I was hopin' it wouldn't come to this."

Air left Kizzie's lungs in a rush. "What do you mean?"

"Joshua says Cain Peterson ain't too pleased with Mr. Charles moving him and his family from their home, and not just because it was one of the nicest houses on the Morgans' land." She pounded the dough she was working on the table with a little added force. "The location gave Cain a good spot for his liquor runs from the mountains to town."

Liquor. She knew all too well the danger of getting between a man and his drink. Had grown up knowing it. A drunk was dangerous. Unpredictable. Mean.

She lowered herself into the nearest chair, Charlie in her arms. "So he wants to frighten me away?"

"I don't see how it's gonna help him none." Nella looked up, her hands deep in the dough. "If Mr. Charles finds out Cain is tryin' to scare you, Cain'll not only lose his home, but his position too. It can't be a clearheaded choice for him, no matter who he thinks he knows in high places." Her attention fixed on Kizzie. "You got a gun?"

Kizzie's face went cold at the implication. "No."

"I'm not sayin' you'll need one." She started kneading the dough again. "But it'd be smart to have one, even if it's only to scare away coyotes." Nella stared out the window, her mouth pressing into a firm line before she looked back at Kizzie. "Here's what we're gonna do. Cain and his folks won't do nothin' in daylight. That's how meanness likes to work best, ain't it? In the dark. So I'm gonna send Joshua and Isaac over this evenin'. I know Isaac's got a heap of math questions for you. And I won't be one bit surprised if Joshua don't give you a rifle and leave Boss with you."

Kizzie's gaze swept to the largest of the Chappells' three dogs, and the only one allowed in the house, as he lay in front of the fireplace in the next room. If the size of the animal didn't scare folks, his bark certainly would. "I can teach 'em a math lesson while they're there."

Nella's chin dipped in assent. "Sounds good."

A twinge of guilt roused Kizzie to defense. "Charles said he'd come tomorrow afternoon."

Nella sniffed, sparing Kizzie a glance. "You're not too keen on that?"

Kizzie shook her head. "I've been a fool about Charles."

"You're young." Nella set the dough aside to rise. "And you acted young. You ain't the first and won't be the last. Time and the Lord will make you smarter, if you let 'em."

Kizzie ran her fingers down Charlie's cheek. "I hope so."

Silence quieted the moment, the sound of the fire crackling in the next room the only interruption.

"You're gonna get through this, Kizzie McAdams." Nella's strong voice broke the silence. "It's gonna be hard. And it's gonna hurt. And the past may tag along with you for a while yet, but there's another side to it all. And you'll get there." Her gaze never wavered from Kizzie's. "But you get to choose how you move to the other side of it. Beatin' yourself up from your own foolishness, or wiser and braver than before." She released a sigh, the energy in her look softening. "God ain't done with you, girl."

Kizzie's eyes stung, and her throat closed up with a sudden rush of emotion she didn't know how to explain. Not sadness. No. Nella's words inspired the same inexplicable response Kizzie experienced when she saw the winter pansies.

The idea that something good waited beyond the hard.

Something strong beyond the weakness.

"Why don't you come on to church with us in the morning? You wouldn't have to be alone then."

The intensity of Nella's words still reverberated in the room, stealing any rejection of the offer from Kizzie's lips. Whether she fit into Nella's church or not, she knew the Chappells wouldn't abandon her, even after what she'd done. And even if Nella knew about Charles staying overnight only three nights ago.

She probably knew. For some reason, Kizzie felt as if Nella had the same inexplicable intuition as her mama.

Mama always knew things.

But even if Nella knew, she still invited Kizzie to join them. The thought bumped into another. Was God the same way? Welcoming? Even to her?

"All right."

Nella's expression failed to change except for the small sparkle in her eyes. "Good."

Good. Was it? Her trembling heart failed to reassure her.

She'd belonged somewhere once, so she knew what belonging felt like, but being an outcast from home, she'd lost her footing, trying to find or create a place of belonging in a story with Charles that seemed now as fragile as glass.

If the morning conversations with Mrs. Morgan and Charles taught her nothing, it reminded her, again, of how little power she held over Charles' choices.

Or his heart.

Kizzie chose to walk home after the Sunday service instead of returning with the Chappells. Besides, they planned to stay for an after-church dinner, and Kizzie's heart squeezed with too many emotions left over from the preacher's message.

Somewhere in the back of her mind, she'd heard the story of the woman who met Jesus at the well, but the way Preacher Jones told it. . . His voice and words reached all the way across the church and hit her right in the heart. Kizzie felt that woman's brokenness, the need to feel superior or sarcastic, her ready distraction when the truth got too close, and her wonder, a wonder that left her dazed and curious and maybe even a little afraid that the promise was too good to be true.

Too beautiful.

Was it all just a story? Did God's love really work itself into broken lives nowadays? Like hers?

It was so hard to grasp. Too big, too out of reach. Nothing as touchable and "real" as the baby in her arms or Charles' kisses.

She stretched out her shoulders as she continued her brisk walk, the deeper ache in her back only confirming what her eyes told her. Charlie was getting bigger.

Of course, he was just over a month old.

A month.

The time seemed fast and slow all at once. Plus, her little boy had started staying awake a bit longer in the day, his bright eyes taking in the world around him. Especially during the church service they'd just left.

Kizzie had never imagined such a lively service. And singing? One woman stood right up in the middle of the offering and started singing "Amazing Grace," like something straight from heaven. And somehow, the piano player followed all her different tones and twists as if they'd planned the whole thing. Kizzie had never heard so many "Hallelujahs" or "Preach it, brothers" in her life. Joy breathed through the little clapboard building, spilling out the front doors, even as Kizzie left.

There was only one other white woman in the service. An aged lady, who stood near the front, face raised to the ceiling and a smile on her face as everyone sang. And no one seemed to mind one bit.

"God loves all His children," Nella had said, a sentiment Kizzie's mama shared too.

But was Kizzie one of His children? A deep ache seeped through her. Those people in the church knew something, had something, she didn't. Like her mama.

A man waited on the front porch of her house, a horse and gig paused just out front. She knew that gig.

Charles.

He met her at the fence, his hair in disarray, his open-collared white shirt rumpled beneath his coat. With a crooked grin, he scanned her from head to boot, the warmth in his gaze igniting a responsive awareness throughout her body.

"Off on a walk this chilly morning?"

It took Kizzie a moment to collect her thoughts at his nearness and teasing, especially after what had passed yesterday morning. "I was coming back from church."

"From church?" His gaze lifted to the way she'd come. "Which church? The churches I know about are back toward town."

She slid past him and unlocked the door then stepped inside with him following. "I went with Joshua and Nella."

He paused in his turn to close the door. "You went with the Chappells? To *their* church?" He tugged off his hat and hung it on a hook by the door. "But you can't go there."

Kizzie placed Charlie in Charles' unexpecting arms and turned toward the fire. "I'd like to go somewhere instead of just be in this house alone all the time."

"But what will folks think of you going to that church?"

"That I must need it, is all I can reckon." She shifted a log into the dying flames to reignite.

Quiet greeted her response until she stood from her crouched position and turned to face him.

"Kizzie, I don't know if it's the best idea for you to attend the Chappells' church. Some folks may not take too kindly of it with. . ." He shrugged and shifted Charlie in his arms. "With some of their other less friendly thoughts about you."

She stared hard at him, wondering if he considered his own participation in her current position. "Would you let me come with you to yours, then?"

He looked away, answer enough.

Law, they were in such a mess.

"They've been real good to me, Charles."

He nodded and swallowed loud enough for her to hear.

"And if you're planning on staying for a little while, I got some leftover biscuits, ham, and grape jam we can share. It'll just take a bit to warm them up over the cookstove."

"That sounds good." His gaze flew to hers, the tension in his face softening. "And I brought a few jars of strawberry jam too, since I know how fond you are of strawberries."

She offered him a smile, pushing back a loose strand of hair. "That sounds like a regular feast then, don't it?"

His gaze searched hers, an almost pleading look sending her pulse into an upswing. What wasn't he saying? He gave a quick nod and then turned toward the door. "I'll go put the horse in the barn and be on back."

Her breath caught at the unvoiced decision. "You're measurin' to stay awhile?"

He paused at the door and looked over his shoulder. "I'd like to spend time with you and Charlie."

And Charlie. The statement hit directly into her new-mama heart.

"And if anybody decides to come back for a visit tonight, I'll be here."

She held his gaze, trying to sort out why a sense of dread followed his somber behavior, while also struggling with the pull toward him. For the night. When she'd sin all over again like she'd done dozens of times before. "That'd be nice."

He stepped out on the porch, and Kizzie followed behind. "I ought to tell you that Boss, the Chappells' dog, is in the barn. Joshua brought him over last night to stay with me in the house and suggested I put him in the barn to guard the animals in case. . ."

Charles jerked his gaze in the direction of the barn. "He won't need to be in the house tonight."

Without another word, he marched off the porch toward his gig, and Kizzie retreated back into the warmth of the house. What was happening? And why did her body tremble with the thought of him staying overnight again? She'd always wanted to spend time with him in the past, always craved his attention and touch, but, well, for the first time, she wasn't sure.

Her attention fell on the covered tin on the stove in the next room, and she made quick work of moving it to a part of the stove that was still warm and then changed Charlie.

She placed her sleepy boy in his cradle and slipped to the kitchen, bringing two plates to the little table just as Charles reentered the house via the back door, his arms laden with brown-paper packages.

"What on earth?" Kizzie set the plates down and rushed to his assistance. "These don't look like jars of jam."

His grin spread into the one she'd idolized since first sight. "Well, there are jams among the packages, and a ham. But I also brought a few gifts."

"Gifts?" She removed the jars from beneath his arms. "But Christmas isn't for a few days yet."

The gentleness in his expression dimmed a little. "You know how bad I am at keeping secrets, and I thought you could do with a little cheering up after all that's happened this week."

For her? To cheer her? Sweet warmth swelled into her cheeks, and she looked away. "I appreciate you being here a whole lot more than any gifts, Charles."

His smile fell altogether then, and he cleared his throat as he walked past her into the sitting room. "Well, maybe this will tide you over until the two of us can spend more time together." He gestured with his chin for her to follow. "Let's eat first, and then I'd love to see you open your gifts while Charlie's still asleep."

She settled into conversation with him, listening to him talk about some renovations to the house and recent business dealings. During the latter, a shadow passed across his face. "We're losing tenants to more of the businesses and factories in nearby towns because folks can earn enough to buy cheap housing near their work. I had to sell off fifty acres last month to offset costs and also have enough to complete renovations on the house."

"I imagine lots of tenants would be interested in purchasing their own land, if you wanted to get back some money that way, and they'd be more likely to stay."

"What do you mean?"

"Well, if their payments to you went toward ownership instead of renting the house and property, they'd be more likely to stay where they are. Most folks want a place that belongs to them."

He gave his head a shake. "I'm not sure I want most of the tenants to own land around me. I can either send the troublemakers away, if I own the land, or threaten to in order to control their behavior."

"But what about the good ones? The ones who've worked for you for years and only helped your business?"

He leaned back in his chair and took a drink of his coffee, his frown deepening. "No, it's a pretty idea, but you don't know how business works. It could end in disaster."

"Ownership creates loyalty, Charles. I saw it, growing up in the mountains. If people feel like they're valued and have an investment in their work, they're gonna work harder and be more content."

"No, let's not argue." His smile returned. "I know your heart's in the right place, but that just won't do." He stood and walked to a nearby chair where he'd placed his packages. "But it does make me think of one of the gifts I have for you."

Kizzie usually ignored his dismissiveness. After all, she didn't understand all the aspects of his business, but during their relationship, he'd shared many things with her. Paired with her own observations as a housemaid, her experience working for Mrs. Cappy, and conversations with her daddy, Kizzie knew enough to at least entertain solid ideas.

But Charles' disinterest in these particular suggestions stemmed less from Kizzie's thoughts being impossible and perhaps more from the fact that Charles liked the class differences between himself and his tenants.

She'd never noticed it before.

Power. Maybe even a sense of deserving.

And certainly a desire for control.

It didn't make him a bad person, but it certainly took a little more of the shine off the man she'd given her heart to all those months ago.

Is that why he chose her and their secret relationship? Control? Her heart pulsed in pain at the idea. No, not completely. She knew he cared, at least in part, but. . . A switch flipped in her mind.

What if he sought to control others because he held such little control where his mama was concerned? Certainly, controlling the tenants gave him a sense of power. And managing any produce sold from the property held power.

Her throat tightened.

And choosing a woman his mother so blatantly refused not only held power but bucked against her control.

"Open this one first." He patted the chair next to him and, once she'd joined him, placed a rather large, unusually shaped package into her lap. As soon as her fingers met the paper, she recognized the curves and shape of a bonnet. She raised her eyes to him, grinning at the way his smile spread to light his eyes, watching her.

The Charles she knew, she reminded herself. The one who cared about her.

The one who wanted her.

She hesitated. But to marry her? Truly? Ever?

"You're not usually this slow to unwrap my gifts." His brows wiggled and returned her to a more lighthearted frame of mind.

She pulled off the ribbon and peeled back the paper to reveal an exquisite and elegant blue-trimmed hat with a wide brim and a few feathers. A simple silver ornament of some sort poised in the center top. "It's called a promenade hat, I'm told." He nodded toward it. "And it is the same color as your eyes."

His comment captured her attention before she slipped her fingers over the soft cloth. He noticed her eyes? She didn't recall him voicing much appreciation for them before. Other parts of her, especially in more intimate situations, but not her eyes. "It's beautiful."

"Let's see it."

She laughed. "I'm not wearing a dress fit enough for something this pretty."

"Your dress is fine." He slipped close, wrapping his arm around her waist. "And everything looks pretty on you, Kizzie."

His kiss shouldn't have taken her by surprise, but it did. The fact that she'd placed her whole future on him left a big unknown on the horizon because the bond between them she used to rely on had shifted into uncertain territory after yesterday. And, for the first time since he'd swept her into a closet and kissed her, she wondered what her future looked like without him.

He drew back, plucked the hat from her hands, and carefully fitted it to her head, his grin broadening to light his eyes.

"It's a perfect shade." He held her gaze, his smile fading. "You look every bit the lady."

A lady. She searched his face. But looking like a lady didn't make her one, did it? Not enough to change his mother's mind.

"Thank you, Charles." She ran a hand over the soft fabric, diverting her attention away from his face. "This is so nice of you."

"Nice?" He laughed, hands on her shoulders, those warm eyes staring back at her. "Kizzie, I know this isn't what you'd hoped, but it doesn't change the truth that I care about you and Charlie."

Care about.

Not love.

"I want to do nice things for both of you."

Her heart hammered in her chest, trying to cling to the thread of hope in his words.

But how long could she live on words?

"And I want you to know I heard your concerns yesterday." He handed her a large envelope tied with a ribbon. "You were right. If something was to happen to me. . ."

She stared at him, almost regretting her previous thoughts. Of course he cared.

"Are you planning on something happening to you?"

"No." His grin tipped. "Stop stalling and open it."

Kizzie pulled her gaze from his and tugged the ribbon loose. She opened the envelope then slid a folded, booklet-like paper from its casing. Printed across the front in bold lettering was the word Deed.

Deed? She blinked. She knew what deeds were. They proved ownership. But what sort of—

She unfolded the paper and skimmed the information, trying to make sense of the wording, the flourish of signatures, and some official stamp.

The house, outbuildings, and five acres—

A surveyor's map showed an area with more descriptive words like "to the Ellison River" and "along Easton Road." Was this a deed to the house?

"Your name is right there." He pointed to a line where someone had typed her full name. Kizzie Louisa McAdams.

She lifted her gaze to his, the reality moving into clarity with the speed of cold molasses. "You've deeded the house to me?"

His grin flashed wide. "And five acres of land. It's yours to do with as you need."

How. . . ? She shook her head to bring the thoughts together.

"I. . .I don't know what to say." She swallowed, looking from him back to the paper. "Apart from that little baby in there, I've not had anything of my own in all my life."

"Daisy and the buggy are included. And anything else in the barn." His smile beamed his pleasure, and Kizzie's heart softened all over again, grasping for the connection to him she desperately wanted.

She placed a kiss to his lips, which Charles quickly took to a more intimate level. Despite the slightest warning rising in her mind, she embraced his affection, his care.

Besides Charlie, he was all she had.

And she needed to embrace what she had. Display her gratitude. Shower him with her love.

Because then maybe her love would prove enough to secure their little family's future.

Kizzie woke in Charles' arms, the cool of the morning just outside the blankets. His chest swelled with his breaths in rhythmic movements against her side as he continued sleeping.

How many times had she awakened to him at her side?

Dozens.

But this morning, a strange pang ached through her at the realization of what she'd done. . .again. She grasped for a description. A picture. The only image fluttering through her mind came in the form of a shadow. A cold shadow. And one just outside the touch of a sunbeam.

Warmth swelled beneath her eyelids. Why?

She owned this house. She was in the arms of the man she loved. She had a beautiful baby.

So why did she feel some deep grief she couldn't explain?

She opened her eyes, and her attention moved across the room. In the dim light of sunrise, Charlie lay bundled and asleep. Her gaze moved to the dresser nearby.

Her mother's Bible still lay there, the deed tucked within its well-worn folds. Kizzie wasn't sure why she'd placed the document there, but it felt right. Safe.

The grief stabbed afresh.

Something was wrong. . .with this relationship, her situation, and. . .her heart.

Like the woman at the well, did God want more for her? Better for her? Even if she'd made so many wrong choices—she felt another of Charles' breaths at her side—over and over again? Was she living off scraps of this world when God had a sweeter meal for her starving soul?

Charles stirred awake and grinned at her as he rolled from the bed. He rubbed one of his shoulders. "Charlie's certainly growing. After holding him a while last night, I'm a little sore." His attention fell on her as she reached for her robe. "I can't imagine how sore you must be."

She looked away from his bare chest, a wave of shame rushing through her in a way she hadn't felt since their first few meetings together. What was wrong with her? "He is getting bigger. That's a fact."

Charles walked from the room, likely to tend the fire, so Kizzie quickly pulled on a simple day dress and socks then moved to the dresser. The deed poked from the top of the Bible. Kizzie drew it from its spot and unfolded it, placing it on the bed to look over as she braided her hair.

Charles told her that he'd had the paperwork drawn up soon after she'd seen his mother. Proof all the more of his affection for her and Charlie. She skimmed over the wording, noting a few extra things she hadn't had the sense to comprehend yesterday.

House furniture was included with a specific mention of the cookstove.

The cow was also listed as hers. And with the inclusion of land to the river, Charles secured her access to water and alternate transportation should she ever need it.

He'd thought of everything.

The gift proved the depth of his care all the more.

She skimmed the signatures at the bottom and paused on the last one. A chill fell over her skin, and she snatched up the paper to take a closer look.

Eliza Morgan.

Charles' mother knew about this? Agreed to it, even?

Why? The woman Kizzie had confronted clearly had no mind to help her at all. So. . .what had Charles offered in exchange?

Charles reentered the room, buttoning his shirt as he came. His grin spread as he noticed the deed in her hand. "I'm glad to know you haven't gotten used to the gift just yet."

"It's the finest gift I've ever gotten." And she was grateful. But what had it cost him. . .or her? "I can't believe your mama agreed to it though."

His smile fell, and he turned his attention toward pulling on his pants. "It took a lot of convincing, that's for sure, but she finally came around."

Kizzie studied him, waiting. His diverted gaze told her more than his words, but was she brave enough to ask for the truth? Did she really want to know?

"Will you be staying for breakfast?"

"I'm afraid not." He tugged on a sock. "I have to get on home to prepare for a trip."

A trip? Why hadn't he mentioned that last night?

Charles pulled on his other sock and then sighed. "I'm gonna have to tell you one way or the other." His gaze came to meet hers. "Mama got notice last evening that her brother is very ill and has requested we travel out to see him for Christmas, in case the worst happens."

Kizzie drew in a breath, processing this new information. "Your mama just found out last night?"

Charles didn't answer.

All of this, right after the scare? As if purposefully orchestrated to drive her away.

"That timing is awfully convenient—"

"It's a stipulation, Kizzie." He looked up, his jaw tight. "One of the promises I had to make to convince her to give you this land. I don't have the power on my own. Everything still belongs to her. We came to an understanding."

Stipulation? So he had exchanged something for her to own the land.

"How long do you plan to be gone?"

He tugged on a shoe. "I imagine a week or two."

She nodded, refolding the deed. "What's the other promise?"

He looked up, his brows raised.

"You said going to your uncle's was 'one of the promises' you had to make." She drew in a breath. "What was another?"

"Isn't the fact you got this house and land to your name enough, Kizzie?" He went back to tying his shoe. "Why can't any of it be enough?"

"It ain't that, and you know it." A heated flicker lit her chest. "I'd give up about anything to be with you, Charles." She waved toward the room. "I have."

And yet, he felt further away than ever.

Silence filled the space as he finished tying his other shoe and then stood, keeping his distance. "You want to know? I promised her I'd keep my marriage options open and agreed to see some of the women she wants me to meet."

Women who were much more appropriate than Kizzie. Proper women. Women who would give him legitimate sons and heirs.

He walked over to her and then sat next to her on the bed, pulling her hands into his. "It's all a game. I play the part she wants for as long as I need to, and then we can be together."

She searched his face. Did he realize how much his choices impacted her? His life went on like normal, no worse for wear, but she bore the brunt of the brokenness and shame as the social castaway.

"Charles, it's not a game to me and Charlie. It's our future." He tried to pull away, but her grip on his hands tightened. "Can you imagine what Charlie's future would look like if your mama lives another five or ten years? How do we explain why he don't carry his daddy's name? What do we say when he's shunned at school because he's got no claim to you?"

He succeeded in escaping her grip and stood. "We'll face that when we need to." An uncustomary fire lit his amber eyes as he turned to her. "You own this house. It's more than most women ever have. It's yours." His voice took on a rumble as he neared her, towering. "And I could have just left you to fend for yourself. In fact, I had several folks suggest I do just that, but I didn't. I've accepted this responsibility."

The words knifed through her, cold and putting her in her place.

"Why can't you just realize I'm doing what I can and all I need from you is to show some gratitude? Some understanding."

Her eyes burned, and she hated it. The last thing she wanted to do was cry, to confirm any weakness. But she couldn't stop the sting. The wave of utter lostness. The dawning realization that the little dream she'd concocted in her head for a year was dissolving before her eyes.

They were both trapped. She was trapped in a world of outcasts and soured hopes. And her presence trapped Charles to a past he thought he wanted, but did he? Really?

Or was this all a game too?

He gave his head a shake and took her hands, drawing her up from the bed. "I'm sorry, Kizzie. I don't want us to end our morning with a fight. Let's have a little breakfast together before I go. Talk a little." He punctuated his words with a squeeze to her hands. "Just remember, I'm doing all of this for us."

Us.

A word that meant two or more.

Then why did she feel so alone?

He didn't stay more than fifteen minutes, talking about the farm more than anything else, before he left.

Kizzie stood on the porch with Charlie in her arms and watched Charles disappear down the road, fresh tears forming in her eyes.

The truth bled painfully clear, changing everything.

The women in the dress shop had called her a kept woman.

But Kizzie hadn't really believed it, until now.

Chapter 7

Kizzie refused to visit the Chappells.

How could she? They'd taken her to their church, and on the same day she'd fallen right back into Charles' arms.

She kept doing that, but this time, she felt like God saw her.

Her skin crawled at the very idea, because she remembered all too well exactly what He saw. And had seen. Each time she'd sinned.

Each and *every* time.

She gave her head a shake and placed Charlie down into his cradle for his nap. Why on earth would He want her if she couldn't do the right thing for one whole day, let alone years?

Because, truth be told, she'd been the rascally one of her siblings. The wanderer and mischief maker. Never in a mean-spirited sort of way, but in a way that likely kept her mama on her knees more often than for the others. Her grin spread just a little.

Well, her little brother, Isom, might best her in mischief, but he still had some years to catch up.

Maybe those childhood fooleries weren't as bad as her choices now, but they'd pointed to a mischievous, rebellious heart, hadn't they? Why would God want someone with a heart so prone to wander?

Yet her mama had always said God forgave. Kizzie had even over-heard her praying for her daddy during one of his bad drunks, and instead of being angry, her mama pled for God to chase Daddy down.

It was her mama's way. To hope. Always hope.

And to pray.

Mama had even said once that nobody could outrun God. *"He's faster, smarter, and can last a heap longer. If He wants you, He'll catch you."*

But Daddy ran from a whole host of nightmares, only a few Kizzie knew about. His history was bathed in rejection and abandonment and growing up much too fast. On his good days, he was the best daddy. On his bad days? Dangerous.

Was God chasing her daddy? Would God catch him?

Her attention shifted to the sunlight filtering through the bedroom window. She didn't have to ask if God chased her. Now that she recalled her mama's words, the sense of someone on her heels made sense. He was after her.

And her heart kept running.

Running so hard because…well, why? Why would He want her? All she had to offer was a bunch of poor choices and a whole lot of regret.

And how would her life change if He caught her?

She turned toward the dresser and ran a hand over her mama's Bible, her fingers curling around the cover. The deed marked a placeholder somewhere near the middle. She searched the page. Isaiah? She looked closer. Her uncle's name was Isaiah!

Her attention fell on a bold number forty-three, and the very next words drew her nearer. She read them aloud. "'But now thus saith the Lord that created thee, O Jacob.'"

Who was Jacob? God had created her too.

"'And he that formed thee, O Israel.'"

He'd formed her too. Her palm went to her stomach. Just like he'd formed little Charlie.

But the next words froze her in place. "'Fear not: for I have redeemed thee, I have called thee by thy name; thou art mine.'"

A chill traveled up her arms, and she slammed the book closed.

Had God been listening to her thoughts only a few moments ago? Had He chased her all the way into this room to call her?

She looked over her shoulder.

Could He really want to redeem *her*?

A knock at the door sent Kizzie jumping away from her Bible

as if God might very well come rising off the pages in some sort of spectral form.

The knock came again, so Kizzie left the room and slowly approached the door. Charles had cut a peephole in the front door with a little sliding bar to cover it and keep out the cold. Unlike the one-eyed peephole at Mrs. Cappy's store back home, he'd made it a little larger to give an easier look.

Surely God wouldn't just come to the front door, would He?

She almost laughed at the fool notion but still took her time sliding the bar over to peer outside.

"If you're tryin' to hide from the world, girl," came Nella's familiar voice, "you picked the wrong family to take on as neighbors."

Kizzie's laugh bubbled out, and she opened the door to find Nella and the three children, with Nella holding a basket of goodies and a knowing look that would make Caroline McAdams proud.

"Boss greeted us in the yard and then skittered off after some squirrel." Nella glanced around the house, a smile growing on her face. "Well, I'll be. Ain't this the prettiest place I ever did see."

Kizzie laughed again, much needed. "You've been inside the Morgan house, and you think this one is prettier?"

Kizzie took the basket and moved to the kitchen.

"I ain't got no use for a castle." Nella followed her, whistling in appreciation as her attention landed on the cookstove. "But this'll do for a family just fine."

"There's an upstairs." Kizzie gestured toward a little door near the kitchen that hid a narrow stairway behind it. "But I don't need that space right now, so I don't go up there."

Nella stepped over and opened the door, peering up the darkened stairway. "It's good you got a door to close off the air and keep the heat down here. That's a good idea too."

"Seems a lot of good ideas went into this house," Ruth offered with a grin.

Nella dipped her chin and set the basket on the counter. "No wonder the Petersons ain't too keen to see it gone."

"But Charles said he set the Petersons up with an even nicer one on the other side of the woods. Bigger barn too."

Nella turned to the boys. "Go on out and poke around in the yard for a little while, boys. You can come in for some math lessons later. You go on with 'em, Ruth."

The girl frowned her answer.

"Git on now. I'll come rescue you from your rascal brothers in a bit." She glanced over at Kizzie. "That gives me and Miss Kizzie time to mix up some sugar cookies."

Kizzie sent a look to the basket, and sure enough, all the ingredients needed for the cookies waited inside. Kizzie grinned at the boys. "And I reckon Boss could do with some of your lovin'."

The boys ran out the back door with Ruth straggling behind, and Kizzie began laying out the items from the basket, avoiding eye contact. "You're too kind, Nella. I really don't deserve—"

"What's all this about, girl?" Nella's hands landed on her hips. "You ain't been by in days, and we expected you for supper last eve."

Kizzie released a long breath and looked over at Nella, who'd removed her hat and gloves.

"Charles came to see me before leaving. He had the house turned over to my name."

Nella's eyebrows shot high. "He deeded the house to you?"

"And land. Five acres. It's—it's mine."

"That's a fine gift. Any person should want to have ownership of their own place, if they can." She reached for the flour and placed it on the counter in front of her. "But that ain't what's kept you away, is it?"

Kizzie stared down at the basket and pulled some sugar from its contents. "He...he stayed overnight again." Her gaze came up to Nella's. "I had put it in my mind to try and do better, but he was so sweet and charming, and I was so lonely..."

"And you was afraid to come see me? Ashamed?" Nella measured out the flour and placed it in a ceramic bowl Kizzie provided. "Do you think you fallin' back into his arms surprises me?"

Her nose tingled with coming tears. "Disappoints, maybe?"

"Why do you think it hurt your heart so much to give in to him this time?" Nella stepped close enough to Kizzie to touch her arm, her expression tender. "More than the past times?"

Kizzie shook her head.

" 'Cause God is after you." Nella's lips tipped ever so slightly. "He's workin' on your heart to put it in order. Right things right. Wrong things wrong."

"But I knew it was wrong, and I done it anyhow. God can't want a heart like mine. I've done wrong over and over again, Nella. I *wanted* to do wrong sometimes, even. I'm a rebel to the good. He don't want rebels like me."

"Don't you go makin' God so small." Nella's dark gaze sharpened on Kizzie. "You're measuring' His ways like He's one of us, but He ain't. His view is much bigger. You think your choices surprised Him?"

Heat rushed into Kizzie's face at the idea of Him knowing what she'd chosen.

"But His love is bigger too. Bigger than us. We place folks in boxes that we think they can never leave. But God ain't stopped by our boxes or our hatred or our rebel hearts. No." She shook her head, her smile growing wider than Kizzie had ever seen. "You'll never get out of this box on your own. You need Him. And your heart is exactly the one He's after."

Her words took on size and volume and filled the room in an impossible way, shoving into Kizzie's breaths like Nella's words wanted to get right inside her chest. "Why?"

Nella sighed. "If your daddy hadn't cast you out, do you think your mama would have taken you in?"

A fresh sting of tears pierced Kizzie's eyes. "I know she would. She tried to talk Daddy into letting me stay. Cried, even, and I've never seen her cry, 'cept when we sent my brother off to war."

"You're sure. She would have."

Kizzie nodded. "No doubt."

"God's love is even bigger than that. What you're craving, He can supply. The joy you're lookin' for, He has. Because His love ain't measured by your ability to love Him back. He loves because. . ." Her smile spread to her eyes. "He loves. And He'll keep loving you. Over and over again."

"But I've made such a mess of my life."

"It's true. And you're gonna have to live with the consequences, like any of us have to do from our choices." Nella squeezed Kizzie's arm, the glow in her eyes somehow transferring into Kizzie's chest. "But your wrong choices don't stop God from makin' things right. Never have."

"I thought…I thought Charles loved me enough to marry me." She wiped at her eyes. "I really believed it."

"I know, but if he loved you, girl, he'd either marry you or show some restraint. Continuing to act like he's your husband without the assurance and protection of his name ain't lovin' you or Charlie at all." Her gaze searched Kizzie's. "And I think you're startin' to know that."

Kizzie looked away, the truth rising into clarity.

"You're takin' all the risk. He's gettin' all the benefits. Love don't work that way." She tapped a finger beneath Kizzie's chin, raising her gaze up to hers. "Real love, God's or otherwise, is a giving sort of love. More than presents, but of ourselves for the other's best. Just like what we celebrate in a few days with Christmas, Kizzie. God gave everything to show us how much He loved us. Everything for our good."

The conversation turned to Charlie, then to Joshua and Nella's dreams, but the whole while a simmering realization bubbled beneath the surface, waiting for Kizzie to acknowledge what her heart already seemed to understand.

God loved her.

Anyway.

He loved her.

Always.

He loved her because He loved her, so there was no way to get out of it.

And—her breath caught on the admission—maybe she didn't want to.

"Your numbers look good, Nella." Kizzie pushed the ledger back toward her friend. "I only found three little errors. That's not as many as last time."

"And you're seein' the growth, ain't ya?" Nella took the ledger into her arms. "Joshua told me to make some dresses to sell. I've been too nervous to try, but he thought it was worth a chance." She tapped the ledger. "And that's what you see over the past three weeks. My dresses

34d Y

have been sellin'. Mrs. Berry took a few last week and told me she's gonna need more right away, they sold so fast."

"Well, it's about time. Ruth bragged and bragged about your skill with a needle and said you were too skittish to let others see your gift, but it's right here." Kizzie tugged at the sleeve of the woman's simple, yet lovely, day dress. "This one's even got puffed sleeves and some detail at the cuffs. A dress a woman can wear every day but still feel a little fancy in."

"If we can just get Joshua a way to start his business, we could finally buy us a place within a year or two."

Nella's statement paused Kizzie's response.

"Joshua just needs access to the river for his mill, right?"

"Sure does. A good spot. But we're too far from the river—"

"But my land." Which still sounded strange to say aloud. "My property goes down to the river. I don't know if the spot is right for a mill, but, well, what if you and Joshua came to look at it?"

Nella's attention zeroed in on Kizzie. "What do you mean, girl?"

"I mean, that if all you need is river access, then you know somebody who'd be willing to give it to you."

"Now, Kizzie, that's your—"

"I didn't have anyone when my daddy cast me out. No place. Nobody willing to take me in." Kizzie took Nella's hand. "But you and your family did more than just take me in and help me with Charlie. You let me be a part of your family. I was alone in so many ways. Didn't know what in the world to do with a baby. And. . ." Kizzie drew in a breath, warmth pooling in her eyes. She squeezed Nella's hands. "Maybe God sent me to help *you* too."

Nella's gaze paused in Kizzie's, the woman clearly speechless.

A wild and wonderful warmth burst through Kizzie's chest at the awareness of her ability to help this family, touch these lives in such a good way. Was this a tiny glimpse of God's joy in rescuing her?

The idea shocked her.

And did He want *her* of all people to give, serve, in such a way? Could He believe in her that much? Love her that much even after her choices?

Was her heart even big enough for such a calling?

A puff of a laugh burst from her. "Getting started a little earlier on that dream wouldn't be so bad, would it?"

Nella shook her head and then released a laugh so big, both her boys looked up from their cookies.

"No, indeed, girl. No, indeed."

Kizzie embraced the awareness, the light, the inexplicable sense of belonging, and released her fears and shame, joining her own laughter with Nella's.

Love, the realest kind, caught her.

White moonlight streaked through the only window Kizzie left unshuttered throughout the night since the unwelcome evening visit almost two weeks before. A halo circled the moon, hinting to another upcoming snow.

Beautiful.

She rested her head against the window frame, the cold of the outside seeping in around the glass, but she only smiled.

Loved.

Beyond her brokenness.

By God?

The newness of the idea radiated a strange lightness through her heart. She raised a sugar cookie to her lips. She'd done nothing to deserve His love. Hadn't expected it, especially since her own father cast her away, but her fledgling understanding grew into something deeper and more real with each additional thought about who He said she was and each passage she read in her mama's Bible.

And, this new identity brought a purpose with it. Something she'd never imagined in all her life.

Helping others.

Sure, she'd helped her family when needed, but her heart had always been so full of what she thought were bigger and better things beyond the mountain that she failed to realize how she could love others well right where she was. But the glimpse of joy in Nella's face when Kizzie had mentioned the land. . .

Well, now she knew.

If God had given her something, either big or small, she had the ability to share.

Give.

Just as God had given to her not only in her spirit but through the care of Nella and Joshua. With a little prayer of thanksgiving, she popped the rest of the cookie in her mouth and then turned toward the fire to add another log.

"It's long past sleeping time, Boss," Kizzie whispered to the dog lying in front of the fire. She ruffled the fur on his head and straightened. She'd not taken two steps toward the kitchen when a low growl rumbled from the dog.

Kizzie turned in time to see something crash through the window where she'd just been standing. A large rock rolled to a stop by a chair near the fireplace, and Boss ran to the front door, erupting in a series of massive barks.

Kizzie pressed herself against the wall. Between Boss' barks, she made out some of the words carried in through the window on the cold air.

"We don't want your kind here!"

"Leave, or we'll make you leave!"

More threats rose from outside, each voice alerting her to another man yelling in the darkness. How many were there?

Another rock flew through another pane of the same window, this time hitting the wall beside her. Her gaze shot to the ceiling in wordless entreaty. What was she supposed to do?

The doorknob rattled, and all warmth fled her body.

What would they do to her if they made it inside?

Her attention flitted to the bedroom. What would they do to Charlie?

With a sudden rush of heat shooting from her stomach to her face, she ran into the bedroom, pushed some blankets near Charlie's ears to, maybe, help curb the noise, and then grabbed the rifle from the corner of the room. She jerked open the dresser drawer and retrieved bullets as well as the pistol Joshua had given her last week.

She had to protect Charlie.

A scraping noise along the side of the house alerted her to more taunting.

She needed to know where the men were, but how?

Boss kept his place at the door, snarling and scratching to escape, but whoever had been at the front must have moved when they heard the dog barking. *Keep your head, Kizzie.*

Her gaze landed on the door that led to the upper floor, so she ran over and dashed up the narrow stairs. Two rooms separated the space, both with large front windows. She moved to the first, the moonlight giving her a much better view of the outside than any of those men could have of her.

Three shadowy figures, one holding a torch, stood in the front yard by her fence. One looked as if he held up a rock to throw. With quick work, Kizzie gently propped open the window and readied the rifle. Squirrel hunting in broad daylight proved a little different than this, but the same technique applied.

Careful. Steady.

The rifle jerked against her shoulder, its blast sending a ring to her right ear, but she hit her target. The fence right beside the man with the rock.

A loud roar came from the man, and three more men ran from out of sight to join the first three.

Six?

And just her.

She squeezed her eyes closed. "Lord, help me. Please."

How could she ever scare off these men when there was only her?

She felt for the pistol in her skirt pocket, and an idea popped to mind out of nowhere. She propped the rifle against the wall and ran back down the stairs, staying within the shadows of the house. With careful movements, she slid the broken window up enough to peer out. Two men stood at the porch steps, arguing. Two more rounded the left side of the house, and the other two, both with guns, moved to the right.

She positioned herself out of sight and raised the pistol, this time taking careful aim for the man nearest the porch. . .and his massive hat. The shot rang out, and she stayed only long enough to watch the hat fly off the man's head before she dashed back up the stairs.

A gunshot fired from outside, hitting what sounded like the wall of the house. She reloaded the rifle and went to another upstairs window.

A voice rose from one of the men. "I thought you said she was alone."

"She's supposed to be," came the response. "Morgan said she was."

Morgan? Kizzie's face went cold. Not Charles, surely.

"Then who's shooting from where?" The man's words came slurred.

Drunk men were especially dangerous, she knew all too well from a lifetime with one. But at least her plan had worked to confuse them. Drunk men were usually easier to confuse too.

The men who had moved right turned the corner of the house, where her bedroom was, so Kizzie landed a shot directly in front of one of them, maybe even caught his boot.

The man jumped back, letting out a string of curses.

"There's got to be more than one. Someone's in there protecting that girl."

Kizzie rushed down the stairs, carefully returning to the broken window. The men had moved away from the house, three with guns raised.

She swallowed, her throat dry, her internal prayers shaking through her as she contemplated what she needed to do next. She couldn't keep firing at them all night. She hadn't the bullets.

One of their shots hit the house where she'd been at the other window, so she took her time, trying to make the next shot count. With another deep breath, she fired. The man released a cry and dropped his gun, reaching for his shooting hand and pulling it to his chest.

"The old woman didn't say nothin' 'bout the whore having someone helpin' her," one of the men yelled at him.

The old woman?

"Your aunt ain't payin' enough to get us killed," said another.

Paying? Aunt?

She didn't have time to fully consider the possibilities. She needed to take advantage of their weakening fight. The men's horses waited outside the fence, so with another breath, she stabilized her shoulder against the window frame and fired at the fence post nearest the front horse, a pale brown one.

The horse reared up as the fence splintered from the shot. It jerked free of its hitch, inspiring the other horses to try to follow suit.

"Catch the horses," one man shouted.

Another man ran through the gate, snagging one of the horses before it loosed itself.

"Ain't doin' no more here, Dean," the man with the wounded hand yelled as he ran to the gate. "The old hag's gonna have to pay for my hand."

"And get her story straight afore I come back with you, Cole," said another, grabbing the reins of another horse trying to free itself.

Cole?

The last man paused at the gate and looked toward the house, the pale moonlight glinting on his face. Her breath caught.

Cole Morgan? Charles' cousin?

Kizzie's breath puffed out, and she lowered the gun. The old woman and Cole?

Kizzie turned and leaned against the wall, Boss' barks still rising from downstairs. Did Eliza Morgan pay these men to try and scare her away? Did she hate Kizzie so much, despise her and Charlie's presence to such a degree, she'd risk Kizzie's life and Charlie's?

Charlie's cries rose over the sound of the barking, and Kizzie moved down the stairs, shuttering the broken window before she went to her baby. She sat in a rocking chair in the sitting room, the sudden quiet rushing through her as she fed Charlie. Her body started quaking, her mind scrambling through a hundred feelings and thoughts.

Boss lay at her feet, as if to reassure her of his presence.

She closed her eyes and pinched her lips against the growing tears. This was no way to live.

No future for Charlie.

She leaned her head back against the rocking chair, scraping through her trembling thoughts for help.

Her breaths began to slow, the shaking too, and the realization of what she'd done cleared through the betrayal and shock she felt from Mrs. Morgan's actions.

Kizzie hadn't cowered. No. God had given her courage. And the idea of how to fight back. She'd used what smarts she had to keep herself and Charlie safe.

She might have made some horrible decisions in the past, but she wasn't stupid.

And she might have weakened under Charles' affection, but she was stronger now.

And she might have been alone yesterday.

I have called thee by thy name; thou art mine.

But she wasn't alone anymore.

She looked over at the shuttered, broken window, an understanding beginning a slow climb into her mind.

She couldn't stay here.

Chapter 8

Kizzie contemplated going to the Chappells' the next morning but decided against it. She had to learn to manage things on her own, and this proved another good test of her abilities.

Besides, her nightly visitors confirmed a growing decision she'd contemplated ever since her confrontation with Mrs. Morgan.

So once she'd cleaned up after breakfast the next morning, she drove to town and inquired of the Berrys for someone who repaired windows. Mr. Berry offered to locate Mr. Clarkson and send him out to the house.

After a few inquiries as to whom she might speak with regarding her deed, Kizzie chose Mr. Berry's cousin, Mr. Davis, a newer lawyer in town instead of the lawyer who'd signed the deed. Charles didn't need to find out about her plans. Not yet. Mr. Davis responded to Kizzie's questions with a bit of surprise, especially noting the deed's recent transfer to her. But an idea continued to form and grow.

Evidently, a very unique idea, from Mr. Davis' response.

When Kizzie returned the next day to direct Mr. Davis to enact the plan and asked if he could have it drawn up by Christmas, he reluctantly agreed. Mrs. Cappy at the store back home had sold two plots of land when Kizzie worked for her, so part of the process held a little familiarity.

But the extra part? Well, at least Mr. Davis seemed to know what to do with that particular wording.

So it was with a great deal of excitement that Kizzie showed up to the Chappells' house on Christmas Day, bundled in a coat and her new bonnet, with Charlie in her arms and a flurry of snow all around her.

The children welcomed her into a house that smelled of cinnamon and sugar. A small fir tree stood in the corner of the sitting room, decorated with pine cones, ribbons, and a few delicate crocheted snowflakes.

"Mama taught me how to make them," Ruth said with a grin. "So while she was busy making dresses for a few folks, I practiced making these."

Ruth's progress showed in the different snowflakes on the tree, moving from less detailed to more as her skills improved. "They're the prettiest things I've ever seen on a Christmas tree, Ruth. Perfect."

"You can't mean that, Miss Kizzie." She lowered her gaze, her cheeks darkening. "You seen the Morgans' tree, and they even use candles to light theirs."

"But they don't have nothin' this special." She touched one of the snowflakes. "When your mama and daddy start their shop, you ought to make these to sell. I reckon there'd be folks waitin' in line to buy 'em. Especially rich folks."

Ruth's eyes grew wide with her smile. "And I'm learnin' to sew like mama too. She says there's money to be had in ready-made dresses."

"Well, I'm sure your mama will make dresses just as fine if not better than the ones in the dress shop in town." And Kizzie wouldn't mind showing that mean woman up a bit either. Enough to knock her off her high horse a little.

"I carved the birds." Quiet Elias shifted closer, gesturing to the tree.

Kizzie took in the various designs. Simple, but each unique. "I don't think I've ever seen such a fine tree in all my livin' days."

"Are y'all gonna stand around talkin' all day, or are you gonna eat?" Nella called from the kitchen where a veritable feast crowded on a new and longer table.

Nella beamed, clearly delighted with the new piece of furniture. "Joshua done gave me my present just in time for Christmas dinner."

And with a wide grin from Joshua, who looked as gussied up as the rest of the family in their Sunday best, they all gathered around the table for ham, potatoes, beans, bread, corn, two different pies, and a whole lot of laughter.

After everybody had their fill of Nella's tasty cooking, Joshua directed them to go sit around the Christmas tree.

Nella plucked a wakeful Charlie from Kizzie's arms.

"You might as well hand him over a while." She snuggled Charlie close, her smile brimming. "Ain't no use hoggin' all that baby-love to yourself."

Isaac grabbed Kizzie's hand and led her to a rocking chair between the tree and the fireplace, his eyes alight.

One bulky package, wrapped in brown paper, lay at the foot of the tree, simple twine tying it together. Another oddly-shaped one stood beside it. She couldn't make out any more, but she figured the family had already opened their gifts first thing this morning like her family used to do.

Maybe their gifts had looked a whole lot like the ones she knew from back home. Simple things. A woodcraft from daddy. An orange. Maybe even a soda pop. A pair of socks and, if things were really good that year money-wise, cloth for a dress or ribbons for the girls' hair. A book for Laurel. Paintbrushes for Maggie. A new knife for Jeb or Isom.

If she closed her eyes, she could see their faces. Hear their laughter.

"It's our custom to read the Bethlehem story after dinner on Christmas," Joshua said, drawing her attention back to him as he took his place in a kitchen chair he'd pulled into the room. His quiet demeanor belied his size as he bent over the Bible cradled in his hands.

The movement, the gentle way he read the words of the story, drew Kizzie's thoughts to a stop. She'd never seen Charles read the Bible, or talk about it. In fact, she couldn't imagine him taking Joshua's humble approach and gently leading his family in a story Kizzie was only now beginning to understand.

The magnitude of Mary's call. The vastness of God's love come to Earth. The shocking impossibility of a king in a stable. Her throat closed with emotion. A hint to what He'd do in the future—the impossible task of taking on the filth, brokenness, and outcasts of eternity and rescuing them.

Like her.

Her smile spread as it had been doing over the last few days. How could she not smile? No matter what happened to her, no matter how hard the choices and consequences, she was loved forever.

Completely safe in His care.

And she belonged to Him no matter where she called home.

He would be her faithful Father. Her protective Lover. Her loving Bridegroom.

"The young'uns done opened their gifts this morn," Nella announced after Joshua finished the story. "But we saved the last two for you and Charlie."

Kizzie shifted her attention to the woman. "What do you mean?"

"Go on, boys." Nella gestured with her chin toward Isaac and Elias.

The boys rushed to the tree and picked up the oddly shaped gift, one on each side, bumbling forward as they brought it to set at Kizzie's feet. "You done so much to help us with our numbers, we wanted to give you something."

"But we couldn't leave Charlie out for his very first Christmas," Ruth added. "So we want to give him something too."

"Y'all know you didn't have to—"

"Miss Kizzie," came Joshua's deep voice, "we wanted to. And we thank ya."

She quieted at his words and turned to the boys, whose smiles took over their whole faces.

"Open it, Miss Kizzie," Isaac urged as Elias pushed the gift closer.

The paper fell away to reveal a wooden rocking horse, delicate in its design, beautiful in its craftsmanship. It reminded her of her brother Jeb and his handcrafts.

"I carved the tail," Isaac nearly shouted. "And 'Lias carved the mane."

"You both did a real good job." Kizzie ran her hand over the wooden mane. Her gaze raised to Joshua, the major crafter of the gift. "Charlie is going to love it."

"In a year or two, I reckon." He grinned.

"I still love mine," Isaac announced.

"But he's too big for it." Elias shook his head as if his brother was the most ridiculous person in the world. "His knees almost touch the floor when he's on it now."

"Charlie is going to love it." Kizzie repeated, nodding to the boys. "And even more so 'cause it came from some good-hearted boys just like I hope he'll end up being one day."

Their grins broadened, and Ruth pushed forward with the other package in her hands. "And this one's for you, Miss Kizzie."

Kizzie breathed out a sigh and gathered the package into her arms. Soft, like a pillow? The paper fell away to reveal beautiful cloth, its pale blue background dotted with darker blue and pink flowers.

Kizzie looked over at Nella, who only stood smiling and bouncing little Charlie.

With careful fingers, she raised the cloth, and it unfolded into the most exquisite dress she had ever seen.

"Mama let me help make it for you," Ruth said, scooting her chair closer to Kizzie, her smile lighting her eyes. "It was my first try at sewing puffy sleeves."

"And she did a fine job." Nella nodded. "She has the makings of a good seamstress."

From the few dresses Kizzie had worn and seen from Nella, she knew the woman had excellent seamstress skills, but nothing prepared her for the beauty of this design.

"Nella." Kizzie breathed out the word, continuing to examine the long sleeves with a delicate V-cut at the hand. Beaded appliqués lined the V-neck front, giving the gown a more elegant style, and a paler blue overskirt offered a soft silhouette to the darker floral print of the underskirt. "Ruth." Kizzie blinked. "I. . .I can't wear this."

"Yes, you can." Ruth nodded. "Mama made it to fit."

"And you can hold your head high when you wear it too, girl," Nella added with a wink. "It's your birthday dress."

"My birthday dress?" But Kizzie's birthday had been in September. She'd turned seventeen.

"For your soul." Nella's gaze held Kizzie's. "You're a new creation, a woman of God now."

Kizzie looked back down at the dress with new eyes, and the idea of how God had taken her from a very broken, sin-stained young woman to claiming her as His child presented itself through this gown. And

Nella knew it. The Kizzie wearing the soiled, stinking dirty rags from that night over six weeks ago proved a very different Kizzie at heart now. She still marveled at the notion of being God's child, but His love and promises shone with the beauty and detail of the finest gown.

Her birthday dress, indeed.

"So you'll always remember who you are." Nella's smile softened, and a watery film came into her eyes. She cleared her throat, and the moment passed. "Now, what do y'all say to singin' a few carols?"

Kizzie blinked her tears away. "Wait." She placed her bundle to the side and stood. "I got a gift to share."

Nella shook her head. "Now, girl. Ain't no—"

"I wanted to." She repeated the words Joshua said earlier. "And I thank you." She nodded toward Charlie. "From both of us, because I don't know where I'd be if it hadn't been for y'all."

She walked to her coat and tugged the envelope from its folds before bringing it to place in Joshua's hands.

"Ours was bigger than yours," Isaac said with a frown.

"Isaac Thomas!" Nella said as Kizzie took Charlie from her arms. "It's the heart of the gift that matters more than anything else."

Isaac's expression turned doubtful, but he pinched his lips closed.

"Go over and open it with your husband, Nella." Kizzie tried to bite back her growing smile but failed. "It's for the whole family."

Ruth walked over to stand behind her daddy, and the boys reluctantly joined too, Isaac looking every bit as if he doubted anything he'd want could come out of that little envelope.

Nella studied Kizzie a moment and then turned to Joshua, who shrugged one of his big shoulders and opened the envelope.

The desire to blurt out the wonderful surprise shook through Kizzie, but she merely clenched her hands together in front of her, watching. "It's a way to get your dream started early. You won't have to wait five or ten years."

"What. . ." Joshua tilted the paper toward Nella.

"It's a deed?" Nella shot Kizzie a wide-eyed look.

"Since helpin' with your budget, I know what y'all got in your funds, so I considered that when I met with the lawyer, Mr. Davis, in town.

He's gonna finish up the paperwork in the next few days and then y'all can sign, if you want. But the basic idea is that, with what you got right now, you'll purchase the acre by the river right away, so you can go ahead and start your plans for the mill." She leaned over and tapped the paper. "And then, you can send me a small amount, there." She pointed again. "Each month, till you own the other three and the house. I'm keeping one acre for myself, is all."

"You. . .you can't." Joshua looked back down at the paper, shaking his head.

"I can." She laughed. "Don't you want to own your own place?"

"Of course we do," Nella answered, blinking.

"And this is a perfectly good offer. Just like anyone else who has land they want to sell."

"Kizzie. . ."

Evidently, Joshua had grown even less verbal than before.

"Your family already has a good reputation in this area, so you ain't bound to have trouble come your way, plus the location is by the river and a bit closer to town."

The room remained quiet, all eyes on Kizzie.

Maybe she'd guessed wrong. Maybe they didn't want to stay around here.

"You. . .you don't have to agree to nothin'. This is just a summary Mr. Davis wrote up so you can study on it a little while before making a decision."

"Are you gonna live with us in the house?" This from Elias, who, normally the quietest, was the only one who seemed to have a working mouth at the moment.

"No." Kizzie shifted her attention between the two frozen parents. "I think it's best if I travel somewhere else."

"What?" This seemed to rally Nella. "Where?"

"I don't know, but it's no good me staying here anymore, for lots of reasons." She'd tell Nella and Joshua about the attack once the children went to bed, so they'd understand even more.

"Are you serious about this, Kizzie?" Joshua's quiet question brought her attention back to him as he held up the paper.

"More sure than I've been about anything else except Jesus savin' me." She rushed ahead. "And it's not only a gift, but an investment too. Into your company and the growth of the town." Her smile bloomed all over again. "But it's mostly an investment in a real good family with a great big dream."

And before she knew it, hands pulled her forward. Joshua, Nella, Ruth, and Elias wrapped her in a hug, while Isaac stepped back and patted her arm, looking from person to person as if they were all a little crazy.

What a wonderful moment, after feeling lost and left behind, to enjoy the sweet welcome and love of this family.

"Thank you, Kizzie," Nella finally said, her eyes bright with uncustomary tears. "Joshua and I will talk about it, for truth."

"But we can't imagine turnin' it down," he added, giving her arm a squeeze.

"I hope you don't." The gratitude in her chest warmed her all the way through. "I think it's a real good plan."

Mr. Davis proved as efficient and helpful as ever. Even more than the first time Kizzie had met with him. Maybe it was the fancy dress and hat that made the difference, or maybe Mr. Berry sent a good word, but whatever the reason, his generosity left her with a proper deed in hand and a promise from him to meet her at the Chappells' at five o'clock to witness the signing.

Only three days after Christmas, Joshua and Nella showed up at the house to accept Kizzie's offer, with a few minor changes related to monthly payments. And now, Kizzie planned to finalize everything and start the new year on a new journey.

Away from Charles Morgan.

And even farther away from home.

On the drive to the Chappells', Kizzie also prayed for forgiveness for entering Sally's Place in her Christmas dress and hat. Sally had fawned all over Kizzie, asking how she could help a "new lady in town" and inquiring after where she had purchased such an exquisite frock. One of the women who had been in the shop the first time Kizzie was there commented on the delicate embroidery on the sleeves. Kizzie smiled sweetly and told her that she'd gotten it from a new dressmaker in town "who has no qualms about serving formerly kept women."

Then the women recognized her, and leaving the two of them standing there with their mouths open, Kizzie left the building.

Her heart hadn't been in the right place at all when she'd done that. And she grinned a little too much at the memory.

But maybe it taught Sally a lesson. Though, after her Bible reading a few days ago, she figured she was supposed to leave those kinds of lessons to God.

Watching Joshua and Nella's joy as they signed the deed and remaining paperwork only secured Kizzie's decision. This was right.

"Kizzie, are you sure about leavin'?" Nella asked after Mr. Davis left and Joshua returned to his work outside. "You know we don't need that house. We can always build us another one on the land we own." She shook her head as if the idea still waited in dreams.

"I can't, Nella. I know that now." Kizzie placed a fully fed Charlie over her shoulder and patted his back. "It's not good for me or Charles. I care about him, and the temptation to love on him is hard to deny when he's nearby. He knows what to say and do to get me to give in, no matter how hard I try."

"Hmm. . . If a man ain't got no control over his mind, heart, or will, then he ain't nothin' more than one of them animals out in the woods." Nella held Kizzie's gaze, her words anchoring Kizzie's decision. "And love brings with it a special power. The power to control certain parts of ourselves, the darker parts, in order to do better by the ones we love, and for our own self-respect. If he cared about you, he'd try."

"I know. Which is another reason to leave. I didn't see it before, but I know now that he cares more about himself and his status than me and Charlie. But I think he's trapped too, betwixt caring for us and putting his mama at ease. He's tore up inside, and I can help fix things for him this way."

"You don't mean to come back then?"

"Not with the way things are now." Kizzie ran a hand over Charlie's soft head. "The only way I'll return is as Charles' wife or not at all. It can't be no other way, for the good of both our souls." She shook her head. "We've already got ourselves in a heap of trouble, and with my past as it is, it's gonna be hard enough to start over somewhere new."

"You got a past." Nella sighed and squeezed Kizzie's arm. "So do the rest of us. But God ain't so shortsighted to waste your past. Oh no, He'll use it to shape you and your future. Always remember how valuable your soul is." She touched Kizzie's cheek. "It's so important that the devil tries to steal it and God sent His Son to die for it. You are precious to Him."

The verses Kizzie had read a little over a week ago flew back to mind. *I have called thee by thy name; thou art mine.*

"So live your life knowin' exactly who caught you *and* who'll keep you." Nella's eyes turned glossy. "Ain't no past can take away your belongin', Kizzie. Find joy in who you *really* are."

"I'm learning. Slow as cold molasses, but I've been reminding myself every day." She chuckled. "Sometimes every hour. That I belonged to God first, and He loves me. Forever. No matter where I go. I belong with Him." Kizzie shrugged her shoulders helplessly. "Which is a good thing, 'cause I ain't quite sure where my next stop'll be."

"You do belong to God, and that's a fact, but it's good to have a plan too." Nella took a paper from the table and placed it in Kizzie's hand. "I sent a letter to a lady I used to work for who lives in The Hollows. It's a town a good twenty miles or more east of here, but if you start early, I reckon you could get there by evenin'." She tapped the paper. "I wrote directions and Mrs. Carter's name there so you'll have it. She's a good lady and will have a room you can rent. She might even have a job for you, but I ain't sure."

Kizzie folded the paper and pushed it into her pocket before pulling Nella into a hug. "Thank you for that." She drew back, taking in a steadying breath to keep the tears at bay. "I already packed up the few things I'm taking with me, but it's not much. Enough to fit in a few small trunks on the buggy."

Nella stepped back and looked Kizzie over. "Well, those ain't travelin' clothes, but you sure do make a pretty picture of a lady." She whistled low. "The dress fits nice."

"Perfectly." Kizzie ran her free palm over the cloth at her stomach.

"And I'd like to buy a few more once you have time to make them. Maybe something in green? Or pink?"

Nella's eyes lit. "Both good colors on you too, but you're about one of the prettiest women I've ever seen, Kizzie. Any color will do."

It wasn't the first time someone had noted her appearance. In fact, before Charles, she'd basked in the idea of being one of the prettiest girls on the mountain. But it was her looks, even in servants' clothes, that caught Charles' attention and led to her being swept away by his attention. Of course, God made her the way He made her, but she was determined to be influenced by wisdom more than charm in the future.

"What did Mr. Charles say about your plans?"

"I ain't told him. He's been gone, and I reckon he won't be back for another week yet. I wrote him a letter though and thought I'd take it over."

"He got back a full three days ago. Ain't he been by to see you?"

Kizzie's gaze shot to Nella's. "What?"

"Sure enough. Three days ago." Nella's eyes narrowed, and she took her time answering. "Joshua said there's a whole host of folks comin' to his house tonight for a belated New Year's party."

Three days, and no sight of him. Kizzie drew in a breath, the realization only confirming her plans all the more. Whatever feelings Charles had for her and Charlie, they weren't enough to spend time waiting for him to honorably act on them or for his mama to become more desperate with her attacks. No. It was time to leave.

"Would you watch Charlie for me?"

Nella's attention shifted from Kizzie to the baby in her arms. "'Course."

"I won't be long." Kizzie relinquished her hold on a cooing Charlie. "I'll deliver my letter through the back door to one of the servants. I'd feel better knowing I did it myself."

Nella's gaze trailed down Kizzie, her lips tipping a little. "Then I'm sure glad you're dressed like a fine lady, because if Mr. Charles does catch sight of you, he'll get a good view of what he's letting go."

"I don't mean no offense to your sewing skills, but if a dress and hat makes him take on some courage all of a sudden, I ain't sure he's ready for a lifetime of lovin' through the hard and ugly."

Nella gave Kizzie's cheek a gentle pat like a mama would to her young'un. "Does sound like you're gainin' some wisdom, for sure. Though the right clothes for a gal never hurt none." Nella's expression sobered. "Be careful, Kizzie. With the way Mrs. Morgan meant to scare you and the fact there'll be a whole host of guests arrivin' at the big house, I'd get there and back quick as a wink. Even *if* you look like you belong."

Chapter 9

CARRIAGES DOTTED THE LAWN OUTSIDE the Morgan house as sunset approached over the mountains. Kizzie gave the house a wide berth and pulled the buggy to a stop along the driveway, turning it so she could make a quick exit if she needed to.

If the Morgans were hosting a party, there was a good chance Cole would be among the guests, so at least she wouldn't have to worry about him. But the Petersons? Mrs. Morgan wouldn't be seen near them, let alone have them in her house.

And with a house party, Mrs. Morgan would ensure their house-keeper, Mrs. Pool, answered the door, in order to show off the Morgan wealth even more.

Kizzie drew in a deep breath and stared at the house. She'd talked herself into going right up to the front door on the drive over. She could easily give her letter to a servant or to Mrs. Pool and be on her way.

Whether he'd refused to come see her when he first arrived or his mama's needs prevented him, Charles' hesitation only drove Kizzie's choice deeper. He may care about her and Charlie, but spending her life on a man's hesitant, ashamed, or leftover love wasn't what she wanted.

Especially when her heart caught a glimpse of a much greater and more beautiful type of love. God wanted better for her too. *His* way. Even if that way meant her and little Charlie living without his father.

With a deep breath and letter in hand, she approached the porch she'd visited only a few weeks before. The sound of laughter filtered from inside along with a piano rendition of "Deck the Halls." Kizzie mounted the steps, her nicest boots making a quiet click against the wood. On tiptoe, she approached the nearest window and peered around the frame into the large front sitting room that was designed specifically for socializing, with its grand piano, fancy furnishings, and glossy floor.

A lovely woman with golden hair sat at the piano, her attention fixed on the music in front of her. Wasn't she Charles' cousin, Theodora, or something like that? To her right stood an older gentleman, and if Kizzie remembered right, he was the "ailing uncle" Charles and his mother had gone to visit. Judging from the grin on his face and the way his foot tapped to the music, he'd recovered awful quick from his near-death sickness.

Kizzie rolled her gaze heavenward and made to step back when her attention landed on a couple at one corner of the room. Dressed in high-class evening attire, looking every bit the gentleman, stood Charles Morgan with a raven-haired beauty on his arm. Had Kizzie seen her before too? Theodora's friend, wasn't she? Kizzie steadied herself with a palm to the window frame, nausea rising through her. This was Charles' life. The fancy clothes and parties. The care for rich friends and society.

Charles leaned close and whispered something to the woman. Her trill laugh resounded loudly enough for Kizzie to hear through the window.

Kizzie looked down at her gown and her delicate gloves. All doubt fled.

New clothes or more proper actions wouldn't make her fit into his world any better, no matter how long she waited.

Fancy parties, fancy dinners—she scanned the folks in the room—fancy people? No, her best memories and most comfortable moments nestled among common folks like the Chappells and Berrys, even her own family. Her gaze found Charles again. Oh, but he was a handsome man! She'd been on the receiving end of that smile and realized now that she didn't regret how he made her feel so special, and that maybe...maybe knowing him and all the hard things she'd learned over the past few months led her to understand what she really wanted.

Was that even possible?

She pressed her fist against her chest and stared at him one last time, attempting to memorize his face. Maybe someday she'd be able to tell Charlie about how his hair curled like his daddy's or how he had the same little bend in his nose. Her vision blurred and she blinked, backing away from the window and returning to the front door.

Mrs. Pool opened to her knock and ushered Kizzie in, clearly mistaking her for one of the guests.

"No, thank you, Mrs. Pool." Kizzie took the letter from her pocket and offered it to the woman. "I'm only here to ask you to deliver this directly into Mr. Morgan's hands, if you will."

Mrs. Pool's hazel eyes grew so wide, a few of the wrinkles flattened out. "Kizzie McAdams?" She scanned Kizzie from hat to boot tip. "Why, you look—"

"I don't want to cause any fuss," Kizzie continued, taking a step back toward the porch, "but I'd be much obliged if you'd get that letter to Mr. Morgan as soon as possible without disrupting his evening. Will you do that?"

The older woman nodded, continuing to stare.

"Thank you."

"Mrs. Pool, Mama's calling for you." Charles' unmistakable voice came from the next room, so Kizzie turned and without another word darted off into the growing dusk. Wind whipped around her with a few flurries spinning through the night air. Golden light from the setting sun still shone enough to light her path for a while yet, at least to get her to the Chappells', and she had a short ride to the house after that.

She'd just reached her buggy when someone called her name.

Her shoulders slumped.

Charles.

With a deep breath, she turned to face him. He ran toward her, coatless, his hair bouncing in the breeze and a paper waving in his hand as he approached. Her letter, no doubt, but he couldn't have read it all in the short time it took for her to leave the house and make it to the buggy.

"What is this?" He waved the paper in the air as he approached. "You're leaving?"

"I explained things in the letter." Her heartbeat ratcheted up, pounding in her ears. "It's for the best."

"For whose best?" He drew closer, his jaw clenched, eyes blazing. "Is this because I went away?" He waved back at the house. "Because of Lorainne?"

Ah, right. That was his cousin's friend's name. Lorainne.

"Your leaving just helped make things clearer, Charles. We can't keep living this way." She clasped her hands in front of her. "I don't want to make this choice, but it's the right one."

"The right one?" He searched her face, his approach slowing, almost predatory. "For who?" His frantic gaze roamed over her face. "Because I don't want you to go."

"And yet I can't stay." A little spurt of fire shot through her. "Have you thought at all about what it's like for me living as an outcast? What it will be like for Charlie?" She waved between the two of them. "This thing betwixt us, it ain't right."

"You're saying love isn't right?" He stepped nearer, towering over her, heat fairly radiating off him.

"Love?" He'd never mentioned love before. Her resolve shifted a little. "Maybe because I love you, I realize the only way you can truly be happy. . .is to be free."

Air shot out of him, his frown deepening. "What?"

"We're both stuck, Charles. Neither one of us can move forward with our lives. You have me and Charlie in the shadows, always reminding you of your past. And. . .I don't think we can belong in your future."

"You belong to me." His words burst out, and then he sighed. "With me."

Belong to him? No, she knew the truth now. "No, I don't. Not in a way that matters to God and the people watching us. Not in a way that I'm willing to live with anymore." She gentled her voice, touching his arm. "I love you something fierce. And I don't want to hurt you at all."

"Then don't." He growled out the words.

Tears invaded her vision, but she raised her chin against the tug toward him.

"By leaving now, I keep you from hurting a lot worse. And I keep

Charlie from hurting worse too." She searched his face. "Can't you see how the hurt will only grow the longer we live in this in-between place? It will hurt Charlie. His reputation, because he's going to grow up and realize that even if his daddy loves him, it's not enough to let him claim his daddy's name."

"Is that what this is all about?" He jerked back from her, eyes narrowed. "Are you trying to manipulate me into marrying you by doing this?"

She stared at him, hoping he'd realize the nonsense of his question. "Mama said you'd try."

"Your mama said?" A fire lit in Kizzie's chest and burst warmth into her face. "She's another reason to set you free, Charles. She already controls so much of your world. Why would I stay and watch her turn you against me and your babe?"

"I appease her so things will be easier for all of us. You can't understand."

"Right?" A humorless laugh shook from her. "Which means you have to choose sides, and that's not the way things are supposed to be. I've already seen how you've been changing toward me because of the fight between your mama's wishes and what care you have for me." Emotions scratched at her throat. "She despises me, and someday she'll turn you against me too."

"That's a bit harsh, Kizzie."

"Is it?" She narrowed her eyes right back at him. "Did you know she's been trying to scare me off? That she's behind the folks attacking the house?"

He shook his head. "What?"

"She's the one who sent men a few nights ago too. Shot up the place. Broke some windows."

He took another step back, continuing to shake his head. "There ain't no reason to make up stories just to justify your choices."

She stared at him, the hard edges of his face, the distrust distancing him even more than the few feet between them. This was only the beginning of his mama's influence, and they'd only known each other a year. What would happen after two years, or five? She'd rather leave with Charles thinking good of her and caring for his little boy with whatever care he had than to have him send her away in disgust or shame. . .or hatred.

"I'm going to believe you know me well enough to come to the right conclusions, but if you won't believe me for who I am, then. . ." She raised her chin. "Ask your cousin, Cole. I think he recently hurt his shootin' hand? A bullet wound, if I'm not mistaken?"

The tension in his face slacked. "How did you—"

"I shot him." She refused to look away. "I didn't know it was him when I shot him, but he was with five other men throwing rocks at the house and shooting into the side of it. They shouted all sorts of ugly things. I don't know who all else was with him, but they meant to run me off." She cleared her throat, the tactile memory of the fear closing off her breath a little. "I was scared and shot at them to get them to leave." Her eyes narrowed. "But I could have killed 'em if I wanted. I'm a good shot. Best squirrel shooter in the family."

His eyes grew wide.

"I heard 'em talkin' that your mama paid them to scare me off, and that's when I saw your cousin's face in the moonlight."

He rocked another step back. "No."

"You don't have to believe me, but that don't mean what I'm sayin' ain't true. You're gonna believe what you want to believe anyway, and I can't change that. But it's all the more proof I need to leave, not just for my safety but for Charlie's. 'Cause if your mama is desperate enough to send men to shoot into a house where a single woman and child live, then she may become desperate enough to do worse." Her eyes burned now, the admission puncturing her control. "And if I have to trick you into marryin' me, then I don't want you marryin' me a'tall."

"Kizzie—"

"I have never been anything but honest with you. And I may have lost knowin' who I was in the idea of bein' your gal, but I'm not lost no more. If I marry, I want it to be because someone chooses me for me, not because he's forced or tricked or talked into it."

"I didn't mean—"

"And if you really wanted to marry me, Charles, really truly. . ." The truth knifed through her as she spoke. "And your mama wanted your happiness, then I think you'd fight a whole lot harder for us. And she'd learn to love who you love, is how I see it."

Which only proved all the more he didn't love her. Not like she'd thought. . .or hoped.

"Please, Kizzie." His voice softened in entreaty, sending an ache through her. "I'm sorry. I didn't mean to accuse. But it's a delicate situation, with social expectations and family land. . ." He stepped close again. "Why can't we go on like we are?"

"Because it's *wrong*, Charles. Don't you see it? All the love in the world can't make wrong choices into right ones. I believe you care about me and Charlie, but you're not free to live your life." She pinched her eyes closed. "And neither am I."

"But when Mama dies—"

Her humorless laugh broke into his mantra. "Your mama ain't never gonna die. She's gonna live forever out of sheer spite, if she don't turn you plumb against me in the process."

"She won't—"

"It's happening right now, with you questioning my motives." She shook her head. "And do you really plan to put your life and mine on hold until then? Five years? Ten? Twenty? Your mama ain't old, Charles."

He fell silent, his jaw tense again.

"I've got to learn to rely on God and my own wits because I can't expect you to rescue or love me in the way you would if your heart wasn't split between two worlds that don't fit together." The tears won then, a strange combination of burning out of her eyes to cool her cheeks. "So instead of forcing you to choose one and live with that guilt, I'm choosing for the both of us. So we can both be free."

He stared at her for a moment, and then his shoulders slumped. "Where will you go?"

"I don't have a set place yet." Nella had recommended The Hollows, but she kept that to herself. "East, I reckon."

A fire lit his eyes. "I want to know because I mean to prove to you that I'm a man of my word." He surged forward, mere inches away. "When Mama dies, I *will* come find you."

Oh, how she wanted to believe him, to trust that his affection for her went deeper than an easy conquest and a sweet thought. "Charlie will know about his daddy. He'll know all the good and wonderful and kind things. I'll make sure he knows."

The tension in his jaw wobbled a little, and he stepped back with a nod. "And make sure he knows that I'm not the one who took him away from his daddy." All warmth fled his expression. "His mama was."

The declaration hit like a blow to her chest, but she refused to bend beneath it. Hurt people were like hurt animals. In their pain, they'd bite the hand trying to help them.

She remained quiet, holding his gaze.

Without warning, he split the distance between them and pulled her into a hard kiss. His arms caged her in, his mouth almost painful against hers. Her body stiffened against his hold before he drew back, the scent of wine on his breath. "You're mine, Kizzie. You'll always be mine, no matter where you go."

After another searing kiss, he released her and marched to the house without one backward glance. Her body shook, her mind reeling. It took a few moments for her to gather her wits and strength to climb into the buggy, tears still coursing down her cheeks.

What had just happened? What sort of new pain gaped wide inside her chest?

She set Daisy into motion at a canter, a sob shaking from her.

You'll always be mine.

His voice, his scent, the steel in his eyes and arms, took on a memory she'd never paired with him, a possessiveness. He had been hurt. Surprised. Surely those behaviors only emerged because of his fear and hurt. His. . .love?

She flinched at the thought. Was it love?

She raised her gaze to the darkening sky as oranges, pinks, and golds mingled into fading blue, another similar phrase rising to combat Charles'.

I have called thee by thy name; thou art mine.

With a smooth of her palm against her cheek to wipe away the tears, she embraced her new life with both hands. She'd never belonged to Charles Morgan. Not fully.

But she did belong to God.

She drew in a shivering breath. And whatever came tomorrow, no matter where she went, He promised to be with her.

Always.

And He would be enough.

Chapter 10

"FIRE!"

The single word shot a chill through Noah Lewis' veins and sent his feet into motion. He ran toward the call. The rhythmic clatter of the knitting machines continued as if unconcerned about the possible devastation ingrained in such a warning, especially in a mill where cotton fibers coated the air in wait of ignition.

Noah rushed between the rows, following the sound of the growing commotion. Smoke rose near one of the back knitting machines, and just as he turned the corner, the sparks from the feeble flames on a small pile of yarn lit a nearby collection of fabric scraps, doubling the fire's size.

"Fire!" someone else shouted, the woman's voice reverberating against the ceilings and the high windows that allowed light into the crowded space.

"Sand buckets," Noah called out to anyone who would hear. "Get the sand buckets."

Pausing only to catch one of the bucket's handles, he continued forward, the flames licking higher. If they made it to one of the machines, there was no way Noah or anyone else could stop the devastation. Each machine stood near enough to another to create a fiery domino effect to take down the entire mill.

"Jack!"

The woman's cry mingled with all the other sounds, diverting Noah's attention to the left. A little boy, no more than three, stood with a skein in hand, the yarn as frozen in his grasp as his expression.

The growing glow of the fire reflected on Jack's spellbound face, the flames moving ever nearer to his little body. Noah dashed the contents of the sand bucket toward the flames and turned to scoop the little boy into his arms, the acrid smell of burning fabric filling his nostrils as he moved.

Noah's actions broke the spell on the boy, and he looked up at Noah as a shudder trembled through his body. "No worries, little one," Noah cooed, stepping back away from the flames. "It's all right."

As if his words gave the child permission, Jack's bottom lip trembled a warning before he burst into a wail.

Amy Lawson ran toward him, arms outstretched, but then her attention shifted to Noah's waist. "Sir, your jacket!"

Her alert sounded at the same time a stinging sensation hit Noah's lower back. He jerked his head around to look. Flames licked at the hem of his jacket, hungrily devouring the material.

"Sand!" Noah shouted again. He shoved the little boy into his mother's arms, jerked off his jacket, and tossed it to the floor, stamping a foot down on the flame. "Hurry. Everyone!"

His cry set more folks into motion. In concert, men and women came from all directions, bringing sand buckets and fire blankets, each worker as aware of the dangers of a spark in a cotton mill as Noah. Too many headlines told of lives lost and jobs destroyed by one flicker in the middle of a cotton mill.

Breathing heavily, Noah bent forward, resting his palms on his thighs as more buckets of sand blotted out the last of the fire. Stretching to a stand, he looked at the people who'd gathered around, a few coated in ash like he was.

"I appreciate your quick actions, everyone." He raised his voice over the sound of the continuing noise of the machines. "Quick work kept the fire from becoming worse, and that's a benefit for all of us." His gaze landed on Amy holding Jack. "And, thank God, no one was hurt."

The young woman smiled despite the tearstains on her face.

"Mr. Camden and I will look for a cause, but everyone else, return to work."

A murmur spread through the crowd as a few men nodded toward

Noah in some silent solidarity. Thank God indeed that no one was hurt and—Noah's gaze rose to the office—that his brother, George, was out of town in Mount Airy today. Otherwise, Noah feared several unsuspecting workers would have lost their jobs, just so George could have held someone responsible.

People dispersed in various directions, several of the younger women tugging their children closer. His eyes pinched closed at the flash of what might have been for Jack. How could he continue to employ these women and protect their children? He'd succeeded in fencing off a portion of one corner for the younger ones to play, but too often a child would escape, looking for their mother.

Lewis Mills needed workers. Mothers with young children were not their first choice, but even with them, there weren't enough to run the machines at an optimal pace. These women, most of them, either had sickly husbands or no husbands at all. As a result, they frequently had to leave work to tend to ill children, cutting even deeper into the company's bottom line.

"What do you think happened, sir?"

Noah turned to find Joe Camden, the mill engineer, at his side.

"I'm not sure, Joe, but it could be a number of things, both human means and mechanical."

"You don't think Peabody took up smoking inside again, do you?"

Noah's attention shot across the room to an elderly man near one of the weaving looms. By all accounts, Peabody hadn't deserved a second chance at his job when Noah had caught him smoking inside the building, a habit which had started a small fire in one of the back rooms four months ago. But the man's penitence paired with the needs of his large family proved too much for Noah's doubts. He'd given the man his job back under strict warning that if Noah so much as smelled the smoke of a cigarette, Peabody would be gone.

Noah's gaze returned to the office space at the far end of the floor, upraised for a full view of the workings of the mill. If Noah's brother had caught Peabody, not only would the man have been out of a job, but he would have beaten him within an inch of his life.

"I'll let the findings speak for themselves." Noah scanned the charred remains of smoking fabric and a wooden chair. "For now, I'm only grateful things weren't worse." He looked at Jack, who rested his head on his mother's shoulder.

Because they could have been much worse.

"True that, Mr. Noah." The man sighed and raked a hand through his brown hair. "True that."

Noah settled his palms on his hips and surveyed the damage again. A spark from the machine? With the trajectory of the fire, it seemed most likely, but conjectures failed to fix problems.

"Joe, would you gather up a couple more men, maybe Lars and Jacobs, and have them help inspect everything?" Noah looked back at the scorched and melted pieces, now covered in sand. "See if the fire started from the friction of one of the machines." He waved toward the scorched knitter. "We can have more frequent maintenance and attempt to keep as much scrap cloth away from the equipment as possible."

"I can do that, sir."

"Good. I'll take a round to look at the other machines."

Joe hesitated, drawing Noah's attention back to the man's face. "Was there some other concern?"

"Not about the machines, sir." Joe shrugged a shoulder. "But it's started snowing again." He gestured to one of the nearby windows. "From the looks of things, it ain't gonna go easy on us neither."

Again? The snow from four days ago still lay on the ground, packed and slick, but the scene outside the window confirmed Joe's assessment. Not only did a new blanket of white cover the ground, a larger problem arose with the way the snow pelted in sheets. In fact, the wind blew with such force, the flakes poured down as if a waterfall of white, which didn't bode well for workers getting home.

Noah gave Joe a nod. "I'll check the roads and make decisions."

"You can't mean to close early, can you, sir? Not after the last time when your brother—"

"I choose our workers' safety over my brother's wrath." Noah offered a tight smile. "I've survived it many times before."

Though his brother's harshness had only grown worse since their father's death two years before, when George inherited not only the mill but a substantial portion of their family's money.

The discrepancy between George's inheritance and Noah's came as no surprise to anyone inside the family. George had always been his father's favorite, but instead of him having a sense of appreciation for his status as one of the richest men in The Hollows, George took to the new position like a tightfisted miser determined to prove even more ruthless than his sire.

As soon as Noah opened the front door, an icy blast of wind charged into him, bringing daggers of snow. No, more than snow. Snow didn't slice with such sting. Ice laced those flakes and—his attention moved to the horizon—as the quick dark of winter-dusk approached, temperatures would prove more dangerous.

Most of the workers lived only a mile or two from the mill, but not all. And there were the children to consider.

Noah pushed the door closed behind him and walked past the machines, taking the narrow stairway up to the office. The hum and noisome clacking of the motors rose with him, the sounds of a business attempting to stretch beyond its current growing pains.

But, much like Noah's mother, Lewis Mills had never fully recovered from Noah's father's death. It needed more workers. More business.

With a pull of a rope nearby, a loud horn echoed through the space, drawing attention from all corners of the room and bringing in a few people from the adjoining smaller ones. The machines slowly came to a stop.

"Everyone, the weather has taken a turn and, I fear, will only grow more dangerous as the afternoon continues. I advise everyone to turn off your machines and start toward home before things become worse."

A mumble rolled over the crowd.

"I know that some of you live several miles out of town. If you need a ride home, please meet me at the front doors once all the equipment has been shut down. Mr. Camden and I will try to help folks get home as safely as possible."

People darted in all directions, each to their tasks in closing up the mill for the night. Noah set to work on his own responsibilities, gathering up paperwork to finish at home. He had always struggled with numbers, so his brother usually kept the books and gave Noah the responsibility of keeping up communication with their employees and purchasers. Sometimes, if George needed an extra hand, Noah would step in, though the work usually took him twice the time it took his brother. But he'd always been good at encouraging and supporting people, so Father had placed Noah in a supervisory role years ago.

And Father had always stressed that employers were responsible for treating their employees with as much respect as was expected in return. Which included doing what they could to keep them safe.

Almost an hour later, the building stood nearly vacant, and the storm continued its wintry assault on everything outside. A handful of people stood by the front door, waiting for assistance, if Noah guessed from the collection of folks. Mr. and Mrs. Dudley, two of the oldest workers in the mill, Jamie Cross with his severe limp, and the three Mitchell girls, who lived two miles outside of town.

"The Dudleys are out your way, Joe." Noah pulled on his coat as he approached the group. "Take them and then get on home to Amy before things get worse."

"Are you sure, Mr. Lewis? I can drop Jamie off too."

Noah shook his head, tying his scarf and sending the others a brief smile. "Jamie is out of your way, and besides, he can play escort." The last thing Noah needed was another reason for George to doubt his professionalism. Driving three young women home by himself, two of them single, wouldn't set the best precedent for professionalism or appearance.

"We don't want to cause no fuss, Mr. Lewis," Emmeline Mitchell said. "Maria's a married gal. Surely she can act as escort, if you're worried 'bout folks."

"Thank you, Emmeline." He tipped his head in acknowledgment. "I appreciate that, but I would still like to take Jamie. I'd rather assure all my workers get home." The next words caught, but he pushed through. "And Mr. Camden has a family relying on his safe return."

"I'll be fine, Mr. Lewis." Joe leaned in, lowering his voice. "If you take Jamie too, it won't get you back home till after nightfall."

"It's all right." His grin spread, though his chest tightened a little. The country roads offered a few treacherous passages in dry daylight, let alone a wet snowstorm. "My mares are hearty ladies, and I have faith in their ability to make quick work of the ride. We'll take the carriage so you ladies can stay dry as long as possible too." He looked back at the group. "Let's be off, everyone. And take care."

The weather proved more piercing than before, and blinding, so Noah stopped by his home, just up the road from the mill, to collect his driving goggles and bring Marty, his stable hand, with him. Thankfully, he was able to stay out of the house. He was afraid his mother would attempt to talk him out of driving and offer to keep all four of the guests in the large Victorian they called home.

At a much slower pace than he'd anticipated, the carriage kept its course. At their insistence, Noah dropped the women off at the end of their drive with their assurance they could make the quarter-mile walk without any trouble. At least, at that point, daylight still offered some assistance, however minimal. Already, just in the last half hour, four new inches of snow covered the ground, and once he'd dropped off Jamie and backtracked toward town, his carriage tracks were invisible.

The acetylene lamp glowed in the blistery white, offering little help in seeing more than ten feet in front of them. Hopefully, his horses' eyes viewed the way with more clarity than his.

Marty sat at his side, cap low, attempting to protect himself from the projectile ice.

"I'll bring the horses to a stop so you can get in the protection of the carriage," Noah called above the wind, pulling back on the reins a little.

"No, sir." The young man, a few years Noah's junior, gave his head a severe shake. "I'll be another set of eyes for you."

Noah nodded his thanks and ushered the mares to keep pace. They had to be close to town, the coming nightfall making visibility less and the air colder. Suddenly, out of the blurry white charged a horse, a single rider on its back. The abrupt appearance spooked the mares, and they reared high on their haunches.

Noah struggled to maintain control, but the rider didn't so much as slow, racing past them so fast Noah only caught a glimpse of dark clothes and a beaver cap. The horses tugged against Noah's hold, and with the combination of snow and the wet ground, the carriage slid to the side of the road. Without traction, the wheels dipped over the edge of the small embankment, taking Noah, Marty, and the mares with it.

The carriage tipped, and everything slowed down.

Noah shoved his feet into the footboard and released one hand from the reins, attempting to grab Marty as the man rose from his seat, but Noah's damp boots slipped the farther the carriage tipped. With a squeal from the horses and a cry from Marty, the entire carriage crashed onto its side, tossing Noah through the air.

His body slammed against the snowy ground, and all went dark.

Chapter 11

Cold.

The first thought to emerge in Noah's mind.

A chill crept over every fiber of his clothes to his skin, slowing his mind. He shivered. Where was he? What had happened?

He pried his eyes open, blinking against the sudden onslaught of snow in his vision. Snow? What was he doing out in the middle of the snow? Thoughts swirled with the same ferocity as the wind, slow to catch. His attention landed on the overturned carriage nearby.

The horseman!

His eyes shot wide as blurry memories cleared into recognition. *Marty!*

Noah moved to sit, and pain coiled up his left leg, nearly crippling him. He paused, allowing a swell of nausea to pass, before adjusting his body to a more upright position. A sharp pain in his shoulder objected to the movement, but he pushed through. His thoughts cleared even more, the ache in his leg shifting from acute to manageable. A sprain, perhaps?

The light dusting of white on his clothes suggested he'd not been unconscious long. A few minutes at most. Maybe less. But he needed to get up and find Marty.

He reached for the nearest part of the carriage, one of the giant wheels, and brought himself up to an even straighter sitting position. At the top of the embankment, his mares stomped nervously, still hitched to the overturned carriage but appearing more annoyed than hurt. Though it was a miracle they stayed upright too.

A sigh shuddered out of Noah's mouth, crystallizing in the air.

Thank God the girls hadn't been with him. His attention shifted back to the overturned carriage with one side crushed in. No woman should be out in this weather. He shrugged his good shoulder. No man, either. Except the crazy ones, it seemed.

And then his gaze caught on a dark mass in the snow on the other side of the carriage, unmoving. His body tensed.

Marty.

He secured his hold on the wagon wheel and attempted to stand, but his first attempt proved futile against the slanted hillside. He barely caught himself before tipping into the snow.

"Marty!" The howl of the wind caught his cry and flung it back to him.

Noah shifted again, leaning his hip against the wheel, almost upright now. He had to get to the man. Pull him out of the snow, at the very least, and under the protection of the carriage.

"Hello!"

Noah jerked his head toward the sound.

Had he even heard it? A woman's voice. He shook his head. It had to be a trick of the wind's howl?

"Are you hurt?"

The voice came again, decidedly feminine.

Maybe he'd hit his head harder than he thought. He searched the direction of the call.

Out of the snowy swirls, a figure emerged, clad in a red cloak.

Noah squinted through the falling snow as the figure grew closer.

It was a woman! She stood at the top of the embankment, and before he could gather his wits, she began a careful slide down the small hill.

He blinked a few times, yet she only grew nearer.

"I was just behind you, using your lantern light as my guide, and saw what happened." She closed in, her dark, damp hair tumbling loose from her bonnet all around her shoulders. Was she a snow spirit? A ghost? Because those large indigo eyes and her pale face looked much too otherworldly to be from this sphere.

She nearly lost her footing as she reached the bottom of the embankment, and he reflexively reached out an arm to steady her. The wool of her cape brushed against his glove.

Well, she felt real.

She looked down at his hand on her arm and then shot him a smile. "Well, here I am, trying to come to your aid, and you end up assisting me."

Noah could only stare. Words completely failed him. And then, from inside the folds of her cape peeked a small set of wide eyes. A baby? The woman stopped in the middle of a snowstorm to help him, and she was carrying a baby?

Words skidded even farther away from him.

"Thank the good Lord you're upright." She gestured with her head toward the road. "Your horses too. With a turn like that one, I'm surprised someone didn't get hurt real bad."

And then Marty flew to mind again.

"Marty." The name puffed out on a breath. Noah spun around, searching for the young man. "One of my men. He's—"

"I see him," she broke in, taking off in that direction.

Noah blinked a few more times and then, with his hand on the carriage for support, made a much slower approach.

"He's breathin'," the woman said, kneeling in the snow beside Marty. "His leg's turned in an awful direction, though, so I reckon it's broke. I can't tell about his head or neck, so I'm scared to move him."

Noah rounded the side of the carriage. "We can't stay here. He'll freeze to death."

Those indigo eyes rose back to his, and she dipped her delicate chin in agreement. "Then we'll have to take the chance there ain't nothin' too hurt in his spine or neck." Her gaze fell to his limp. "You can't make it up that bank without help neither."

He attempted to stand taller to prove his ability, but his wince contradicted his intentions.

She dipped her chin and straightened her shoulders as if readying for the task. "But I don't think I can get him up to my buggy on my own."

If at all. Noah stiffened against a surge of panic and searched the area. His attention landed on a blanket half spilled from the open carriage door. "Let's drag him."

Her gaze followed his, and a smile brightened her whole face, pausing his thoughts all over again. "That's a good start, but you think you're able?"

He forced his brain into motion. "I will be."

She held his gaze as if measuring his determination, and he refused to look away. He'd have to work through the pain in his leg. There was no other option.

"All right." With a nod, she marched over to the blanket and pulled it from the door. Noah released his hold on the carriage and limped forward, biting back the pain in both his leg and his shoulder as he helped her shift Marty's limp body onto the blanket.

"Are you sure *you're* able to help?" He flitted his attention down to the baby's wide blue eyes, so similar to the woman's. "I can try on my own."

Her grin tipped a little. "Charlie's used to me working with him strapped in. If it gets too tough for me, I'll settle him in the buggy, but he's getting so wiggly, I'm afraid he won't stay."

"You need to promise that you won't put either of you in harm's way. If it gets to be too much for you, stop. I'll make do as best I can."

Her dark brows rose. "Mister. . ."

"Lewis, Noah Lewis."

"Mr. Lewis, it's impossible to live without being in harm's way sometimes, and I think helpin' out a neighbor in need is one of the best reasons for risk, don't you?" And with that, she turned and started tugging the blanket with Marty up the hill.

Who was this woman? Maybe she truly was a snow spirit. . .or an angel? And as soon as he reached his home, she'd disappear with the wind.

Noah hobbled to her side, taking the other corner of the blanket. After a few slips and stumbles, they made it to the road.

"I reckon we'll all have to bunch up on the buggy seat together, but at least the buggy's covered, so we'll keep Marty from getting more snow on him." The woman's breaths pulsed into the air, her chest rising and falling with her deep breaths from the effort to get Marty this far. She stretched out her back, dropping the corner of the blanket into the snow at her feet and then opened her suit jacket beneath her cape to check on the babe. The little one's attention fastened on Noah again. "He's trying to figure you out too, Mr. Lewis. With the snow covering about every inch of you, he ain't never seen a snowman before."

Humor? At a time like this?

And yet, if he guessed right, she'd paused long enough to not only catch her breath but give him a moment to catch his too.

"He'll lose all interest once I'm thawed, I suppose."

Her quick smile unfurled again, and she looked back at the carriage. "Is there any way to unhook one of those lanterns to help us get the rest of the way into town?"

"I can try." He moved in that direction, grateful the front of the carriage still rested partially on flat ground. "We're only a mile from my home."

Another rush of wind pushed them both back a step and set them into motion. The woman took hold of the corner of the blanket again. Noah helped, and they finally got Marty beneath the shelter of the buggy while they sorted out what to do next.

"How about if I hitch my mares to the buggy along with yours. That'll help us move through the storm faster."

"As long as they'll all play nice together. The last thing we need is a bunch of fussy ladies when we already got a wounded man and. . ." Her attention settled on him. "A limping one."

His laugh almost burst out despite himself and the situation. "I'll have a good talk with them before we commence to make sure they play nice."

"Well, womenfolk can be testy sometimes, I hear." Her smile flared.

With another puff of a laugh, he helped her navigate the tedious transition of an unconscious Marty to the buggy seat. The woman slid in next to Marty, guiding his head to rest against the side of the buggy before dismounting to take the blanket and tuck it in around him, as much to keep him warm as to secure his head position.

Then she hopped down to help Noah with the horses.

In just a few minutes they were seated in the buggy and finally in motion. The wind had quieted a little, enough for them to see farther ahead, but snow fell at such a rate that Noah wondered if, even with the three mares' strength, the buggy could push through the drifts. Already, at least five inches had fallen in some places, if not more.

Any attempt to increase speed led to the buggy slipping on the ice layer beneath the new snow, and all they needed was another ten minutes. Then he could get everyone into the house, phone the doctor, and have his mother get Marty settled. Even if the doctor couldn't make it to Noah's house, perhaps he could offer some advice on how to help Marty.

The woman pressed against his side, the three of them wedged in the small seat made for two. Something about her red cape and those blue eyes carried an almost haunting combination, like a veritable Red Riding Hood emerging from outrunning the wolf, though, with her fortitude, she may have killed the wolf before setting out on her snowy drive.

"I don't mean to be rude, but what were you doing out in the storm alone?"

She pulled her gaze from tucking the now-sleeping babe more safely within the folds of her cape. "The snow started when we were about four miles outside of town. At least that's what the sign said." She shrugged a shoulder. "There wasn't much else to do except move on at that point, since I didn't see no other place to stop."

He kept his face forward but nodded. The storm had come on all of a sudden, and there was no other town within a ten-to-fifteen-mile radius of The Hollows.

"It's a good thing I kept moving forward for your sake." She shot him a grin. "Now I know exactly why we got caught in the storm."

His attention shot back to her. "What?"

"Well, when the snow started falling so hard I started getting worried. But I kept reminding myself that God's got me and Charlie right where He wants us, so He's bound to use even the storm for His good." She waved toward him. "And look at what good He's done. I've only ever rescued my little brother Isom from drowning, and once, a trapped rabbit from a gum." She wrinkled her nose with her frown. "I just couldn't abide trapping those little rabbits, even if it brought in good money." Her gaze flew back to him. "What a better story to rescue two grown men."

Noah's jaw slacked, his pride prickling just a little at the notion of being rescued by her, and then his laugh burst out. "Who *are* you?"

Her eyes grew wide. "Who am I?"

"Surely *you* know. I'm the one who hit my head, not you."

Her grin brightened, lighting those eyes.

"If you don't tell me who you are, I'll be forced to call you Red Riding Hood." He gestured toward her cape with his chin. "Or an angel?"

"Angel?" At this, she laughed, a light and dulcet sound. "I ain't no angel, Mr. Lewis. Though, with the Lord's help, I'm a heap of a lot better than I was." She snickered again and shifted in the seat a little to face him. "My name is Miss Kizzie McAdams." She raised her cape a little to showcase the sleeping babe. "And this here's Charlie McAdams."

"Well, I'd hate to think you were put in danger in order to rescue me and Marty, but I am grateful for your timing." Almost as if his declaration held power, the buggy's movement grew more sluggish. The horses pulled against the growing weight of the snow.

"We may have to walk after all." Miss McAdams steadied herself with a hand to his arm.

"See that roofline up ahead, through the snow?" He pointed. "We only need to make it there. It's home."

A frown puckered her brow. "You mean, you don't live in the town proper?"

"I live outside the town a mile to be nearer the mill my brother and I run."

"So I'm not too far from town then. That's good." She nodded as if taking in the information. "'Cause I don't think me, Daisy, and this buggy are going to make it much farther tonight."

The glow of the gaslight both inside and outside the house pierced through the growing dark and wild flurries. "Miss McAdams, you won't make it to town tonight unless you try by foot."

Her eyes rounded, and for the first time since meeting her, the glow in those uncommonly blue eyes dimmed. "Well then. I'll just have to go by foot. Charlie can't be out in this storm for much longer, and I sure don't have plans to cuddle up in the buggy for the night."

"Of course not." He laughed. "No. The only course for you right now is to stay with us."

"Stay with you?" Air crystallized around her from the force in the words. "Mr. Lewis, I can't stay at your house. . .you and me being. . . I can assure you, I don't live like that no more, and I ain't keen to sully a perfectly fine gentleman's reputation."

Well, there was a lot to unpack from that statement.

"My mother lives there as well, so you have nothing to worry about as far as reputation, Miss McAdams. And. . ." He tightened his hold on the reins as the buggy slid again and the horses nearly crawled to a stop. "There is no way I or my mother will allow you to walk to town tonight. So prepare yourself to be our houseguest."

How had she run right from one sticky situation into another?

Staying at an unmarried man's house? No matter the weather, she'd just chosen to walk away from such a life and now. . .here she was?

"My mother lives there as well, so you have nothing to worry about as far as reputation."

At least God provided a chaperone to prove Kizzie's reputation had changed, should someone drum up her past and attempt to hurt not only her but good Mr. Lewis. She sent him another look from her periphery.

He had kind eyes.

And he didn't seem to be a scoundrel, so hopefully he told the truth about his mama. At any rate, they had to get poor Mr. Marty somewhere to check on his wounds, because bouncing around in a buggy wasn't the best idea.

She drew in a breath, reminding herself of what she'd prayed only a little while before when the storm hit. God had her and Charlie right where He wanted them. All she needed to do was keep choosing Him and His ways.

She looked out into the blurry evening, barely able to see anything except snow and more snow. Despite her reservations, the safest course for her and Charlie was to stay at Mr. Lewis'.

Up ahead, light glimmered into the snowy veil, taking shape as they neared.

Kizzie squinted into the snow.

The building kept growing taller and wider and broader with each horse's step.

Was that a house? Or a hotel?

She'd never been to a big town, and the one closest to her home growing up only had a little hotel, no larger than the general store. But this? This brick, three-story building rose into the snowy sky with a large porch almost completely around the whole front and a. . . Was that a tower rising up on one side?

Where on earth had God brought her?

She'd thought the Morgan house a grand place, but this. . . "Law, is this your house?"

Mr. Lewis shrugged. "Well, it's my mother's, but my father had it built ten years ago when we first came to The Hollows."

"It's beautiful," she whispered, placing her palm over the place where Charlie's head rested beneath her cape. "I ain't never seen nothing like it before in all my livin' days."

"Mr. Noah." A call came from the front of the house as two men ran, or attempted to run, toward them through the snow, but the snow's depth slowed them. "Thank God."

The horses seemed to recognize their nearness to shelter. They jolted into a faster pace, meeting the men on the front drive of the massive house.

"The carriage overturned a mile back," Mr. Lewis announced as the men reached the buggy and kept pace alongside. "Marty's injured. We need to get him inside."

The younger of the two men, who had dark curls like Marty, shot a look to the unconscious man. "We need the doctor?"

"The doctor won't make it here," Mr. Lewis responded, drawing the buggy to a stop. "And we can't make it there. Case, follow me to the stables."

The younger man nodded.

"Taylor, take Miss McAdams inside and let Mother know we'll be carrying Marty in." He gestured toward Kizzie. "And ask Mrs. North to prepare a room for Miss McAdams. I'll explain everything when we settle Marty inside."

The older of the two men, probably more like Kizzie's daddy's age, glanced at Kizzie before turning to Mr. Lewis. "Yes, sir." The curl of his accent gave off a similar sound as Mr. Angus from the mountain. Was he from across the pond?

"I'll have your trunks brought to you, Miss McAdams." Mr. Lewis' attention raised to the man he'd called Taylor. "And Taylor, I'll need some assistance getting from the stables to the house on account of my own minor injury."

"Yes, sir," Taylor responded with a nod.

"Allow me to help you down, Miss McAdams." Mr. Lewis turned to Kizzie and offered her his hand.

She stared at his outstretched gloved hand, the simple movement hinging in her mind like the courtly gesture she'd sung about in old ballads back home. Her gaze raised to his, the man's pale hazel eyes holding hers with the same patience as his outstretched hand. With the slightest hesitation, she slid her fingers over his, and he assisted her to a stand.

"Taylor?"

Kizzie turned at Mr. Lewis' word to find Taylor ready to help her to the ground.

The snow reached to the top of her boots as her feet landed on the ground. She glanced back up at Mr. Lewis before turning toward Taylor, her palm rising to the place where Charlie's head rested. Her little bundle began to wiggle beneath her touch, warning of his coming need for food. Mr. Taylor led the way as Mr. Lewis and her buggy disappeared around the side of the house, presumably to find the stables.

Stables.

Even the Morgans, in their relative wealth, didn't have stables.

Their few horses went into a barn like most everyone else's.

Her gaze trailed back up the length of the house. But, she supposed, folks who lived in houses the size of hillsides could afford stables.

Mr. Taylor held the door for her to pass, his posture stick straight and his expression, well if an expression *could* be stick straight, his was.

A small entryway, with stained glass windows on either side, led through double doors into a large room with a grand spiral staircase of dark wood that twisted up and out of sight. Her attention caught on a chandelier dangling from two stories up, three times bigger than the one in the foyer of the Morgans' house.

"Please wait here, miss."

Kizzie looked over to find Mr. Taylor gesturing her through an arched threshold into one of the prettiest parlors she had ever seen. Lush green furnishings, thick ornate rugs, and a fireplace big enough to fit a horse greeted her from the first room, with another arched separation opening into another elegant room to the left. Another sitting room? Even larger?

Kizzie glanced behind her, where a doorway led to a hallway, hinting at more rooms.

"May I take your cape, miss?"

Kizzie stared at the man as if he spoke some foreign language. She understood the words, but somehow, they didn't fit the position she'd held her whole life: mountain girl and servant girl. Maybe it was his accent that caused the trouble.

She pushed up a smile and unfastened the clip at her throat. "Thank you kindly."

He took the cloak and was in the process of dipping his head when his attention fell to Kizzie's chest. She followed the shocked man's attention and found Charlie peering back at Mr. Taylor with a similar wide-eyed expression.

"This here's Charlie, Mr. Taylor."

And, as if on cue, Charlie unrolled one of his biggest smiles for the man.

Mr. Taylor's brows shot even higher.

"Well, he must know you're a good sort, because he's only started smiling over the past week or so, and he cut you a nice one on first look."

Mr. Taylor's mouth jerked around like his lips and his brains wanted two different things, and then, with another dip of his chin, he backed toward the foyer.

Kizzie drew Charlie from his place within her day suit jacket, the warmth of his body leaving a sweat stain, or she hoped it was a sweat stain, on her blouse beneath. The house fell quiet, and the room seemed to grow in size at the silence.

She sat on the nearest little settee and discreetly fed Charlie while noises happened around her, but no one entered the room. She'd just finished caring for Charlie when a woman, near her mama's age, walked in. She wore a purple gown as exquisite as the one Nella made for Kizzie, and her soft brown gaze moved from Kizzie to Charlie as Kizzie stood.

"Miss McAdams." Her accent lilted with that otherworldly sound too.

"Yes, ma'am." Kizzie stepped forward. "Are you Mrs. Lewis?"

"I am." The woman folded her hands in front of her and nodded. "And I am particularly grateful for the kindness and courage you showed to my son and our servant Martin."

"I'm just glad I happened to be going by."

Her lips flickered with the faintest smile. "And this is your child?"

"Yes, ma'am." Kizzie shifted Charlie so that Mrs. Lewis could get a better view of him. "How is Marty?"

"He's still unconscious, so it is difficult to ascertain his injuries, and there's no way the doctor will make it here tonight with the storm still in full force."

"Is there something I can do?"

Again, the press of the woman's lips softened. "That is very kind of you, but I believe you've helped a great deal already this evening, and I'm certain you are tired." She waved toward the stairs. "I've had Mrs. North prepare a room for you and Charlie. She'll also bring some supper to your room." She gestured for Kizzie to follow.

"Thank you kindly." Kizzie followed the woman up the grand stairs. "I'm sorry to be such trouble."

Mrs. Lewis paused on the landing and turned. "Please, you are no trouble at all. I am grateful for you. There is a good chance you not only saved Martin's life, but Noah's as well."

She resumed her walk.

"My father was a doctor, and I would often assist him when I was younger," Mrs. Lewis continued, oblivious to the fact that the beautiful surroundings kept pausing Kizzie's attempts to keep up with her. "I'm not certain, but I think Martin's spine is fine. However, to ensure his mental faculties are in order, we have to wait for him to wake."

A fact Kizzie had learned from witnessing a few falls. Hezzy Clark fell from a tree once and was never the same afterwards, but he'd stayed unconscious four whole days before coming to. Hopefully, Marty would wake up soon.

Very soon.

Because he'd already been unconscious at least an hour.

Mrs. Lewis stopped in front of an open door and gestured to the room. "Will this do for you and Charlie?"

Kizzie peeked into the room of gold and blue. Wallpaper covered the high, wood-trimmed walls, a bed bigger than any she'd ever seen stood in the center of the room, and a marble fireplace sparkled with a healthy fire and blinked light over velvety carpeted floors.

Kizzie felt pretty sure she'd stepped into a fairy story.

"It's the most beautiful room I've ever seen."

"Good." One corner of Mrs. Lewis' lips tipped up, almost transforming into a full smile. "And you can see that your trunks have already been delivered." She waved across the hall. "The washroom is there."

"Thank you." Kizzie barely got the words out, her head spinning with the wonder of it all.

Mrs. Lewis paused in her turn and folded her hands again. "Noah told me that you traveled alone tonight."

A sudden wariness tightened Kizzie's spine. "Yes, ma'am."

"Are you alone in the world?"

Kizzie swallowed and nodded. "Except for the Almighty, ma'am. I am."

Her attention flickered to Charlie and back. "And. . .is there a Mr. McAdams?"

Kizzie stifled a sigh and offered a smile much brighter than the lump gathering in her throat suggested. "Well, there is, but he's my daddy."

Her eyes flickered wide for only a second, and if Kizzie hadn't been paying such close attention, she may not have noticed. "So forgive me, but am I right in understanding that you have never had a husband?"

Kizzie drew in a deep breath. How she'd hoped it would take longer than a day for her reputation to come to light in a new place. "Yes ma'am, you are, but God's seen fit to put me on the straight and narrow despite my wrong choices, so I aim to move forward in a way to please Him, if I can."

The rush of shame flooded from Kizzie's boots all the way to her hairline, as if she stood right back in front of her mama and daddy, hoping love would overcome prejudice. But at that moment, she knew the truth.

"I see." The woman's gaze held Kizzie's almost as if her eyes delved into Kizzie's soul, trying to dig up something broken. Well, she'd find a whole lot, but hopefully, she'd see a woman trying to do right too.

God would accept her in her brokenness. He already had.

And a few other people who knew forgiveness might accept her too.

But finding a good and decent man with a good and decent family to take her just as she was? Well, that was as likely as finding white wildflowers in a snowstorm.

She closed off the dream and tucked it far back into her heart, where impossible dreams were kept.

Yes, impossible.

Chapter 12

A CRASH SHOOK KIZZIE FROM staring out the window into the night as she nursed Charlie. At the sudden interruption, his drowsy suckling took on new vigor for only another minute before he drifted back into contented slumber despite the sudden shouts coming from downstairs.

Kizzie buffered Charlie in the middle of the bed, surrounded by the lush blankets, her attention dropping to the little pocket watch she'd laid on the bedstead.

Two o'clock.

The shouts erupted louder followed by another crash, but Charlie slept on, so Kizzie grabbed her robe and started for the door. On the threshold, her attention landed on one of her travel bags.

The herbs Nella gave her.

Kizzie took a ginger root wrapped in a thick cloth and ran from the room. Following the sounds, she rounded one of the hallways only to hear a string of expletives coming from the nearest room.

"He—he ain't never talked like that, Mr. Lewis," came a young voice. Case, perhaps? "I promise you."

"Marty, it's me. Noah," Mr. Lewis' familiar voice followed, calm and warm and much gentler than when he'd been trying to talk over a storm. "We're home."

Kizzie peered around the doorframe to find a group of three men around the bed where Marty lay, red-faced, with one hand gripping Mr. Lewis' arm and the other grasping the air. A string of unintelligible words erupted from him before he screamed, "The horses. I can't find 'em." He jerked Noah forward. "Who hit me? I've been hit. The horses ran over my legs."

A flash of memory pierced through her of her uncle coming to after his wagon overturned. He'd been unconscious for days, not hours, but the confusion and fight looked the same. What had Mama done? Said?

Kizzie stepped into the room, her movement catching the attention of all three men, but she held Marty's gaze. "You're safe, Marty. Right now, you are safe."

The man's dark eyes widened as he stared. "Am I dead?"

Kizzie's body shook a little as she attempted to calm him. Could Marty prove as unpredictable as her daddy on a drunk? Could he be as violent? The white-knuckled grip he had on Mr. Lewis' arm suggested a strength beneath his lean frame. She drew in a breath, but three men were nearby to help, and God had placed her here. In this moment.

She had Marty's attention, so she drew closer. Whatever she was doing seemed to be working at least to calm him a little. Maybe the fact he had no idea who she was helped. Mama used to say the "startled factor" could work magic sometimes. She'd used it quite a bit on Daddy's hard head, not to mention while raising nine young'uns.

"No, you ain't dead." She kept her voice soft, her words slow. "You hit your head somethin' fierce out in the snowstorm, and Mr. Lewis brung you here till you are fit again."

"I ain't. . .I ain't dead," he echoed, releasing his grip on Mr. Lewis' arm and relaxing back into the pillows.

"No, sir. You just bumped your head when you fell from the carriage."

He flinched, his fists tightening on the blanket at his waist. "The ghost carriage."

Ghost? She flipped her attention to Mr. Lewis' hazel gaze. Whether from the way they'd met or some other means, she felt a connection to him.

He dipped his head as if feeling her uncertainty and turned to Marty. "We were in the snow, Marty." Law, the way that man's voice smoothed out his words could calm a whole host of wounded men, snow ghosts, or wild horses. Was it his voice, or the underlying gentleness couching his words? "No ghosts, just a snowstorm."

Marty nodded slowly, his hands fisting and unfisting the blanket. "The horses?"

"They're fine," Mr. Lewis continued. "Safe and warm in the stables."

"They…they didn't run over my legs?" His words trembled in a pitiful sort of way before he sucked in a quiet sob. "My legs. Where are my legs?"

Case turned wide eyes to Kizzie as if she knew what to do, but as far as she could tell, Marty's legs were right beneath his blankets. She looked back at Mr. Lewis, and after a moment, he gently touched Marty's hand.

"Marty, do you feel this?" Mr. Lewis touched the man's thigh and then moved his hand a little farther down. "This?"

The weeping man nodded.

Mr. Lewis moved his touch down below Marty's knee. "And that? Do you feel that?"

Marty sniffled and nodded again.

"Those are your legs. They are right here with you."

The man relaxed into the raised pillows, his shoulders shaking a little from his sobs.

Case backed toward the door and leaned near Kizzie. "Has he lost his mind?"

Well, Kizzie didn't have a heap of experience with folks who'd hit their heads, but she hoped for a sound guess. "Probably not lost, just shook up a bit."

And then, out of nowhere, the idea to pray for the weeping man popped to mind. Kizzie only had a couple weeks of solid praying experience, and she'd never prayed out loud in front of other folks before, but since Marty was scared and Case seemed worried…Well, she'd read something about God helping folks with both of those ailments, so why not ask Him for help?

"Mr. Marty." She approached the bed, near enough to note the massive welt on the man's forehead in the dim light. "Would you mind if I pray for you?"

The room fell quiet for a moment before Marty whimpered. "I *am* going to die."

"No." Kizzie lowered herself to the bed. "But I hear that if we're afraid, God wants us to let Him know, so He can give us courage. And

I reckon it can't hurt none to ask Him to help your head and legs too. Would you be fine with that?"

The man nodded despite the fact his eyes grew as wide as skipping stones.

Well, at least God understood her intentions. So if her words came out wrong, He'd take care of the rest. She kept her prayer short. Simple. Thanked God for His protection of Marty and Mr. Lewis. Even the horses. And asked for His favor on their healing, ending with prayers for any folks out in the storm and gratitude for Mr. and Mrs. Lewis' kindness in allowing her to stay with them.

When she opened her eyes, Marty lay back against the pillows, eyes closed and incredibly still. A chill swept over Kizzie's whole body. Was he dead?

And then the man's chest swelled with a long breath.

"Well, I see everything is well in hand."

Kizzie looked over her shoulder to see Mrs. Lewis standing in the doorway, tea tray in hand and pale brow raised. She stepped into the room, and her son walked to her side and took the tray from her hands. Mr. Taylor followed behind her, gripping a large cloth sack. He immediately began clearing a broken lamp from the floor near the head of the bed. Likely the result of one of the crashing sounds.

"I suppose the chamomile tea is not as effective as prayer at calming a man's nerves." Mrs. Lewis sent Kizzie a soft smile.

Kizzie stood, folding her hands in front of her. "I reckon God can use chamomile tea too."

Mrs. Lewis' lips quivered wider, and then she gestured toward Marty. "At least he's resting again."

"And, despite some odd behavior, there was some coherence blended in with his confusion." Mr. Lewis placed the tray on a nearby table. "Should we attempt to wake him for the tea?"

Mrs. Lewis approached the bed, her tall, willowy body poised so perfectly Kizzie thought of what a lovely statue she'd make. She'd seen pictures of marble statues in a book once and wondered how on earth any person held the talent to make rocks so lifelike. Though her daddy and Jeb shared the ability to turn wood into beautiful creations, so she reckoned talent to work other small miracles of creativity waited in all sorts of places and people around the world.

"I'm not sure, but my first inclination is to let him rest." Mrs. Lewis studied Marty. "I recall Father speaking about how the brain heals during sleep, but I think it's good for someone to stay by his bed, in case he wakes again. He may still be confused."

"I'll stay." Case stepped forward. "He's my brother, and I need to be here."

"Case, you were on your feet all day." This from Mr. Lewis. "While he's resting, you should too. I have a feeling he'll need lots of help as he heals, and you'll need your strength."

"I'll stay up with him so y'all can catch a few winks," Kizzie offered. After all, Charlie should stay asleep the rest of the night.

"No, dear girl, you're our guest." Mrs. Lewis commanded attention with the lift of her chin. "I've slept a few hours, so I'll take the first watch."

"Mother—"

Her look stopped Mr. Lewis' response. "You'll do no good if you're exhausted either, Noah. You can take the next watch." She plucked a book off the tea tray. "Besides, I can catch up on my reading."

Mr. Lewis conceded to his mother's wishes without another word. Kizzie studied them. Was Mr. Lewis under his mother's power like Charles was his? What was it about men and their mothers? Her brother, Jeb, certainly respected Mama and would submit to her wishes most times, but out of respect, not fear.

Which was it for Mr. Lewis and his mother?

"I'm sorry we woke you, Miss McAdams," Mrs. Lewis said.

"Truth be told, I was already awake with Charlie. With the traveling today, he's off his schedule a little." Kizzie looked down, remembering the bag in her hand. "Oh, and I thought this might help." She presented the bag to Mrs. Lewis. "It's a small piece of ginger root."

Mrs. Lewis' smile filled her face. "Ah, for tea. For the pain?"

Kizzie nodded as the woman took her offering. "Mama always used it to help with pain of all sorts. If I had some willow bark, I'd offer it too." She gestured toward Mr. Lewis. "Ginger tea might do Mr. Lewis' leg some good too."

Mrs. Lewis swiveled to look at her son, her expression dawning with understanding. "I'm afraid I've been so intent on Martin, I completely forgot about your injuries, Noah."

"Mother, I will be fine." But even in saying it, he placed his hand on the back of the chair for support.

"Hmm . . ." Mrs. Lewis noticed too. "Miss McAdams makes a solid point. Noah, you, Taylor, and Case will need your strength for whatever work needs to be done once the storm stops. Getting at least some rest tonight will do you all good. And your twisted ankle and sore shoulder have some healing to do." She turned to Kizzie. "I suppose you can make ginger tea?"

"Of course, ma'am. I can make a poultice for Mr. Lewis' shoulder too, if y'all got some onion and garlic or turmeric. Smells somethin' awful, but it's been known for treating aches and sores, even helps with swelling."

"Well . . ." She turned to Mr. Lewis. "You're in pain, Noah. It's obvious." She waved toward the tea tray. "Take that to the kitchen, if you will, and allow Miss McAdams freedom to make you some tea and a poultice."

"I'll bring some for Marty too, if you like," Kizzie offered.

Mrs. Lewis nodded. "Yes, he is likely to have a headache."

"We could make a chamomile and lavender poultice. We could place it on his head while he sleeps, and maybe it will help him rest better and lessen the pain."

"How did you learn all this?" Mrs. Lewis asked, her smile a bit on the surprised side.

Kizzie shrugged a shoulder. "My mama and granny had mountain remedies passed down. Being so far from town, we learned to make do with what we had."

"I heard my father speak of such remedies back home in England but never witnessed them." She studied Kizzie carefully, almost as if she was trying to sort something out.

With their previous conversation and Mrs. Lewis' knowledge of Kizzie's past, perhaps she was trying to figure if Kizzie still lived in her sinful ways. A woman of her social status had to take care to protect her family's name, didn't she? Like Mrs. Morgan and Charles?

Kizzie knew this story, so she'd tread carefully with any conversations or friendships in this home.

And keep her expectations matched to what she knew.

A person should steer clear of becoming too comfortable with people outside their status.

"I think a poultice for both would be excellent, Miss McAdams." Mrs. Lewis released Kizzie from her stare, renewing her smile as she turned to her son. "Noah?"

"I'll lead the way." He dipped his head, his submission not of the same ilk as Charles'.

More like Jeb with Daddy in the workshop.

Like Laurel with Mama at the stove.

A good kind of kinship.

She gave her head a shake. No need spinning thoughts too far. Oftentimes they became tangled in poor assumptions or misplaced hopes.

She'd let God handle things like futures and tomorrows and intentions, because He was the only one who really saw that far and deep.

Besides, most likely, the Lewises offered simple politeness because the storm kept her here. They seemed like decent folk and unlikely to cast her and Charlie out to the elements, no matter how much they inwardly scowled at the state of her life, her past.

And she'd always have a past.

She could try to hide it, but it would find her, and she'd learned the value of forthrightness. It might sting at first, but it kept a whole lot of misconceptions from tangling up later on.

If she could keep more tangles out of her already knotted life, she would.

She followed Mr. Lewis from the room, his strong shoulders and gentle curl to the ends of his brown hair an interesting contrast. But they fit what she'd seen so far. Strong and gentle.

Her heart twinged at the awareness, and she looked away.

The last thing she needed was to entertain any silly notions with a family of this type, or any family at all, actually.

Charles still took up space there. A wounded space, but space all the same.

And a wounded heart knew better than to seek love from a place where it would only be wounded all over again.

Noah's cane clicked on the glossy hallway floors as he turned toward the kitchen, his neck tingling at the idea of Miss McAdams close behind him. He wasn't sure why she set him on edge. Perhaps, it was those eyes, or her overall. . .beauty, simply put. Or the directness in her stare.

Or the way she'd emerged from the hallway in her soft blue robe, hair tumbling around her shoulders and a look so. . .what was it? Innocent? Eager to help?

Apart from his mother, he'd not seen a woman in her night-robe since Elinor. He cleared his throat. Whatever the feeling, it left a strange sort of ache in his broken heart, and he wasn't certain what to do about it.

"The kitchen," he said, switching on one of the gaslights to illuminate the space. He rolled his eyes at himself. As if the woman couldn't tell from the stove and sink and assortment of other items that this was the kitchen.

Miss McAdams crossed the threshold and scanned the room before sending him a crooked smile. "You sure Mrs. North don't mind me riflin' around in the kitchen?"

He grinned, in part due to her quick humor and in part at the idea of Mrs. North's interest at all in the kitchen. The idea of Mrs. Candler, however, finding a strange woman in "her" kitchen in the middle of the night brought a renewed grin. The long-time cook could be quite possessive about the room. "One never wishes to skew the gentle balance of one's cook, Miss McAdams, but since Mother made the suggestion, I do believe we are safe."

She nodded, moving more fully into the room but keeping a solid distance between them. Whatever had happened to place her in her current situation had left her careful and guarded but not scared. No, she didn't seem afraid. How curious.

"I don't have much experience with housekeepers, so I'll trust your observation on the subject, though the one housekeeper where I served last was sweet as honey."

She'd been in service? But the clothes she'd worn when they'd met didn't fit the style or price range of a woman in service. From what little he'd been able to learn about her from their unconventional and brief meeting, she presented as a puzzle. A single mother in a snowstorm without a husband, from what his mother shared, but confident in her faith and modest in her presentation.

What was her story? And what brought her here?

He shifted forward to one of the cupboards and then turned in time to catch her looking at his leg. "Maybe you should just go on to bed, Mr. Lewis. I can fix tea and a poultice on my own and leave them for your mother to bring to you. It wouldn't do you any good to tire out your leg even more."

"I'm fine." He shrugged. "Besides, my mind is too busy to sleep just yet, and the idea of tea and perhaps some leftover bread and jam sounds like a good idea. I missed supper."

"Well, starving sure ain't gonna help you heal none." She moved, navigating the kitchen much more easily than he did. Before long, he sat dutifully on a chair by the counter with tea in hand while she "put a plate together" for him.

Already, just the scent of the chamomile began to uncoil his taut muscles. He took a sip and raised his gaze to her profile as she spread jam across a piece of bread. "Thank you."

"You thanking me?" She shook her head and added a slice of cold ham to the plate. "You and your mama are kind enough to keep me and Charlie for the night. Fixing some tea and a plate is the least I can do."

Ah, yes. She'd been placed in the Blue Room. Small, but nearer the stairs. "Is your room comfortable?"

"Gracious." Her smile flashed wide, lighting those eyes, and she walked toward him, plate in hand. "I ain't never set foot in a place so handcrafted for comfort. I could fit almost all my siblings in that bed upstairs."

He coughed out a quiet laugh. "And how many would that be?"

She set the plate in front of him on the counter. "There's nine of us all told." The glow left those eyes along with her smile. "At least, I think there's still nine of us. My big brother had just gone off to fight in the war last time I was home."

The war. Yes. Quite a few lads had gone. "I had friends who volunteered, but Father's death was so recent, I stayed back for Mother's sake."

"Lots of boys chose to stay for different reasons, but Jeb, well, I think he had an itching to get out of the mountains like me, 'cept he made wiser choices."

The silence blanketed her confession a little. Another nugget of information to apply to the growing picture he was making of Kizzie McAdams.

He released a sigh. "But nine! I can't even imagine."

"Yeah, it was quite the clan." She moved back to the counter and began working on another concoction. The poultice, he presumed. "They wouldn't know what to do with a place like this."

His father's visible proof of wealth. Noah relaxed in the chair and took a bite of the bread. A house much too big for their family and much too pretentious for Noah's liking, but he'd gotten used to it—the elegant woodworking and arched entries. The nooks and crannies to escape unwanted guests or conversations. "It's certainly the grandest house we've ever lived in. Much nicer than the town house in Richmond we owned before moving here."

"To build the mill?"

He nodded at her as she looked over her shoulder. "Land was cheaper here with less competition at the time."

"At the time?" She'd begun boiling water, using the spigot with clear awareness, so she must have previously served in a relatively modern house. "Competition has come in?"

"With better pay and more modern conveniences. And both of those incentives have wooed workers who can afford the longer distance away from our mill."

"Which creates a nasty circle, don't it? You lose workers, then you can't make as much product, so then you lose money, which means you can't give raises to the workers, so you lose more workers."

He met her gaze. "Precisely." Curious thing, speaking to this woman about business. And her even being interested in conversing about it at all. "It's a mercy tomorrow's Saturday so we don't have to close the mill for the snow and the workers won't risk their necks to get there."

"Walking a good distance in snow definitely tires out the body." She rolled her shoulders, as if sore. "Not to mention freezes the toes."

His grin crooked at her quaint phrasing. "I imagine you must be tired as well. It's been quite the night."

"Fact, but, like you, my mind's too busy for sleep just yet." She chuckled—a soft, contented sound—and then she returned to the pot, now steaming. The scent of garlic traveled the distance to him. "What sort of mill do you run, Mr. Lewis?"

Mr. Lewis felt much too formal for their current situation. "Please call me Noah. Most folks around here do, except for some of the house staff."

She took in the request with a nod. "Kizzie."

Kizzie. He'd never heard that name before. Was it short for something else? He gave his head another shake at the unbidden curiosity. "We're in the process of turning it from cotton to a vertically integrated mill. My brother liked the idea of keeping everything in-house and providing every service possible for the community."

"Vertically integrated?"

"It means we oversee multiple stages of the production process from knitting and spinning to the finishing productions. My brother, George, thought to build on what our father started by streamlining the process and growing the mill's production options, such as adding dyeing and seamstresses to create a finished product instead of only materials such as yarn, thread, and fabric."

"You say that with a frown." Her brow rose. "Don't seem like you're too keen on it."

"With the costs what they are and the workers leaving, expansion didn't seem the wisest of choices, however. . ." He paused. "Well, my brother tends to aspire to grand ideas."

"Grand ideas are all well and good when you've got the legs to hold them up." Her dark brow curved upward, her gaze capturing his in a knowing look.

"Did you travel far to get to The Hollows?"

She returned to kneading some sort of dough. "Not too far. 'Bout twenty miles, from what I can tell."

Twenty miles. On her own. Was she running away from something? His spine stiffened with a sudden defensiveness. From someone? The sizzling of the contents of the pot sounded in the quiet.

"I ain't in no trouble with the law or nothin', if that's what you're thinking."

That wasn't the direction of his thoughts at all.

"I made a good and proper mess of my life, Mister—" She glanced back at him before returning to her work. "Noah." Her body bent a little as if the thoughts weighed on her. "I wasn't alone in making a mess, 'cause it takes two folks to make a baby, but then things got so mixed up and wrong. Even wronger than they'd been before. So I had to leave." A sad little chuckle rose from her. "A stink hole is still a stink hole no matter what we call it, but when you're in it long enough, you just get used to the smell." She shook her head. "It took God pulling me out of it to see how awful things had gotten, and the more time and farther away I am, my hindsight gets clearer and clearer."

She turned then, those indigo eyes holding him in place, cup halfway to his lips. "Why is it we can't see when we're so close? That it takes stepping back a little ways to get a better view?"

He placed the cup in its saucer, attempting to piece together what he could from her admission. "I suppose it's like seeing this town from one of the nearby mountains. From down here, I can't see how another road might lead to a shortcut, but from up there, I can get a more comprehensive view."

"Yes. Exactly." She returned to her work, her movements a bit slower.

Curiosity itched in the back of his mind, but he wouldn't pry. Shouldn't.

He took another few bites of ham and bread. Her work at the stove made quiet sounds, each long silence urging his curiosity into a near frenzy.

She gathered something into her hands and walked toward him. A wariness creased her forehead as she approached. "These are quite warm, but they will work best if we use them now." She placed them on the counter beside him, the garlic scent tickling his nose. "If possible, place it directly on your skin, where the soreness is worst."

"But didn't you make those for Marty?"

"I told your mama I'd fix one for you too. You've been favoring one side since I found you in the snow, and since we've been in here you reached up and held it twice."

"You're observant, aren't you?"

She looked away. "In service, you learn to pay attention."

And then the idea grew into realization. Service. Running away. "Were you. . .was it. . .your employer?"

Her gaze shot to his, the answer in those depths. Her face paled.

A fiery heat stiffened him from boots to ears. "Did he. . .force himself—"

"No." She backed away, a flush darkening her cheeks. "It wasn't like that. I wasn't even fully aware of what was happening until it. . .well. . ."

His jaw tightened in an effort to control himself.

"And I didn't do anything to entice him." Her attention caught in his. "Or if I did, I didn't know. But I—I didn't stop him either."

"Don't you see? He took advantage of his position over you." Noah stood, narrowing the distance between them, watching her face. "As an employer of any virtue whatsoever, he should set an example. Guard himself."

"I suppose that's the truth of it, though I can't see why he'd pick me out of the bunch. I wasn't nearly as well spoken as some of the other servants. Nor as proper."

"Can't you see why? You're beautiful." Was she truly so blind, or was she playing a part? Drawing him in, even now, as she'd done to this employer of hers.

Her gaze flew to his, eyes wide, not a hint of pretense written on her features.

No, even as he considered it, the logic failed. She'd helped rescue him and Marty, putting herself in danger in the process. She'd come to offer aid to Marty and him with the poultices and tea. And even now, in the way she spoke with him, her frankness mingled with hints of naivete that rarely paired with a woman who sought. . .more.

Instead of basking in the compliment, her brow creased. "But Mary, one of the other maids, she was a lot prettier than me and knew how to—" She waved a hand in the air. "Woo much better than I ever could."

He doubted many women compared to Kizzie McAdams' beauty. He'd rarely seen an equal. His jaw tightened again. "An easy conquest is rarely what such men are after." The words ground out of him, a truth he'd witnessed too often from inside his very mill. Yes, he'd been able to protect a few such women, but not all. Some refused protection and ran headlong into the danger.

"I think there was a part of him that truly cared for me. . .and then Charlie." She nodded, stepping back from him. "Until life and the expectations became too hard."

True or not, the man took clear advantage of the woman. The young woman. What was she? Seventeen? Eighteen? Her eyes held cares and wounds older than her face. Noah leaned a palm against the counter to offset the weight to his leg. "He's a bit older than you, I'd wager."

She tilted her head, studying him. "Older than you, I'd reckon."

Old enough to know exactly what he was doing.

"Miss McAdams." He cleared his throat and relaxed his shoulders with a sigh. "Kizzie," he corrected. "I don't know what your future plans are, but if you mean to stay in The Hollows, I would give you one solid piece of advice."

"All right." She placed her hands on her hips, evidently preparing for his insight.

"Watch out for my brother."

Chapter 13

NOAH OPENED THE TOP DRAWER of his dresser as he did every morning, his fingers instinctively wrapping around his grandfather's pocket watch. The quiet ticking of the hands as they moved forward always brought his grandfather's consistency and faithfulness to mind, traits which seemed a bit out of reach in the last year.

A twin blend of grief and gratitude wound its way up through Noah's chest as his attention shifted to a small black-and-white portrait tucked in the corner of the same top drawer. Elinor's lovely dark eyes stared back at him, the photo's lack of color failing to highlight their soft brown hues.

He closed his eyes against the memory of holding her frail body in his arms and tried to push better thoughts to the surface, but watching life leave those eyes haunted him. The images of burying his new bride along with their stillborn son never seemed to fade like so many of the brighter memories.

The pain still slashed through him like a blade, but he'd grown accustomed to it now. Accustomed to the ache of a missing life, an unfinished love.

Time offered a strange sort of comfort, a blend of the distance from loss' acuteness and the longing for what once was. But, to some degree, he'd begun to sleep again without reliving Elinor's cries in his dreams. He'd rediscovered his whistle, offering a tune to the songbirds on the walk to work, and he'd started looking forward instead of back.

And he'd begun to breathe in life. Accepting his place among the living instead of thinking his survival was more of an accident. It was a strange lot to be a young widower. Not uncommon, unfortunately, as too many men lost their wives in childbirth, but unsettling.

To have the life before and the life after.

The man he was before, and the man now.

No one could look on the outside of him and tell there'd been a change.

Same appearance, more like his mother than his father.

He enjoyed many of the same things. Chess, working with his hands, music, reading.

Yet there were pieces of him that would never be the same even a year later. And, for the most part, he didn't want those places inside of him to disappear.

He wanted her imprint on his life forever.

He closed the drawer as images of last night slipped into the ones of Elinor. His attention unexpectedly gravitated toward Kizzie McAdams. Something in her manner, her honesty. The way she'd stepped into the chaos of the overturned carriage and Marty's confusion as if some sort of soothing force.

And her prayer. Gentle with a tinge of strength infusing her words.

Like she truly believed them.

He shook his head to clear his mind of Kizzie's face. Whatever spell she'd cast on his thoughts needed to go. George would never approve of any connection with the likes of an unmarried mother, let alone one who used to be in service and probably didn't offer any financial benefit to the match.

Living beneath George's control raked over Noah's nerves, but he only needed to wait one more year for his inheritance to mature. One year, and he'd receive enough money to start over somewhere without George's influence, meddling, and criticism.

Maybe then, he could focus some time on his heart.

But not until then. Not until he was free.

He tucked the pocket watch in his jacket, picked up the cane, and raised his gaze to the ceiling, offering a simple prayer for guidance and patience before leaving his room.

As soon as he stepped across the threshold into the hallway, he froze. Laughter?

He looked back at his bedroom. Was he still asleep?

More laughter rose up the stairs. His mother's laughter along with another woman's. What had happened in the few hours he'd slept? He pulled out the watch. Five hours, to be exact. He'd slept longer than anticipated. So long, the sunlight glimmered through the large upstairs windows into the galley hallway.

He rubbed at his shoulder, less sore than the night before, his grin taking brief flight. The poultice had worked its magic. The tea too, or else he'd have been up with the sun.

But her little remedy had worked. Exhaustion on his part probably helped too.

He descended the stairs and slid into the back hallway the servants usually took from the kitchen, which would give him a more subtle entry into the dining room. Mrs. North met him along the corridor, her dark brows high in silent inquiry, but he raised a finger to his lips, stilling her questions. With a tilt of her head, a slow smile dawned from her lips to her eyes, which paused his forward momentum.

What was that look about?

She seemed to read his thoughts and leaned forward. "It's been a while since this house has heard laughter, aye?" Her whisper curled around her highland accent. "But a babe and a joyful heart tend to bring it along, don't they?"

He peeked around the doorway and paused with his hand on the frame. There his mother sat at the dining table in the ornate room holding little Charlie in her arms and teasing smiles out of him by shaking the long necklace she wore.

He hadn't seen his mother smile this much in months, maybe longer.

"He just started smiling in the last week or so, but he's taken quite a shine to it." Kizzie took a bite of the oatmeal in front of her as Mother held Charlie's attention. The younger woman's simple blue dress looked plainer than the one she'd worn last night, but the hue still brought out the color of her large eyes. No wonder Marty had wondered about what side of heaven he was on when she'd appeared, dressed in a pale robe, all that hair in disarray around her shoulders. . .

Even at the memory, Noah's face grew warm. Why did his heart have to prove he was ready for a relationship at this juncture in his life? When he wasn't at liberty to make choices without his brother's influence. And why this woman? A stranger with a past that almost scoffed at his family's status and. . .brokenness.

"He certainly has," came Mother's response, her own smile wide. Even the creases around her eyes looked less pronounced.

Could Kizzie McAdams and her son be what his mother needed to help her through her grief of losing not only her grandchild but her daughter-in-law too? Plus. . .her only daughter leaving.

Noah's attention shot back to Kizzie. Maybe all this strange interest had nothing to do with romance.

He nodded to himself. Merely a way to support his mother. Help her heal.

"It's like he's just waiting to laugh, ain't it?" Kizzie's light response pulled his attention back to her face. Her hair hung in a long thick braid over her shoulder, much less distracting.

"He does seem ready for it. He smiles so easily, it wouldn't surprise me if he didn't start laughing early." At her words, Charlie cooed out a response, and Mother's entire expression softened even more.

"I think he likes you, Victoria. He doesn't talk to just anybody."

Victoria? They were on a first-name basis now?

His mother chuckled at Kizzie's teasing and ran a finger down the baby's cheek, inciting another coo. "He reminds me how very lovely smiles are, especially in babies."

"Their laughs are wonderful too." Kizzie sighed. "I remember my youngest siblings laughing as babies, but I don't recollect when they started. Do you happen to know when laughing usually starts for babies?"

"I'm not certain, but I feel as though Noah laughed relatively early, and his sister wasn't far behind." She tickled Charlie's chin, inciting another dimpled grin. "George took much longer, but that is no surprise. He seems to have an aversion to joviality as a whole."

Noah grinned. A trait his brother carried into adulthood.

At the mention of his sister, pain squeezed his chest. Another missing life.

"What a horrible way to live, don't you think?" This from Kizzie.

"It's difficult to smile when your focus is on things that rarely lead to joy."

"Well, that's something we ought to stitch on a pillow." Kizzie's ready chuckle bubbled out with his mother's joining in.

"Indeed." And then his mother saw him. "Noah Lewis, at some point in your life, I know I taught you that eavesdropping is rude, didn't I?"

He stepped into the room, glancing in Kizzie's direction before dipping his head. "I didn't wish to interrupt with your adoration of little Charlie there."

"Are you afraid his dimples might overshadow yours?"

He nearly missed sitting in the chair he'd just pulled out. His mother? Joking with him? That behavior had been less frequent over the past two years and rarely in front of guests. "It's been a while since you teased me so openly." He hoped his smile reassured her. "And"—he nodded in Charlie's direction—"if I must succeed my claim of the best dimples in the house to anyone, I can think of no one quite so cute as Charlie."

The laughter warmed the space grief still touched within these walls.

"Very true." Mother touched Charlie's cheek. "And I do believe that more laughter is a sign we are moving forward to the other side of grief, where the pain bows to memory."

A quiet settled between them as their gazes met, the wounds still fresh. But hope waited just behind Mother's eyes. Perhaps they both understood the need to step forward. To welcome more laughter in the house again.

"Life's full of that, ain't it?" Kizzie took another bite of oatmeal. "Having to choose to keep living in the 'afters.'" She sent his mother a gentle smile. "They aren't easy, but I'm hoping they become easier as we go on."

"I think they do with the right mindset." Mother sighed, patting Charlie's hand. "And the right people."

"And the right perspective," Kizzie added, meeting Noah's gaze. "I'm glad I'm a little smarter than I was in the 'before,' and despite a snowstorm and an accident among strangers, I'm glad my 'after' has started with making such nice acquaintances."

His gaze caught in hers against his will. Those eyes, or perhaps what shone behind those eyes, captured his attention, redirected his thoughts. Part of him wanted to ask her to tell more of her story, but the other part dodged the inclination. The last thing he needed was another reason to argue with his brother. One more year. Just one more, and he'd be free to forge his own future without the power of the will's stipulation.

"I hope we are all smarter as we learn from hardships." Noah sat back in the chair, his emotions twisting too tight to keep the conversation going much longer. He turned to his mother. "How is Marty this morning?"

"He's been awake for an hour, and Case is with him." She looked over at Kizzie with a teasing grin. "He's still convinced Kizzie is a ghost, but I think he's starting to make some real improvement, though I'd feel better if Dr. Palmer could see him."

"Which brings me to my plan for this morning." He nodded toward Mrs. North as she approached with a breakfast plate. "I plan to take Case with me to attempt to salvage what we can of the carriage, unless you think I should hitch up the sleigh first thing and get Dr. Palmer."

"Last night, perhaps, I would have given a different answer, but this morning I'm not as concerned. His leg is broken, I believe, so it will be good to have the doctor here to set it, but he's making sense when he talks and has even eaten some breakfast."

"That's good news." His gaze pulled to Kizzie. She offered him a smile as she took a sip of tea.

"Are you and Case capable of retrieving the carriage on your own?" This from his mother.

"I'm not sure, but we have to at least try. The longer it stays in the elements, the worse it will be to repair."

"If you need some extra hands, Mr. Noah," Mrs. North said as she poured coffee into his cup, "my grandsons are sledding out back. I can send them along to help you."

"I thought I heard their laughter." Mother grinned. "They do so love that hill, don't they, Mrs. North?"

"Indeed, ma'am. It's the best for sledding within a mile of their house."

"But aren't they quite young for the task of pulling a carriage from the snow, Mrs. North?" In addition to the carriage being stuck on an incline in the snow, Noah wasn't certain how much more snow wedged it even more.

Mrs. North's smile bloomed. "If passion and the promise of hot chocolate and cookies can turn into power and energy, then I feel they'll be some of your best helpers. Clarence's nigh on twelve, and Cody's only a few years behind. They're young, aye, but they're keen to help when they can."

"If hot chocolate and cookies are promised, I'm tempted to throw in my hat to help too." Kizzie laughed. "Those are some mighty fine rewards."

Mother chuckled and stood. "Indeed, Kizzie."

"Well, I'll take their help." Noah winked at Mrs. North. "And the cookies." He looked over at Kizzie, her welcome smile a surprisingly pleasant start to his day. "And bringing Charlie and his dimples into the house for Mother's benefit should certainly be rewarded with some hot chocolate and cookies."

The sound of women's voices met Kizzie as she rounded the hallway toward the kitchen. Victoria Lewis kept a hint of reservation in her demeanor, which seemed just a part of who she was, but watching Charlie soften the woman into smiles eased some of the concern Kizzie had nursed since Victoria's questions about her past.

Of course, those concerns were justified, and Kizzie would continue to face them over and over again, but the idea of having her entire personality judged on the basis of one mistake grated on her and, at the same time, strangely exalted the grace she'd come to understand. Her humanness wanted to scream to the world that she had strength and wisdom now she didn't have before. A type of love she hadn't known before. But the new part of her heart reveled in God showing his goodness through her brokenness, rescuing her despite her immaturity and selfishness.

An ongoing, lifetime battle, she supposed.

She yawned as she approached the voices, her travels and lack of sleep weighing on her as the afternoon waned. Even when she'd finally curled up in the massive bed upstairs, it had taken her an hour to get to sleep. Her mind kept replaying her conversation with Mr. Lewis. . .Noah.

Looking back at the scenes of her life since meeting Charles Morgan, little hints created a patchwork answer to the question why Charles chose her. Noah's mention of her beauty only held a partial answer. Charles using his position as her employer provided another part, and one which brought with it a wave of shame. But despite all her silliness and inexperience, she wanted to believe Charles held some true care for her, some desire to do right by her.

No one forced him to secure a house for her. Or give provisions.

He visited of his own accord, even if those visits were few.

So the answer probably waited in some mixture of the three parts.

And despite the fact she'd wanted to keep her past private for as long as possible, she didn't regret Noah knowing the truth.

What he did with that information, she couldn't know, but she trusted him.

She probably shouldn't.

Trust had gotten her into her current predicament. Trust and an overzealous love of kissing.

Heat rose into her cheeks at the many images stirring through her mind of when she'd indulged quite thoroughly in the kissing part.

But she'd learned her lesson. Noah's observations only pressed the lesson deeper. If God ever brought her a chance to love again, she wanted it to be for all the right reasons.

Her gaze rose to the ceiling. With the kissing parts added in too, if God didn't mind too much.

Mrs. North and another woman stood working side by side. The younger woman looked to be glazing a ham, while Mrs. North peeled potatoes. The bits of conversation Kizzie heard involved some story about runaway sheep, some angry bees, and Mrs. North meeting her husband.

"Well, Miss Kizzie." Mrs. North welcomed her in with a smile. "Are you going mad stuck in this house all day?"

"No, ma'am. With the number of books y'all have in your library, I think it could be a while before I get too restless." She waved toward their work. "But I'd like to help here, if you need another hand."

"Far be it from us to ever turn down help." Mrs. North gestured with her paring knife to a nearby bowl. "I imagine Mrs. Candler wouldn't mind you kneading out the dough for biscuits, would you, Mrs. Candler?"

"Pleased to have you." Mrs. Candler's accent sounded much more familiar.

Kizzie slipped into the familiar work, thankful for the task and conversation, though she listened much more than she talked. The women talked a little about Mrs. North's upbringing in Scotland and how her grandfather had been a long-time servant of the English Lewises before she was recommended to take up service with them when they moved to America a generation ago.

Kizzie couldn't fathom traveling across an entire ocean. Moving over a couple mountains seemed big enough.

"So I've been a part of the current Mrs. Lewis' life since she married Mr. Lewis, and have seen all the children raised." Mrs. North directed her words at Kizzie.

"And did your husband come from Scotland too?"

Her smile grew. "I met him within five years of living in America, back when the Lewises lived in Virginia. He's a blacksmith. Mrs. Lewis convinced her husband to allow the marriage despite his reservations about having married staff, and for that, I am forever in her debt, because it's allowed Caleb and me to live in a way we wouldn't have with only one income."

"And allowed her to send her children to college, even," Mrs. Candler added.

"College?" Kizzie arranged the dough circles on the pan. "Now that's something, for sure."

Mrs. North preened at the praise. "Am right proud to say one of my sons has become a doctor and the other a lawyer. The youngest, the lawyer, lives here in The Hollows. It's his sons who are out helping Mr. Noah this morning." She shook her head and stirred a pot on the stove. "Heaven knows, Mr. Noah could use all the help he can get with trying to manage this house and the mill."

"Doesn't his brother help?"

The women exchanged a glance before Mrs. North returned her

attention to Kizzie. "With the mill losing workers, Mr. Noah's taken on more and more of the work while his brother travels to nearby towns and gets his new house ready for his new wife."

"Or causes trouble with other people's wives."

"Joyce!" Mrs. North shot the younger woman a look.

George Lewis certainly carried quite the reputation.

"What about the sister?" Kizzie surveyed each woman. "Is she near enough to help?"

"No, unfortunately, she's not." Mrs. North's tone ended any further questions on the subject.

"And what brings you to The Hollows, Miss Kizzie?" Mrs. Candler asked, softening the moment with a gentle smile. "You got friends here?"

How to answer without giving too much of her story away? "Mrs. Carter is expecting me."

Yes, accurate and vague. Folks would learn about her past soon enough, but she'd prefer to keep things private for as long as possible, hopefully long enough to build a reputation to help offset her past a little.

"Mrs. Gayle Carter? The owner of the general store?" Mrs. North asked.

Before Kizzie could answer, a thud struck one of the windows.

"What in the world?" came Mrs. North's exclamation as she stopped her work and moved to the window.

Another thud sounded, and then a shout.

Kizzie followed her, with Mrs. Candler close behind.

Two boys ran through the wintry yard, stopping only long enough to gather up snowballs to throw behind them. The elder's aim proved more accurate than the youngest's, whose next launch hit the front porch column, just visible from the kitchen window.

"Those boys." Mrs. North sighed, but judging from the tilt of her smile, it was half-hearted exasperation.

Kizzie laughed. "Who's chasing them?"

As if in answer, Noah emerged into view, limping after the boys and pelting them with his own snowballs. Her smile pinched into her cheeks as she watched his ready grin and heard his laughter through the windowpanes.

Mr. Taylor came into view, driving the crippled carriage toward the house.

"The man can barely run, but he's bound and determined to entertain those boys." Mrs. North sighed.

"He has such a kindness about him, doesn't he?"

Kizzie hadn't meant to voice her words aloud, but after her last meeting with Charles and the memory of her father, kindness and playfulness from men seemed horribly absent, except for Joshua Chappell. The kindness part anyway. Kizzie never saw any of his playfulness.

"Aye. He is kind," came Mrs. North's slow response as she studied Kizzie.

"You won't find finer in all of The Hollows, I reckon," added Mrs. Candler, turning back to the cooking.

Both boys braved the snowballs and barreled into Noah, knocking him to the ground. Kizzie pressed her fingers into her grin. The world could certainly use more kind, playful men. Good men. Some good woman waited for the love of such a man.

"Well, I pray his brother recognizes it soon." Kizzie touched the windowpane, smoothing away the fog her words made on the glass. "Good things should happen to kind people."

"Aye, they should." Mrs. North stepped closer, lowering her voice. "But I warn you, don't be setting your sights on Mr. Noah."

Kizzie flashed the woman a look. "I don't mean to set my sights on anyone for a long while, Mrs. North." She turned back to the window. "No man wants the burden of my reputation or past. And I wouldn't wish it on him." She swallowed through her tightening throat, accepting her future. "Besides, my focus needs to be on taking care of Charlie, not learning how to take care of a husband too."

"Not everyone judges by pasts, but some of the kind ones are controlled by those who do." Mrs. North's voice lowered even more, drawing Kizzie's attention back to her face. "There are hurts in these walls which cannot be undone. Ones that nearly destroyed Mrs. Lewis." She held Kizzie's gaze, warning tightening the lines around her eyes. "Keep to your kindness, but guard your heart."

Chapter 14

Mrs. North's words weighed on Kizzie's mind as she excused herself to check on Charlie. She kept to her room for the next little while, waiting for the dinner bell to ring and giving her heart a much-needed redirection.

She wasn't attracted to Noah. She knew the sense of attraction.

No, she merely appreciated his kindness and care.

Both of those were reasons to keep her distance, because a man like him made attraction grow too easily.

Kizzie squelched the hint of longing. Mrs. North's warnings hit their mark. She knew all too well how social status influenced decisions about hearts and future. She didn't need to nurse a notion of any fancy for Noah Lewis. . .or anyone else at the moment. She had enough to do with starting her life over.

Charlie cooed beside her on the bed, enjoying the discovery of his fingers, and Kizzie turned her thoughts back to the book she'd taken from the library downstairs. *David Copperfield*. It had the prettiest cover in the expansive Lewis library, a far cry from the one wall of books in the Morgans' study. A library in a house! It was beautiful and would dazzle her sister Laurel.

She sighed at the thought. Part of her wished the ache for home could dim a little, and the other part was afraid it would. She carried her family with her wherever she went, fought thoughts about them every day, sometimes every hour.

And now, the only way to reach them was through memory.

She closed her eyes and breathed out a prayer for them, that someday, somehow, she'd see them again.

After a little while, once Charlie slipped back into slumber, Kizzie closed the book and walked downstairs to see if she could relieve Case from watching Marty. But one peek into the room revealed both brothers asleep, Marty in the bed and Case in the nearby chair.

The sight was sweet.

"Mother says Marty ate well for lunch."

Kizzie spun around at the whispered voice to find Noah nearby, sleeves rolled up and a streak of dirt across his cheek.

Her breath caught, and she stepped away from the doorway to keep from disturbing the brothers' rest. "I'm glad to hear it. Eating is sure to help with the healing process."

"Yes, that's what I thought too." He searched her face before taking a step back. "I didn't mean to startle you. I should have made my presence—"

"It's fine, Noah." His name rolled off her tongue in such an easy way, those hazel eyes of his so warm and welcoming... Maybe her heart wasn't as safe as she thought. She took another step back. "I saw the carriage roll in earlier."

"It has a few broken pieces, but it's mendable." He shrugged a shoulder and gestured toward the hall. "I just finished hitching up the sleigh to fetch the doctor and was wondering if you might need anything for the baby."

Her heart trembled at his consideration. So simple. And it should have been natural. But it hit her with such force, she folded her arms across her chest as if to keep her heart from weakening into water. "That's awful kind of you, but—"

A sudden slam of a nearby door broke into her words.

"Noah!"

Noah's head shot up, and he stepped in front of her, as if blocking her from some unseen force in the next room. She didn't need to ask the identification of the voice.

His behavior screamed it loud and clear.

George Lewis.

"Noah, where are you?"

Noah turned and placed his hands on her shoulders, bringing his face close to hers, the energy radiating off him increasing her pulse. "It would be better if you stayed out of sight." He searched her face then released her and disappeared around the corner of the hall.

"There you are," the voice blasted again. "What's this I hear of you sending workers home early yesterday?"

"George, even you must see how keeping them for a few more hours could have led to worse—"

"We lose money for every hour we reduce production. You know this. Do I need to physically pound it into your head?"

"We would lose more production if a third of our fledgling work-force died in the snow." Noah raised his volume to match his brother's, refusing to cower.

Kizzie grinned from an inordinate sense of pride swelling in her chest for this man. Of course, she didn't know him a heap of a lot, but witnessing his tenderness and then hearing him stand up to a thick-headed tyrant made her want to cheer.

"I left you to keep the process going, not cost business." The harsh, deeper voice erupted again. "We can hire more people."

Air lodged in Kizzie's throat. Had he just dismissed people's lives?

"From where?" came Noah's quick response. "We're having a hard enough time keeping the dwindling numbers we already have. Every person counts."

So did every hour.

But not at the cost of a life.

A roar sounded with such fury, Kizzie peeked around the corner just in time to see a broad man grab Noah by the suit jacket and jerk him closer. "What about your life? Do you care about that? I have the power to take everything away from you."

Noah stared back, unflinching. What did Mr. George Lewis mean?

"George!" Victoria emerged from the hallway, her blue gown flying around her, her face ashen. "Let go of your brother this instant."

George released him with a shove, sending Noah stumbling into a nearby table and knocking a vase of artificial flowers onto the floor with a crash.

"If we don't improve our business, we could lose everything." George ground out the words, his face red from his forehead to his beard. "We can't lose any time. Father entrusted us with this business."

"Then perhaps you shouldn't have taken on so much debt to build your new house," Noah shot back as he righted himself. "No one should live above their means, George. Father entrusted us with making smart decisions too."

George made to rush toward Noah again, but Victoria's hand flew against his chest to stop him.

"Boys!"

"And what do you have to say about the fire?" George growled as he stepped away from his mother's touch. "Are you covering for your precious poverty-stricken nobodies, or worse, the outcasts you champion behind my back? You know they're all the same. Liars. Tricksters. Just waiting to find a way to take our money. Your softness for them only increases their willingness to take advantage of—"

"Stop this at once, George Lewis." Victoria's voice broke into the argument again, this time silencing both men.

Noah grounded himself, readying for another attack from his brother.

Long before his father's death two years ago, Noah had stepped into the role of defender. Not of his business ventures, per se, but of the weak and the right. Sometimes it had been the workers. At times, the business dealings. A few times, his own mother. But his father's forceful personality and his brother's desire to emulate him thrust the innate peacemaker within Noah onto the battlefield.

Three years ago, he would have attempted gentle responses to his brother's irrational accusations. Acquiesced to the demands of his father. Three years ago, he may have cowered a little.

But losing Elinor, their sister, and their father forced Noah to take a stand, over and over again. To raise a voice of reason and compassion.

True compassion cared with a steel spine.

His brother's tyranny had only gotten worse since his engagement to Beatrice Malone, belle of The Hollows and daughter of one of the richest men in town. More outrageous. With an apparent need to prove to the Malones and the entire town that he deserved such a social advancement.

Charlie's cry suddenly sliced into the argument. Heat fled Noah's body, and three things happened at once.

George's eyes grew wide, Mother exchanged a look with Noah, and Kizzie dashed from the hallway toward the stairs.

"Have you brought one of those vagabond children to stay in this house?" George dodged Noah's approach and started for the stairs, only to run directly into Kizzie blocking his path. She stood one step above him, placing her almost at eye level.

"There are no vagabonds here, Mr. Lewis." She raised her chin, her eyes as cool as steel. "Only strangers who got lost in the storm last night, so if you'll kindly control yourself and stop scaring my young'un, I'll go quiet him."

George froze, eyes growing wider as he stared.

Noah moved closer, ready to rise to Kizzie's defense, but his brother didn't move, barely seeming to breathe. Merely stood there in a stare-off with a woman half a foot shorter than him. Though, from her current stance and the fire in her eyes, Noah wondered if Kizzie would be a force to reckon with.

"I beg your pardon, Mrs.. . ."

"Kizzie McAdams, sir." And with another withering look, she dashed up the stairs.

George's attention followed her until she disappeared from sight, and then he turned, blinking. "Who is she, and why is she here?"

"As she said, George," Mother interjected before Noah could respond, her tones low. "She met Noah on the main road after his carriage overturned last night in the storm, and she helped him and Martin home. There was no making it to town once they arrived here, so I invited her and her son to stay."

"The carriage?" George's gaze switched to Noah. "What were you doing out on the road in the middle of the storm?" His expression dawned with awareness. "You weren't taking workers home from the mill, were you? Do you realize the waste of resources you've created in damaging the carriage? Have you no care for our situation, brother?"

Noah braced himself for another assault, but Mother stepped between them again.

"That is enough." Her whisper was harsh.

"Not nearly," George seethed, holding Noah's attention. "But I will forgo the conversation until later for the sake of Mrs. McAdams."

The creak of stair and shush of a gown brought their attention to the stairs, where Kizzie slowly descended, Charlie in her arms. Her gaze flipped from George to Noah and then back again as she pulled a sniffling Charlie up against her shoulder. Noah stepped forward, but George bypassed him, reaching the bottom of the stairs at the same time Kizzie did.

"I apologize, Mrs. McAdams, for my previous behavior." He sent a glare to Noah. "I had no idea there were guests in the house."

A curl of nausea rose in Noah's stomach at his brother's saccharine response. His charm worked on so many women, especially the young ones. How many lives had he ruined with a compliment and the promise of something he'd never give?

Kizzie's eyes narrowed for only a moment before she offered a reserved smile that was nothing like the one she'd given him before George stormed into the house. "My mama says that our true self rises to the top when we're mad or when no one's looking. I certainly hope what I just witnessed doesn't prove true in your case."

Noah had been on the verge of coming to Kizzie's defense, but in the wake of her response to his brother, he almost grinned.

Kizzie McAdams wasn't in danger of cowering to his brother. Something twinged inside his mind, an awareness he couldn't quite place.

His brother appeared in similar shock, but instead of being affronted, a look of pure fascination brightened his expression, and the nausea in Noah's stomach took an aggravated turn. "I intend on proving that it doesn't, if for no other reason than to replace whatever unpleasant thoughts are whirring in your pretty little mind about me."

"I hope your motivation for improvement is a whole lot deeper than my thoughts about you, Mr. Lewis."

Noah nearly laughed. His mother met his gaze with a hint of humored surprise.

George's smile dimmed only a moment and then flickered wide again. "One motivation could certainly spur another." He gestured toward the sitting room. "May we start over?"

"Actually, I believe we've overstayed our most kind welcome, and I feel Charlie and I should get on with our plans." She turned to Noah. "Could we ride with you into town on your way to fetch the doctor?"

A twin blend of disappointment and relief flooded through him. Getting her away from George, especially with the sudden shift in his behavior, was a good idea, but despite all inner warnings, he wanted to know her better. Understand the fire in those eyes, the confidence that spurred her to a new life, to a different future.

He wanted to know more about the strength that sent her fleeing the man who used his power to his advantage over her. Kizzie McAdams was no wallflower.

His Elinor had been a gentle, quiet soul, weaving in and out of his world like a whisper. Dying in the same quiet way. But Kizzie bloomed with a passion and resilience, capturing his attention as much with her confidence as her beauty.

His heart twinged again, as if working through emotions to find the right one, but his head knew the best course of action. Get her away from George.

"Of course. I'd be happy to," he heard himself say. Yes. Good choice. Best one.

Safer for everyone.

"The doctor?" George spun to face Noah, his attention shifting to Mother and back. "Why do we need the doctor?"

"For Martin," Mother answered as Noah stepped toward Kizzie. "He was seriously injured in the carriage accident, and his leg requires a set."

"I'll let Taylor know of your plans." Noah lowered his voice. "He'll have your things loaded into the sleigh, and we can leave as soon as you're ready."

She searched his face with those large, curious eyes. Charlie's head wobbled as he turned to look Noah's way too. Same eyes. "Thank you. I reckon we can be ready in half an hour."

"And perhaps it would be good for you to return to your house, George," Mother added, gesturing toward the door. "I'm sure you have things to work on there in preparation for your wedding?"

George stepped back, his smile tight. "Excellent idea. And I'll go by way of the mill to have my own little investigation about the fire yesterday." His attention swept over Kizzie. "I look forward to our next meeting, Mrs. McAdams." With another glare in Noah's direction, he crammed his hat on his head and marched from the room.

"I'm sorry you had to witness such a spectacle, Kizzie." Mother placed her palm on Kizzie's arm, her attention resting on Charlie. "What a horrible way to wake up from a kip."

"It ain't the first time he's been startled awake by a loud noise." Kizzie sighed as she gave Charlie a little bounce. "By some folks with the same thinking as your son." Kizzie raised a brow and looked at Noah. "Not that son. I can already tell he's the good sort."

The compliment caught him off guard. "At least fumbling toward good, I hope."

She offered him the smile he'd seen a few times before, the one he felt all the way through him. The feeling in his heart grew, like someone opened a window inside his chest and flooded its shadowed recesses with light.

And he couldn't look away. Didn't really want to.

What was happening? Surely it was just a response to her wit, her vibrance. But no. The ache pooled deeper, soul deep, reaching beyond the shattered pieces of his grief toward the surface. Her honest faith interrupted his world, his planned path. His heart wanted whatever hope and strength she held within those eyes. Wanted. . .her?

His brain paused on the thought. *Her*?

A single mother with a child barely two months old? A woman running from a past he didn't fully comprehend? After all these months, why did his heart suddenly respond to Kizzie McAdams?

His gaze fell to Charlie, the baby offering a smile as if he somehow recognized Noah's internal bewilderment.

"Ain't we all fumbling, some days finding our feet a little better than others, but all holding on to hope that God is making each step stronger and better than the one before?" Her gaze held his, some deeper understanding passing between them. "I sure hope so, because I don't want to go back to where I was."

Words failed him. His mind still struggled with the very real awareness of wanting to win her. At the mental admission, his pulse took off on a race, like a windup toy set free.

He was completely crazy!

"You really don't have to leave," his mother urged, drawing Kizzie's attention away and releasing him from whatever hold she had. "We'd be happy to have you stay with us another night."

Which sent him back to seeing her in her robe, hair long and wild. His throat tightened at the memory. *Beautiful.*

He was completely useless at the moment.

"That's kind of you, but if I'm going to start over in this new life of mine, I better go ahead and begin. Besides, once Mr. Lewis figures out I'm not a 'Mrs.,' he may not be too pleased I stayed here at all."

Noah drew in a breath and stepped back, Kizzie's words sending an unintended reminder of his precarious place in the family and his brother's unpredictable behavior. The interest on George's face for Kizzie had little to do with her marital status. How the man could portray an upright life for the small social circles of The Hollows and live in complete opposition in private kept the two of them at odds, especially when it came to the young women at the mill.

They proved easy prey for George's roving eye.

But once Noah gained his inheritance, he'd change things. Protect the workers. Maybe even start his own mill where the employees wouldn't have to worry about people like George in power.

Now his situation trapped him.

The women needed incomes to serve their physical needs, but the job placed them in danger of George's anger and insatiable interests.

And Noah had no financial means to make a difference.

Someday, but not now.

Oh God, please help me know what to do! Sooner rather than later.

His attention landed back on Kizzie. He had to protect her too.

"I think considering everything. . ." He waved toward her. "It's best for you to leave as soon as possible."

"Yes. Of course." The glow left her eyes, somehow deflating his chest a little. "That's probably best."

"I'll bring Daisy to you once the snow clears," he continued. "It will give you time to sort her lodgings. I don't recall whether Mrs. Carter keeps a horse or not."

Did she *want* to stay?

"I don't want to cause any trouble with her being kept here."

"No trouble at all." He searched her face, attempting to bring back the light in her eyes.

Kizzie looked from him to his mother. "Thank you for your kindness to me and Charlie. But it's time for me to step into whatever's next in my life. . .to start over."

Chapter 15

LEAVE AS SOON AS POSSIBLE.

She attempted to pinch her heart against the sting, but it flared a little. Another reminder of how her past kept impacting her future. Of course Noah Lewis wanted her out of his house. If his brother felt so strongly about associating with people like her, he wouldn't support his little brother doing the same. Or his mother.

And Noah knew more about her than anyone else in The Hollows.

She shook her head and closed her mind against the worries. One truth she clung to, when the self-doubt and shame screamed accusations, was that she belonged to God. He called her His.

His beloved.

And that truth trumped every other label or slander.

She sighed out the hurt and glanced over the snow-covered country-side as the sleigh moved toward town, a picture straight from heaven to her insecurities. *Though your sins be as scarlet, they shall be as white as snow.*

On the horizon, the mountains rose in frosty peaks against the brilliant blue sky, the sunshine almost blinding against the stark white of the wintry world. Almost as if God wanted to get her attention. Remind her of His truth.

Her smile stretched wide, and she closed her eyes, breathing in the chilled air.

"A penny for your thoughts?" Noah tossed her a grin as he steadied the horses' reins. The sleigh moved with smooth dips and swells across the new snow.

"Everything is just so beautiful." She drew her attention away from his face, holding on to God's thoughts about her. "I've always loved snow."

"I would have thought after our harrowing adventure, you might take a dimmer view."

"I met you and your mama." She shrugged. "That's been a nice surprise."

He sent her a look from his periphery, his smile brimming with his nod. "I'm happy to hear that."

"Besides, the fresh, untouched snow. Well, it reminds me of hope."

His expression sobered, and he stared ahead, brow furrowing a little. "I'm sorry about my brother. I trust you know Mother and I do not share his views on many things."

"Though he's louder about his feelings on the subject, his view is the more common one." Charlie wiggled against Kizzie, trying to pull himself up, so Kizzie placed him on her shoulder closest to Noah and more couched from the wind.

"Common doesn't mean right."

"And right doesn't mean accepted."

"True." He nodded. "So I think it's all the more fitting you're staying at Mrs. Carter's."

Charlie's capped head wobbled as he looked around, and then when his eyes met Noah's, his little lips spread into a bright, dimpled smile. The dimples Noah's mama had mentioned earlier blinked in response for a half second. Too quick to get a good peek at them, but just enough to increase her curiosity.

What was it about a man having dimples? And only ones that sneaked out on rare occasions? It felt like a little secret only few and special folks got the chance to know.

Not that she was special to the likes of Noah Lewis, but the idea didn't hurt her none. A nice little daydream to think on every once in a while, that some good man in the world didn't think too badly of her, despite knowing her past.

"He's such a happy baby." Noah's soft voice carried over the thrum of the horses' hooves.

Emotions gathered in her throat at the tender sentiment. "I used to think what I'd done would make him a sad baby. That my sin would somehow transfer to his disposition as punishment." She kissed Charlie's head. "I'm glad that's not been true."

"I think he knows how much you love him."

She sent Noah a look. His smile was gentle, not holding any of the censure she'd heard from his brother. "I hope that's true. And maybe Jesus' love in me crosses out the sin that brought little Charlie here, so he can be happy." She sighed. "Besides, this little man and the Lord are all I got in this world."

Noah's expressions sobered. "Despite my brother's behavior, please know you have friends in me and my mother."

She dipped her head in acceptance but didn't hold a lot of confidence in his claim. She didn't doubt his sincerity. He'd already proved to be an honest and kind sort of man, but with a powerful brother and a company to run, his good intentions weaved through the hands of someone else's control.

Besides, Noah and his mama barely knew her.

But the sentiment was nice.

Charlie's little hand reached out, and his fingers snatched a hold of Noah's coat sleeve. Noah's smile brimmed wider, giving a longer view of those dimples. Kizzie's lips couldn't help but respond. It was a real nice secret to know.

"He's happy—and strong, judging from the grip he has on my jacket."

"I don't reckon you've been around babies very much, since you and your brother aren't married?"

He transferred the reins to one hand and jerked the free hand's glove off with his teeth before raising his fingers toward Charlie. The baby took a double-fisted hold of Noah's large hand, bringing out the man's dimples again. "Quite the grip there, little man."

Something inside Kizzie's heart melted.

"He's got a good one. Believe me, I've felt it every time he grabs a handful of my hair."

Noah's attention rose to her hatted head and then lowered to her eyes. "He's strong like his mother, I'd say."

Those hazel eyes bore into hers as if trying to nudge some confidence her way. She looked down at Charlie, smoothing his little head with her palm. "I'm stronger now, but it took breaking first."

Noah's sigh released a cloud of cool air. "That's certainly one way to become strong."

Charlie took that moment to bite down on one of Noah's fingers, enticing a chuckle from Noah. "Strong and feisty."

Noah's brow rose as his gaze flitted to hers, and she wondered if he didn't pair the latter word with her too. Feisty. Her daddy used to call her his spitfire, an endearment meant just for her. He never used it during a drunk, which made the word even sweeter.

She looked away.

She reckoned she'd need to recall some of that feistiness to make a new start on her own.

The clanging of the horses' tug straps and buckles made a welcome sound in the special silence only a snow day provided.

"I had a son."

His declaration pulled her attention from the view to focus back on his profile. *A son?*

"A little over a year ago, my wife died giving birth to our son. Born a little early." He worked his jaw, his words coming in halts and stops. "He. . .he was already gone. She died soon after."

Kizzie stared at him, a deep ache carving out space inside her chest.

A double-knotted loss. Wife and child. Her palm instinctively tightened on Charlie's back.

Mama birthed one stillborn child. A girl. Born between Isom and Suzie. The irony of such a scene in one's life wounded like nothing else. It carried a strange sort of silent grief. Too silent when the sound of a life should have rung the air.

Seeing her daddy at that moment, his strong, larger-than-life frame bent beneath the loss, his strength and protection insufficient to change the outcome, created a memory that burned into her mind. She'd never seen him cry, except then, and it had been a quiet cry. Two big tears rolling down his careworn face. Eyes wide and lost, he was as helpless as the rest of the people in the room.

"I'm so sorry," she whispered, watching as Charlie continued holding

Noah's hand. A bittersweet picture. "What was your wife's name?"

His Adam's apple bobbed just above his scarf with his hard swallow. "Elinor."

Elinor. Beautiful. "Sounds like an angel's name."

His attention flitted to hers for a second before he twisted his hand free from Charlie and tapped the baby's nose. "She liked the snow too."

He replaced his glove and turned back to the horses.

What sort of man was Noah Lewis? More like her brother, Jeb, she reckoned, than her daddy or Charles. She didn't know a great many men very well, but when pairing the four together, Noah's gentle but sturdy character matched Jeb's the most.

A hard worker and thinker, like Daddy, but with a sweet spirit binding all his strength and compassion together. And he had to be strong to keep his smile after bearing such sorrow.

She couldn't have fully appreciated it until she held a child of her own.

Losing one's reputation was one thing.

Losing one's child was another.

"There's The Hollows." Noah gestured with his chin, and Kizzie followed his gaze as they crested a hill to reveal a long collection of buildings clustered in the valley below.

The town grew from a large flat land poised between mountains. Three steeples vaulted into the blue sky at various points along some large street. Brick, white-paneled wood, and a few stone buildings of various sizes and shapes created the collection of shops, businesses, and homes large enough to house a few hundred people.

If not a thousand.

She'd never been in a place so big.

Her shoulders relaxed a little. Maybe a bigger place meant an easier spot to start over, to disappear among the crowd.

Yes. Nella had known what she needed.

"Looks like they've tried to clear the snow from Main Street, so we'll have to go around the back way to Mrs. Carter's, since we're in the sleigh."

"Is her shop on Main Street?"

He nodded. "One of the oldest shops too. A great location, as she's sure to tell you." Noah offered a grin, a twinkle deepening his hazel eyes.

"Mrs. Carter and her late husband bought the shop about twenty years ago. She has a good mind for the people, and he had a good head for business, so they made a fine pair for shopkeeping."

"Late husband? He passed away?"

"About six months ago." His frown deepened. "And from what I hear, it's been a difficult transition for her, since she doesn't have as solid a business mind as he did. A few months ago, a woman from church stepped in to help her and then ran off with some of Mrs. Carter's money."

"How awful." Why couldn't people just be decent to each other? "Does the boardinghouse do well?"

He hesitated. "I believe she could earn a better income from it if she didn't—" He pinched his lips together. "Mrs. Carter is known for taking in women who need a safe place to start over." He looked over at her. "She's been in the business of helping them for a long time."

Mrs. Carter helped women like Kizzie? Had Nella been one of the women she'd helped? Is that why Nella understood grace so well?

"She uses the top floor of the boardinghouse for those women to have a low-cost place to live, but—"

"Rescuing folks like me doesn't lead to a great deal of profit," Kizzie finished.

"Not of the financial sort, usually." He guided the horses to the left and bypassed the main street, the snow becoming less smooth the nearer the town became. "But her interest is in a reward of a much higher nature, I believe."

Noah spoke like a man who talked to God, who understood. It had never occurred to her how sweet such a shared love could be. And Mrs. Carter kept growing more and more interesting. "It sounds like she may have her priorities in the right place."

"I believe you're right, Kizzie McAdams." Noah's lips crooked. "She's as unique as she is magnanimous. I think the two of you are going to get along very well."

Noah promised to deliver her trunks the next day, since he couldn't get the sleigh close enough to the shop entrance due to the snow, so she carried a few items in her small carry sack to get her and Charlie through until then.

She oughtn't to think about Noah's fine face or eyes. Or the way his smile dimpled. Thoughts like that had gotten her into her current predicament, but Noah Lewis proved the easy sort for daydreaming. Too easy. And his heartbreaking history made him take up even more space in her mind.

She pinched her eyes closed against the pull. No! Noah Lewis wasn't the sort to fancy romantic notions about someone like her. Besides, after Charles refused to marry her for so long, she didn't need to set her sights on matrimony for anyone else in her near future. Clearly, she wasn't the sort a good man wanted to marry, and dreaming about the warmth and welcome of a home of her own would only end in heartache.

She walked toward the direction he'd pointed her. The boarding-house stood behind the general store, trees framing it to give a more secluded feel from the business of Main Street. A fence hedged in a backyard blanketed with untouched snow. Kizzie rounded the two-story clapboard building to find a front porch the length of the house, complete with two rocking chairs poised at one end.

Welcome.

Kizzie smiled. What a generous, kind woman Mrs. Carter must be to create such a nice spot.

A gunshot came from inside the house, startling Kizzie to a stop at the corner of the porch. Someone yelled, and the sound of glass breaking followed.

What on earth was going on? Kizzie pulled Charlie close, stepping back to somewhat hide herself behind the corner of the building. Another shout shook from the other side of the wall, followed by another shot.

Heaven and earth!

Suddenly, the front door crashed open and out ran a young man, shirtless, trying to button his pants as he nearly fell down the front porch steps.

"That's right, Jake Murphy, you come back into my boardinghouse, and I'll do more than scare you, boy!"

Tagging along behind the voice was a small, gray-and-brown-haired woman wearing an apron over a calico dress. In one hand she held a rifle and with the other she pulled a young woman out onto the porch. "As for you, Molly Edwards, you've lost your last chance." The younger woman's loose red hair hung around the shoulders of her underclothes, a balled-up dress in her hands. "I don't run a brothel, girl. And you knew the rules about menfolk in your rooms."

"But I didn't mean to, Mrs. Carter," the woman cried. "He was such a sweet talker. I couldn't help it."

"If you don't start taking responsibility for your own stupidity, you ain't never gonna get smarter, girl. And I ain't got the patience or time to try and teach you."

"Please don't cast me out. I ain't got nowhere to go."

"You should have thought of that before you let him onto my property with plans to give yourself to him." The older woman pulled Molly to the porch steps. "Jake Murphy ain't no man for any woman."

"But he promised me he'd marry me this time." Molly stumbled to the bottom of the steps with the older woman keeping her by the arm and upright.

"Men will promise a great many things when they're thinking with the wrong part of their bodies."

"Please, Mrs. Carter. Just one more chance."

At that moment, as both women reached the bottom of the stairs, the older woman's gaze found Kizzie. She looked from Kizzie's face to Charlie, and she released a loud sigh.

"Well, we got a vacancy for you, Miss, if that's what's brought you here." The woman released her hold on Molly. "Molly's just leaving."

"Please, Mrs. Carter," Molly cried out again.

Kizzie stepped forward, reaching into her pocket for Nella's letter. "Mrs. Carter?"

A few wiry sprigs had fallen loose from the woman's bun and poked in various directions around her face, her large gray eyes wide. "I am."

Kizzie looked over at the teary-faced Molly, who stood at the end of the stairs, hands clasped in front of her, as if waiting for Mrs. Carter to change her mind. An immediate kinship bloomed in Kizzie for the young, misguided woman who was looking for affection in the wrong place and in the wrong way.

"I'm Kizzie McAdams, sent by Nella Chappell." Kizzie offered the letter.

"Nella Chappell." The woman's entire face transformed with her smile. The stern lines around her eyes softened. "Ah, a telegram arrived from her just yesterday saying I should expect you soon." Mrs. Carter gave Kizzie another look from head to boots. "You're a might bit younger than I figured you'd be, but if Nella trusts you, I got no reason not to."

"Mrs. Carter, please."

Molly's cry came again, and the older woman turned toward her, pointing the envelope like a finger. "I ain't interested in supporting your sin, girl. If you ain't got the decency to follow my rules, I can't jump inside that thick skull of yours and help."

"But I've learned my lesson." Her green gaze flipped from Mrs. Carter to Kizzie and back, the desperation in them reaching out and snatching at Kizzie's heart. "I promise, Mrs. Carter. Please."

She knew that look, that need. And the realization that even the very best plans failed to change reality.

"What if I take her under my wing, Mrs. Carter?" The words popped out so fast it surprised Kizzie as much as it seemed to surprise both of the other ladies. Well, might as well dig a little deeper. "I know you don't know me yet, but I'm more than willing to give you a hand in helping any of your girls make better choices. I've had to learn the hard way, and maybe God wants me to help other girls learn too."

Mrs. Carter's gray eyes narrowed for a full five seconds, her steely look prickling the hairs on Kizzie's arms with its scrutiny. Then, with a glance back at Molly, she said, "One more chance, girl. And that's only 'cause Miss McAdams seems to think there's more to you than kisses for brains. But this is your last chance, because my reputation is tied to this place. Do you understand?"

Molly nodded her head so fast it made Kizzie dizzy. "Yes, ma'am. I promise."

Mrs. Carter rolled her eyes and then shooed her away. "Now go get some clothes on so you don't catch your death." Then she turned back to Kizzie, one brow sitting high. "Now, Miss McAdams, Nella's telegram mentioned you know shopkeeping business."

Shopkeeping business? Had Nella intended to provide Kizzie a job as well as a new place to start over? "Shopkeeping business?"

"I'm in need of a person with a business mind to help me get untangled from my current mess, and I mean to interview you for the job."

Kizzie blinked and riffled through her brain. "I did shopkeeping back home. For a general store in the mountains. Helped with stocking, cleaning, ordering, and bookkeeping."

"Bookkeeping, eh?" Both brows swung high. "Now that's even better."

"I've always been decent with numbers. Daddy had me help him some when purchasing things." Kizzie stepped forward. "And I've worked in service for a year, besides growing up in a house full of young'uns, so I know how to clean and tend house."

"Good, good." She nodded, raising a wrinkled finger to touch Charlie's cheek. "You sound like just the right person for the job."

"You mean. . .you'd really hire me?" Kizzie gestured with her chin toward Charlie. "Even me being the way I am?"

"I can only take you part-time to start, but I can provide you free lodging above the shop. If you're working for me, sleeping someplace other than the boardinghouse would suit better." She shrugged, her grin wrinkling her whole face. "I know the value of a second chance. Sometimes the very best folks rise out of a second chance because they know what they've been forgiven of. I believe in humility. Keeps people from putting on airs. I reckon that's why God likes it so much."

Tension rolled off Kizzie's shoulders in a giant wave, and the emotions scratching at her throat began a steady climb into her eyes. "My mama would like you a whole bunch."

" 'Zat so?"

"Yes, ma'am. She used to say that humility was knowing God's place and knowing your own place and not getting the two mixed up."

"I think I'd like your mama too." Mrs. Carter chuckled and gestured with the letter toward the brick two-story building across a little path in front of them. "Let's get you and that babe inside by the stove, and we can discuss whether you want to work for me or not." She shot Kizzie a wink and then showcased the rifle in her hand. "After this introduction, you may just reconsider."

Chapter 16

Gunfire?

Noah had only gotten the horses into a trot when the sound echoed through the thin woods to the right of the path only two streets back from Main Street, a path untouched by wagons just yet. He drew the horses to a stop and turned to look in the direction he'd come. Who would be firing gunshots in town?

Another shot shook the air, carrying over the snow like the sound of thunder.

Had he left Kizzie in a dangerous situation?

His eyes shot wide. Or was Kizzie protecting herself? She hadn't mentioned owning a gun, but she seemed the sort to have one.

He gave the reins a tug and turned the horses, urging them into a canter, or as much of a canter as the snow allowed. Before the horses even came to a stop behind the boardinghouse, he'd jumped from the seat and tied the reins to the nearest fence post.

To his right, a shirtless man ran at an unbelievable speed through the snow toward the woods, his feet as bare as his chest.

What was going on?

Noah pushed through the snow, down the little hill behind the boardinghouse, and rounded to the front. Footprints in the snow proved a small group had been standing there. One set of prints went in the general direction Noah had just come from, but the other footprints, a set of two, disappeared toward the general store.

No blood.

His breath released in a puff of frozen air.

He followed the pair of footprints to the back door of the general store, proceeded around to the front, and entered the large space with a jingle of the bell above the door.

The usual scents of licorice, tobacco, spices, and woodstove hit him right away. He'd always loved the atmosphere of this place, the warmth and quaintness. Barrels sat in various places along the floor, boasting bulk goods for sale. Along the right, to appeal to the women of the town, Mrs. Carter housed a dry goods section, with some of the Lewis Mills fabrics, yarn, and thread on display. The back right corner featured hardware, and running along the left side of the building was a long counter, featuring candies, various canned vegetables, and other foodstuffs. But most of all, paused in conversation and staring at him, stood Mrs. Carter and Kizzie McAdams, both safe and whole.

At their wide-eyed expressions, heat took a steady course from his chest into his face. He cleared his throat and stepped farther into the warmth of the building.

"Mr. Noah?" Mrs. Carter tilted her head. "Are you all right?"

The heat in his cheeks heightened, and he removed his hat. "I. . .I heard the gunshots and came to. . ." He gestured with his hat toward Kizzie. "Make sure everyone was fine."

Mrs. Carter's gaze flipped between him and Kizzie. "Well, aren't you a good sort." She waved him forward, and his attention flitted to Kizzie's face.

Her smile beamed him closer. . .and increased the heat in his face.

He should have known she was fine. Ridiculous.

"I'm sure Kizzie appreciates you ensuring she's safe from me and my rifle." Mrs. Carter grinned, her eyes alight.

"You fired those shots?"

She looked down at the rifle lying on the counter and nodded. "One of the Murphy boys saw fit to enter my boardinghouse with designs on one of my girls. I had to convince him to leave."

A laugh burst out of him. "Your methods prove most effective, Mrs. Carter."

She patted the rifle and sent him a wink. "Ain't failed me yet."

"I didn't mean to worry you, Noah." Kizzie stepped around the counter to meet him on the other side. "But I appreciate your kindness in making sure I wasn't victim to Mrs. Carter's wrath." She leaned close, her eyes sparkling with humor. "She's about as terrifying with her rifle as my mama."

"I already thought I'd like your mama, and now I'm even surer." Mrs. Carter patted the counter with a laugh.

Ah, the teasing between the two already confirmed a healthy start to their relationship.

"Well, I won't keep you." He took a step back, sending a nod to each woman. "I need to get to Dr. Palmer before the day gets later than it already is."

"Is your mama all right?" Mrs. Carter's gaze sharpened. "I know she's had a rough go the past two years."

"She's fine." He retreated another step, cramming his hat on his head. "Kizzie can fill you in on the snowy adventure which led to her staying over at our house and my stable hand's broken leg."

"I can't think of a better house in which to find refuge from a storm · than the one where Victoria and Noah Lewis reside." Mrs. Carter's attention shifted again between Noah and Kizzie, like she was attempting to sort something out.

But what?

"Kizzie, you walk the man on out. I'll send him along with a soda pop for the ride back home." Mrs. Carter reached into the nearby cooler, drew out an RC Cola, and handed it to Kizzie. "It won't warm you, but the fizz'll keep you awake." She tugged Charlie from Kizzie's hold. "And let me see this young'un so he can get better acquainted with his Auntie Gayle."

Kizzie's eyes grew wide, and she chuckled, shaking her head and walking over to Noah by the door. The swish of her frock was a whisper among the other sounds nearby, like the carriage traffic outside or the cooing of little Charlie. But the whisper blared above the other noises, as if his rebel heart already tuned in to her presence despite his efforts to keep his head rational.

There was something entrancingly good about her, a light pouring from her eyes which told of the battle with brokenness from which she'd somehow emerged as victor.

He knew how.

Her faith.

And the genuineness in which she embraced and lived that faith.

"Are you sure you're going to be all right here?" He squinted over at Mrs. Carter as Kizzie neared, his grin itching for release. "She's known for being a bit on the bossy side."

Her chuckle warmed the space between them as she pressed the cola into his gloved hand. "Bossy doesn't bother me. Besides, she kind of reminds me of one of my grannies." Her gaze held his as she drew even closer. "She's offered me a job helping with shopkeeping."

"A job?" He ought to encourage emotional distance and refuse to cultivate this interest, but his curious heart refused logic altogether. "Have you experience?"

"Actually, I do, though not with such a fine facility as this." She waved toward the room. "But I worked several years for the owner of a country store back home and particularly helped with her bookkeeping, since I got a mind for math like my daddy."

"That's excellent, Kizzie. Already making your way in The Hollows, and you've only been here two days."

"I'd say there's a whole lot of God's good grace wrapped up in my good fortune." Her smile softened. "Especially meeting you and your mama. I'm real grateful for that."

"If you need anything"—his fingers itched to touch her arm, to show her the earnestness in his words—"you have friends."

"Thank you," she whispered, searching his face, seizing him with the glow of gratitude in her expression. "It's good to have friends." She drew in a breath and stepped back, gesturing toward Mrs. Carter. "I have a feeling I'll be making another one here."

"I hope so." The spell broke, and he withdrew another step. "I suppose you'll be in the boardinghouse?"

"Actually, she has an apartment over the store, right beside her own. She's putting me and Charlie there, overlooking the street. I've not seen it yet, but with the size of this store, I reckon it will be a nice-sized apartment."

Good. The idea of her staying over the shop brought much more comfort than in the boardinghouse along with whatever guests came along needing room and board.

He opened the door, and the cool air swept over him. "I'll see you later then."

"Let me know how Marty's doing, if you will."

"I will." And with a dip of his head and the image of her face captured in his mind, he closed the door and started for the sleigh.

As soon as the cold air hit his face, he lifted his face to the blue sky and cast a voiceless cry to the heavens. He knew what attraction felt like. He'd known it with Elinor. A quiet, gentle sort of feeling. She'd come into his life as a friend of the family seven years before, and they'd simply grown into love.

But this?

If he thought about it too long, he feared whatever spark came to life when he met Kizzie would burn like a lightning strike, leaving an open wound only she could heal.

He closed his eyes. This was all ridiculous. Utterly. They'd only met yesterday. She was an unmarried mother a few months into parenting. And George had the power to destroy Noah's livelihood if he turned a serious mind toward someone like Kizzie McAdams.

And yet, he wanted to know her better.

Laugh with her.

Ensure she and Charlie were safe.

Tickle Charlie's chin to see that dimpled smile again.

He pulled his coat close around himself and marched up the hill to his sleigh. He should have just kept riding toward Dr. Palmer's all along. Of course Kizzie would be safe.

What had he been thinking? Rushing in like some sort of hero. He rolled his gaze heavenward again and mounted the sleigh, glancing at the horses as he sat down.

Nugget stared back at him as if she knew something Noah refused to even contemplate. "Don't look at me like that. I was simply being a concerned friend." He clicked his teeth and, after a slight hesitation, the two horses started up the path.

It wasn't until Noah got out of the sleigh at the good doctor's small house on the edge of town that he noticed Kizzie's trunks in the back of the sleigh. He could have walked them down to the store, since he'd gone inside anyway.

Nugget's whinnying almost mimicked laughter.

Noah cut the horse a glare but refused to say another word.

The only thing he needed to feel even more ridiculous was to attempt to argue with a horse.

"I think we're going to get along just fine." Mrs. Carter placed an extra quilt on the bed in Kizzie's new home. "We have a shared bathroom in the hallway. My husband had it installed about three years ago."

Pride tinged the woman's words.

Kizzie placed Charlie on the bed and drew a clean diaper from her bag. "How long were the two of you married?"

"Forty years." Mrs. Carter's gaze grew distant as she stared out the window. "Good years." She clicked back to attention and patted the iron railing of the bed's footboard. "And three children."

Kizzie stared at the woman, seeing beyond the wrinkles and hardened lines to peer into the face of a new bride, a new mother. Forty years. Her mama and daddy had been married thirty. Unfortunately, Daddy's alcoholism overshadowed the sweetness their marriage could have held. But the faraway smile on Mrs. Carter's face spoke of the dream in Kizzie's heart she dared not nurture.

"Are any of your children living nearby?"

Mrs. Carter blinked back to the conversation, and Kizzie worked on changing her wiggling baby's diaper.

"I have a daughter nearby, but she and her husband are talking about moving out west." A shadow passed over her face before she continued. "My son lives about an hour north of here, and my oldest girl, well, she died giving birth to my granddaughter twelve years ago this month."

"I'm so sorry, Mrs. Carter."

"Gayle," the woman corrected. She reached to grab one of Charlie's kicking feet. "It's what started me and my husband helping girls living with the same mistakes our daughter made. She had a family who helped her through being a pregnant woman without a husband." She sighed. "But we got Gloria, and she's been the sweetest gift that could ever come out of such pain."

"The world sure ain't easy on women like me and your daughter." Kizzie looked up at her as she pulled Charlie's clothes down over his chubby legs. "But your daughter was blessed to have you love her through it all. Gloria too."

"My youngest daughter took Gloria in, and she's been a good fit for their growing family, but you'll see her plenty enough around the shop too." Gayle studied Kizzie and then opened her arms for Charlie. Kizzie complied, the muscles in her arms thankful for another reprieve. "You have family?"

"None that I can go home to."

"Well then." Gayle nodded and started toward the stairs. "If you're as good at bookkeeping as you say, I imagine you, me, Charlie, and Gloria can make up a little family of our own." She grinned down at Charlie, who offered her another one of his signature smiles. "You go on and get yourself settled, and I'll take this little man downstairs with me for a bit. I'm gonna see if I can scrounge up Gloria's old cradle."

And with that, she left the room. The floor creaked as she took the steps to the storefront.

Kizzie sat down on the bed and looked around the little room. It wasn't tiny, as she'd expected. Big enough for two twin beds, a dresser and nightstand, a table with two chairs, a woodstove, a washbasin, and even a bookshelf with a rocking chair by the window. Two woven rugs decorated the oak floors with rainbow colors, one in front of the fireplace and another by the bed.

She stood and walked over to one of the large windows overlooking Main Street. Buildings stretched either way, and a few shops stood close enough to make out what they were. A barbershop and a dress store. A millinery and a furniture store. A little white building a few shops down looked like a restaurant.

Kizzie leaned her head against the window frame and breathed out a prayer of thanksgiving. God had already given her much more than she could have imagined in her move to The Hollows. He'd shown His care in small ways like a sleigh ride through the snow and giving her the chance to sleep in that wonderful bed at Noah's house. But He'd also shown grace in big ways, like keeping her and Charlie safe in the storm and giving her this job.

A job that, though part-time, had room and board included and gave her ample funds to use for her and Charlie's needs, and maybe even some to save. She pressed a hand to the purse in her skirt pocket. She already had a sizable amount from her sale of the land to Joshua and Nella, and she planned to deposit it into a bank as soon as she could, but God couldn't have given her a better position.

Shopkeeping.

Bookkeeping.

She'd always been good at tending things like children and inventory.

But tending her heart? She was only now beginning to understand, because of God's love, how little she knew about real love betwixt a man and woman. The wholesome, beautiful kind she imagined Mrs. Carter may have known with Mr. Carter.

It was certainly not whatever unhealthy relationship she'd had with Charles Morgan.

And, maybe, she hadn't been as much in love with him as dazzled by him. The decision to leave, along with his behavior before she left, had dusted off his shine and left behind a much more realistic picture. Love didn't look like that.

Her attention followed a carriage moving slowly across the uneven terrain of snow and dirt on Main Street. A few people walked alongside the street, their voices rising to create a welcome hum of activity.

Home?

She embraced the present and sighed out what she couldn't change. For now, this would make a fine home.

"Why does the house feel so quiet all of a sudden?"

Mother's question pulled Noah from staring down at his bacon and eggs as they ate breakfast in the large, ornate dining room. He'd wrestled with his interest in Kizzie McAdams all night long, praying for God to take the desires away, but the morning left him in the same befuddled state.

People didn't have an overwhelming preference for someone they only just met, did they? His experience with Elinor proved as different as night and day to this. He'd loved her, but it had been a quiet, deep sort of affection, nothing nearly as noisome as the current now clashing in his head and his heart.

How could he even propose to pursue something with her? George would never allow it. And his livelihood hinged on George's place as head of the Lewis funds.

He shook his head to clear it and looked back at his mother. "What do you mean?"

Though he already knew. He'd felt it too.

"How could Kizzie and Charlie's presence make such an impact?" She pushed her uneaten eggs around on her plate. "They weren't even with us a full twenty-four hours."

But a lot had happened in those hours. His chest twinged with the interest he kept trying to squelch. "It wasn't a typical visit, Mother. I suppose that's what made it more memorable."

She sighed and took a sip of tea. "It was nice to have them here, Noah. It was nice to laugh again."

A loneliness edged her words. Since the elopement of his sister, Clarice, and his father's death, Mother had led an even more solitary life than before. She'd never bonded with some of the higher society ladies of The Hollows, and with the absence of his sister, her social events consisted of church and occasional trips into town for shopping.

She lacked female companionship, a truth Noah had failed to notice or even consider before Kizzie's presence brought the starkness of his mother's quiet life into focus. She didn't complain. He bit back a growl. But he *should* have noticed. He was the son who tried to mind those particulars.

"I suspect we could invite her to dinner sometime, perhaps ask her to help with your garden plans this spring."

His mother's face brightened. "Do you think she'd agree?"

"I think she may be surprised by the offer, but she's in need of some good friends." *As much as you are, Mother.* "You could do her good."

The idea hit its mark and bloomed into a smile on his mother's face. "Of course. That's an excellent notion, isn't it? A young girl who is new to our town could do with companionship." His mother picked up a piece of toast and nodded, the light in her eyes warming a place in his heart. "We can ask her today when we take her trunks to her."

He raised his gaze to her, suddenly trapped in his own tangle. "We?"

"Of course." Mother sliced a piece of her bacon, her voice slipping into a chipper pitch. "We'll go near enough to Carters for church, and I haven't been into town in two weeks. Besides, it's proper to give a lady some advance notice about something as significant as being a dinner guest. And we ought to smooth over a bit of ruffled feathers from George's nasty little fit yesterday, don't you think?"

"Kizzie seems to have managed George's fit much better than most, Mother."

"Dinner would still be a nice way to apologize." Mother shrugged a narrow shoulder and took another bite of eggs, her appetite suddenly restored. "Why the scowl, Noah? Surely you're not prejudiced against her because of her past choices, are you? You've never been the sort—"

"No, Mother. I believe Kizzie has grown a great deal from her past." Heat from the steam of his coffee somehow attached to his cheeks. "From what I can tell, she's a very admirable young woman."

Her gaze bore into his profile as he took a long drink of water in an attempt to cool his face.

"The two of you seemed to get along very well from what I could tell."

"Well enough." He crammed a much-too-large bite of eggs into his mouth.

"Excellent." She looked at him over her teacup, her smile turning in such a way it twisted his stomach. "Perhaps Kizzie and Charlie McAdams could do us both good in healing from our own pasts."

Footsteps clacked against the entry followed by the sound of the door closing. Heavy and quick footsteps, which only meant one person.

George rounded the archway into the dining room, his dark hair slicked back, his brown suit fitted to his broad frame.

Noah stiffened in his chair. Mother's cup returned to its saucer with a *clink*.

"Have you seen the damage from the fire?" His voice boomed too loud in the silence of the room.

"Good morning to you too, George," came Mother's gentle response as she waved to the chair nearest her. "Would you care to join us for breakfast?"

A rush of air released through George's nose like a frustrated snort from Nugget. He moved toward the chair but, instead of sitting, grasped hold of the back of it and looked from Mother to Noah. "We don't have time or funds to cover such carelessness, Noah. You're floor manager for a reason, and that is to keep things like this from happening."

"You know as well as I, George, how easily a small spark from one of the machines can cause what happened. I examined the damage myself after dropping off Dr. Palmer, and from what I can tell, the fire came from the machine."

"From what *you* can tell?"

"So I will make plans to ensure we clean them more regularly than what the manufacturers suggested." Noah pushed forward, refusing to bend beneath his brother's penetrating stare. George spent far more time managing the books than actually navigating the equipment. "The damage was small, and no lives were lost. Two things for which we should be grateful."

"Grateful?" He white-knuckled his grip on the chair. "We lost half a day of production, some needed fabric, and a knitting machine. How do you expect me to be grateful?"

"With a great deal of self-control," Mother interjected, her gentle smile in contrast to the steel in her eyes. "You are a business owner, George. You are not only responsible for production but for the lives of those who work for you. One thing can be replaced. The other cannot."

"Then those workers of mine better be grateful that I sold a bulk shipment to two new department stores in Mount Airy." He pushed back from the table and settled his attention on Noah. "Father entrusted the ownership of Lewis Mills to me, which means you are my employee too, Brother. If you can't keep the business going as it ought, then perhaps I'll need to find someone else."

"George!" Mother protested. "How dare you even consider such a thing? You know it was your father's direct desire that you two run the mill together."

"Desires change." George's gaze never left Noah's.

"Perhaps you ought to nurture the desire to spend time in your mill then, so you can examine the machinery yourself, since you have such little faith in my abilities." Noah stood, their matching heights a boon to his confidence. "Or would that put a damper on the time you need to cultivate your inflated reputation?"

"How dare you?"

"Does your fiancée know the shape the mill is in? That you refuse to raise our workers' wages and so we're losing them by the month? That profits are becoming smaller?"

"Don't you dare speak to me—"

"Don't complain about the mill's earnings or losses if you're not willing to curb some of your own spending for the better good." Noah edged closer, pulling from his own frustration. Since losing Father and Elinor, his patience with his brother's selfishness continued to shrink. "Actions speak louder than words."

Noah should have seen the fist coming.

Should have expected it.

But the impact still took him by surprise.

He stumbled back for only a second, and then launched forward, catching his brother with a fist to his mouth and sending him slamming against the nearest wall.

"Boys! Stop this at once." Mother rushed forward and placed herself between them as she had the day before.

Noah's chest pumped with his breath. George's too. Noah tasted blood. George's upper lip was busted, a stray strand of dark hair falling over his forehead.

"You both would make more progress if you had a civil conversation instead of a brawl." Mother lowered her arms, looking between the two of them, her attention finally landing on George. "No matter what Beatrice Malone wants, George, you cannot give her what you do not have. If the mill fails, there will be no money for you or Noah. No funds for the latest suits and the detailed archways in a house too large for your income."

George's gaze flickered to his mother. "We came here nearly penniless. I will not have us return to being laughed at and scorned as outsiders when we are seen as important as the Camdens or Jacksons or any of the others."

"Then work together," Mother pled.

George straightened and smoothed back his hair, his attention never leaving Noah's face. "I've given you fair warning, Brother. Get in my way and, blood or not, I'll see you out of a job. Then there will be no one to protect your precious outcasts."

Chapter 17

GAYLE ENCOURAGED KIZZIE TO ATTEND her church with her, one of the three on Main Street. Kizzie had never stepped foot in such a large building, with a steeple so tall it towered up into the pale sky. Light brick with nearly twenty steps rising to the double front doors. She made sure to wear one of her nicer dresses, since the size of the building carried with it a certain air of importance.

She'd never heard an organ in all her born days and nearly jumped to her feet when the first chords played through the massive space. Gayle proved no help at all. She chuckled so loudly, several folks in neighboring seats paid notice. Charlie behaved as good as gold until the last little bit of the service when the preacher really got wound up. Then, whether he thought the man was singing or asking for comments, Charlie started calling right back to him with such volume it echoed through the church.

Kizzie drew him up in her arms and skedaddled right outside so as not to cause any further commotion, and wouldn't you know it? As soon as the church doors closed behind them, Charlie grew as quiet as a church mouse.

Kizzie paused on the expression.

She'd dealt with too many mice in her day, and all of them were loud, scratching at walls and eating through almost everything.

So where did the expression "as quiet as a church mouse" come from?

She shook her head and continued her walk toward Carters Mercantile, only about a block—as she was learning these spaces in town were called—away. Charlie tucked his head into the crook of her neck and sucked on his fist as Kizzie nodded a good morning to folks she passed.

Most everyone appeared friendly in The Hollows, or at least the ones she'd greeted so far. A few young men gave her interested looks, but once they caught sight of Charlie, they turned away.

Which was good. The last thing she needed was someone courting her while she attempted to navigate a new town and a new job and at the same time learn how to be a good mother. Besides, any of the men interested in courting would likely lose interest as soon as they heard her story.

She frowned, the idea pooling a teensy bit of nausea in her stomach.

Maybe someday, with the passage of time and distance from Charles' memory, she could think about romance and marriage. Little Charlie deserved a family. A loving father. Her gaze shot heavenward. *Someday, Lord?* She'd happily wait for someday, if she knew it waited for her.

She'd just made it to the front of Carters when a carriage pulled up alongside her.

"Kizzie."

Kizzie turned to find Victoria Lewis staring down at her from the carriage seat, her beautiful burgundy hat so large it boasted not only one peacock feather but what looked like the peacock's entire collection. Kizzie's bottom jaw dropped, her stare so focused on the hat that she didn't notice Noah rounding the carriage to assist his mother until he stepped in front of her.

"Quite the hat, isn't it?" he whispered, his grin slanted in the teasing way she was beginning to recognize. A shadow darkened the other side of his face. "Take care how you respond. It's her favorite."

Kizzie smiled as he offered his hand and assisted his mother to the pavement.

"I've never seen such a grand hat in all my life, Victoria."

Noah rubbed a palm over his mouth to, no doubt, curb his grin, but Victoria preened as if Kizzie had offered her the best compliment in all the world.

"I know it's a bit out of fashion, but Mr. Lewis bought it for me during an anniversary tour of New York, and I'm a bit partial to it." She raised a matching burgundy glove to the rim. "It used to be quite the fashion statement."

"I can't imagine it being otherwise." Kizzie refused to look in Noah's direction, because even in her periphery she could see his shoulders shaking from barely contained laughter.

"Do you mind if we step inside the store to visit with you for a moment?"

At Victoria's request, Kizzie glanced back at the shop and then scanned down the street toward the church she'd just left. "Of course. The store will be nice and warm." She led the way with Victoria and Noah following, but it wasn't until they'd entered that she saw Noah's full face.

Or rather, Noah's left eye. Which was all shades of blue and swollen into a little slit.

"Either you got into a serious wrestling match with the Holy Spirit this morning, or someone wasn't too pleased with you, Noah Lewis."

His laugh shot out like a cough, and he shook his head. "My brother and I didn't see eye to eye on a certain situation."

"I'd say if he looks like you, neither one of you are going to be seeing too clearly for a while."

His grin spread wide, slowly, and lit those hazel eyes of his in such a way her heart tremored a little at the sight.

She quickly turned her attention to Victoria.

"It's difficult when both are being so hardheaded, Kizzie," Victoria said, tugging at her gloves. "But at least one of them has a soft heart."

"A soft heart your brother ain't too keen on, I'd wager."

Kizzie's attention returned to Noah, the answer clear enough on his face. She drew in a breath and turned toward the shop. "I'd offer you to sit over here by the potbelly stove like the old men did this morning before church, but I'm not sure it's the right place for such a fine lady as yourself, Victoria."

"Oh, pish posh." She waved away Kizzie's words. "The hat deceives you. I'm not as fine as you think I am. I grew up on a sheep farm in the midlands of England. A rocking chair by a potbelly stove will do quite well for me, but our business will not take very long." She turned to her son. "Noah?"

He blinked at his mother and then appeared to rally, sweeping off his derby. "Mother and I would like to invite you and Charlie to our house for the afternoon next Saturday, including dinner. I will be happy to collect you and bring you home, if you are available?"

And here she'd thought they'd have little to do with her once they'd given her over to Mrs. Carter.

"Well, I'm not sure what Mrs. Carter has planned for my schedule. We're still sorting it out." Kizzie focused her attention on Victoria, hoping her desire showed on her face. "Charlie and I would love to visit with the two of you, but if it wouldn't be too much trouble, could I plan for the week after? Just to give us more time to figure out our new place?"

"Of course." Victoria smiled, taking Kizzie's free hand in hers. "And should you need a place of refuge, please consider our home open to you." She squeezed Kizzie's fingers as if trying to add emphasis to her words. "Truly."

"Thank you kindly, Victoria. Charlie and I are most grateful and. . ." Her attention flitted to Noah. "We look forward to spending more time with both of you."

Victoria took Noah's arm and sent Kizzie a thoughtful look. "How did you enjoy church this morning?"

Kizzie paused, shuffling through the experience. "It was certainly big. I about jumped plumb out of my skin when that organ took off, but then I was just amazed." She shrugged. "But I ain't sure Charlie and I are the right fit for such a proper place. Mrs. Carter says she ain't set on any of the churches around here, but I feel as though I ought to find one to settle into, don't you?" Her chuckle escaped as a memory popped to mind. "When me and my siblings were younger, we'd hop from church to church on the Sundays Mama couldn't come with us, looking for the ones that had food after service, but then, we never really got to be known or to know anybody else. And, after reading my Bible a might bit more, it seems to me God wants His family to know each other."

Charlie took that very moment to begin a fuss, and no wonder. He likely needed a diaper change. And from the way he smacked his lips, he wasn't interested in waiting much longer for food either.

"Well, we attend a smaller church at the edge of town. In fact, it's called Friendship Church," Victoria said, moving with Noah toward the door.

"George isn't too keen on us attending a place where more farmers and mill workers take up pews than the fashionable folks." Noah's wink came as such a surprise, her cheeks sparked from cool to scorching in no time at all.

Clearly, Noah Lewis didn't know the power of his winking skills.

She hadn't known it either.

But now she did.

And he ought to be ashamed.

Her grin twitched at the very idea, as a flush of appreciation heated her cheeks.

It was a good thing the man couldn't read her mind, because he'd label her about as bloomin' crazy as women went.

"Sounds like you're awful keen to rile your brother, Mr. Lewis." She grinned, holding his gaze as she walked with them to the door. It was so easy to talk freely to him. "And I look forward to spending more time with y'all."

Charlie's fussing took an upswing into crying, and Noah started tugging his mother more quickly through the door. Kizzie stood in the doorway, watching how he took such care with his mama, gently coaxing a smile out of her and sending Kizzie exaggerated expressions as his mama warned him to be careful with her hat.

A tightening in her chest, like the gentlest squeeze, pressed through her as the carriage pulled away from the store. Other than Charles, Kizzie had little experience in romance, but this ease and friendliness with Noah came as a pleasant surprise. She didn't feel inferior or silly with him.

She sighed.

How would it feel to be loved by a man like him?

Her former notions of charming and romantic crumbled against the slow truth she was beginning to see in him. How could she have been so blind?

So desperate for love?

Glancing back as the carriage pulled away from the pavement, Noah doffed his hat, his gaze holding hers for longer than it ought. She looked away.

She wasn't ready for his heart.

And he shouldn't want hers, with all its many wounds still mending.

But. . .maybe someday?

She stepped into the store before Charlie went to caterwauling and slipped up the stairs to her apartment. Once she changed his diaper and then wrapped him in a warm blanket, she settled into the rocking chair near the stove and window and leaned her head back. Prayers pooled through her. Praise for God's provision and kindness. For new friendships and a job. For Charlie's sweet disposition and a warm little apartment of her own. She prayed for her family, the same swell of longing that accompanied each thought of them nearly bringing her to tears, but she prayed for their safety and for Jesus to catch her daddy. But she stopped the prayer before she voiced the tiny piece of her heart still vulnerable and afraid. The part longing for the love of a good man, for a family of her own.

Someday, she'd be ready.

She'd work to deserve it.

Yet her longing needed a place to land, so she prayed for God to give her work to do for Him.

And maybe, the other would come along in time.

A stack of ledgers with loose papers sticking from between the pages teetered on the brink of toppling.

After breakfast, Gayle Carter ushered Kizzie into a tiny office at the back of the store and urged her to start sorting through six months of untouched bookkeeping. Evidently, either Gayle had been so overcome with grief that she refused to look at her husband's desk, or she really didn't like ledgers.

Some people didn't.

Kizzie's sister Laurel feared Daddy's ledgers, but Kizzie loved them.

Keeping track of the books, watching how items and money came and went.

And using these fancy fountain pens of Mr. Carter's only made the job even more exciting. The ink flowed so smoothly onto the paper, and she was pretty sure they made her handwriting look better.

Gayle took Charlie right out of Kizzie's hands with a grin.

"I'll put him to nap when I see he's fussing, so you can work, because I know I've left you with a tangle. But you can hear him when he wakes up, because the piping carries voices from the room upstairs." Gayle waved toward a pipe running along the ceiling and disappearing into an adjoining wall. "That's how my Howard always knew when Gloria was awake."

Kizzie had met the little brown-haired, freckle-faced girl the day before. A quiet, shy little thing, her smile bloomed readily, and she loved her "Granny Gayle" with such sweetness. It was good the two of them had each other to grieve the loss of Howard Carter.

"And I think Charlie's taken quite a liking to that cradle, don't you?" Gayle asked, stepping toward the door of the room.

Her happy baby had. He'd snuggled right into the blankets Gayle found for him and slept from nightfall almost to sunrise for the first time in his life. But even with the added rest, Kizzie's back ached as she stood from the bed—likely from carrying around the ever-growing Charlie—and she didn't have much of an appetite. However, Gayle proved a difficult person to refuse, and Kizzie found herself eating a ham biscuit from the restaurant next door along with some home fries.

As the week progressed, Kizzie's schedule began to take shape.

On Wednesdays and Fridays, she took Gayle's place as shopkeeper, and on half days of Monday and Thursday, she kept the books. On Saturday, she and Gayle took turns with the shop, but that was the day little Gloria's presence came in handy as another person to watch after Charlie.

And Gloria took to snuggling Charlie like a duck to water. In fact, the little girl kept finding ways to visit with Charlie when she got home from school each day.

Over the first week and a half, besides digging through the many bills, receipts, and notices, Kizzie started understanding a little more about the workings of the store and boardinghouse too. Gayle had hired another one of her boarders, Hettie, as a part-time cook and housekeeper, which was likely more for Hettie's sake than Gayle's. Hettie had two children, one five and the other three, and, as with Charlie, Gayle found ways to assist with them. On the surface, one would think Gayle didn't care much for the young women who stayed in her boardinghouse. Her sentences came in curt, direct commands or requests, and her smiles for them weren't particularly frequent. But beneath all the bossiness, she found ways to offer the women some stability, by paying one of them to hem garments brought in for secondhand purchase, another to stock shelves.

She boarded four women in addition to Molly.

They paid her a minimal fee or worked for their lodgings, but they knew they had a roof over their heads as long as they kept to Gayle Carter's rules.

Otherwise, Kizzie didn't know the full extent of how else the boardinghouse worked. Guests who were passing through town stayed on the first floor of the boardinghouse. The young women, "Gayle's Girls" as some folks called them, came and went via an upper, external stairway from the second floor. Evidently, the women had a separate entrance that kept them out of the way of the downstairs boarders.

Kizzie offered reading lessons for Molly and Susan, two of Gayle's girls, and math for another, Pamela. All bright enough to learn. Teaching them reading, writing, and math would open their job opportunities.

After her second lesson with the women, as Kizzie sat by the window nursing Charlie and watching the evening sky eclipse the sunset, a realization dawned.

Perhaps God had created her for just this moment with these women.

To help Gayle Carter with her grief and her business.

To teach the other young women skills to assist in their futures.

And to offer Victoria Lewis friendship.

Tears stung her eyes, so she closed them and leaned her head back against the wood of the rocking chair. When she'd left Charles, she was scared, uncertain, and alone, and in under two weeks, God had filled her life with more purpose and people than she could have imagined.

He just kept surprising her.

And she just wanted to keep embracing the gratitude. The hope.

Beneath the newness and lessons, she began to feel the slightest inkling of an idea growing in her mind.

Belonging somewhere might not just be about a physical place.

Or the presence of a certain person in her life.

Maybe belonging had a lot more to do with accepting where God had placed her and loving His plan in the best way she could.

If she thought about it that way, then the disappointment weakened and the fear disappeared, because if she was in His hands—and, as she'd read that morning from her mama's Bible, nothing could snatch her from His hands—then she was right where He wanted her.

And that's exactly where she wanted to be.

Chapter 18

SHE'D WORN A DEEP BLUE ensemble, simple and elegant.

And the color continued to draw Noah's gaze to Kizzie's eyes.

Or that was the excuse he kept telling himself.

Yes. She had unique eyes. Expressive eyes. Eyes that somehow held him captive without any hint of seduction on her part.

They held a sort of internal glow which somehow reached into his broken heart and started it beating again. She brought out his laugh, even his teasing.

And the idea of it all was preposterous.

Yet here he sat, enjoying the lovely, snowy afternoon with her by his side on the seat of a wagon on the way to his home.

They crested the hill, the house before them, and just beyond stood the mill.

"That's the mill?"

Kizzie's question pulled his attention toward the large, box-shaped edifice he knew as well as his own home. "It is. Father wanted the house nearby to keep close for any of the mill's needs."

"I reckon having it so close is both a good and bad thing."

"Indeed." Her insight kept impressing him. "He had a tendency to overwork himself. And he expected perfection, from himself and everyone else."

Her gaze warmed his profile. "I was going to ask whether you or George was more like him, but I think you just answered that question."

He turned to her, grin in place. "Did I? You don't think I work hard, Miss McAdams?"

"I've not seen you work, Mr. Lewis," she shot back. "But I suspect you're a hard worker. I just think you probably know when to stop and how to set the proper priorities."

He hoped so. Unlike his father.

"I do believe you're teasing me, Kizzie."

Her grin crooked. "Turnabout's fair play, I hear." She nodded toward the mill. "It sure is a sight though. A whole lot bigger than what I thought a mill would look like."

"You mean, you've never been in one?"

She shook her head. "I've never been in a house the size of yours either, so maybe that will give you an idea of my little world." She paused and stared out over the landscape. "Well, it wasn't little. I always thought it was growing up, and I felt trapped in it, but we had views as big as the sky and stories to match. So I guess part of the problem was just how I saw my world. You know what I mean?"

It was as if she spoke directly to his slow-healing heart. "Often times it's difficult to see a different perspective when it's all we've known. I didn't realize how much my father was driven by status and social acceptance until I watched him drive away my sister. Then all the times he directed us away from certain people or enforced certain trivial rules began to take on a new meaning. That it wasn't about keeping his family safe as much as keeping up appearances."

Kizzie's gaze focused on him, but she waited, in that quiet, unnerving way she'd done before. Not pushing for an explanation, but giving him time to decide how far he wanted to go in the story, how much of the brokenness he wanted to share.

Up ahead, Mother emerged onto the front porch of the house, her smile wide.

"Ah, it looks as if Mother can barely contain her excitement." He nodded, and Kizzie followed his attention. "It's remarkable how God took an overturned carriage in a snowstorm and turned it into a way to bring my mother out of her shell."

"God tends to do things like that, doesn't He? Work out life's tangles into a better plan than we could ever make." She drew in a deep breath. "I realize I'm in my own predicament because of my choices, but He loves me so much that. . ." Her pause drew his attention, and the watery film in those blue depths captured him, heart and soul. "He'd give me this job and the opportunity to serve those women at the boardinghouse, and. . .friends like you and your mama. It's kind of like getting the Christmas presents you never expected because you'd been so bad all year long."

What a heart! Had he ever met anyone like her before? A beautiful mix of confidence and humble. Of grateful and humorous. Of penitent and hopeful.

And all he wanted to do was spend more time beside her, basking in the glow flowing through that hope she carried around like a badge.

"Sounds exactly like what Christmas is all about, doesn't it?"

Her smile bloomed, full and wide, the resident glow lighting those eyes. "That's right. It sure does. Getting something amazing when we aren't looking and don't even deserve it." She sighed again and then raised her chin to gesture toward the mill. "Is it all just one big room, or do you have it broken up into smaller rooms?"

She really had no idea of a building he knew so well? His surprise must have shown on his face, because she leveled him with a look. "Where I grew up, seeing a two-story house was a sight. And the nearest town was barely a third the size of The Hollows. I reckon the town didn't have enough people in it to justify a mill, so there wasn't one to be seen, unless you count a saw or gristmill."

"It's very different than those types of mills." He hesitated, glancing up at the house. Most women who didn't work in the mill weren't overly interested in touring one. But despite his brother's larger portion of it, Noah was proud of his father's work and the jobs they provided for those in the community. "Would you like to see it?"

Her attention rushed to his face. "Could we?"

She even looked excited. "It's truly nothing spectacular, but if you're curious. . ."

"I sure am. Taking the opportunity to learn more about my new home and the people who live and work here is worthwhile. 'Specially as I continue to grow in my business learning at Carters."

"Well, you're starting off well with Mrs. Carter, I believe. When I collected you from the store, she couldn't stop singing your praises. Your organization and resourcefulness." He tipped a brow. "Both excellent qualities for a businesswoman."

"A businesswoman?" Her light laugh warmed the space between them. "That makes me sound like I own my own business." She looked over at him, her raised brow challenging him a little, but the playful light in her eyes softened the edge. "You reckon it's silly to think I could own my own business someday?"

"Do you think it silly for me to want to own mine?"

Her eyes narrowed. "Not the same at all."

"True." He chuckled. "I think you are quite capable of doing a great many things, Miss McAdams. Why not own a business?"

He drew the carriage up to the front of the house. "If you truly want to see the mill, we could leave Charlie with Mother while we tour. She'd love the opportunity to tend to him, and if you feel the need of a chaperone, we could ask Mother's lady's maid to join us."

"I'm not worried about going alone with you, but I don't want to cause any trouble."

"You'd delight Mother beyond words. I didn't realize how much she missed the joys of children until I saw her that first day with Charlie. She had such high hopes for my child. . . ."

"Well then, let's cheer her heart with some sweet Charlie dimples." Kizzie gave the baby a little bounce, and he showed off those dimples with a grin.

Victoria happily took Charlie and, with a smile, shooed Kizzie and Noah off toward the mill. Kizzie hadn't thought much about needing an escort, since she wasn't likely to draw attention from such a fine man as Noah Lewis anyway, but as Noah sat so close on the carriage seat and his warm scent of soap and some sort of leathery spice squeezed into the small space between them, she started to wonder if a chaperone might have been a good idea.

Not for safety.

Heavens, no. She trusted Noah Lewis.

But maybe for her own mind and the way his kindness and nearness spiraled her good intentions into daydreaming about sweeter things. She decided to breathe through her mouth and keep her focus forward. Maybe that would help.

Because the last thing she wanted to do was appear like she was the kind of woman who threw herself at men. Going right from thinking she loved one man and bearing his child to sparkin' another within a month of leaving the first didn't look too good for her reputation at all. Or her desire to do God's will.

So she focused forward. At the large, square-shaped building standing quiet in the middle of a field with the backdrop of mountains and a river snaking past it on the far side. The brick building stretched long with tall windows everywhere. Rows and rows of them, twelve or more on each of the three floors with a tower on either side of the structure, like bookends to all those rows of windows.

"I thought your house had a lot of windows, or the bank downtown, but I ain't never seen so many of them in all my life."

His warm chuckle jumped across the space between them with as much sneakiness as his smell.

"The windows provide some ventilation and additional light, though we are not as up to date as more modern mills. Which is one of the reasons we are losing our workers at such a rate, despite the security a mill job provides over agriculture."

"What do you mean?"

"Places in nearby Mount Airy or White Plains provide more up-to-date facilities, better pay, and housing. It makes sense the men and women want a safer workplace and better pay." He waved toward a small collection of buildings near the mill. "And those other mills built successful mill villages, unlike the few buildings Father erected before he died."

"Mill villages? The workers live there?"

He nodded. "They create community among the workers, all these families living side by side together. The villages make it easier for their workers to get to work, provide education for their children, and save money. Father wasn't in a hurry to build one because it cost so much money and The Hollows wasn't too far from the mill, but I believe it has been to our detriment long term. That sort of security and provision is a real draw to young families, in particular. Though Father had secured Dr. Palmer's weekly visits to offer some sort of health care. Working in an environment with machines and the fiber-filled air of the main floor can lead to all sorts of medical needs."

"At least he wanted to offer them health visits."

He brought the carriage to a stop in front of the nearest towered entrance. "Healthy workers are more productive, which is why better ventilation is next on my list of updates, as soon as I can afford it."

She nodded as he climbed from the carriage and rounded it to help her down. "I'd say happy workers are even more so."

He offered his hand, and the same strange thoughts of knights came to mind as they did during their snowy evening together. She slid her gloved fingers against his palm, and he guided her to the ground in front of him, keeping hold of her hand until her footing was secure. . .and maybe a little longer.

Or did she just want to believe some wonderful man like him would want to hold her hand a little longer?

Silly Kizzie. Stop this nonsense.

He stared down at her for a moment and then stepped back. "Exactly. Yes, happy workers do better work." He retreated another step or two. "But I'm afraid George has lost sight of that. Just before he died, Father cut the working hours from twelve a day to eleven. We had our largest number of workers then. Folks felt appreciated and paid fairly for their work."

He offered his arm, and with only a slight hesitation, Kizzie slid her hand to hook about his elbow. She never remembered walking in such a way with Charles. Of course, they never walked places together, really. Their meetings had been clandestine and fueled with more passion than real friendship. In fact, she didn't remember ever having as many genuine conversations with Charles in the whole of knowing him as she'd had with Noah Lewis during their short acquaintance.

The realization nearly ground her feet to a stop.

How was it possible she'd given her most intimate self to a man who didn't know her, let alone truly respect her? What lostness or emptiness had driven her to value herself so little?

And how was it, that in only a few months, God's work in her heart, Charlie's birth, and the mixture of situations surrounding her life, including meeting the Lewises, matured her into even recognizing these things?

But they had.

She drew in a breath, walking a bit taller.

She was not the girl she'd been a year ago, or even four months ago.

She truly was a new creation, from the soul out.

"It's even bigger the closer we get," she whispered. "All brick and windows."

"Just wait until you see inside." He tipped his head toward her. "Bricks, windows, and *machines*."

The front door swung open to reveal a tall, broad-shouldered man, wearing a dark gray uniform. He looked to be in his fifties, perhaps, with black hair peeping from beneath his bowler hat. His dark gaze shifted from Noah to Kizzie and back.

"Mr. Noah." He nodded, removing his hat.

"Good afternoon, Sykes." Noah turned toward Kizzie. "Mr. Sykes is our watchman who keeps an eye on the building during off-hours. He and Mr. Jones are the mill's two watchmen on salary." He turned to Mr. Sykes. "Mr. Sykes, this is Miss McAdams, a recent friend of my mother's, and she is curious to see the mill."

"Very good, sir."

"Nothing to report, Mr. Sykes?" Noah asked as the man stepped aside for them to pass into a small entryway with a set of double doors directly in front of them.

"Quiet as a churchyard."

Mr. Sykes nodded to Kizzie and then disappeared up a stairway to the left.

"The stairs lead to the floors above, one for offices and another for storage and some smaller machinery," Noah offered, continuing forward through one of the double doors.

"And the tower on the other side is the same?"

His eyes lit, as if her observation pleased him. "Yes. Ease of access and additional escape, if necessary."

Additional escape?

He must have noticed her expression, because he paused before proceeding. "There's always a risk of fire."

She looked up at the sturdy brick walls and envisioned what a fire might do from the inside—turn the place into an oven? A shudder ran through her. "That's what your brother was talking about. A fire?"

He squeezed her arm. "I work hard to keep the employees safe, but with the machinery, fabric, and cotton, and the lint floating in the air, fires are always a possibility."

They continued their walk into one of largest rooms Kizzie had ever stepped into. Wide and light, its tall ceilings reached high above to showcase two stacks of windows on either side.

Various odd-looking machines lined the space, leaving a walkway down the center.

"Gracious sakes alive," she breathed.

He chuckled and gestured toward the room. "Here we have the largest production space. We make yarn here and the fabric here. In the back room there is a cotton bale breaker, so we can create the fabric from raw cotton all the way to the finished product." He walked ahead, his feet and words faster. "The cotton is carded then threaded through the spinning frames." He gestured at a machine as he spoke, his knowledge and excitement almost infectious. "Then the thread or yarn is sent to the loom to be woven into fabric. And, of course, we have a weaving shed and a dyeing room before fabric is sent to the finishing machines."

"And it all happens here?"

"All of it." He paused, glancing around the room. "We used to have more production when we had more employees, but we are still able to create excellent fabric, which is sold for miles around. Father's technique was admired, and his name carries the weight of the sales, I think."

"It's fine fabric, for sure." Kizzie stared at a machine that looked to hold rows of massive spools of thread. "Mama uses a loom, but it doesn't resemble anything like any of these machines."

"And thankfully not. These are miracle workers." He walked over to one of the machines that looked like it had rows of fishing poles sticking out of it. "Most of the workers are monitoring the machines as they take the materials through the process."

She stared at him, her smile brimming a little more. "So you love this work?"

He shrugged. "I enjoy working with people and seeing a job well done." He sighed. "But even with adding a few additional vents and trying to keep up morale, I don't think it's going to change our trajectory if we keep losing workers."

She studied him a moment and then looked around the massive space, trying to take it all in. "From what I can tell, your brother doesn't feel the way you do?"

He gestured for them to continue walking. "I believe he wants the money from a successful mill, but he's so consumed by financial success, he can't see how short-term expenses will lead to long-term gains."

"Like higher pay and finishing the mill village?"

"Exactly." He offered his arm again. "He carries a lot of expectation since our father's death, but with our sister gone, and now his engagement to Beatrice. . .well, he's just not been reasonable."

They walked through a door into a little hallway, the quiet shifting between them. Kizzie finally decided to give in to her curiosity. "What happened to your sister?"

Noah paused in their walk, just in front of another door. A smaller one. "Clarice. My father's pride and joy. George says she broke Father's heart and that's what led to his death."

"How?"

The lines deepened around Noah's mouth with his frown. "She fell in love."

Not the answer Kizzie had expected. "A mighty evil choice, for sure."

His lips quirked at her response. "With the wrong person, or at least wrong to Father's mind."

If Charles had married Kizzie, could that have happened to Mrs. Morgan? Death by disappointment? She seemed too mean to die over something that simple.

"A good friend of mine," he continued. "Lucas Becker. A German."

He said the words as if they mattered in a way Kizzie should under-stand. "And being German mattered to your daddy?"

He drew in a breath. "Kizzie McAdams, I think you are one of the most genuine people I've ever met, and simply wonderful."

The compliment moved from her ears all the way down to her heart and then flooded like warm water all over her. She'd been complimented before, but it usually had to do with her looks. Noah's compliment encompassed more of *her*. She tried to keep her composure. "I don't see how that makes me wonderful at all, Mr. Lewis."

"With the war going on, some people have taken to mistreating and shunning their neighbors of German descent. Lucas is an excellent businessman and was a good friend of our family until the war broke out. Then Father's attitude toward him changed, leading to George's opinions changing as well. When Clarice announced her engagement to Lucas, Father refused the match."

"Just because he was German?"

He dipped his chin and opened the door into a vast storage room with shelves filled with finished fabrics, spools of yarn and thread, and even a few garments.

"He gave Clarice an ultimatum."

Kizzie's breath caught. "Her family or her fiancé?"

"Yes. And despite her love for us, she left with Lucas. When Father discovered her letter announcing her elopement, he was so furious, his heart gave out. He died after three days in a coma, and we've not heard from Clarice since."

"I'm so sorry." She touched his arm. "And you lost your wife and son? You've gotten more heartache in your young years than most folks feel in a lifetime."

"It has been. . ." He swallowed so hard she heard it. "Difficult, but I pray God has used and will continue to use my hardships to stir up my strength, compassion, and trust in Him." He waved toward her. "As He's done with you."

And again, his simple statement proving he saw beyond just the superficial in her touched all the wounded places in her chest. A gentle touch. Healing and confidence-building.

His gaze held hers a moment before returning to the room. "Obviously, this is where we store finished product." He led her through another door which opened into a large room of shelves and counters, much like a general store, except it only held textiles of various types. Socks, fabrics, some linens.

"And here is our mill store, where we sell our products and—" He paused, focusing on something across the room.

Kizzie followed his attention to a counter holding a huge cash register. The money drawer hung open.

Noah rushed to the register then moved to a shelf housed behind the counter, his movements frantic.

"What's the matter?"

"The register money is gone." He drew a metal box from the shelf, dug into his pocket, and pulled out a key ring. After a little finagling to find the right key, he opened the metal box and looked up at her, his brows drawn almost together. "And so is the cash from the money box."

She scanned the room as if some robber might still be hiding in the shadows. "But how? I don't see a broken window or anything like that."

"How indeed?" He walked past her toward the door that led outside from the mill shop.

Kizzie followed.

Noah turned the knob and opened the door. "This is unlocked." He looked over at her. "We never leave this unlocked."

His gaze trailed from the carriage, along the side of the building, and over the area in front of him. He stepped forward, studying the ground. "Wagon wheel marks and footprints." He pointed to the ground, still half covered in snow. Then he knelt down and picked up something from the mixture of snow and rock. Something small and white.

Kizzie drew closer.

A cigarette?

He raised another item for her view.

A blue-and-gold button.

Chapter 19

AFTER A BRIEF CONVERSATION WITH Mr. Sykes, who appeared as shocked by the robbery as he did, Noah returned to the house with Kizzie, asking her to keep the current situation private from his mother until he could pursue further investigation.

Kizzie excused herself to feed little Charlie while Mother went to change into something with less baby spit on it, so Noah took the opportunity to phone the police department in town.

From what he could tell, someone stole at least one hundred and fifty dollars, and what was more disturbing was the fact that there was no sign of a break-in.

He needed to discuss the findings with George and make next steps.

Noah rolled the button around in his hand. A fine button. Not something from someone without either means or fashion interests. Or perhaps, a clothing item passed down from someone of means to a mill worker? A sliver of gold dotted the center of the button. Unique. Recognizable, if he could find a match on someone's jacket.

Kizzie assured him that she would keep her eyes out for a match too, though he felt certain finding the culprit through a button was akin to locating a mouse in a field. The mill had only been robbed once before, three years ago. The culprit only got away with a few pieces of fabric, two dollars, and the storekeeper's secondhand boots.

But with the amount stolen this time, how did Sykes not see anything or anyone? And the burglar must have been an expert lock picker too.

"I've already invited Kizzie to dine with us next Saturday, Noah." His mother rounded the corner, tugging at the sleeves of her blue gown. "Just so you will be prepared."

"I appreciate the preparation, Mother, but, if you'll recall, I have a meeting out of town next Saturday." He walked forward and bent to kiss her cheek. "So you'll have to make do without me."

"Oh yes." She nodded. "What is it about again? Some sort of new machine?"

"Yes. An advanced type of ring spinning frame. Keith swears that it's faster and more cost effective than the mule, but he tends toward exaggeration."

"Keith Lancaster? The mill owner in Mt. Airy?" Mother rolled her eyes. "Indeed, he does. Well, I'm sure you'll know best, but I doubt your brother will be quick to buy a new machine when the mule is still in working order."

Noah shrugged a shoulder. "I can do my job and still research new advances. If there's a way to help our production and the mill workers, I mean to try."

She reached up and patted his cheek, her hand cool against his skin. "You are such a good man." Her lips tilted. "With a good heart in need of the right sort of tending, I do believe."

His attention shot to the gleam in his mother's eyes. "Mother."

"I'll not attempt to force you to look in any particular direction. . ."

"Mother—"

"But, there's already some obvious interest on your part."

"I am not having this discussion with you." He stepped around her and started for the dining room. "Besides, she has barely left one relationship. I sincerely doubt she is ready for another."

The glint in his mother's eyes deepened. "I didn't even have to say her name." Her smile stretched to dangerous proportions. "And perhaps being a part of a very wrong relationship only primed her heart for the right one."

"You certainly know how to take a notion and forge ahead like a steam engine, don't you?"

"If I think it would make my son happy? Then yes, I do." She caught his arm as they stood on the threshold of the dining room. "I know you invited her here primarily to cheer my heart, but perhaps God sent her and Charlie for the both of us."

"I won't presume upon her heart, Mother." He tugged his arm free but held her gaze. "Not after what she's been through. And if we began any relationship and George failed to approve, he could ruin me."

"Ruin you?" She laughed. "You're too smart and too hard a worker to be ruined, my dear."

Her faith in his abilities proved much greater than his own.

George had the influence and the power.

A creak from the stairs pulled both their attention as Kizzie approached. She'd worn her hair down, as he'd seen while giving a tour of the mill, but without her coat and hat, it flowed in long dark tresses over her shoulders in contrast to the burgundy of her dress.

Her beauty staggered him.

It bloomed from the inside out.

He couldn't tame the desire to spend more time with her, enjoy more thoughtful conversations and teasing.

Could her heart truly be ready?

He shook his head and met her at the bottom of the stairs.

Not likely.

Not yet.

But in a year? When he was free?

"Charlie fell asleep, so I laid him on the bed upstairs, if that's fine."

"Of course." He offered his arm. "And may I escort you and Mother into dinner?"

Her eyes shot wide as she slid her hand into the crook of his elbow, the feeling as welcome as it had been that afternoon. "That's sounds mighty fancy."

He tilted his head to study her. "But not bad, I hope."

She raised her chin, a smile lighting her eyes. "I ain't used to such finery, but that don't mean I'm not willing to get used to it."

He chuckled and joined his mother, offering his arm to her, and the moment lingered in his mind long after the meal began.

Could Kizzie McAdams' heart be ready for the taking?

The week moved along even better than the one before. Kizzie tackled another month of reconciling paperwork, closing in on present day with each passing week. At some point, she'd dig out from Gayle's stacks and stacks of ledgers and bills and invoices while also managing the current shipments.

But amidst all the tangle, she found she loved the rhythm in her life. The busyness and feeling of accomplishment.

Earning her own money and managing the affairs of a business.

Having conversations with Gayle and learning more about the operations of a store and boardinghouse, as well as the workings of The Hollows. In fact, Kizzie discovered that because of The Hollows' strategic placement between Charlotte and Virginia, it boasted a popular stop-off point before travelers and businessmen crossed the mountains. The boardinghouse stayed full, as did the two small hotels in town. If the rich and influential of The Hollows wanted to make some real money, what they needed to do was build a larger hotel to meet demand.

Whether from Gayle Carter's evident approval or Kizzie's own desire to welcome folks into the store, no one seemed at all concerned about Kizzie's past. Or, at least, not the folks who came into Carters.

And, as promised, she'd also begun befriending Molly Edwards. In fact, the older and more active Charlie became, the more Kizzie liked the idea forming for Molly.

Keep her busy and out of trouble?

Well, Kizzie had a good idea how to do that and serve her own purposes too.

She caught the girl, who was no more than sixteen, as Molly carried some linens from the washroom toward the boardinghouse one morning.

"I heard you've been asking around for more work to do."

The girl turned, her round eyes almost too big for her olive-toned face. "Me and Mary both."

"What happened with Mary?"

Molly pushed her fiery braid behind her head so she could lean forward and tickle a smile out of Charlie. "Well, since I was watching

Mary's young'uns so she could work as a washerwoman, I lost my job too." Molly drew in a deep breath, preparing for her dramatic story. Just from the short time Kizzie had known Molly, she recognized a spinner of stories. Long stories.

Molly loved attention.

"My errand for Mrs. Carter ran too long, so I wasn't able to get back in time to tend Mary's young'uns for her to go to work. Which means Mary missed two days in one week and Mrs. Landers"—Molly's nose wrinkled in a frown—"who ain't too keen on none of us boarding-house girls noway, fired Mary on the spot."

"Couldn't Hettie have watched the boys?"

Molly exchanged her armful of linens for Charlie, drawing him into her arms with a smile in contradiction to her words. "Hettie was tending her granny over in Mount Airy way, so she wasn't around."

"Poor Mary."

"And me too, since she can't pay me to watch her young'uns no more." Molly's eyes grew wider. "I got to make money to pay my rent just like Mary. But nobody'll hire me 'cause of my history."

Kizzie switched the linens from one arm to the other and tilted her head to study Molly. "What history?"

A sheepish expression spread across the girl's face. "Afore Mrs. Carter found me, I was a street thief."

Kizzie coughed out her surprise. "A street thief?"

Molly gave an emphatic nod and turned her attention back to Charlie, who kept reaching for her braid. "Never knew my daddy. My mama died when I was ten, so me and my brother started living on the streets." She tickled beneath Charlie's chin enough to incite one of his new giggles. A wonderful sound in comparison to Molly's story. "My brother hopped a train about three years ago, but I wasn't fast enough to catch it, so I was left here in The Hollows. Kept thievin' until Mrs. Carter caught me one day and brung me here."

"And you've been helping with tending the boardinghouse ever since, haven't you?"

She stood a bit taller. "Sure have. I promised Mrs. Carter and the

Lord I wouldn't thieve no more, so she gave me an upright job here at the boardinghouse."

Kizzie's palm went to her hip. "And how upright is it to go sneakin' menfolk up to the second floor?"

A rush of pink flew into her cheeks, highlighting a dusting of freckles. "Well now, I only tried that twice, and both times Mrs. Carter caught me afore. . .well, afore things got too far." She raised her chin, leveling Kizzie a stare. "But I done promised Mrs. Carter and the Lord I wasn't gonna do that no more either."

Kizzie pinched her grin into a frown and nodded. "Well, that's mighty good to hear, because if I can't trust you, there's no way I can give you another job to do."

She blinked those big eyes. "You can trust me. I promise. There ain't no way I'm gonna find me no husband if I can't earn enough money to dress like a lady."

"The right men like smart and kind women too, Molly."

Her face fell. "Well, I ain't got no schoolin' worth talkin' 'bout, Miss Kizzie."

"Smart comes in all shapes and sizes. Just like we've been learning in lessons."

"Well, I'm sure glad to be reminded." Molly laughed and gave Charlie a little bounce. "But maybe you can teach me how to talk more ladylike too?"

"Well, I'm not too sure about the talking part, but if we keep up on our reading and writing lessons, it may carry over some into your talk."

"Well, howdy do!" Molly exclaimed into Charlie's face, causing the little boy to giggle all over again. "I'm gonna become a lady, Charlie."

"Or smarter, at any rate." Kizzie chuckled, coaxing Charlie back into her arms and giving Molly the linens. "But about the extra money."

"Whatever you need, Miss Kizzie."

It still felt strange having this girl who was only a year younger than her call her Miss Kizzie. "I have a lot of work to do for the store business, and I could use an extra hand with Charlie, especially as he gets bigger."

Her eyes popped wide again.

"And since you're in need of some extra work, I wondered if you'd help watch him on the days I'm tending the store and Mrs. Carter's running errands?"

"You can count on me, Miss Kizzie."

Kizzie raised a brow. "Which means you have to keep on the straight and narrow, Molly. Little eyes are gonna be watching what you do."

Molly dipped her chin with a few deep nods as if she felt the weight of the request. "Like I done said, Miss Kizzie, I promised Mrs. Carter and the Lord." Her smile brimmed. "Besides, if you're gonna teach me to be a lady, then I better start learning how to think like one."

As Molly bounded off with the linens, Kizzie released a laugh with Charlie joining in.

"You think she's going to be a good one to watch that boy?" Gayle came around the corner, wiping her hands on her apron as she approached.

"I think she will be. She just needs something to do to keep her out of trouble."

Gayle glanced out the window in the direction Molly disappeared. "She's grown a lot since she came to live here, but there's still so much of that little girl seeking someone to love her."

"Ain't we all lookin' for that?" Kizzie kissed Charlie's cheek. "Until we know how much Jesus loves us, I reckon we're all seekin' for the same thing."

Gayle nodded and sighed. "It's so hard for them to keep jobs. They work hard at first, trying to prove their place, but something always happens. Folks aren't as gracious with the fallen ones. It's almost like they're waiting for the girls to make a mistake so they can dock their pay or cast them out."

"And you can only offer so much work before you're losing more money than taking in." Having seen the ledgers, Kizzie knew the cost.

"But they need someone to give them a chance, some hope." She crossed her arms over her chest, the hardened facade she sometimes announced to the world softening in the lines of her face. "None of them have ever been able to get a job that would raise their status. People only hire them for kitchen help or washerwomen. A few I've had even dressed up as boys to work on the trains."

"Then we need to pray we think of somethin'." There had to be more options for these girls. Some kind of consistent work to give them a step up. To place them in the way of good men who wouldn't turn their noses up at their backgrounds. "But in the meantime..." Kizzie reached into her pocket, pulled out a few bills, and pressed them into Gayle's palm. "Use that to cover some of Mary's expenses until she finds another position."

Gayle looked down at the money, and her lips tightened. "Those girls don't want or need handouts."

"I don't want to give them handouts." She raised a challenging brow to Gayle, her lips tempting to crook. "I want to give them hope. So give her some extra chores to do around the shop and count that toward her pay."

Gayle's eyes narrowed despite the hint of humor in her expression. "You may be more softhearted than me, Kizzie McAdams, and that ain't good for us keeping a strong front."

"I'll try my best to keep my soft heart warned, Gayle Carter. But I'm as determined as you to help these girls."

Girls like her.

And yet, they were in a much worse place than Kizzie, because as Kizzie saw her life now, she recognized God had placed her in a better position than anything she could have ever had back with Charles.

A job, an apartment, friends.

Her smile grew.

And now she knew with even more certainty why God had placed her in Mrs. Carter's shop in The Hollows.

To help women like herself find hope.

The consistent clicking of the machinery hummed through the room, as workers kept to their positions, some attempting small conversations over the noise of the machines. Others quietly kept to their repetitive work. Even the mule scavengers, mostly ten or eleven years old, appeared more serious than usual as they slipped beneath the spinning mule to retrieve fallen pieces of cotton before the carriage returned to the creel.

Usually, the boys raced the carriage to the creel like a game.

News of the theft had made its way through the mill, sobering most folks, because any hit to the overall production had the possibility of hurting their pay. But Noah was determined to keep any more docks in pay from happening. He had to, or they'd lose even more people.

His gaze traveled to an empty knitting machine on the other side of the room. Another family gone. Left only a few days ago to move to Mount Airy. Better pay, better support, and a mill village where their children could receive an education. In fact, that mill village even had a YMCA, with one of the most popular baseball teams around. He stifled a groan. How could he compete with that? Especially if someone was stealing from their mill and George refused to make needed changes.

Who was it?

One of the workers?

What evidence did he have? A button and cigarette butt.

His attention moved to Peabody, but the older man wasn't the only smoker in the mill. His gaze trailed the room, pinpointing others, but Noah had known most of them for years and none of them fit the profile of a thief at all.

Jones, the other watchman, assured Noah he'd keep an eye out for any hints of who the culprit or culprits might be.

"The Carpenters left?" George stood from his desk as Noah entered his brother's office. "When?"

"Their last day was Wednesday."

George slammed a fist down on his desk. "But he was one of the best spinners we had."

"I'll make inquiries in town for more workers, but you can't expect to find a replacement for Peter Carpenter's skills anytime soon. He's been with us five years and worked as a spinner five years before that somewhere else."

"We must have someone to take his place, Noah. We can't allow production to slow."

Noah attempted to tamp down a sudden rise of fury. "Then you're going to have to pay for a replacement. No one's going to come to our limping mill for the pay Peter received for the past two years."

George's jaw tightened, and he pushed back from his desk and stood. "Fine. Write up an advertisement and list it in town for whatever you think will bring us someone fast."

Noah stared, waiting for his brother to change his mind, but George was silent. "Do you have any idea who might steal from us, George?"

His brother released an exaggerated sigh and took his time looking up to meet Noah's gaze. "How many names from our current riffraff of mill workers do you want?"

Noah drew in a breath, attempting to calm himself. A fight wouldn't help anyone right now. "Someone who either knows how to pick locks or has a key."

George narrowed his eyes. "Someone with a key?"

"That's the only other way besides lock picking that anyone could get into the store. No windows were broken. And Jones said he'd ensured all the doors were locked before he finished his shift and Sykes took over."

"Maybe we should examine the whereabouts of our watchmen, then?" George released a humorless laugh. "Noah, don't make this more complicated than it has to be. A simple thief could have broken in to that store and taken our inventory, and there's no way to track any of it, so we're going to have to chalk it up to another loss."

Something in the way his brother's gaze shifted or the tone of his voice put Noah on edge. Did George know more than he was admitting about the robbery?

Was he protecting someone?

A chill swept through Noah's body.

Or was he somehow involved in stealing from his own mill?

Chapter 20

THE LEWISES' CHURCH STOOD AT the edge of town. It was smaller than the ones on Main Street, but the familiar white clapboard structure reminded Kizzie of home.

Her family attended a church with the same look, only smaller and poised on the edge of a view that went on forever. Oh, how she wished she'd recognized things about God back then. The view would have probably been even more beautiful, the love for her family even deeper. The hope for her daddy's rescue even stronger.

If she closed her eyes, she could almost see the view.

Feel the cool, honeysuckle breeze wafting up from the valley.

Hear her mama's humming as she washed laundry or her younger siblings' giggles as they played in the yard.

The familiar ache nestled deep, but she had learned to live with it and pray through it to fight for the joy she knew God provided. The joy He'd helped her find in her new life.

But the present sweetness and quality of her current world never took away the longing for her family, to know how they were. It played through her mind like an unfinished melody. A story without an ending.

In the back of the church sat a few young mothers with infants on their laps, some she recognized from seeing them at the store. She joined them, already feeling a bit more comfortable with the intimate surroundings and folks dressed more commonly than richer congregants in Mrs. Carter's church downtown.

The preacher talked to the congregation without getting too loud, like having a conversation with them about the Bible. His style reminded her of Reverend Anderson back home, though, much to Kizzie's chagrin, she'd paid more attention to the boys or scenery or other girls' clothes than the sermons growing up.

But now her heart opened to the teaching, drinking it in like the freshest milk.

The preacher warmed the room with his words and his knowledge of folks in the congregation, especially through his prayers, and made little comments to set people at ease. For example, when one of the babies near Kizzie started making loud noises, as if singing, during a prayer time, the preacher seamlessly said, "Thank you, Lord, for the evidence of life in this church by the sounds of our children. May we rejoice over their voices raised when all too many have been silenced by illness or mistreatment."

She met Victoria outside the church, and they took her carriage to her house to spend the day together. Despite her wealthy lifestyle, Victoria never created social distance between herself and Kizzie. And since spring hovered on the cusp of the next month, Victoria took Kizzie on a tour of her walled garden and they spoke of plans for flowers and spices. Kizzie told her how she always allowed some wildflowers freedom to grow in any garden.

"Why is that, dear girl?"

"I've always loved them, especially now," Kizzie answered as they walked around the space. Kizzie had only imagined a walled garden when Laurel read her a book about it once, but seeing one in real life made the story even more real. An easy place for romantic thoughts and secret meetings.

And beautiful images of God's creation.

"Wildflowers are everywhere on the mountains back home. Azaleas and rhododendron, in their big bunches to brighten up the mountainside, but also the smaller ones. The ones that grow in the most unlikely places. Even through cracks in rocks or in the snow. Like phlox or trillium or bluebells and blue violets." She sat down on the bench in the middle of the sleeping garden with Victoria joining her. "They seem to grow and survive no matter what."

"Resilient," Victoria whispered, but her attention wasn't on the winter growth around her. She stared at Kizzie, a soft smile on her face that made Kizzie want to lean in for a hug. "I see it in you and the way you have grown since coming here. Your faith has bloomed as bright and strong as the sturdiest rhododendron."

"It feels more like the tiny bluebell, but I like your thoughts on the matter." She relaxed against the bench. Charlie napped in his regular spot in Victoria's guest bedroom, giving Kizzie's back a little rest. She'd been so tired lately, and she couldn't blame it on Charlie one bit. He'd been sleeping through the night consistently for two weeks.

"Did your husband have this garden built for you?"

Victoria glanced around the space. "Actually, Noah did. Several years ago."

Noah. He just kept getting sweeter and sweeter.

Victoria turned on the bench to face Kizzie. "I know George hasn't left a pleasant impression, but you've noticed that Noah is quite different from his elder brother."

Noticed Noah? Lord, help her. She had a hard time *not* noticing him. She'd even begged God to help her stop noticing him so thoroughly, but she loved their conversations, and his smile, and the way he lit up when he saw Charlie. Kizzie looked away, afraid Victoria had the same mind-reading abilities as her mother. "I ain't never met any man so kind and hardworking as him."

"He is. Both." She nodded. "If only his teachers had recognized that in him. He's struggled with reading his whole life. Math too. It's not that he can't do them, but both tasks take more effort and time."

He struggled with reading? Math? He sounded a little like her brother, Isom. "I reckon that's why he's so patient then."

"You've told me a few things about your past and Charlie's father, but are you still bound to him in your heart?"

Kizzie looked up, pondering the words, searching over her feelings. "I reckon I'll always feel a connection to him because he gave me Charlie. And I did care about him in my young-minded way, but I know now, whatever it was I felt, was more daydream and fancy-thinking than love." She sighed and raised her gaze to the blue sky just beyond the oak branches above them. "I imagine me and Charlie will be on our own for a while yet, if not forever. It's hard for a good man to stomach my past, and I can understand it, so I'm asking God to help me learn to be content with Him and Him alone."

Victoria's quiet chuckle brought Kizzie's gaze around. The woman gave Kizzie's arm a gentle squeeze. "I wouldn't give up all together, Kizzie. If the Lord loves us in all our brokenness and creates good for us even when we are not, then don't you think He is also able to create a man to love you in your brokenness too? And you very well may be exactly the woman some man's heart needs most. Your joy, your desire to find hope in even the most difficult situations of life? Mind my words, my dear, any *good* man should find your heart a treasure to possess."

"I ain't considered myself a treasure before, 'cept in God's sight. And that's still a new notion."

Victoria's smile gentled. "Don't place your value on your past, Kizzie dear. And don't underestimate God's grand love for His children. The Bible says He lavishes His love on us. Do you know what lavish means?"

"A bubble bath in nice warm water." Kizzie grinned. "I never had one until I came to work for Mrs. Carter, and I'd say that's about as lavish as anything I've ever felt in my whole life."

Victoria laughed. "Well then, think of a bubble bath and even more when you imagine God's lavish love. He means to give us more than we can imagine, and usually in the most unexpected of ways." She touched Kizzie's cheek. "He brought you to me out of a snowstorm, and I didn't even know how much my heart needed you in my life."

Heat burst into Kizzie's eyes, blurring her vision. She leaned in and wrapped her arms around Victoria. It had been too long since she'd been hugged by someone like a mother. She buried close, breathing in Victoria's rose scent. The soft texture of the lace of Victoria's gown rubbed her cheek.

"I needed you too."

Victoria's palm slid down Kizzie's hair, the way Mama used to do, and Kizzie rested in the moment, holding it close. It had been so long since she'd felt. . .*this.*

Victoria pulled back first and sniffled before she stood. "Now, I would imagine Mrs. Candler will not be too pleased if we are late to supper, for she has cooked up one of her most famous specialties, chicken pudding."

Kizzie laughed as she wiped at her eyes. "A cook like Mrs. Candler deserves our ready respect."

"And praise." Victoria grinned and offered Kizzie her hand. "Come, my girl."

Kizzie took her hand and then, after she checked on a happily sleeping Charlie, joined Victoria at the dining table. Victoria shared stories of George and Noah as children and a few about her daughter, Clarice. The sadness in her eyes as she spoke of her youngest child pierced Kizzie's heart. Did her own mama feel the same about her "lost daughter"?

Surely, Mama prayed for her. Sometimes Kizzie wondered if she gained strength on special days when the longing for home grew stronger because her mama was praying extra hard that day. If God's Spirit lived in all His children at the same time, then maybe the Spirit took Mama's prayers and gave them a message as quick as one of those amazing telephones could do, except instead of communicating from ear to ear, it was from heart to heart.

Kizzie told some tales about her siblings and growing up in the mountains.

They both shared stories of being mamas of little boys, though Kizzie didn't have near the experience of Victoria yet. Though she missed Noah's interjections and company, the time spent with Victoria Lewis warmed her heart.

Charlie's fussing drew Kizzie from the table.

But after tending to him, upon her return to the dining room, she found George Lewis seated at the table.

He stood at her entrance, though somewhat reluctantly.

She still wasn't used to men standing when she entered a room. Back home, the boys would have laughed their heads off at such a notion.

"Kizzie, dear." Victoria's smile grew tight. "George stopped in on his way from town, so I thought he could join us for the end of our meal before he returned home."

"Of course." Kizzie resumed her seat, settling Charlie on her lap. "It's nice to see you again, Mr. Lewis."

He tipped his head toward her, holding her gaze. "A pleasure, Miss McAdams."

Her entire body stood on edge. From the vulturelike look in his eyes to the superior tilt of his head, George Lewis brewed with danger and arrogance. And the way he'd pronounced "Miss"? He must have heard her story. Maybe her daddy burned with trouble when he was on a drunk, but Mr. Lewis carried a very different type of threat.

"George was just sharing how he should be finished with his new house by the end of March with plenty of time for his new bride to furnish it to her liking before the wedding, isn't that right, George?"

"Indeed." He took a sip from his glass. "One of the finest houses in The Hollows, I'd venture to guess."

What to say? "When is your wedding, Mr. Lewis?"

"May." He placed his glass back on the table, eyeing her as he did so. "Beatrice longed for a spring wedding or we would have already been wed. I'm not sure if you know Miss Malone?"

"I can't say that I do, but I may have seen her if she came into the store."

His smile took a humored turn. "I don't believe she would frequent Carters. Her tastes run in a more refined direction for purchases and clothing."

Kizzie may not be refined, but she knew exactly what he was saying. "Well, I wouldn't discount your fabric, Mr. Lewis. We sell it in Carters, and it's some of the finest I've ever seen. No wonder it costs so much."

Though the price still ran too high. She hadn't yet approached Gayle regarding some of those purchases over the last few months. Not with Lewis Mills having so much trouble with keeping their workers.

He flinched the slightest bit, or perhaps she'd only imagined it, and then he tipped his glass toward her before he took another drink. "Are you enjoying your work with Mrs. Carter and her. . .*tenants*?"

The way he curled the word turned Kizzie's stomach, and she already felt a little sick. The chicken pudding tasted delicious, so she hoped the nausea didn't originate from Mrs. Candler's excellent cooking.

Perhaps she was just tired.

Or sick of George Lewis' glares.

She knocked the thought away.

Sorry, Lord.

"I've learned so much and am grateful for the position. She's a good businesswoman, and I'm happy to help her get her books back on track."

"Books?" He lowered the glass, more slowly this time, and sat up.

"I'm her bookkeeper as well as shop assistant."

"Kizzie's a wonder at numbers." Victoria gestured for Mrs. Candler to bring in some sort of dessert. Kizzie's stomach took another turn. She frowned. She loved desserts.

"Gayle Carter raves about how Kizzie has already started to economize and get the finances of the store back on track after her husband's death."

"It seems you've fallen on your feet," Mr. Lewis said. "How convenient for you, given your newness to our town."

Ooh, she didn't like him, and she had enough of her daddy in her to have to nearly bite her tongue in half to keep from showing that side.

"Why don't you tell us about your recent trip to Charlotte, George? Is it truly as large as people say?"

Mr. Lewis blabbered on about tall buildings and paved streets. About electric lights and buildings so tall a person could see the whole city from the top of them. The idea of folks crowded on top of each other like ants didn't entice Kizzie at all. Living on Main Street in The Hollows was as crowded as she cared to be. And someday, she hoped to live away from the town enough to have her own yard and garden. Space to breathe and a room with a view of the mountains.

Kizzie ate very little of her dessert. The sweet smell of the apples bothered her stomach for some reason, or perhaps it was just the presence of Mr. Lewis—she fetched Charlie from his nap.

"Oh, dear, Mrs. Candler wrote down the recipe for chocolate chip cookies you'd asked about last week." Victoria rose from the table. "I'll have Taylor call the carriage while I find it for you."

"Thank you kindly." Kizzie wrapped Charlie in a blanket in preparation for the ride. "I think Mrs. Carter could do with selling a few in the store."

As Victoria disappeared down the hallway, Mr. Lewis moved closer to where Kizzie was standing at the threshold of the dining room.

"I'll see Miss McAdams out, Mother," Mr. Lewis called.

Every hair on Kizzie's neck stood on edge, like she'd just heard the cry of a coyote in the forest.

A hunter. Looking for prey.

"That's very kind of you, Mr. Lewis." She tugged Charlie close. "But I can see myself out, and Case will help me and Charlie into the carriage."

"Nonsense." He gestured for her to walk ahead of him. "Since Noah isn't here to do the job, it will be my pleasure."

She reached for the door, and he placed his palm against it, stopping her escape. "I don't know why you're in such a rush, but I'd be happy to drive you home to get to know you better."

She studied him before creating a little more distance between them. "I'm sorry to say this, Mr. Lewis, but I'm not sure I want to know you any better."

His brows shot high, and then his smile slid wide. "Ah, tossing away all pretense, are we? How resourceful. No wonder you're such a good *shopkeeper*."

She tugged at the door again, to no avail. With Charlie in her arms, she couldn't use both hands. "All the more reason for you not to dirty your nice clean reputation by riding into town with the likes of me. And I'm sure your fiancée wouldn't appreciate it at all."

He leaned closer, his gaze roaming her face. "Oh, I know how to play by the rules quite well enough to keep Beatrice happily ignorant and my tastes. . ." His gaze trailed down her. "Fully satisfied."

"I don't think there's a woman in all the world with enough to satisfy you, Mr. Lewis." She pushed him back and reached for the door. "And I'm not your kind at all."

"On the contrary." He snapped the door closed. "You're just the kind of woman who inspires my interest most."

"What?" She offered a humorless smile of her own. "The fallen kind?"

He leaned forward, attention dipping to her lips. "The reluctant kind."

Charlie took that moment to swing a fist in Mr. Lewis' direction. Kizzie almost grinned.

"Well, I'm not reluctant." Mr. Lewis dodged the little hand, giving

Kizzie another pull at the door. She slid through the small opening, Mr. Lewis on her heels. "I'm completely resistant."

"Resistant?" He laughed as she crossed the porch toward the steps. Kizzie searched the growing dusk for any sign of the carriage. *Case, where are you?*

"Don't you know what I could offer you, silly girl?"

"I am sure as shootin' that whatever you got to offer me, I don't want to ever see." She made it to the porch steps.

"What is it you want then, I wonder?" He grabbed her arm as she moved toward the porch steps, nearly knocking her hold on Charlie loose. "As you play house with my mother. If you're not after a little secret affection to boost your status?" His eyes trailed down her and back, hardening into two dark orbs within the shadows of the porch. "Then you must want something much more secure." One of his dark brows rose. "I didn't reckon you the power-hungry sort, but I see I've been wrong."

"I ain't got time to listen to your trickery, Mr. Lewis." She pulled against his hold, but he only tightened his grip.

She bit back a wince, refusing him the knowledge that he hurt her.

"I'm not the tricky one, Miss McAdams. You are."

Kizzie twisted her arm in an attempt to free it. "Just what a tricky person would say."

"Do you think your attention to my brother goes unnoticed?" He loomed over her, taking up all the space in her vision. "Don't you know that the whole town is waiting for you to ruin his excellent reputation by placing him in a compromising position in order to marry you?"

The fight drained from her. "What are you talking about?"

"It makes perfect sense to use your wiles to prey on my brother's position and wealth." His smile turned into a nasty curl as he pulled a cigarette pack and matchbook from his jacket pocket. "I would commend it, even. Excellent playacting as the broken and destitute woman misused by one man and in desperate need of the protection of another, who is conveniently rich and would elevate your place in society."

Her insides shook at his claims. They weren't true, of course, but did folks really believe that? Was that what was going around about her past and her purpose? Did they think she had designs on Noah to ruin him?

She'd never hurt him or his family.

Well, maybe she'd hurt George Lewis, but only if God didn't stop her with a healthy slap from the Holy Spirit.

"I ain't got no plans of the sort." She succeeded in jerking her arm free of his hold.

"That's not what the world sees." He struck the match, raising it to the cigarette, the match glowing against his face to reveal his shadowed smile. "And if you cared at all about my brother, you would distance yourself from him before you damage his reputation even more than you already have. As you likely already know, he tends to want to rescue broken things, and an association with you would sully our entire family's reputation."

The sound of the approaching carriage crunched against the gravel in front of the house. Kizzie refused to respond to Mr. Lewis and instead turned and marched to meet it. She kept her comments scarce on the ride home, her smile ready for Case's benefit. But as soon as she made it into her apartment, the internal shaking emerged in a sob, and she snuggled Charlie close as she cried on her bed.

Her past had cost her many things.

Her family. Her reputation. Her home.

But she'd thought starting over offered a fresh start, hopefully to move beyond the weight of those costs.

Giving up her friendship with Victoria and Noah Lewis proved yet again another price to pay. But she'd do it. To keep them from the shame she understood so well.

"We've got to think of a way to protect those young children, Mother." Noah removed his coat and walked into the sitting room after a full day at the mill. Taylor took the coat and disappeared around the corner as Noah sat down across from his mother in front of the large marble fireplace. "I jerked a little three-year-old out from underneath the spinning mule today. He'd escaped his mother to chase after his older brother."

Mother pulled her attention from the fire, where she'd seemed lost in thought. "What on earth was the older brother doing beneath the spinning mule?"

"He scavenges for me after his school day. It's a way the family can earn a few extra dollars in the week." ·

"Good heavens, the poor boy must be exhausted after a full day of school, then to scavenge beneath the mule for another two or three hours?"

"I tried to convince them otherwise." Noah's palms came up in his defense. "But the family are in debt to their landlord, Mr. Malone, and you know how Beatrice's father is." He narrowed his eyes and growled out the name. "So there will be no grace for them with him, as everyone knows."

"Can an older sister stay home with them? Or an old aunt?" His mother sat up. "The mill is no place for those little ones."

"Most of these mothers have no one to tend to their children." He sighed back onto the couch. "But I'm not sure how much longer we can function without a true catastrophe happening to one of them. It's a wonder George hasn't seen any of the near disasters already. With his magnanimous nature"—he raised his brows to his mother, sarcasm lathering his words—"he'd find a way to blame the workers, which would only drive more of the families away."

"George." His mother's eyes closed, but she quickly opened them to focus back on him. "What if you hired someone to see to the children?"

"With what money? I've already given up part of my salary to give a raise to some of the weavers we've had for years. I could try speaking to George again, but he won't listen. I can't understand him. In his effort to conserve funds, he's going to kill the mill, and there's nothing I can do about it."

"Well, I'm full up with George and his horribleness. I plan to meet with my solicitor as soon as he is back in town and go over our family's resources. Your father wasn't the most magnanimous of men either, but he knew how to run a business, and the mill has lost more money in the two years since your father's death than I can understand."

"What do you mean to do?"

"Investigate." Her fists came down on her lap. "How is the family money and mill ownership truly distributed? Who owns what? I was in too much shock from your father's death and Clarice's elopement to remember anything from the reading of the will, but I'm not as muddleheaded now. I've never even questioned George's claim to the full inheritance but blindly trusted him to take all the weight of everything from my hands because I could barely manage my own emotions." Her lips pinched into a grim line before she looked back up at him. "Was there a trust? Do you recall?"

"George took over so many of the conversations with the lawyer at the time, I wasn't privy to more specifics." Did something in particular trigger her sudden curiosity about the business, her apparent frustration?

"I know I own this house, but I want to make sure I know what else is going on, because something is not adding up with George's behavior, the mill's loss of workers, and these thefts. It's almost as if George is..."

"Sabotaging the mill?"

His mother's gaze flashed to his. "Do you think he'd stoop to such a level? To his own family?"

"I hope not." Though his business choices would suggest otherwise. "But perhaps there's a desperation or some business or personal decision he's trying to cover?" He studied her as she stared into the fire, hands fisted tightly together on her lap. "Mother, what's going on?"

She turned her gaze on him. "Do you realize that Kizzie avoided us yesterday after church?"

"You saw her? I searched but didn't—"

"I don't believe she wanted us to notice her, but I heard Charlie's laugh in the middle of the service and looked back and saw her."

Tension knotted in Noah's stomach. "Perhaps she had business to attend to."

"She rushed out after the service, Noah, without a word to us." His mother shook her head. "She's not the sort to act in such a way unless provoked. She's too forthright for such behavior."

"Provoked?" He sat up straighter. "By what? Who?"

Mother rubbed her forehead, pausing a moment before looking back at him. "Case overheard part of a conversation George had with Kizzie last week when she was leaving after dinner with me. I think it may have caused her to keep her distance."

"Last week?" Noah sat up. "And you're just learning of it now?"

"He mentioned it to Taylor this morning, and Taylor suggested Case discuss it with me." Mother ran a hand down her face. "Her choice to avoid us only proves her good intentions all the more, but I refuse to allow her to think that we believe the same thing George does. I've grown to care for that dear girl, as I know have you."

The knot in his stomach burst into flames and poured heat through his body. He stood. "What did he say to her?"

Mother relayed what Case shared, inciting a groan from Noah as he paced in front of the fire. "Investigate, Mother. Find some way to put reins on George, because if we do not find a way to catch him, so help me, I may end up proving how much stronger I really am than him."

It was true.

George had spent the two years since Father's death sitting behind a desk and driving to meetings around the county.

Noah had worked, learning all the aspects of the mill, helping in every area. Pulling the weight he could to ensure the mill continued to function.

"And what are we to do about Kizzie?"

Noah looked out the window into the darkness. "First thing in the morning, I'll pay a visit to Carters and work this out."

After an early breakfast, Noah proved true to his word. He had Case saddle one of the stallions, and as the dawn peeked over the mountains, Noah rode toward town.

He barely made out the slightest glow of a gas lamp as he peered in the front window of Carters and then knocked on the door. After the third knock, the door opened to reveal Gayle Carter with a very unwelcome expression.

"Noah Lewis, my front sign clearly states we do not open the shop until seven o'clock on Tuesday mornings."

Judging from her clean and pressed clothes and tidy bun, plus the smallest smudge of jelly on one cheek, Mrs. Carter had been awake for some time.

"I'm sorry to bother you so early, Mrs. Carter." He removed his hat and hoped his expression matched his appeal. "But I need to speak with Kizzie, if I may."

"It's too early for a decent visit." Her eyes widened. "Unless you've come a-calling? And if that's the case, I'd say it's about time."

"About time?" Noah's jaw dropped. Kizzie had only been in The Hollows for six weeks. How on earth was Mrs. Carter coming to such conclusions?

"And you're a good catch for her, boy. So I'll give my approval upfront." She nodded, opening the door wider. "I wouldn't have agreed to a lesser man, but you're worthy of her, as long as she can keep working at my store."

He coughed out a laugh. Had Mrs. Carter and his mother been scheming? "I'm honored to have your approval, Mrs. Carter, and if the time should come that I choose to—" He ran a hand through his hair. "Right now, there's been a misunderstanding, and I need to speak to her."

Mrs. Carter's brows rose, and she placed both hands on her hips, giving him a threatening look from his hairline to his boot tips. "What did you do to her?"

He stumbled a step back, hands in the air. "No, not me. I'd never do anything to hurt her."

Her other brow shot high to meet the first. "No?"

"No." He shook his head for emphasis.

She gave him another long look and gestured for him to come inside but leaned forward as he passed. "You better catch her while you can, Noah Lewis." Then she closed the door behind them, turned toward the inside of the shop, and called out, "Kizzie McAdams. Somebody's here to see you much too early in the morning."

Kizzie emerged from a back hallway, Charlie in her arms. She wore a simple blue dress, and her hair lay in a long braid over her shoulder. Her feet came to a stop when she saw him, breath pulsing so that her shoulders rose and fell in quick movements.

"Here, let me get this one out of the way of the conversation." With barely a pause, Mrs. Carter plucked Charlie from Kizzie's arms and disappeared into the hallway from which Kizzie had just emerged.

"Is. . .is everything all right with you and your mama?" Her gaze searched his before flitting away.

"I've come to clarify something." He stepped closer. "And to apologize for my brother."

Her attention returned to his face. "Your brother?"

"I'm afraid he behaved very badly to you last Sunday. And I've come to let you know that whatever he said isn't true."

Her brow puckered with her frown. "Did *he* tell you?"

"Case overheard something and told Mother about it this morning. I don't know all the particulars of it, but I know the gist, and he didn't do himself any favors by acting like an entitled idiot."

Her gaze flashed to his, the smallest hint of humor lighting those beautiful eyes before she lowered it again. "I don't want to cause trouble for you or your mother. I'd never want to do that."

"I know." He closed the distance, almost reaching out to touch her. "And you're not. My brother is the one causing undue trouble."

"I know what my past brings." She looked up at him, searching his face. "I can't change that, but I can change how it impacts the people I care about, by distancing myself."

The people she cares about? He shifted another step closer. "Kizzie."

"You're a good man, Noah. Your mama is one of the finest ladies I know. I won't hurt you."

"You'll hurt us more by taking away your friendship and Charlie's dimples."

Her frown deepened, her gaze pleading with him. The struggle with her heart was evident on her face. He wanted to smooth away the pucker on her brow and almost lifted his fingers to try. "I have a question for you, Miss McAdams."

The pucker deepened.

"If my brother attempted to manipulate me the way he tried with you, what would your advice be?"

She narrowed her eyes at him. "You're not a fallen woman with a past, Noah."

"But let's say he told me I wasn't strong enough or smart enough to attempt to run the mill on my own and that I should give up altogether.

How should I respond to that?"

She folded her arms across her chest, pinching her lips closed.

"Cower to him?" He matched her stance. "Believe his wild rantings?"

The tension in her mouth and around her eyes softened. "Of course not."

"Then why don't you heed your own advice?"

"If you. . . If I keep visiting with you and your mama, people are gonna start to talk."

"People are always going to talk, Kizzie." He took her hand for a brief squeeze. "What would be worse, inflammatory remarks by the narrow-minded of The Hollows, or refusing my mother and me a friendship with you and Charlie?"

Her shoulders deflated despite the slight tilt to her lips. "You had to toss Charlie into the lot, didn't you?"

"I felt it beneficial for my cause."

Her smile blossomed, and then her expression grew serious again. "Fine, but I'll not have things grow worse for my friends, so I reserve the right to retreat if the two of you get hurt from association with me."

"Well, I don't agree with your reasoning, but as long as you agree to join Mother and me for dinner on Saturday, I'll not argue about it anymore." He wiggled his brows. "*Today.*"

Chapter 21

NOAH HAD HOPED FOR A quiet, relaxed dinner with Mother and Kizzie on Saturday, but as soon as he met his brother in the office at the mill on Friday morning, George informed Noah that he and Beatrice would be joining them. Beatrice wished to discuss some of the wedding plans.

And when Beatrice wanted something, George made sure she got it.

Unfortunately for Beatrice, George's dedication proved more related to his determination to move among the richest circles in The Hollows rather than any true devotion to his fiancée. Noah knew all too well how unfaithful his brother's affection had been in the past. . .and the present.

"You could have refused to come, Kizzie," Noah offered as they neared the house. "I gave you fair warning back at Carters when I collected you."

Charlie grinned up at him as he drove, and he nearly touched the baby's round cheeks. His large eyes mirrored his mother's. His smile too, except for his dimples.

"I could have, but I considered what you said, and I realized the good in it."

She'd worn green today. "It's nice to have my advice so thoroughly taken."

She chuckled and rolled her eyes for his benefit. "Well, a solid half-hour talk from Mrs. Carter helped too."

"Ah." He released an exaggerated sigh. "Mrs. Carter's words proved more powerful."

"Both of your words proved powerful." She grinned over at him. "But it's hard to fight what I know God says about me with what I feel I've done to my own self. If God"—she looked over at him—"and you and your mama aren't worried about an association with me, then I need to believe you truly accept me for more than my past and what others may think about our...friendship." Something in her features softened. "I want to believe it too."

His gaze caught in hers. Was it possible her heart was turning toward him?

She cleared her throat and looked ahead. "And I ain't never been keen on bullies, so I didn't want to give your brother the benefit of thinking he'd won against me."

"That's the spirit, Kizzie. We'll face my pigheaded brother together." He winked, and her smile spread even wider. "What do you say?"

"I say I'm awfully glad we're teaming up against him tonight and that I ain't alone."

He sobered. "I won't leave you alone with him. And perhaps, if Beatrice's wedding talk becomes too tedious or George begins to monologue about his house, we can find a way to escape their company by..." He looked up at the sky. "How are you at chess?"

"Chess?" Her nose wrinkled. "I'd never heard of it until I started working at Carters and saw a chess set for sale, but I can play checkers."

"Checkers it is." He nodded, clicking his tongue for the horses to pick up the pace. The idea of secluding her for a game of checkers completely reframed his opinion of the entire evening. "But, if you're game, I could teach you chess."

She raised a brow in challenge, and the overwhelming urge to kiss her nearly had him breaching the distance.

"I'm game."

"And, of course, we shall use the Episcopal church for the ceremony," Beatrice Malone continued, detailing her family's extensive plans for her and George's nuptials.

Noah stifled a groan into his glass and caught Kizzie's gaze across the table. She failed miserably at cloaking her expressions, which only made her more endearing. No pretense. She looked utterly unimpressed and perhaps a little bored.

In fact, just as he met her gaze, she was attempting to hide a yawn in her teacup.

Her eyes grew wide at his observation of her blunder, so he shot her a wink.

She attempted to smother her smile.

And he embraced then and there this new love growing inside his heart for her.

As ridiculous as it sounded, he *wanted* to win her.

If they had to wait a year to marry, he could do that, as long as he knew she waited with him.

"Doesn't your family attend the Baptist church, Beatrice?" This from his mother.

Beatrice turned her bright blue eyes on his mother, the same look of superiority she always wore pasted on her porcelain face. "Yes, but the Episcopal church will hold more people and, as you know, we will have a large number coming in from out of town for the occasion. My mother's New York family plan to stay for a month."

"Did you know she has connections with the Vanderbilts?" George said, touching Beatrice's hand. "Beatrice and I have discussed taking a train to Asheville to see George Vanderbilt's grand estate during our honeymoon tour."

Beatrice slid her hand free from his grasp and gave him a disapproving look.

Kizzie glanced over at Noah. Yes, she'd caught that too. Not the first time Noah had seen the behavior, however. Beatrice Malone ruled the relationship with her money and personality, and despite Noah's attempts to convince George otherwise, his brother was determined to connect himself to a family beyond his status and a woman who seemed rather cold and controlling.

"It must be nice to have such a large family willing to travel down here to celebrate with you," Kizzie said. She'd remained quiet for most of the meal but watched everything. No doubt coming to her own conclusions.

Beatrice barely offered her a look before returning her attention to Mother. "Of course. We all are highly supportive of one another, and Father wishes to show the family his new bank." She looked over at George. "However, I'm not sure how long we'll remain in The Hollows, as Father is making plans to move farther south for more lucrative banking opportunities in Charlotte. My uncle expounds on the fact that Charlotte will be one of the financial capitals of the South in a few decades, and who doesn't want to take advantage where advantage is available?"

Moving?

George looked away, his expression steeling. Had he known about this? Why build an expansive home if he had no intention of staying?

From his pallor, perhaps the news came to him with as much shock as it did Noah.

Had George invested all this time and money and debilitated his father's mill for a house he'd have to sell within a year? Maybe two? For a status he wouldn't even hold in The Hollows anymore? What had his brother's desire for rank cost him?

Cost *them*?

"That is why we have been able to create our legacy. We take opportunities as we see them." Beatrice's gaze slid to each person at the table, finally landing on Kizzie. "And refuse anything that would weaken us." Her smile took a humored direction. "Survival of the fittest, as Father says."

Noah started to interject in order to pull Beatrice's attention from Kizzie, but Kizzie responded first.

"That's certainly a fact where I grew up in the mountains. The survivors are the ones who run the fastest from the cougars and bears. Though I reckon if you lose someone you care about while trying to save your own skin, you lose all around. I reckon that's why most folks ought to help each other as they can."

"Or learn to run faster." One of Beatrice's golden brows edged northward.

What had George gotten himself into with this one?

"If our eyes are focused on ourselves, then that would definitely be the best option, Miss Malone, but I tend to think we create a happier world when we're willing to help those alongside us. Outrunning everybody else may have you win, but it's a lonely place in the end."

"Kizzie." Noah broke into the stare between the two women just to rescue Kizzie from further conversation. "If you're finished with your dessert, I'd love to show you the chess set I told you about earlier today."

Kizzie bestowed on him such a knowing smile, he couldn't help but reciprocate.

"I'd like that." She placed her napkin on the table and stood, sending the others, except Mother, a much less welcome smile. "If you'll excuse me."

They'd barely made it into Noah's study when Kizzie released a deep sigh. "I ain't never heard so much talk about dresses and parties and money and food before in my life." She turned to him, her eyes wide. "And I'm from the mountains. We love to talk about food."

His laugh burst out as he followed her across the room, leaving the door open so Kizzie could listen for Charlie. "I think Miss Malone is becoming much more comfortable with her position as George's fiancée, because all pretense appears to have flown out the window."

He gestured toward the chess table, where two comfortable chairs poised on either side. Kizzie followed his direction, shaking her head.

"But here's something I don't understand. If your brother has his sights set on high society, then I reckon he's got a good catch, but why did *she* choose *him*? He ain't so up in money as her, though he puts on enough airs for it."

"Land." He took the seat across from her.

"Land?"

"What is less known is that the Malones own buildings, but not a great deal of land in this area." He adjusted some of the pieces on the board. "Father purchased over one thousand acres surrounding the mill. Valuable property, especially with its placement along the river and with its forests. There is always money to be made with land."

"So she wants to marry him for the land?"

"You noticed her personality. She'll take control of it as soon as they're wed and likely do whatever her father says they ought to do with it."

"Where will that leave you and your mother?"

"This house and the two acres adjacent are hers. And though I don't inherit anything as vast as George, Father left me twenty acres of river-front between the mill and town, as well as some funds. I inherit them on my twenty-fifth birthday in November."

"Good." She sent him a satisfied smile. "Even if what you get is smaller, you'll use it better."

"I hope we still have a mill and workers left for me to manage, or I may have to start over with a new venture once I inherit."

"You'll do well with anything you put your mind to. I'm sure of that."

He warmed at her ready confidence.

Kizzie lowered her chin to her palm and studied the chessboard. "You still looking for more workers?"

"Certainly. We can't manage with our dwindling numbers long-term. Already, we're faltering."

The light in Kizzie's eyes deepened, and she leaned forward. "I have a good idea about new workers, Noah Lewis. But you're gonna have to convince your brother about it."

He studied her, his white button-down rolled up at the sleeves, his tie forsaken. He looked at leisure. Comfortable.

With her.

And the intimacy of the room only added to the feeling. It was too easy to imagine them in their own home, studying over a board game and sending sweet glances to each other while they talked and teased and loved each other.

And he was the type of man who was made for loving something fierce.

Because he'd love back in all the ways that mattered most.

"You've got that mischievous look in your eyes, Miss McAdams, so I'm bracing myself."

Her grin spread a little wider at the humor in his tone. "If your brother is desperate, he should be willing to take anybody, ain't that right?"

Noah's eyes narrowed a little. "Mm-hmm."

The tilt to his lips inspired a sudden kissing thought out of nowhere. Heat rushed into her face, and she looked down at the strange figures on the board in front of her. "So, some of Mrs. Carter's boarders need jobs."

"You mean Mrs. Carter's girls?"

Yep, they had a reputation.

"That's right." She held his gaze, attempting to weigh his reaction. "To stay at her boardinghouse, they can't practice sinful lifestyles of their past and they must earn their keep by tending to the rooms of the other guests, but they ain't making a lot of money. Few folks are willing to hire women with shadowy pasts and no husbands to show for their young'uns."

Noah released a long breath and ran a hand through his soft brown hair. It bounced almost back into place, except for a few random sprigs here and there. Kizzie pulled her gaze from the tiny shift in his hair, her cheeks a little warmer than they were a few seconds before.

She didn't need to be thinking about Noah Lewis' hair or his eyes or his smile any more than anyone else's, but for some reason, his face was the only one that kept causing a whole lot of trouble in her thoughts and her cheeks.

And it would only lead to a heap more trouble to her heart.

Girls like her didn't aim for boys like him.

Well, they might aim for them, but they didn't win them.

"Are they good workers?"

"They are." He actually entertained her suggestion? Maybe he wasn't as afraid of his brother as she thought. "All of 'em. And I've heard two talk about having work experience in a cotton mill too."

"But don't they have young children?" His shoulders fell. "We can't manage the ones we have, Kizzie. It's putting those small ones in danger every day. Adding more will only pose greater risks."

"Well. . ." She drew out the word, steepling her fingers as she spoke. "I have an idea about that too."

"Why did I even doubt you?" He laughed, giving a helpless shrug. "Go on."

Her lips twitched, and the gaslight glimmered in his hazel eyes, drawing her closer. "Is there a room free in the mill somewhere? Not large, but well ventilated, with windows?"

"What are you plotting?" he asked, matching her position.

"I have two half days of the week that I'm not working at the store, and one full day. What if I work those days to watch the children in the mill? It would keep the younger children away from danger but also keep them close to their mothers for tending."

"What about the other days?"

"I think I could get Molly to take two or three of them, and maybe one of the other girls at the boardinghouse too. She's good with young'uns." She nodded, working through the idea that had been forming over the past few days.

"There are two twelve-year-olds who work alongside their mothers at the mill, but perhaps they could alternate."

He was not only embracing her idea but adding to it.

"Aren't they in school?"

He shook his head. "Both struggle with academics, so their parents felt they would do better to start learning a skill, so they've worked at the mill."

After what Victoria said about Noah, the plight of those girls hit Kizzie in the heart. Maybe she could give them a few tips when she worked with them.

"And I feel certain Mother would love to help."

Her jaw slacked. "Do you think she'd be willing?"

"I think she'd be highly offended if we didn't ask her."

Kizzie laughed and released a sigh. How refreshing it was to speak together as equals and come up with solutions together, like a real partnership. "Oh, I like her a whole bunch."

His gaze held hers, all warm and welcoming with that smile. "The feeling is mutual."

And then the realization weakened her breath. Was Noah Lewis sparkin' her? Even just a little? "I'm glad."

"I've heard of something like this in one of the other mills in a nearby town. It proved considerably helpful. If we could get the village school in working order, we could move the children there." He tapped the table. "But I don't have a lot I could pay those watching the children."

"*I* won't need anything. And your mama won't." She firmed her lips with her resolution. "That would cost you less."

He narrowed his eyes as if in doubt.

"I make enough from Mrs. Carter to meet my needs and don't have any housing expenses, since she provides the rooms over her shop. I'd prefer giving a little of it up, if it meant helping you and these girls."

Kizzie didn't know why she kept calling them "girls" when some of them were older than she was, but for some reason, she felt like she needed to care for them. Help them. Prove to them that there was more to their lives than the messes they'd gotten themselves into.

"We'll work that part out as it comes, I think." He started to say something else, but George stepped into the room, his gaze moving between them as his lips took a mocking turn.

"Don't the two of you look rather chummy together."

Noah sent her another quick smile before turning to his brother. "Kizzie and I have been brainstorming a way to increase our workers at the mill, George." He relayed the information, and George scoffed.

"I'm afraid women of their ilk would cause more harm than good. Distract the men from their work."

"No more than men are distracted by women anyway," Kizzie shot back.

"And none of these women are living in their past ways now," Noah continued. "They're trying to start over, and we need workers. In one sweep, we could hire a few."

"And they'd bring others too." Kizzie rushed ahead, seeing a hint of interest on George's face. "If they knew they had an opportunity for jobs. They've stayed away because they knew you wouldn't even consider hiring them."

George narrowed his eyes at her, but Noah intervened.

"You know as well as I that between the robbery and the loss of workers, we're not going to survive another year, George. You may not want these types of workers, but we need them. Father entrusted this mill to us. And it's our job to honor that."

George's attention flashed to Noah, and his features softened ever so slightly. "New workers would help us earn back what we've lost."

"Exactly." Noah paused and then looked over at Kizzie. "And we could open up the three cottages as homes for some of the women too.

If you're worried about their characters, that would keep them close for observation."

He was handsome, kind, and brilliant. What a remarkable combination. Kizzie nodded at his statement. "And they'd surely be more dedicated to their jobs if they had their own place. It would give them a sense of dignity, and it would open up more space in the boardinghouse for paying guests."

"And all the children we'd inherit from this endeavor?" The doubt in George's voice stiffened Kizzie's spine.

"Kizzie has already worked up a solution to keep the children out from under foot and watched after without costing *you* more money."

For the briefest of moments, a look of sadness crossed over George's features. He glanced from Kizzie to Noah. "I don't like it." His shoulders slumped. "But it seems I have few choices." He raised his head and pointed to Kizzie. "But I expect their wages to be docked to pay for their accommodations."

Kizzie nodded, afraid to say anything else in case he might change his mind.

George turned to Noah. "And I'm holding you personally responsible for them, Noah, since you're so keen on this idea."

"I'll take that responsibility." Noah sat up straighter.

"Mr. Lewis!" A call came from the front of the house, followed by a slam of a door. "Mr. Noah!"

George bolted from the room with Noah on his heels, and Kizzie followed.

Mr. Sykes stood in the foyer, out of breath, his hair disheveled and a stream of dirt lining one side of his angled face.

"Sykes?" George reached him first. "What on earth is the matter?"

"The thief, sir." He breathed out the words. "I caught him running from the mill store."

"Where is he now?" Noah ran toward a nearby closet and removed a coat. "Which direction did he go?"

"I. . .I lost him, sir." Sykes shook his head. "In the woods."

And that's when Kizzie noticed something about Mr. Sykes' jacket. The way the gaslights glimmered off his shiny buttons.

Her face went cold.

Buttons that were blue and gold.

And about three-fourths of the way down his jacket, there was a blank spot where a button should have been.

Sykes!

Noah's suspicions were already on high alert after the reported second robbery, especially from the way Sykes and George kept sending knowing looks to each other. Their answers flowed in synchrony, his brother's concern too sedate.

And the fact that there was no trace of an intruder, not even footprints, in the direction Sykes pointed, despite the damp ground, deepened Noah's suspicions.

The knowledge of the missing button only confirmed those suspicions.

But why? Why would Sykes join forces with George? And why would George steal from his own business he claimed to want to save?

Noah took the next few days to look for his own clues, even questioned Jones, and after some prodding at the man's hesitancy, Jones admitted to concerns about Sykes and George.

"I ain't sure, sir, but I just overheard a few things. They talked at different times, all after work hours." Jones shook his head. "And Mr. Lewis gave Sykes some money. I saw that plain as day."

But how to prove it?

Cash wouldn't leave a trace.

And Sykes wouldn't implicate himself by betraying George.

He'd told Jones to keep a close eye on any exchanges between Sykes and George and to await further instruction.

If he could get proof, he would not only have answers, but perhaps even use the knowledge to change George's ways.

And save the mill.

Chapter 22

Kizzie barely had time to turn her mind to Mr. Sykes and the thief. She'd told Noah about the missing button on Sykes' jacket, and he'd shared his concerns about George. Then, he'd surprised her by stopping at the store later that week to inform her of what he'd learned from Jones, as if her opinion was important to him.

She liked the notion that she mattered enough for him to go out of his way to get her opinion. Especially since it gained her the attention of a man she admired so much. But no evidence pointed to Sykes or George. Or at least, not enough to incriminate them.

Though Noah planned to use Jones to keep a keener eye out for more evidence.

Even though there was little they could do about the robberies, there was a whole lot they could do about getting more workers for the mill. Over the next two weeks, Kizzie, Victoria, and Noah readied the mill cottages and discussed plans for the women to start their new jobs. Noah mentioned how George asked when the workers planned to start, which Noah saw as a good sign.

Or at least a sign that his brother bowed to necessity over convention, which proved positive for Gayle's girls as well as the mill overall.

Noah held a private training with them on the Saturday evening they moved into the cottages in order to make their transition to work on Monday as successful as possible.

And it was. Hettie and Mary brought five more women with them, including Mrs. Carter's newest boarder, Jessie, a seventeen-year-old with a one-month-old baby to tend.

The two twelve-year-olds proved indispensable, with Noah pulling from his own limited cash to pay the babysitters.

Mrs. Carter even volunteered to help one morning a week.

And Noah kept growing dearer to Kizzie with each day.

Watching him oversee the mill and relate to his workers only strengthened her admiration. He genuinely cared for them, asking personal questions about family members or inquiring after an illness.

Hardships had changed her, but they'd also made her stronger. Wiser. She noticed things now she'd have never noticed with Charles. The way Noah treated his mother meant more to her. The kindness he showed to all classes and stations. The diligence in his work and care for others.

Telling a woman her bonnet strap was loose and too close to the machines.

Warning an older worker of a slippery spot on the floor.

What other employer would notice things like that and make a point to protect his workers?

Charlie appeared to enjoy the engagement of the other children. Since he'd grown enough to sit up when propped against something, he could watch the toddlers and other children's antics. And though the additional work with the ten small ones who were too young for school or the mill offered Kizzie a sense of service for those women bringing in the most money they'd ever gotten, her body ached. She'd even gotten sick a few mornings before taking off to the mill and wondered if breathing in some of the fibers didn't sit well with her.

Or maybe she was overworking herself.

Tending the store and keeping the books became her more restful days, where she could ease into her schedule, enjoy alone time with Charlie, and befriend more residents of The Hollows.

But watching the women she'd grown to care for gain confidence and friendships through not only working in the mill but also managing their own little houses cultivated a deeper burden for other people like them.

Some of the women had even found themselves objects of admiration by a few of the younger men. In fact, Noah's servant, Case, couldn't keep his eyes off Molly anytime they were in the same place together.

Noah praised the progress. Having the children out of the machines seemed to lighten some of his worry, especially since he already had to live beneath the precarious whim of a volatile personality. Though Noah commented that George had seemed more subdued and less snappish over the past few days.

Perhaps seeing Noah's work and the ladies' willingness to serve the children with minimal pay humbled him?

Could he possibly be regretting his choices? Kizzie could only hope that the same change the women continued to show made its way to George, for his own sake, but also for his mother and brother. Repentance was beautiful to behold, much like the early spring flowers taking advantage of the warmer late-February days.

Though a part of her wondered if Granny's old adage about the calm before a storm was true.

After a month, Noah's plan to move the children to the empty schoolhouse turned into a reality, removing the children from the noise and polluted air of the mill. Once the new childcare spot was secured, Mrs. Carter wrangled in some helpers from the ladies' group at church, inspiring them to serve the Lord through ministry to children, which meant Kizzie's shifts reduced to only two half days, giving her enough time to get back to reconciling the books Mrs. Carter had left in disarray.

The few quiet moments Kizzie had with Noah at their Saturday afternoon meals usually included talk of changes to the mill or for the children, though he had succeeded in teaching her to play chess over the last month.

A little.

He soundly beat her every time, but she was improving.

It was a thinking game. She liked those.

And recently, when he returned her to the shop, he'd lingered a little longer, playing with Charlie or teasing Mrs. Carter. Just being near.

Like he wasn't quite ready to leave Kizzie and Charlie just yet.

Kizzie couldn't hold back her grin as she took the path to the store from the bank. Could it be true? She turned her gaze heavenward and offered God one of her biggest smiles, and since He saw her heart already,

He knew how grateful she was at even the possibility of someone like Noah Lewis waiting around to spend time with her.

And her little boy.

She sighed and adjusted the belt of her skirt, which fitted more tightly over the past few weeks. Perhaps she needed to refrain from joining Mrs. Carter at Lola's restaurant so often, but the fried chicken tasted so much like Mama's, Kizzie could never get enough. And Charlie loved the mashed sweet potatoes, or any type of potato. Pudding brought out his dimples too.

She'd just turned the corner to her street when someone grabbed her by the arm and pulled her into the shadow of the building. With a step back to break contact, she looked up into the face of Cole Morgan.

Charles' cousin.

The man she'd shot.

"I thought that was you, Kizzie McAdams." He stuck out his hand. The pinkie finger was missing. "How 'bout we greet each other with a proper handshake, like *friends*."

Kizzie pulled her purse against her chest and readied herself for. . .well, she wasn't sure what he might do, but thankfully, they were in the middle of town in broad daylight, so that helped. "I don't recall us ever being friends, Cole Morgan."

"Well, that would explain the little surprise you gave me then, wouldn't it?" He wiggled his fingers. "Charles was good enough to let me know 'bout you bein' the only one in that house, so I reckon you're the one who gave me this gift."

"I think your gifts were just as friendly."

A ruthless grin curled his lips in a slow movement from one corner of his mouth to the other until his sun-leathered face wrinkled in an unwelcome way. "Same ol' Kizzie McAdams, 'cept all fancied up now, are you? I didn't expect to see anyone I knowed in these parts, but when I caught sight of you walkin' down the street as if you was one of them fancy ladies, I barely recognized you at first." He took a step closer. "But it's hard not to remember a face like yours."

She retreated another step from him, thinking of how to get by him.

"You got yourself a new man in this town?" She made an attempt to sidestep him, but he moved to stop her. "I reckon that means no." He ran a hand over his chin, tilting his head to give her another look. "Still pining over my cousin, are you? Well, you better give up that dream, darlin', 'cause he's done got hisself engaged."

Kizzie's body went completely still. Charles was engaged. In a little over three months since last she saw him, he was engaged.

She looked away, digesting the information. Had his mama's plan worked so well?

"I reckon you didn't matter as much to him as you thought."

She blinked.

"Engaged to his cousin's friend from out near Nashville. High-end lady. Good money. And much more than you could ever give him."

If Cole meant for his statements to sting, he'd find Kizzie's indifference highly disappointing. Whether Noah ever meant to care for her beyond friends or not, she'd learned what the heart of a good man truly looked like. And perhaps she didn't have to settle for anyone else.

Rising to her tallest height, which still wasn't impressive next to Cole Morgan, Kizzie pushed her brightest smile into place. "I wish him all the happiness in the world." And to her own surprise, she meant it.

The news didn't hurt as much as she'd thought it would.

In fact, had she expected it all along? Despite his grand declarations of coming after her, of waiting for her, deep down she'd known she wasn't enough for his mother. . .or him.

And maybe she wouldn't have known that if she hadn't grown from her experience in The Hollows. Hadn't built her confidence and independence through work and service and seen what a real gentleman looked like in Noah.

The knowledge gave her an odd sense of freedom, not just from her past, but from whatever thread of connection her heart still held for Charles. He'd moved on.

And she was glad it wasn't with her.

Cole's smile fell. "Just like that."

"Just like that. Charles has moved on, and so have I. I'm real glad he's found what he's been lookin' for." Kizzie raised her chin. "Are you looking to move this way, Cole, or are you just passing through? 'Cause

I can't imagine Charles ever casting off his right-hand man."

"Charles is looking for better places to sell his cotton. Sent me to check on some of the newer mills. Them or the dying ones." He folded his arms across his chest, taking her little "compliment" with enough pride to loosen his tongue, she suspected. His grin returned. "Either they're too green to know when they're being swindled, or they're too desperate to care."

So Charles had sent Cole to find people in The Hollows to cheat? That didn't seem like Charles, did it? He wouldn't try to swindle anyone, would he? He may have been selfish and weak, but greedy or desperate?

He wasn't those things. He already had status and money. And he didn't seem to need to show off his wealth to folks like George Lewis tended to do. Besides, Charles or George would have to prey on ignorant people. Or those who were distracted in some way, because most folks knew what a good deal was or not.

It'd be a shame for any employer to become so desperate or rotten to swindle vulnerable people.

And then she stopped on the notion, a strange recollection coming to mind from the books she'd been reconciling for Gayle. It was easy to take advantage of a despairing person.

Especially one who didn't know how to keep their records.

"Please send my regards to Charles and his lady." Kizzie rounded him and only made it a few steps before she paused and turned. "And, Cole, I'm real sorry about your hand."

With that, she nearly ran to Carters.

For the past receipts, she'd just been looking at numbers to see if they matched the bank. She hadn't been looking to see if anything was amiss or not. It hadn't occurred to her that something might be.

Of course, as she'd started taking over current purchases and inventory, she'd found ways to save money, barter prices, and look for inconsistencies. But some memory in the back of her mind hinted to a discrepancy that Cole's words resurrected.

She took out the ledgers from the first six months since Mr. Carter's death and skimmed through the numbers. First month, nothing unusual. But the second month. . .

Prices for all inventory purchased from Lewis Mills increased. Not an exorbitant amount per item, but in total, substantial.

An extra dollar to socks. An additional fifty cents to fabric. A quarter more on linens. She pulled out the receipts she'd saved from the time, matching them to the dates. And each signed by George Lewis.

He'd raised his prices on Gayle Carter in her grief because he must have known she wouldn't notice. But if he increased the prices to much higher amounts—which, as the owner he could do—why was the mill suffering from low funds?

Unless George Lewis skimmed off the top of the extra costs.

And the only way Kizzie could figure that out was to talk to Noah.

Gayle Carter wasn't angry.

She was furious.

But after Kizzie had talked the rifle out of her hands, Kizzie suggested they get their wits together before making her discovery public knowledge. She needed to talk with Noah first and get his perspective. Perhaps there was a logical reason for such a cost hike to a woman who everyone knew wasn't too keen at keeping the books.

But Gayle thought of another plan.

A few other business owners she'd spoken with had also experienced unexpected high costs from Lewis Mills over the past few months. So over the next several days, Kizzie covered the shop so Gayle could meet with them.

Of the six who had cost hikes, four had reasons that their bookkeeping had fallen behind.

One was due to the husband being ill. Another was because the wife had died and the husband struggled with keeping the books in his grief. Another couple whose business was already failing didn't realize they'd been overcharged, because their son had died in the war, and he'd been the one managing most of the business before he left. The last was because the wife had given birth to twins and couldn't tend to the books for a few months.

Ignorant or despairing. . .and too busy.

George knew the people of the town and preyed upon the ones who were in difficult circumstances. Took advantage of their weaknesses.

No wonder he'd gotten away with it.

The wronged people gave their records to Gayle without hesitation.

George Lewis' signature marked every one of them.

All the pieces came crashing together.

George's constant complaints about needing more money but wearing the latest fashion. His unwillingness to raise the mill workers' salaries yet affording his massive new house.

He had to have gotten the money from somewhere, and a few robberies wouldn't have been enough.

With the paperwork in her satchel and Charlie on her lap, Kizzie got in her buggy and sped to the Lewis' house. Noah must have seen her approach, because he met her at the door, his forehead crinkled with concern.

"What's the matter?"

She thrust Charlie into his arms, which resulted in a grin from both of them, and then raised her bag for his view. "I think I've figured out a way your brother's getting extra money. I'm not sure, and it will take some searching on your part, but. . .I've got an idea."

"What?" His gaze flashed to her face, and he took a step over the threshold and gestured her inside. "I'll get Mother. She's uncovered a few things herself."

"I can't believe he'd stoop to such a level." Victoria sat on a nearby chair, looking over the ledgers. "Those poor people."

Kizzie scanned the papers, trying to piece together why in the world George Lewis would try something that hurt his reputation in such a small town but also, if someone knew what to look for, was easy to find. *Desperate people don't always use their best brains,* as Daddy used to say.

"If that's even what he did," Kizzie reminded her. "I mean, all we've got to go on is the fact he charged some folks in town more than others, but we don't know if he skimmed off the top of those charges unless we can see the mill's books."

"And if he did, is it even illegal?" Noah waved to the papers scattered on the desk in his office. "He charged them, and they paid the price he charged. Any business owner is allowed those liberties from a legal standpoint."

"He *stole* from them, Noah." Victoria's response edged with contained fury. "From our neighbors, using our business."

"I ain't the smartest person in this room," Kizzie interjected. "But if the other business folks start talking, some reporter's gonna have a grand time sharing this information, and I'd say the news wouldn't fare too well for George or his future."

"Or Lewis Mills," Noah added, releasing a sigh. "But if we can control the narrative, it would cause less damage. And if George paid back what he overcharged, we might still have a chance to keep the repercussions small."

"Your reputation and your mama's will help counter George's, I'd say." Kizzie looked at them. "Everyone in The Hollows thinks the two of you are some of the best people in the world. And like you said, Noah, if the information comes out honest and worded rightly, then it will sting George, but not kill Lewis Mills."

"We hope," Victoria said. "Though, if it does kill the mill, the fault will fall on George's head, and he won't have the collateral to bail himself out."

Kizzie glanced between the two of them. "What did you learn?"

Victoria held out her arms for Charlie, who Noah finally relinquished.

The way they passed around her little boy as if he was part of their family shone the sweetest bright spot into this moment. What would it feel like to find a family like this to love. . .and in which to be loved?

"George is in such debt, the bank wouldn't offer him any more loans." Victoria pressed a kiss to Charlie's cheek. "So he must have been desperate enough to steal from his own mill. I'm meeting with the solicitor to go over the particulars of the will and see exactly how all the property was divided."

"I plan to look into some of the other banks next week to investigate whether George has taken out loans anywhere else," Noah added. "But this. . ." He pointed to the desk. "We can easily pair these costs with the ones we've charged other people and show the purposeful overcharging without any exaggeration to the story at all."

"But even if we prove that he overcharged them, we need to check the ledgers. Then we'd have proof of whether or not he's pocketing the money and stealing from the company." Kizzie stepped closer to him, drawing his attention. "Once word gets out that we know something, George will be sure to get rid of any evidence lickety-split."

He stared at her, taking in her words, appreciation warming those hazel eyes of his. "Which means we need to search his office tonight." Noah drew his watch out of his pocket. "The watchmen change over in a half hour. If we get there early, I think I can convince Jones to distract Sykes for the time we need to sneak into the office. Bribery for the good, right?" Noah winked at Kizzie. "And Jones can help give us the time we need to search."

"We?" Kizzie looked up at him, still a little distracted from the effect his wink had on her pulse. "You want me to go with you?"

A wonderful feeling bloomed through her chest and ignited her smile.

He grinned down at her. "You'll make sense of the numbers much faster than I ever could." He searched her face, his voice gentle and welcoming. "That is, if you're willing to go with me and have Charlie stay with Mother."

Kizzie looked over at Victoria, who answered by kissing Charlie's round cheek again. "We'll be right here, safer than either of you."

Kizzie blinked a few times and shrugged her shoulders before turning back to Noah. "I'm willing."

Chapter 23

Victoria gave Kizzie a black coat to wear instead of the green one she'd worn to their house.

"It will hide you better," she said, sending a wink to Noah with an added glint to her eyes.

His mother's knowing look, tinged with a little matchmaking mischief, ignited all sorts of sparks in Noah's chest he shouldn't have while taking Kizzie into a dark mill to secretly search for evidence of his brother's villainy. Not to mention also trying to avoid being caught by a crooked watchman.

Instead of drawing attention by taking the carriage, they walked the short distance from the house down to the mill, keeping to the shadows as best they could.

With quick work, Noah filled Jones in with an abbreviated version of the current situation, and the older man, a contemporary of his father's, grumbled through a few unsavory comments related to George's and Sykes' ungentlemanly and abhorrent behavior.

Instead of being offended, Kizzie attempted to hide her humor behind her gloved hand.

And Noah fell a little more in love with her.

Because, without a doubt, he was.

Falling. Sometimes, even jumping in with eyes wide open. How his heart could love two such different women as Elinor and Kizzie only proved the bigness of God's ability to grow a person's heart through grief and trial.

Of course, he wasn't the same man he'd been when he'd first courted and then married Elinor. Life, grief, and a great deal of growing up had changed him, so perhaps Kizzie was exactly the perfect woman for the man he was now.

Jones agreed to help keep Sykes distracted and, at the half-hour mark, ensure he was far away from the office so Noah and Kizzie could slip out of the mill and back to the house without Sykes knowing about it.

The plan sounded fairly foolproof, but since Noah had never delved into sleuthing of any sort, his confidence quivered a little. However, Kizzie didn't appear nervous in the least. In fact, she plunged toward the office stairs without a hint of hesitation.

They got to the second floor just as the sound of a door closed below them.

Sykes was early.

Kizzie looked over at Noah, and without a word, he grabbed her hand and drew her the short distance down the hallway to the office he and his brother shared. Strange as it was, Noah spent little time in the large room, as most of his work kept him on the production floor. So his side of the room was fairly sparse. But George's side was crowded with a large rolltop desk framed by two bookshelves and a massive window on one side.

Noah led her to the desk and dug into his pocket, retrieving a key.

"I've never used this key for Father's desk because I hadn't any need for it, but I'm certainly glad he gave both George and me a copy of it now." He unlocked the desk, and the top rolled back to reveal nooks and crannies crammed with papers, ledgers, receipt books, and Noah wasn't certain what else.

"We might need more than a half hour for this," Kizzie whispered, studying the disorganized conglomeration.

"I have an idea." He looked at her, the fading glow of sunset highlighting the room in gold. "Since you read numbers faster, why don't you take the ledgers, and I'll take the receipts. If there are any letters, I'll give them to you too. You can read them faster than I can."

He wasn't certain what he'd expected from her response, but the look of admiration she sent him settled in his chest like winning some sort of award. His weaknesses failed to diminish him in her eyes. In fact, if he guessed right from her expression, she didn't think badly of him at all.

"All right." She drew out a ledger.

"Perhaps this will help." He tugged a flashlight from his pocket, catching Kizzie's attention.

"What in the world is that?"

He grinned and held it up for her perusal. "A flashlight."

Her nose wrinkled with her frown, inciting his grin. "A what?"

He flipped the switch on the small tube and watched her eyes widen as a dim light poured from the other end. "Well, look at that." She peered closer. "How does it work? I didn't see you light a match."

"Batteries." He shone the beam over the papers before them. "But I'm not sure how long we have with it. I've never gotten one to last long before it turns off."

"Then we better stop talking and start working."

A few minutes in, Noah found a receipt to Mr. Lawrence, one of the shopkeepers in town his brother had overcharged. He tilted the paper toward Kizzie.

"Those dates fit the timeline," she said. "We'd better take that one."

He nodded, folded the paper, and tucked it into his shirt pocket.

"When did George start courting Miss Malone?"

Noah thought. "Six months ago."

"So I'd imagine he didn't start hurting for money until after that, so. . ." She closed the ledger. "These dates would be too old." She moved through two more while he scanned other papers.

"Here." She turned the book so he could see. "This one has some of the dates we're looking for."

He shifted a step closer to her in order to shine the light more fully on the book, but his hip rubbed against something on the desk, and a pile of books and papers crashed to the floor.

Noah met Kizzie's wide-eyed gaze.

"Did you hear that?" A voice rose from downstairs, carried up from the production room floor.

Sykes.

"Where did it come from?" Jones' voice rose too loud, like he was attempting to warn them.

"Upstairs." They heard rushed footsteps.

Noah scanned the room, searching for a hiding place. He grabbed Kizzie's hand and rushed across the room to the little closet behind his unused desk. After tugging her inside the cramped space, he brought the closet door to a close just as the footsteps made it to the hallway.

"Your flashlight." Kizzie looked down at his free hand, light glowing through his fingers because of the way he held the light.

He switched it off just as the clipped footsteps entered the room. A glow swooped from beneath the closet door, giving Noah a better view of Kizzie's silhouette beside him, though her fingers wrapped around his certainly highlighted her nearness. He gave her hand a squeeze and tugged her a little closer, turning so his body created an additional buffer between her and the door.

She edged against him, likely to orient herself in the tiny space, but he rather liked the nearness. The touch.

"See anything?" This from Jones. Footsteps, heavier ones, likely Jones moving near the closet. Did he suspect they hid in there?

Good man.

"A mess on the floor by Mr. Lewis' desk."

More footsteps. Kizzie's fingers tightened in his. He brought his free arm around her waist to assure her. The subtle scent of lavender invaded each breath, and he leaned a little closer. How soft was her hair? Or her lips?

"Seems to me, the noise was nothing more than Mr. Lewis' papers and a couple of books falling out of an overcrowded desk."

Noah stilled. But did George usually leave his desk closed and locked? He racked his brain to recall such a simple answer.

"I've warned him to keep it closed, if not locked," Sykes murmured. "We can't cover every inch of the mill all night long, and if he wants to keeps his papers safe, he ought to lock the desk."

"Perhaps he left in a hurry." Jones continued on, his footsteps moving away from the closet. "You know how these young business owners can be."

"He's always in some kind of hurry, ain't he?" A sound like a snort followed. "If his father could see him, he'd be none too pleased, is all I have to say."

"Should we clean up, or leave it for morning?"

A large sigh sounded. "I suppose we'd better at least get them off the floor." Sykes growled out the words, and the sound of papers swishing followed. The steady roll of the desk cover came next followed by a click of the top in place.

Noah's shoulders dropped. If they opened the desk again and the papers or books fell out, Sykes would certainly know someone had been in the room.

"I heard tell Mrs. Morris left some of her sponge cake in the store," Jones said. "Why don't we have a piece before I head off for the night? No one makes sponge cake like Mrs. Morris."

A grumbling assent followed, and the footsteps left the room. Noah waited. They should give the men a few minutes to make it down to the first floor again. Kizzie's hair brushed against his chin as she shifted, and he tightened his hold on her waist.

Their hiding spot was now in complete darkness, with only the smell and feel of her to tease his senses.

But that was more than enough.

Her breath hit his chin, which meant she must be looking up at him.

His free palm slid up her arm to her shoulder, his fingers brushing against her braid. Soft. Smooth. Like glass.

As he touched her chin, her breath caught, and the sound, high-lighted in the dark, brought him nearer. He didn't need to see to know exactly where her lips were, but. . .would she let him kiss her?

Kizzie's heart thrummed in her chest.

At first, the beat pounded because of Sykes' entrance into the room outside their hiding spot and the fear of discovery.

But then, as the footsteps disappeared down the hallway, her pulse shuddered for a new reason. Noah's pressure against her back gentled, changing from a protective hold to something. . .sweeter. She hadn't been this close to a man since Charles.

And never to one she admired as much as Noah.

Admired? She raised her chin, his face lost in the darkness. No. Even more than admired. She loved him.

In a way unlike anything she'd known with Charles.

Stronger and deeper.

One of his hands gently moved to her shoulder, sending tingles over her skin and awakening her pulse to an even faster thrum.

And then, his fingers touched her cheek.

She drew in a quick breath at the warmth, the intimacy, at the way her entire body hummed to life from his skin against hers.

"Kizzie?" His whispered word rasped, and her body rose to meet the entreaty.

"Yes?" She barely voiced the response.

His face had to be terribly close. The hand around her waist smoothed up her back, the movement catching her breath completely. "May I kiss you?"

The sweetness in his request, the tenderness in his voice, stung her eyes. He didn't take from her or coax her into a response. There was no guilt, manipulation, or bribery.

He merely offered himself.

In his own sweet, wonderful way.

And himself was all she wanted.

She released her hold of his hand and slid her palm up to his chest, grasping the lapel of his coat. The heat in her eyes turned to warm tears.

Could God really offer her something so beautiful? Someone so. . .extraordinary?

"If you want."

His palm smoothed over her cheek, followed by the other, framing her face, warming her cheeks. "Oh, I want." The rumbled words held her captive, reverberating in her chest and skittering her pulse into a faster beat.

She wanted too.

His kiss. Him. This unbelievable affection and care she didn't deserve. Her breath caught just as their mouths touched. The fresh scent of soap tinged with a leather scent wafted over her in time with the soft brush of his lips against hers.

Barely a stroke of skin against skin, but enough to incite an explosion in her chest. So gentle.

At first.

But only at first.

Because then, as if the brief taste failed to serve its purpose, one of his hands slid down to capture her waist, drawing her even more tightly against him. Her free arm slipped up his chest, hooking around his neck, cherishing the full and incomparable feeling of being held...kissed by him.

Warmth cascaded through her, wrapping her heart in as much of an embrace as Noah's arms, promising something she'd missed far too long.

Home.

She hadn't felt home in so long and never expected to find it in a person, but as certain as the sky was blue, her heart belonged to Noah Lewis.

He pulled back only enough for her to feel his lips spread into a smile against hers. He wanted her. To kiss her. And, as if for further proof, he kissed her again, lengthening the embrace a little longer. Another second. Or ten.

A wonderful cascade of flutters poured through her and then. . . something different.

Another fluttering. Different.

She drew back this time, her mind foggy from his thorough attention. How did she know that feeling? It was strangely familiar.

"I suppose we ought to get out of here before Sykes returns." Noah pressed another kiss to her lips.

"We'd do more harm for ourselves if we were caught in a closet together, Mr. Lewis."

His chuckle warmed the space between them, and he shifted away from her toward the door, bringing her with him.

The room lay in shadows, the last bits of sunset barely bleeding into the space. Noah turned back to her, his face close enough for her to make out the smallest grin.

"I believe I've developed a newfound appreciation for closets, Kizzie McAdams."

She stifled her laugh and squeezed his hand. "I certainly never paired them with kisses, but I'm perfectly fine with the idea." Her gaze slipped to his. "Especially if they're yours."

His grin spread wider, and he looked as if he might lean over and kiss her again but then caught himself, offering her a wink instead. "We'd better take advantage of what time we have left. If I start kissing you again, I may lose all sense of time and place."

Her cheeks heated at the implication. "I can certainly see that as a nuisance at the moment."

"Indeed. A nuisance to have to wait to indulge a little longer."

And then her whole face caught fire. Lord, have mercy. "Noah Lewis, if you keep talkin' like that for much longer, I may melt plumb into my boots." She waved toward the desk. "So we'd both better get our minds off of kissing for now or we'll be in a heap of trouble, and I don't aim to fall into the same trouble God's got me out of already."

"Kizzie, I'd never put you in that position." He tugged her back against him, searching her face. "You know that, don't you? I care too much about both of us for that. I want us to do things God's way."

Her face cooled, her breath growing shallow.

Which meant marriage? To her?

Could it be true?

She smiled up at him, not trusting her voice for more, and then he pressed a kiss to her cheek and gestured toward the desk. "Should we attempt to open it again and have another look?"

She shook her head and raised the ledger in her hands. "We have this. I think it will be enough to get us started."

Noah kept hold of her hand as they slipped down the hall and the stairway, careful to listen for Sykes or Jones, before making it out the front door of the mill and back to his house.

Once Kizzie, Noah, and Victoria gathered around the ledger on Noah's desk and paired their findings with the documentation of the customers in town, George's actions surfaced in full detail. Though he'd charged the shopkeepers the outrageous prices per their records, in his ledgers he'd marked a lesser cost and then pocketed the difference.

And according to the ledger, what he took from the mill along with the overpriced items equaled over a thousand dollars.

At least.

"Oh, George." Victoria sank into the nearest chair. "He's ruined us all."

"Not if, once the truth is out, we pay back those he's wronged, Mother." Noah paced. "If we are forthright about the information and present it to the police or reporters ourselves, laying out our plan to make amends, then perhaps we can salvage our reputation."

"And reporters are so prone to virtue." His mother rolled her eyes in a very unladylike way.

"Casper Jackson is." Noah turned to her. "And he's one of the most respected newsmen in The Hollows or the area in general."

"And how will you pay them back?" Kizzie looked up from Charlie, who sat on her lap. "I thought funds were tight."

Noah and his mother shared a glance, and then he sighed. "I need to investigate some of the other banks to see if George attempted to take out any more loans and—"

"And if we must, we'll sell the house."

What? Kizzie glanced at Noah before turning to Victoria, but the woman continued. "I've loved this house, but it's too large for me and Noah anyway, and with the profits of the sale, we could pay back the difference to those George has wronged and purchase a house more feasible for two people and a few servants."

"Maybe it won't come to that." Kizzie turned to Noah, as if to reassure him too.

"I'd rather sell George's house." Noah chuckled and then paused before approaching the desk again. "Do we know which bank he used for building the new house?"

Mother shook her head. "I thought it was our regular bank, but evidently he'd already exceeded his credit there before getting very far on the house."

"So he must have used those loans for the new carriages and horses." Noah resumed his pacing, sliding his fingers up and down his suspenders as he walked. A trait which always piqued Kizzie's grin. "And the stables. As you recall, he built the stables and carriage house before starting on the house so that he could have a place to stay and oversee the building."

"And the carriage house is not small, so I'm certain it cost more than he had in ready money."

"Here's what I think we should do." Noah approached the desk, his hands bracing each suspender at the waist. "I will investigate any other bank information with Mother as my assistant, because if George had to seek a loan from another bank, it makes me wonder if he used Mother and me as leverage in the process. I'll also talk to Casper. He's discreet and will give solid guidance on the matter. Before we make anything publicly known, we need to have all the information we can."

Kizzie nodded, pulling Charlie close as she thought. Could George incur legal charges against him for this? The situation was certainly wrong, but illegal?

Another flutter moved through her abdomen, more pronounced with Charlie against her.

And this time, it had nothing to do with Noah's kisses.

No.

Kizzie drew in a shuddering breath and stood. "It sounds like that's a good plan, and I'll wait for your word on how I can help." She stepped toward the door. "It's getting late, so I'd better get on back to town."

Noah followed her to the door. "Are you all right?"

"You can always stay with us, Kizzie dear," added Victoria, rising from her seat.

Kizzie pressed on a smile. "That's awful kind of you, but it's my shop day tomorrow." She looked from Victoria to Noah. "If you need me, let me know."

Kizzie walked to the foyer, and Taylor presented her with her and Charlie's coats. She wrangled Charlie's little arms into his and then Noah assisted her with hers. Then he walked her outside.

"Are you certain you're all right?" He searched her face as they stopped at the buggy.

"I think I'm tired." Which wasn't a lie. Her soul felt too tired to believe what might be true.

"Of course." He smiled his beautiful smile and bathed her in a tender look. "It's been an unexpected day." He shrugged a shoulder. "And certainly not all bad."

She lost her worries in the adoration on his face, and with a quick dip of his head, he pressed a kiss to her lips. And then, at Charlie's giggle, he added another kiss to the little boy's head.

The flutter came again. Stronger.

Impossible, wasn't it?

But memories of feeling the same flutter over the past few weeks came to mind, and episodes she'd discounted as indigestion or nerves. Nothing serious.

But she knew this feeling. She'd had it once before.

And only once.

Her gaze dropped to Charlie.

"Here, let me take this little man while you mount." Noah plucked Charlie from her arms and offered his free hand to her as she climbed to the seat of the buggy. She looked down at him, all smiles and kindness, with her little boy in his arms.

Emotions rose into her throat, gnawing at her breath.

Noah would make a wonderful father.

Husband.

But. . .what if. . .

"Be careful." Noah patted the side of the buggy. "I'll stop in at the shop tomorrow afternoon so we can talk."

She held his gaze, thankful for the shadows of dusk to hide the growing sting in her eyes. "I'll see you then."

He nodded and handed Charlie back up to her. She edged the horse forward.

Her mind raced. Her heart pounded in her head.

Was it possible? But even as she asked the question, her past flew into the present.

She'd only been with Charles twice since Charlie's birth, maybe three times, and Nella said it was unlikely for women to get pregnant so soon after having a child.

And if she was pregnant? The cool air hit her damp face as she calculated the possibility. Around five months ago.

Five.

She pinched her eyes closed.

No wonder she'd been overtired and her skirts were tighter.

It explained her morning and nighttime nausea too.

As she turned the curve in the road, she glanced back to catch one last look of Noah, the large house rising behind him aglow in gaslight.

One last look of how he saw her then, with their kisses new and wonderful between them.

Because tomorrow, once she confirmed what her heart already knew...

Tomorrow, she feared, everything would change.

Chapter 24

THE EXTENT OF GEORGE'S DESPERATION left Noah utterly bewildered. Mother too.

In the middle of his madness, George had placed the entire mortgage for his new house in Mother's name, which allowed her to uncover a few more ways he'd used her name on various documents. But also made her financially responsible for the house's mortgage.

But, apart from keeping himself out of financial obligation, why did he keep using Mother's name on all the accounts? Unless Mother had some executive power over the estate? Which sent Mother into a deeper investigation into what the will really said.

Had she held power all along?

As they delved even deeper into the paperwork, they found documentation to suggest that George had sold twenty acres of their family land, again, with Mother's forged signature as verification for the sale.

His debt was staggering.

At least Noah still had the property he was meant to inherit from his father. That was some leverage, if he needed money. He pinched his eyes closed, pushing the fury and hurt down to keep a clear head. He and Mother had to figure out how to manage the information in the best way at the least cost to them and the mill. Was there a way to take this knowledge of George's crimes and use it to help him make amends? Even if he had to go to jail, if he willingly sought to atone for his mistakes, then perhaps the outcome could prove better than Noah feared.

After taking Mother home to consider their next steps, Noah returned to town to visit Casper at the *Daily News*. He wasn't ready to go to the police just yet, but Casper knew enough of the legal world to give some insight.

"You're going to have to confront him, you know." The dark-haired man looked up from the information Noah had just given him and shook his head. "It would be better coming from you than seeing it in newsprint first or, worse, having the police come to his door. There are other crimes besides extortion here. Forgery, fraud, falsifying documents—"

"I know." Noah ran a hand through his hair and sat down across from Casper's desk. "I'm just not sure how he's going to respond."

Casper grimaced. "Probably not good."

"No, probably not."

"This information is going to come out within the next few days no matter how hard you try to keep it quiet." He waved the papers. "You've stirred the pot with your questions. The bankers will talk. The shopkeepers will talk." He shrugged. "Probably already have."

Noah's stomach dropped. He should have considered the way word spread in a small town. Not everyone would prove as discreet or concerned as him and his mother. Which meant George may already be aware of his and Mother's knowledge.

He needed to get to Mother and prepare her.

Kizzie too.

Noah stood. "I'd better go."

Casper nodded and pushed up from his chair. "When do you want me to print this? I can't say I'm not a little selfish in wanting to officially break the news first."

"Can you give me twenty-four hours?"

Casper rounded the desk and placed his palm on Noah's shoulder. "Forty-eight, if you need."

What about a week? Month? But no amount of time could change the bombshell readying to explode. "I'll ring you if I need longer, but if you don't hear from me, do whatever you think is best."

Within five minutes, he marched through Carters' front door, his thoughts moving from one step to the next. Tell Kizzie and encourage her to keep a watch out for George. Noah didn't think his brother would resort to violence, but desperation led to unforeseen responses.

Molly worked the front counter and directed Noah up the back stairway to Kizzie's little apartment. Charlie's babbling met him through the closed door, and he grinned, something he'd neglected doing all morning.

Despite the circumstances, he'd done quite a bit of grinning the evening before, especially when recollecting the delightful memories of a closet and Kizzie's lips. After today, he'd likely not have anything to offer Kizzie but his heart, his good name, and his work ethic, because his brother had taken almost everything else, but something told him those things didn't matter as much to her.

He gave the door a light rap and, after a moment, it opened.

The smile stilled on his face.

Kizzie looked up at him, eyes red-rimmed, tears still wet on her cheeks. Heat left his body, and he took her by the shoulders. "What? What's wrong?"

She pulled in a shaky breath, fresh tears forming in those cerulean eyes. "I'm. . .I'm so sorry, Noah. I didn't know. I promise, I didn't. If I'd known *you* could be in my future, I—I never—"

"Good heavens, darling, what's happened?"

She shook his arms free and wiped a hand over her face. "I. . .I went to the doctor this morning."

His entire body froze. Doctor? What was it? Cancer? "Whatever it is, Kizzie—"

"I'm pregnant." The declaration shook out of her with such force, he didn't fully comprehend.

Pregnant?

"It must have been from the last time Charles and I were together." She pulled back another step, Charlie's little voice still humming through the room. "I didn't know. I wouldn't have. . . I'd never have entertained loving you at all, if I'd known. But. . .but. . ."

"You're pregnant?"

"Dr. Palmer said I'm five months along, at least." She shook her head, more tears running down her face. "I promise you, Noah, I didn't know until last night and I started feeling the baby move. That's when. . .I wondered."

"You're five months pregnant?" He said the words aloud to fully comprehend them. Five months. November? Long before she ever met him.

And had she said she loved him?

His mind wrestled with the two competing thoughts. He wasn't certain how to fully respond. His care for her hadn't changed. His desire to be with her still anchored him to his resolution. But the news of her pregnancy took some time to digest.

"I don't expect you to renew your. . .affections from last night."

His gaze shot to hers. "What?"

"I was ruined goods when I came here. I already have a reputation, Noah." She wiped at her face again. "And when the news gets out about your brother, you'll have enough dirtying your family name." She waved to her middle. "If folks keep seeing us together, you know exactly what people will think about this baby. They'll think—"

"That I love you?"

The words slipped out effortlessly. They'd nearly choked him to get out last night. And now in the middle of her revelation, news which should send him stepping back a little to regain his footing propelled him forward. Nothing had really changed, had it? She was the same woman she'd been yesterday, the one he'd slowly been falling in love with for months.

Charlie still needed a father.

The only difference now was he'd become a father of two.

And was the brother of a criminal.

Plus, the little fact he was nearly penniless.

And, at the moment, he'd never been happier.

"I love you, Kizzie; that's not changed at all."

Kizzie's heart had broken into a million pieces at having to tell Noah the news which was bound to end any hope of their future together, and now, her mind swept completely blank and her reprimand died on her tongue. What had he said?

"You—you love me?"

He shifted a step closer to her, his gentle smile turning into a quiet laugh as if he'd just realized it too. "I do."

Perhaps the situation with his brother had addled his thinking. She shook her head, new tears blinking free. "You can't."

"I hate to disagree with you, Kizzie, but I can." He gathered one of her hands in his. "Actually, I do."

"Still? Even with the news I'm carryin' another man's child?"

"I know it's not what either one of us would prefer, but it doesn't change what I already know about you."

He loved her and Charlie? He wanted them to be a part of his life and family? Still? It couldn't be possible.

The look in his eyes almost weakened her fight, but she placed a palm to his chest, stopping his growing nearness. He wasn't thinking straight. Men didn't give up their lives for women like her. "You can't mean that." She shook her head, new tears blurring her vision. "You'll lose everything. I can't let you lose everything."

"Everything?" His smile turned so sweet her breath stalled. "I don't think so, Kizzie. If I must let go of those things to gain something even better, I'd call it a good deal." He squeezed her hands. "I'd have your lovely self as my bride. And get to be the father to"—he waved from her stomach to Charlie—"these children."

Her heart pulsed a painful rhythm. He was offering her everything she could have ever dreamed, and she couldn't take it. No good person took advantage of a crazy man, and that's exactly what he was to not even flinch at the news she'd given him. Crazy.

"You. . .you can't mean to marry me, Noah Lewis. If you do that, you're just gonna confirm what rumors folks will think once they know I'm carrying another child. You're innocent to such charges and plumb crazy to pair your name with a woman twice fallen." Her eyes widened, her face growing hotter as she spoke. "Then it'll hurt your mama, and there ain't no telling what your brother will do."

"My mama will be fine. In fact, she's likely been praying for this outcome for a few weeks now."

What? Victoria wanted her and Noah to marry? Even as she was?

"And my brother's already created enough trouble for himself not to worry about mine."

Doggone it! If the man didn't keep shooting down her arguments like a regular straight shooter. "Which is all the more reason why you *can't* think to marry me." It was the most outlandish, foolhardy thing for a decent, respectable, good-hearted man to contemplate, let alone actually voice. "George's choices are already going to hurt you and your mama enough. Why add this—me—to make things worse? Folks will tear your family down, Noah. I know what it feels like to have them tear you down. I'd never want to be part of causing that for you."

He gathered her hands into his in complete contradiction to her arguments. "Do you love me, Kizzie?" His soft hazel eyes searched hers, the tenderness nestled within those greens and golds so real it captured every piece of her broken heart.

"Of course I do." She responded without hesitation. "How could I not, but the truth still—"

"Kizzie." The faintest smile curled his lips. He looked at their braided hands as if the answer pleased him. Loose hair curled over his forehead as he raised his gaze back to hers. "Then it doesn't matter what anyone else thinks except you and me and God."

Her heart nearly puddled to the floor, her fight dwindling with each confession, each touch.

"Noah Lewis, you're a whole lot smarter than to want such a tomfool thing. *Especially* now." Yet she didn't let go of his hands, didn't pull away. Her body already accepted what her mind couldn't believe. Emotions squeezed in her throat, the idea too big for her heart. Too beautiful.

Still? Want her? "What good could marrying me bring you?"

"A little family of my own?" He brought her hands to his lips, a look of sheer delight on his face. Her eyes grew blurrier as he spoke. "Your love, Kizzie?"

Her breath trembled out on a sigh. "But what about your reputation? Your status in this place?"

A humorless laugh burst from him. "I've had all the benefits of wealth and station, but what have they given me? An estrangement from my sister? A heartbroken mother and a tyrannical brother? You brought value of a measureless sort into my life. I don't want a future without you and Charlie in it."

Her arguments dissolved into smithereens.

"Well, this is quite the interesting story, isn't it?"

Kizzie looked up to see George Lewis standing at the top of the stairs, arms crossed and leaning against the nearby wall. An unfriendly smile curled his lips, and his gaze took its time moving from Noah to Kizzie and back.

George's lips dipped into a sneer. "Unwed mother pregnant once again and my brother playing the Good Samaritan? Or has he lost his virtue to a pretty face?"

"George?" Noah dropped Kizzie's hands and turned.

"Good of you to make an honest woman of such a fallen spectacle, Noah."

"How did you get up here?" Kizzie asked, stepping forward to the apartment doorway near Noah.

One of George's dark brows rose. "The sweet little thing in the front sent me up when I told her I was looking for my brother and it was an emergency." He straightened from his position. "You can't mean to marry her, Noah." He took a step closer, and Noah shifted to place himself between Kizzie and his brother. "Bedding a woman like her is one thing. Legitimizing things is quite another. I will not have you bring someone like her into our family to dampen our status."

"You're doing that just fine on your own, George. You don't need my help."

"Ah, so you're the one who slandered my name, are you?" He rubbed a hand over his chin and drew in a breath. "Because, you see, the oddest thing happened about an hour ago. Mr. Lawrence stopped me on the street to let me know the police would be serving me papers soon, as he intended to sue me for price gouging. And then, when I went to the bank, they informed me that you and Mother had left this morning. . .with my accounts."

"Not yours. Mother's, since almost everything is in her name. She was rather surprised to discover how many things she's been purchasing without even knowing it." Noah shook his head, continuing to create a wall with his body between George and Kizzie. "How could you, George? After all she's already lost?"

Something flickered on George's face. He looked back at Kizzie. "If you marry her, you'll see nothing of your inheritance, you know that? Father would never have approved of her. I'll be forced to disinherit you just like Father had to do to Clarice."

"Funny thing about my visit to the bank, George. It seems I've already lost the money Father left me. It seems Mother, unbeknownst to herself, reverted my inheritance to a business account that has been depleted considerably. So your threat is powerless."

The smile vanished from George's face.

"Exactly," Noah continued. "I know about it all. The overcharging vulnerable customers. Stealing from the mill. Forging my name and Mother's name on bank documents. I imagine there's more we haven't uncovered yet."

George's face paled a few shades. "You don't have any proof."

Kizzie looked up at Noah, whose only response was to fold his arms across his chest.

"What?" George matched his brother's stance.

"Mother has legal access to any documents in her name." Noah shrugged. "We should have caught things before now, but we didn't think our own flesh and blood would stoop to such a level. I suppose the bank didn't either, to take all this at face value. And for what, George? Status? Prestige?"

"If you share what you know. . ." George loomed closer, and Noah stood to his full height.

"If Mr. Lawrence and the bank already know, do you think it's going to be a secret for long?" Noah released a sigh. "And the worst part of it is that you've not only ruined your own life, but you've stolen from dozens of people. Mother and I will lose the mill and property Father worked so hard to purchase, and the mill workers will lose their livelihoods."

"What do you mean?" George gave his head a severe shake, as if not fully hearing. "Once Beatrice and I marry, I'll have the prestige of her family, and then I can do what I want with the mill."

Kizzie stared at George. Did he really not know? Even Kizzie with her narrow upbringing and experience read between the lines of Noah's statements. If George's debts proved substantial, which it certainly seemed they were, the creditors would seize everything in his name—or in this case, his mother's—to use as leverage against debts.

Everything.

Including the mill, the land. . .everything he owned.

"George, if she smirked at the very idea of sharing a table with Kizzie"—Noah's voice softened with entreaty—"do you truly think Beatrice will have anything to do with you once this news comes out? You'll be labeled a criminal."

"It's all a mistake. An easy fix." He sneered. "I'll sell the land. We have hundreds more acres. I can sell Mother's house too."

"The house isn't in your name to sell," Noah reminded him. "And even if you sold the land, you can't change the reputation you've made for yourself now. Laws you've broken require justice." He sighed, taking a step toward George as if approaching a wild animal. "We'll have to start over, George, with whatever is left after the debts have been paid."

"Start over?" George yelled so loudly, it startled Charlie, and his cry broke into the sudden silence. "I will not start over. I will not lose what I've created. This is all your fault." George rushed forward, and before Kizzie knew what was happening, he hit Noah across the face. Noah stumbled back into Kizzie, and she steadied him as best she could.

"You just wait." George's face distorted into a deepening frown. "I'll speak to Mother, and we'll see about this."

The man's voice cracked like a whining child's. He turned and raced down the stairs.

Noah stumbled toward the door after him and then looked back, but Kizzie waved him away. "Go, you need to get to your mama."

"We'll finish this conversation later, Miss McAdams." He nodded and pointed at her. "I know what loss feels like, so I have plenty of fight in me to not lose what is worth saving. And you and Charlie are worth it all to me."

With that, he followed after his brother. Kizzie took a sniffling Charlie up in her arms and then dropped into the nearby chair, the overwhelming urge to laugh and cry crashing together inside of her chest.

He loved her. Wanted to marry her. She was worth saving.

She pinched her eyes closed against the hope dangling too close. It was impossible.

Even as her hand palmed her protruding abdomen.

Too wonderful for *her*.

But the joy barely took a foothold when a sudden rush of questions followed, assaulting her. Who are you to deserve something this good? Who are you to accept it? What have you ever done to earn the love of such a fine man? Don't you know he'll come to regret marrying you?

Who are you?

She pulled Charlie close, kissing his head, new tears blurring her eyes.

She knew what the voices called her. She'd heard their condemnation enough to recall it from memory. They repeated the same names, the same hate.

Her gaze fell on her Bible, and a sudden light pierced her spirit.

But what did God say? Even if she didn't feel like anything wonderful, His voice needed to be louder than anyone else's.

Louder than George's. Noah's. And even her own.

Chapter 25

NOAH ARRIVED AT THE HOUSE, but his brother never came.

The blood from his busted lip easily washed away.

The pain would take a little longer.

But the uneasiness about George's next choices lingered in every moment. Noah went through the house, locking windows and doors, and put all the servants on alert. Within the next two days, George's entire life would fall apart all around him, and, from what Noah could tell, his brother hadn't counted the cost of his choices.

He'd played a hand against the whims of the world and lost, horribly.

Certainly, as Father's golden child, George reserved the honor of getting most everything he wanted, with no consequences for small mistakes. Or at least none from which Father didn't rescue him. So perhaps George thought skimming a little extra money here or there or forging Mother's name to acquire funds or neglecting the needs of the mill to feed his own faux status were acts that wouldn't come back to roost.

Yet here they were.

Noah stared out the window, taking in the sight of the mill, branding it into his memory.

There was nothing he could do to stop the imminent doom.

"Do you remember what George used to do as a child when he found himself in trouble?"

Noah turned as his mother walked into his study, the lines around her eyes deeper than usual.

"Blame me?" Noah shot her a humorless grin, and she responded with a sad smile.

"Well, besides that." She joined him at the window. "He'd have a little fit and then attempt to run away."

Noah braced himself with the revelation. "You think he'll run away?"

"He's never been good at facing up to his mistakes." She sighed. "Your father indulged him so. After two babies dying before George's birth, I suppose it was your father's way of healing. I wouldn't be surprised if he hasn't already disappeared."

Noah turned toward her. "And remain in hiding for the rest of his life, perhaps?"

"I don't know." She rubbed her forehead. "I suppose it all depends on how deep his stubbornness and anger run."

"Or his fear." He returned his attention to the window. Sunset glinted off the dozens of mill windows, reflecting back the scene of a mountain silhouette. After all the discoveries, in the quiet afterward, grief began a steady climb into his chest. "I hate disappointing the workers, Mother. Having them lose their livelihoods."

"Maybe they won't."

"What?"

She turned and walked to a nearby chair. He followed.

"Your father's solicitor discussed the will with me today. I've been a fool." She rubbed her forehead. "I just believed George, allowed him to take over everything, assuming your father had left it all to him, but. . ." She looked up. "*I* am the sole inheritor of everything except for the land left to George."

"The land he sold was his own?"

"Some of it. Your inheritance is safe, though, and I'm grateful for that." She nodded. "But that's why he forged my name so often. I was the one who had to sign for loans or to release funds, because I inherited it all."

"It was yours all along?" Noah lowered into the chair across from her, allowing the news to sink in. He wasn't completely ruined. His inheritance was safe.

She nodded again. "I wish I'd been sounder of mind when your father died. If I'd paid better attention, none of this would have happened." She sighed. "Or at least we might have caught it sooner."

"You can't blame yourself, Mother. You had not only lost your husband but your daughter as well." He took her hand in his, emotions lodging in his throat. "I thought for a few months there, I was going to lose you too."

She'd become so ill, at one point Dr. Palmer suggested that George and Noah prepare themselves for the inevitable.

Her expression gentled as she squeezed his hand. "I'm sorry I left so much of the burden on you during those months, Noah. You were grieving too."

"I didn't mind being strong for you. I only wish I'd recognized how much of a mess George was making of things before now."

"How could you have known? The worst of his behaviors only started when he began courting Beatrice, but at that point, I believe he realized what a financial disaster he'd created and became desperate."

"So do you have any idea of the outcome? The cost?" Noah released her hand and sat up, preparing for the blow of the truth. "Will we lose everything but the house?"

"Not. . .everything." The hesitation in her voice didn't bode well. "Since all the property and funds are in my name, I am responsible financially, at this point, so the solicitor and I have worked out a possible plan, assuming you agree." She drew in a breath and steadied her attention on him. "I will sell the mill and its connected acreage plus George's house. We may be forced to sell more land, but if what the solicitor and bankers said is true, the first two should provide enough to cover debts and pay back what George overcharged. It's possible we can salvage this situation with our dignity intact and some money to live on as we sort out our next steps. But we can't keep the mill."

Noah had expected as much, but the declaration still hit like a blow to his chest. He'd worked so hard to manage the mill in a way to make his parents proud and had endeavored to support the workers and community, only to have it end like this?

"I hate being forced into the choice, Mother." Noah squeezed her hand, accepting the good and right decision over the desired one. "But this way, people will keep their jobs, and we can do what is right by those George has wronged."

"Exactly." Her expression softened. "And, perhaps, clear our names while we start afresh without any debt hanging over us."

"And you can keep *your* beloved house." He gave her hand another squeeze.

Her eyes grew glossy, and she gripped his fingers. "I do love this house." The faintest smile returned to her face, one brow winging high as if to nudge him along. "And it's quite large enough for a ready-made family."

Noah drew in a breath and released his mother's hand. "About that."

"Noah, please don't bring any other heartache today."

"It isn't heartache so much as being unexpected. . .and difficult for some people to accept." He paused and then leaned forward again. "Kizzie's pregnant."

"What?" Mother covered her mouth with her hand, eyes widening. "You. . .you. . ."

"The baby is from Charlie's father. She didn't know she carried another child until yesterday when she started recognizing certain symptoms."

"But that would mean she's at least four months along."

"Five," Noah corrected. "And she's refusing to marry me because she doesn't want to wound our already-vulnerable reputation."

"You asked her to marry you?" Mother's eyes widened.

"I know we've not known each other as long as some, but I care about her, Mother. Deeply."

"And you're unfazed by her news?" Air burst from his mother's lips.

"Unfazed may be too simple a term." He'd mulled over the news on his drive to the house, accepting her choices as part of the unredeemed and naive woman she'd left behind. Not the new woman he'd grown to love. "I'm grieved for her because of the shame she is constantly battling, but it doesn't change how I feel about her or Charlie."

"Of course it wouldn't matter to you, would it? Your heart is so good and big, you would love them all." His mother's smile brimmed, and a tear spilled over her cheek. And then she chuckled, and her chuckle grew into a laugh. Despite the tears running down her face, she laughed still.

"Mother?"

"Poor Kizzie, worried about our reputation when your brother has soundly trounced every part of our name in ways I would have never imagined." She wiped at her eyes and leaned her head back against the chair, sobering. "Wouldn't it be nice if this story of your life and mine and Kizzie's earned a happy ending after all this heartache?"

"You truly don't mind? About Kizzie?"

"Mind? That girl may be a diamond in the rough, but her true heart shines through." Her grin returned. "If I had any small doubts before working with her at the mill, they disappeared. Seeing how she cared for those children and worked with the girls and fought for the future of those women?" She sat back up and grabbed Noah's hand again. "Her faith is truly resilient. It has bloomed in the most unlikely ways and places, yet beautifully. And you'd give me one of the most wonderful gifts in all the world."

Her teasing smile spread to his lips. "What is that?"

She sent him a wink. "Grandchildren."

He laughed, a much too absent action over the past few hours, and then with a sigh, he leaned forward and kissed her cheek.

"I'm going out to search for George." His attention held hers. "Lock the doors. Just in case, and alert Taylor and Case to keep watch."

Case showed up at the store the next morning in search of Kizzie.

"Case?" She approached him where he stood near the canned goods by the front window. "Is everyone at the house all right?"

"Yes, ma'am." He nodded, removing his cap. "It's just that Mr. Noah wanted me to deliver this note to you as soon as I could get to the shop this morning."

Kizzie took the proffered note and thanked Case before he left.

Gayle looked up from her place at the counter. "I told you last night while you was weeping like a willow that Noah Lewis is the sort to know a good catch when he sees one. And in this case, he gets three for one."

Kizzie rolled her eyes and approached the counter. "You've already heard what folks are saying about George, Gayle. I don't want them thinking awful things about Noah too."

"Well, I suppose you're right." Gayle sniffed and turned to straighten a row of cans that were already perfectly straight. "You don't want to marry no weakling."

"Weakling?" Just the idea of Noah's strong arms around her or the way he stood up to his brother over and over again proved Gayle's statement completely false.

"Sure." She focused on another perfectly straight can. "If you think he's so weak to buckle 'neath the censure of folks whose opinions don't matter anyway, then I wouldn't want you to marry him either."

"Ooh!" Kizzie groaned and narrowed her eyes at the woman before turning away from the counter to open the letter.

My darling Kizzie,

Darling. He'd called her that yesterday. No one had ever called her something so sweet. Her smile pinched into her cheeks, and she felt Gayle's eyes on her, so she angled herself away from the woman a little more.

George is missing. I'm searching for him in all the places I think he might hide. Mother and I are both concerned for his welfare. I'm sure you've already heard by this time that Beatrice Malone called off their engagement, which means all of George's grand plans have not only come to naught but ruined him.

Mother and I travel to Mount Airy and a few other towns today in an attempt to find him, but Mother is afraid he may have taken a train out West to truly disappear. I hope she's right because I'd rather him disappear than harm himself. A man on the run has the hope of redemption, at least.

We've closed the mill for the next few days as Mother and I work through some particular details related to George's decisions. I'll explain as soon as I get back into town.

Before you entertain any thoughts to the contrary, I want to reiterate my intentions and thoughts from yesterday. The time and distance of the last hours have failed to temper my passion with logic, as I'm sure you feared. No, my darling, my logic and my passion are equally in unison with the fact that I love you and Charlie and would love for us to become a family.

The choice is yours, but my mind is set.

So, would you make me the happiest man and marry me, Kizzie McAdams?

Yours,

Noah

PS: Mother knows and agrees with my proposal, so if you are going to question my logic, you will have to question hers as well.

PPS: She's particularly enamored with the idea of spoiling grandchildren.

"See there?"

Kizzie swung around to find Gayle peering over her shoulder, a look of pure satisfaction on her face. "That boy's stuck on you." Her brows wiggled. "You'd better run from such weakness, is all I have to say."

"You ain't helping at all."

"I sure am." Gayle planted a fist on her hip. "I'm helping you use some sense." She waved a cloth in Kizzie's direction and returned to her place behind the counter. "We all got pasts, Kizzie. But we got futures too. Don't get so hung up on the past that you discount God's mighty good love in the future. Your heavenly daddy ain't prone to giving stingy gifts, so what I'd do if I was you, is just thank Him."

Kizzie reread the letter, her smile unfurling all over again. The sweetest warmth pierced through her doubt. Noah loved her. And he still wanted to be with her even though she carried another child that wasn't his?

Too wonderful.

She should look for it again in her Bible. Anything with the phrase "too wonderful" sounded like it ought to be worth rereading.

Kizzie had just come back from a brief lunch break when Molly rushed through the front door. Her bright gaze landed on Kizzie sorting through some of the hardware items, and she nearly vaulted forward, her eyes growing wider the nearer she came.

"Kizzie, is it true?"

The bell over the door rang to alert her of another customer, so she tugged Molly close to keep the girl's volume from disrupting the entire store. "Is what true?"

Molly's attention dropped to Kizzie's middle.

Already? George sure made his rounds, didn't he?

Kizzie released a long sigh and braced her hand against the nearest shelf.

The bell rang again, so Kizzie tugged Molly even farther away from the front. "What exactly did you hear?"

"It's all over town." Molly's whisper wasn't nearly as quiet as Kizzie wanted. "You and Mr. Noah are gonna have a baby."

The resurrection of her shame infused liquid heat into her cheeks.

"That's not true at all." Kizzie tried to keep her voice calm. She'd known the news would make quick fodder, but oh, how she'd hoped for a few more days to prepare herself for it. "This baby ain't betwixt me and Noah. I've been carrying this little one since leaving my old home and just found out yesterday about the fact I was with child at all."

"You mean, you've been carrying a little one all this time and didn't know?" Molly's entire face scrunched. "But you and Noah Lewis are sweet on each other. Hettie heard him declare himself yesterday when she was listening from the kitchen."

So much for privacy. "Be that as it may, Noah Lewis did nothing inappropriate. He's always been a complete gentleman to me."

"But the baby?"

"Has the same daddy as Charlie." Kizzie huffed at the girl's immaturity, her own frustration rising to the surface. "I got pregnant back before coming to The Hollows and before I ever came to know the Lord." Her throat tightened as the shame deepened from her face to her chest. "But I had no idea I was expecting at all, not until yesterday, because I thought I was just tired or adjusting to my new life."

"But if Mr. Lewis ain't your baby's daddy. . ." Molly tilted her head, trying to sort out the story. "Who is?"

"I am."

The voice pulled Kizzie through the past year of her life. A voice she'd once longed to hear speak such words of love and dedication Noah had delivered yesterday.

And in one rush, all the heat in her face drained away.

Molly looked over Kizzie's shoulder, her wide eyes blinking in quick succession.

"Kizzie?"

Kizzie pinched her eyes closed and swallowed.

She hadn't expected him to keep his promise.

To find her.

But Charles Morgan had said he'd come for her.

And he had.

A tremor in Kizzie's chest moved through her body.

"You can imagine my surprise when Cole came back home two days ago and told me he'd seen you." Charles stepped forward, gaze locked on hers. "Said you were set up nicely and even looked the part." His gaze trailed down her, so she folded her arms across her chest to still a little of her trembling. "I came to see for myself."

She drew in a shaky breath and stood up taller. "How have you been, Charles?"

"Better now, Kizzie." His lips crooked into a charming grin she knew all too well.

"I reckon the two of you may want to carry this conversation to a more private part of the store." Gayle stepped near enough to place her palm on Kizzie's arm. "The back porch might be a good spot." Gayle held her gaze, infusing some sort of strength into Kizzie's body. She wasn't alone. She wasn't destitute or desperate anymore.

Kizzie had choices, friends, confidence, and the Lord. "Yes, that'd be good."

"And if I hear anything ungentlemanly"—Gayle eyed Charles like the protective mother hen she was—"I'll be sure to investigate myself, but I warn you, boy." She pointed a finger at him. "I sell cast-iron skillets of all sizes."

Charles' brows rose, his eyes lit with humor, before he dipped his head in acceptance of the threat.

As Kizzie entered the hallway, she heard Gayle say, "And Molly, don't you go repeating nonsense. If you ain't got nothin' worth sayin', don't say nothin' at all."

The hint of levity dissipated as soon as Kizzie reached the back porch. She gestured toward a set of chairs, but Charles laughed.

"Why are you acting so formal, Kizzie?" He stepped forward as if to embrace her. "It's me."

"We ended things betwixt the two of us, Charles." Her palm rose to stop him. "When I left."

His gaze dropped to her middle. "Doesn't seem like anything's ended." He reached over, picked her up, and swung her around. "In fact, we got a whole new beginning growing inside of you."

"Not for you and me." With another push against him, he let go. "You're getting ready to be married."

Something he'd never offered her.

He studied her a moment and looked away while removing his hat. "I ain't engaged anymore."

"You ain't?" Something wasn't right. "That was an awful quick change from Cole's words two days ago to now."

Had he ended the engagement because he found Kizzie? Her breath paused. Because he wanted to marry her now, after all? And wouldn't that fix everything? Charlie would have his daddy, Noah his reputation, and Kizzie her happily ever after?

The thoughts crashed in her aching head.

But was it a happily ever after? Especially now when she understood loving and being loved so much better.

"When Lorraine heard Cole's news of finding you, she didn't take too kindly to the notion of me already having a child that wasn't hers."

How could she continue to be so naive? Charles hadn't broken the engagement for her. "So Lorraine called it off, did she?"

"Kizzie." He took her hands in his. "You know how Mama is. She gave an ultimatum, and I had to make a decision to keep her happy."

"To marry Lorraine?"

"She was Mama's choice for me, not mine." He squeezed her fingers, his smile returning. "We got along well enough, but you were the one who always had my heart."

Kizzie tried to pull her hands away, but he held fast. "So you'd marry a woman you didn't love while loving one you wouldn't marry? Or. . .is it love at all, Charles? Seems more like me and Charlie are things you own, more than people you love, especially when we're a second choice."

"You're turning this against me." He released his hold and ran a hand through his hair. "I came to find you so we could be together. As a family."

As a family?

"You mean to marry *me*, then?"

She read the answer on his face.

No.

Not marry her.

Good enough to bed, but not wed, as George had said about her.

And she saw Charles then. Even better than she had four months ago.

Perhaps a gentler type of George, but the same internal drive. Pleasing himself without counting the cost to others. Weak in character and morals.

Unsteady in self-control.

Driven by passion and pleasure.

But not love.

Not the hard, selfless, pain-bearing and joy-giving love she'd come to understand by living in the community of The Hollows and in the friendship of Noah Lewis.

"I can't marry you. Not yet." He released a long sigh. "But I'll not expect anything. . .intimate until we *can* wed." Though his gaze sent the opposite message as it trailed down her again, as if cotton and lace didn't stand up against what he knew lay beneath. "How about that?"

Poor man. He had no idea what love really was.

"Your mama wanted to scare me off by having men shoot guns at a house where me and your baby stayed. That ain't no way to raise young'uns, Charles. Living under your mama's wrath? Worried that when the next time she gets mad she'll choose better gunmen? Acting like we're married when we're not."

"I've given Mama an ultimatum too." He leaned forward, pressing his finger into his chest. "If she targets you again, then I'll run away with you and she won't see me again."

"You'd give up your inheritance for me?" That couldn't be true. "Seems that's the whole reason we can't marry in the first place."

"We'd never get to the point of actually having to run away." He looked away and shrugged a shoulder. "She doesn't really *want* me to go." He regained her hands. "Can't you see? I want you with me. In my life. I need those children to know their daddy." He softened the edge in his voice, the gentle Charles rising to the surface. Pleading. "I'll do about anything to get you to come home. You belong to me."

"*About* anything. About? Except marry me and give your children a name?" Her voice rose, the utter selfishness of his declarations driving out any fear his presence brought. "Except stand up to your mama to legitimize the family *you* chose to start but aren't brave enough to claim?"

"That ain't fair," he growled, stepping back. "If I lose my inheritance, then I won't be able to take care of you at all."

Then clarity struck and hit her like a knife to the chest. How had she been so stupid? "Charles, your mama would never disinherit you, would she?" Her eyes wilted closed, a deep sorrow growing through her chest. "You're her only child. Her pride and joy."

"I wouldn't put it past—"

"And the two of you play this game of back-and-forth to manipulate people and situations for your own benefit." Kizzie ran a hand down her face, the truth blooming clearer. His mama had mentioned him being with girls before Kizzie. Were there other children too? Other women he dangled along with unkept promises?

"That ain't true, Kizzie." He moved toward her. "I care about you. I've always cared about you. I just have to make sure Mama—"

"Let's walk out together right now, Charles." She waved back in the direction of the store. "Let's you and me walk down Main Street, and I'll introduce you to some of the shop owners round here and tell them you're the daddy of my child. It'll clear a good man's name, and you can prove your boast." Kizzie started walking toward the front of the store. "Let's make that right at least."

"Now, Kizzie." Charles grabbed her arm and turned her around.

"There ain't no cause to do that." His cheeks darkened. "I still got some business in this town, and I don't want to get things off to a rough start."

And the answer came clear as day. He'd never meant to marry her. Not from the start. Not ever. And even if Noah came to his senses today and decided not to marry her, Kizzie knew she wanted more than the scraps of a selfish man's affections.

Better that she have no man at all.

"You know what?" She looked up at him, the small part of her heart still connected to him aching a little. "I believe you do care about me in your own way, Charles. I believe that if your mama made things a little easier and I wasn't such a poor mountain girl, you'd actually consider marrying me."

"Kizzie—"

"But that's all I'd ever be. A consideration. A last resort. And I won't be that for you or anyone else."

"You're not—"

"And these children don't deserve to be a last resort either." She stood taller, closing in, confidence steeping her words. "They deserve a man who won't be ashamed to call them his."

"Now, Kizzie—"

"And part of it ain't your fault." She laughed, a sudden lightness pushing through the pain. "You couldn't have known that by leaving you, I'd learn what real love looks like. That I'd discover the pure joy of having someone put me and my son first, to choose us over everything else, even his own reputation. That I'd meet a gentle man who listened and supported my ideas and even found ways to spend time with me and Charlie just because he wanted to. You couldn't know it would change me. That I would learn—" Tears tightened her throat. "That I would believe I'm worth a love like that."

He searched her face, his jaw clenching and unclenching. "I could love you like that, if you'd just give me the chance."

"You had the chance," she whispered.

"You just wait, Kizzie." He leaned close, eyes narrowed. "Whatever you think you have with this *gentleman* won't last. He'll change his mind. When the rumors come and the nasty looks happen, he'll feel the sting.

It may not start out that way, but over time, the truth that these children aren't his, that you really belong to someone else, will beat away at whatever you think he feels for you. That's how it works in the real world. Good men don't give up their reputations for another man's used goods."

All pretense fled. Despite his grand declarations, he finally disclosed the truth of his real thoughts about her. Used goods.

Another label to add to the list of names others called her.

She smiled. But she knew better names too. Ones to eclipse the others.

Beloved. God's. Redeemed. Whole.

Darling.

"It doesn't matter, Charles." Even though Noah could change his mind any second, Kizzie knew now that she wasn't what Charles or George or anyone else called her. She belonged to God, and she wasn't used goods or unlovely to Him.

She was His beloved child.

"I'm not going to go with you. I'd rather live on my own than live in the shameful and belittled place of a woman others consider not worthy of respect, love, or marriage. I'm not changing my good world right now for a future without those."

"But—" Charles drew back as if she'd hit him. "You belong to me. The children are mine, and so are you."

Fear wavered a second in her heart, but she shoved it away. "No, I'm not. I belong to God, and because I know that now, I can choose His path for me. Not yours."

He nearly singed her with his glare. "You'll change your mind." He laughed, a humorless sound as he backed toward the doorway. "When you get knocked off of your high horse and you really need someone, you'll come back to me, and then you'll take whatever I've got to give you." He raised his finger, drilling it into the air. "And I'll do what's right for my children. I'll take care of them despite their mama's ways. You'll get tired of living your life alone, and then *you'll* find *me*."

Chapter 26

Kizzie swept the store floor as the workday came to an end. She'd set Charlie up in a little box nearby, where he played with a set of wooden animals Gayle bought for him, his happy little noises mixing in with the sounds of people passing on the street on their way home from work or shopping.

She'd spent the afternoon and evening of the day before going over her meeting with Charles, and with each recollection, her heart freed a little more from the guilt hovering over his arrival.

Even if Noah returned and had changed his mind about a future with her, her conscience and heart were clear. She knew how to respond to the question "Who are you?" And the answer truly was too wonderful.

Within the folds of her mama's Bible, God kept repeating the truth over and over.

She belonged to Him.

He had called her by name. She was His.

And as she'd read Psalm 139, the words poured over her healing heart.

Thou hast searched me, and known me. . .and art acquainted with all my ways.

Which meant God had known about her baby when He'd given her forgiveness and helped her start over in The Hollows. He'd known Charles would come and offer her an escape from reliving her shame in her new world. And God had known she'd fall in love with Noah.

And by showing her what love truly looked like in so many forms,

He'd taught her about herself.

Thou hast beset me behind and before, and laid thine hand upon me. Such knowledge is too wonderful for me.

God was all around her. Knew her through and through, and still loved her. A tingle started at the bridge of her nose. He loved her anyway.

And deep inside, she knew Noah did too. That he was an example of how human love could look on this earth. In God's best way, where two hearts blended together to beat as one. Patient. Kind. Selfless.

It truly was "too wonderful" for her.

Kizzie basked in the newfound security as she continued to sweep. Gayle's pastime of listening to the radio at the end of the day filled the room with a collection of music different from what Kizzie had heard back in the mountains. And she liked it. Her mama would have liked it too. Sweet and fun, most telling stories like the ballads back home. As Kizzie finished up the sweeping, the familiar melody of "Till We Meet Again" filled the room. Charlie cooed to the tune, so Kizzie put the broom aside and swept her little boy up into her arms, dancing with him around the barrels of flour and beside the shelves of Campbell's soups.

" 'When the clouds roll by I'll come to you.' " She sang to the music as Charlie offered a wide double-dimpled grin. The tiniest tooth peeked through his bottom gum. " 'Then the skies will seem more blue. Down in lovers' lane, my dearie, wedding bells will ring so merrily.' "

The doorbell jingled, and she turned toward the sound as the male voice sang the next line.

Ev'ry tear will be a memory.

Noah stepped over the threshold, his smile spreading from one dimpled corner to the other.

So wait and pray each night for me.

Till we meet again.

Noah moved into Kizzie's little dance with Charlie, encompassing them in his arms. She sighed out all her worries about whether he'd still want her when he returned, and her entire body relaxed into him. His warm scent traveled through her, and she pressed closer, burying her face into the soft skin of his neck. She belonged right there in his arms, grounded by his strength and love.

His.

"Hello, my darling," he whispered against her hair.

Heated tears stole her words. The moment, the love, too wonderful to describe.

It took the rest of the song for her to gather enough composure to find her voice. She looked up at him, and he tilted his head, examining her face before he gently brushed a tear from her cheek. "How are you this evening?"

"Better now that you're here."

"I do like the sound of that." His palm paused on her cheek, and he raised a brow. "I'm feeling better now that I'm here too."

She pressed her cheek into his palm and sighed. "Did you find George?"

"No." His smile fell. "Last anyone saw him, he was boarding a westbound train."

"I'm sorry, Noah."

He gave his head a shake and shrugged. "There's nothing else to be done at this point but to let him go and pray he finds his way back someday."

Charlie reached out for Noah, and without hesitation Noah took the little boy into his arms. They made a pretty pair, all four dimples on full display.

She'd never seen a sweeter sight. That was what home looked like right in front of her. "What happens next?"

His gaze caressed her face. "Well, first off." He leaned down and kissed her soundly on the mouth right in the middle of the shop.

She grinned against his lips as he pulled back.

"And secondly, Mother and I have worked out a plan to make things right. It will mean selling the mill and some of the land, but in the end, we'll have enough to keep a piece of the property and my inheritance. While we were in Mount Airy, we made connections with a much wealthier company who is interested in purchasing the mill, so that means the workers can keep their jobs and get a raise in the process."

She slipped a palm up his arm. "Bittersweet, then?"

"But right." He nodded as Charlie reached for his chin. "And much better than what Mother and I thought might happen." He grinned down at her, his hazel eyes alight. "What do you say I take you and Charlie to the house for dinner and explain everything?"

"I'd love that." She stepped out of his arms, preparing herself to share her own news. "I have a few things to tell you too, one of which is Gayle's desire to sell the store to me."

"What?" He laughed out the word.

"Her daughter's asked her to move closer to be near them when her next baby comes, and because of all I've done with the shop and how well the girls are doing, Gayle asked if I'd be interested in purchasing it."

"Kizzie, that's marvelous." Noah slipped his hand around her waist and pulled her into a hug.

"Well, I didn't give her an answer, because I wanted to talk to you first. See if it fit. . ." She hesitated and caught his gaze. "Our plans?"

"Definitely sounds like an excellent discussion to have over dinner." He scanned the shop with a growing grin. "And I'll be free from the mill to try my hand at shopkeeping."

"Maybe even expanding the boardinghouse into a hotel?"

His brows shot north. "I think we've got conversations for dinner fully covered through dessert and maybe breakfast tomorrow morning."

"Besides Gayle giving me such a good deal on the shop, I have some money saved too." Kizzie laughed and rocked on tiptoe to kiss his lips. "With more on the way."

"Do you?"

"It ain't a great lot, but enough to start, especially if you wanted to go in with me to help." She nodded. "I invested in some friends' new gristmill back where I used to live. They bought some land from me and plan to pay for the rest as they grow their business."

His thumb slid over her cheek. "You're just full of surprises, aren't you?"

"I don't know about that, but I'll tell you what my heart is filled with right now." She slipped close again, and his arm linked about her waist, pulling her against him with Charlie happily squished in the middle. Well, Charlie and the next little family member. "Love for you, Noah Lewis."

His laugh filled the room until his lips met hers again, sweet, strong, and promising more than her dreams ever imagined.

Being here, with him, fit together perfectly. This shop, their little family.

This was home.

Exactly where she belonged.

Epilogue

March 1920

"I SHOULD BE BACK BY tomorrow night." Noah zipped his duffel bag closed and turned toward the foyer of the house his growing family called home. Complete with a very happy grandmother to coddle the children to her heart's content.

"I packed you a sandwich for the train." Kizzie stepped forward with Charlie hopping behind, his grin wide and as welcoming as ever.

"And a slice of cake," Mother added, following with a wide-eyed baby Julia in her arms.

Well, she wasn't as much of a baby anymore. Over a year now. And she wouldn't be the baby of the family come summer. His gaze dropped to Kizzie's middle, where the next addition grew. His smile spread with the gratitude in his chest. *His family.*

"I can eat at a restaurant if I need something, ladies." He chuckled, dropping the bag at his feet as they approached.

"Daddy's going!" Charlie hopped close enough for Noah to sweep him up in his arms. The little boy's giggles never grew old. Neither did the word *daddy*.

"Only for *two days*." He emphasized the words as he met his wife's gaze. "And Molly has already agreed to help out some more at the store, so you can be free to check on the hotel construction."

Kizzie set the lunch bag on top of his duffel and sent him a saucy look. "Are you afraid I can't handle everything without you, Noah Lewis?"

He captured her around the waist and pulled her close. "I'm certain you can, but I just don't want you getting used to it."

She pressed a kiss to his lips. "I don't plan on it."

At her clear display of affection, Charlie planted his own kiss directly on Noah's mouth too.

"A man who's loved so well will always make short trips." Mother stepped forward to give Noah access to his little girl.

She boasted the same dark hair and large blue eyes as her mother, and her smile proved every bit as active as her big brother's.

"And don't forget, next week your sister and her husband are coming for a visit, so you can't stay gone too long anyway."

As if he'd ever want to.

He grinned at his mother, living in her element. Surrounded by family. Clarice had seen the news about George in the papers and come home to be with her mother, reconnecting their families in a way they'd only hoped might happen.

They still hadn't heard anything from George, but an anonymous envelope of cash arrived several months after he left with the initials G.L. signed on the paper wrapping it, so at least he was alive.

And trying to make amends in his own way.

Julia's little hands reached out to him, and unable to resist the pull of his little girl, Noah swept her into his other arm.

Arms full. That was how his heart felt too.

Julia joined the sweet farewells by offering a sloppy kiss to his other cheek.

"Gracious sakes, you're gonna have enough sugar to last you a whole week." Kizzie tugged Charlie free and placed him back on the ground, but the little boy only ended up grabbing Noah's leg.

"I can't imagine having enough kisses to keep me away that long, my dear Mrs. Lewis."

"I going too, Daddy." Charlie looked up.

"Not this time, little man." Noah ruffled the little boy's head.

"Me go." Julia added.

"Look at all this fuss you're causing, Noah Lewis." Kizzie shot him a wink. "If you're gonna catch your train, you need to be off." She took

Julia from him, but not before he'd placed a kiss on his daughter's head and another, slightly longer one, on his wife's lips.

Oh, how he loved her!

"Right." He took the sandwich bag in one hand and tossed the duffel over his shoulder.

Charlie and Julia followed behind as Kizzie walked Noah to the carriage, with Marty at the helm to drive him to The Hollows train depot.

"Two days," he said, more for himself than her. He'd not been apart from them since the day she'd agreed to marry him while they danced in the storefront of Carters Mercantile, now Lewis Mercantile. And though they'd had their own bits of adjusting to do as newlyweds and an instant family, he knew he wouldn't have changed a thing about his choice. The woman loved with such open and generous affection, he couldn't imagine ever receiving anything better on this earth. "If Mr. Laws is serious about selling his store's inventory to us at low cost, it will be a worthwhile trip all around."

"Then the faster you set off, the quicker you'll get back."

He pulled her to him for one last embrace as the children hugged his legs, and then he joined Marty on the wagon seat.

If his plan worked out as he hoped, perhaps he'd come home with much more than just new inventory for the store.

The meeting with Mr. Laws went well, and they made arrangements to have the inventory shipped to Lewis Mercantile within the next few weeks. Noah paid the first half for the inventory with plans to pay the other half upon delivery. The entire business deal was finished by supper, as Noah had hoped, so he took the last train west to a small town at the edge of the mountains called Flat Creek.

Once Noah took supper in the hotel's restaurant downstairs, he climbed the stairs and readied for bed. All he knew about Kizzie's family was a list of names, descriptions, some of Kizzie's memories, and the knowledge that her father had cast her out two and a half years ago.

Otherwise, he had no idea what the journey looked like, how her family would receive him, or if he could even find the McAdams' home.

But he had to try. For Kizzie.

If nothing else, to know they were alive.

First thing the next morning, with directions from the hotel owner, Noah hired a horse and took a well-worn path up the mountainside. Early spring buds sprinkled the evergreen forest with hints of color and mingled blooms with the scents of pine. Birdsong greeted him through the cool morning air as he climbed higher up the mountainside, the natural wonders attempting to loosen the tension in his body. As if to completely shock his nervousness away, the trees on his left gave way to reveal an endless horizon of blue mountains upon blue mountains, swathed in morning fog and sunlight.

He'd never seen the world so vast and beautiful.

Their busy home inside a crowded town must have been such an adjustment for her, but he'd never have known it. She hummed and smiled and radiated joy in it all.

Even when she'd been used to. . .this.

He brought the horse to a stop and gazed out over the waiting world, wondering how far he could see from this lofty height. How he wished he'd brought a camera to capture the view for her, but the grandeur wouldn't transfer in black and white.

But why was he surprised at his wife's personality? Whatever strength God forged inside Kizzie through her past and hurts, He'd bloomed into an impenetrable joy she poured into those she loved, and he was a happy benefactor.

Joy, love, laughter, wit, and the constant supply of Kizzie's daily cookies.

"To make the day sweeter," she always said.

He sent God a grateful prayer over the blue-hued vista before continuing his trek.

The trail continued, rising higher, until he came to a flat area consisting of a collection of various buildings. A white two-story building offered a sign which read STORE, and another nearby rock structure looked like a blacksmith's shop. A little way through the trees, a white building—perhaps a school—stood on a hillside with a small house poised near the bottom of the hill.

Where to go next?

After a moment's pause, he approached the store and dismounted. A bell jingled his entrance, and a young girl stepped behind the counter from a back room of the shop. The room was about a third of the size of his and Kizzie's store, with, of course, much less inventory, but canned goods, some hardware, and a few reams of cloth were all featured in various places throughout the room.

"Can I help you, stranger?"

His attention traveled back to the girl. Something in her eyes looked familiar. Not the color of Kizzie's, but the same shape, and her hair was slightly lighter than his wife's.

"Good morning." He stepped closer, watching expressions he knew so well travel over a new face. "I'm looking for the family of Sam McAdams."

The girl's gaze sharpened on him, and a wariness tightened her young features. How old was she? Sixteen? And which sister? Maggie?

"Why are you looking for Sam McAdams' family?"

"My name is Noah Lewis." He drew another step closer and offered his hand. "I'm married to Kizzie."

The girl's body froze, and then as the information sank in, her eyes widened. She braced her hands against the counter and continued to stare until her bottom lip trembled. "You're. . .you're Kizzie's husband?"

"I am."

She blinked a few times, her eyes growing glossy. "She's. . .she's alive?"

"She is." He nodded. "And the mother of two."

A sound like a cross between a laugh and a sob erupted from the girl's lips, and she attempted to catch it.

"She doesn't know I'm here because I didn't want to disappoint her if, well, if your family wasn't willing to see her, but I thought I had to at least try. So I'd like to talk to your—"

"I can't leave, since Mrs. Cappy's gone," came her quick response, those dark brown eyes still wide. "But Daddy's helping Jeb with repairing his barn after a tree fell on it. Laurel and Jon's there too. It ain't but a little over a mile up the mountain." Her bottom lip trembled again. "We didn't know nothin' about her. If she was alive or not."

He sighed, the tension he'd been carrying about some confrontation dimming a little. "She's happy. I'm certainly happy to have her in my life."

The girl's smile burst wide. "That's real good news, Mr. Lewis."

"Noah, please." He offered his hand. "And you are. . .Maggie?"

She sniffled and nodded, wiping her hand on her apron before taking his. "That's me." She gave her head another shake. "Oh, how I wish I could see Mama's face when you tell her. To know her lost girl is found and fine. That'll do her heart a heap of good."

Maggie's response hit him.

Several times, as she'd cried over the loss of her family in their private moments, he'd held Kizzie in his arms and attempted to work through a way to help her heal. At times, her father's actions sent him to his knees to help curb the fury. All the while, he'd created some sort of scenario about her family and her life that, perhaps, his hurt for her had misconstrued a little.

If Maggie's reaction gave any indication of the longing of most of the family, if her words about their mother proved an inkling of the desire for restoration, then perhaps they'd been aching as much for a different end to the story as Kizzie.

Maybe not her father, but the rest of the family.

He swallowed through the rising emotions in his throat, his chest tightening with a fight against those emotions.

Perhaps he should have come sooner.

But he'd only begun nursing the idea a month ago and had waited until he had an excuse to go overnight from Kizzie and the children, so that if the trip proved unsuccessful. . .or worse, she'd never know.

She wouldn't get hurt all over again.

After asking Maggie to repeat the directions one more time, Noah mounted his horse and followed the path past the church and beyond a rock house Maggie labeled as Jon and Laurel's place. The briskness of the morning softened with the warmth of the sun finally breaking through the trees as he continued his ascent. No wonder his wife held an otherworldliness about her sometimes. This place carried a strange sort of old and distant feel to it.

The rhythmic sound of a hammer striking wood reached him first. A woman's light voice echoed over the breeze saying something about. . .sun tea? The trees parted to reveal a large clearing with a beautiful two-story white house to the right, a covered porch lining the front, and a sprinkling of outbuildings across a field, all encompassed by a fence. Well organized. Tidy. With a mountain climbing up behind it on one side and a view over the trees with a small glimpse of sky on the other.

Barking pulled his attention toward the barn where three dogs charged at him and his horse. He slowed his approach, keeping a firm hold on the horse's reins. A little girl with golden curls stood on the porch, her calico dress blowing in the breeze. A pair of little boys, clearly twins, sat near her with a ball passing between them. Suzie and the twins?

"Down," came a firm voice from the barn.

The dogs immediately stopped in their tracks but kept their eyes on Noah, as if weighing whether he came as a friend or foe.

Up ahead a young man in overalls and rolled-up shirtsleeves walked forward, a broader and older man a few paces behind. Still farther behind followed another young man, light hair and more refined features, whose crisp clothes gave off more town than mountain.

The young man in overalls came to the fence line first, keeping his distance, and sent a look up and down Noah before offering a curt nod. "Can I help you?"

With a deep breath and another prayer, Noah dismounted and glanced back toward the house. The little assembly on the porch had been joined by a young woman with wild curly hair holding a baby and a blond woman, about the same age, wiping her hands on her apron.

Noah named them all as best he could guess. Jeb, the young man in overalls, and Mr. McAdams, the elder. He had no idea about the refined man or the curly-haired woman, but the family resemblance in the golden-haired woman likely meant she was Laurel.

Noah approached the fence and offered a smile.

"Good afternoon. I'm looking for the McAdams family of Maple Springs."

"You found 'em." The younger man dipped his head. "I'm Jeb McAdams." He gestured back with his chin as the older man approached. "This here is my daddy, Sam. And following up behind him is my brother-in-law, Jonathan Taylor."

"A pleasure to meet you all." Noah offered his hand and swallowed through his tightening throat. "My name is Noah Lewis. I'm—I'm married to Kizzie."

Both Jeb and Sam froze in place, from their expressions all the way down to their feet, much like Maggie had done. No one moved, except Mr. Taylor, who joined them at the fence, his smile wide and hand outstretched. "Jonathan Taylor."

Noah pulled his attention away from the other two men to take Mr. Taylor's hand. His accent sounded English. What on earth was an Englishman doing back in these mountains? "Noah Lewis."

"You're. . .Kizzie's husband," Jeb repeated, his gaze boring into Noah's.

"Yes, we've been married almost two years." His attention shifted from Jeb to Mr. McAdams. "Kizzie doesn't know I've come, because I wasn't certain of the welcome, so I didn't want to get her hopes—"

"Kizzie's alive?" The question burst out of Mr. McAdams' throat on rasped air. "She's all right?"

Noah had stiffened at the man's explosive response and then released a nervous laugh as his positive response made its way into Noah's comprehension. "She's wonderful." The answer emerged before he could catch it. "I mean, except that she misses her family, and. . .I thought if I could see. . .if perhaps you'd be willing to see her—"

"Mama!" Mr. McAdams turned his face toward the house, his voice carrying over everything else. "Laurel, git your mama. Git her quick." The older man rounded the fence and in two steps grabbed Noah in a hug.

The strength in those arms held Noah fast. His throat closed for a whole different reason.

For Kizzie.

When Mr. McAdams released Noah from his hold, the man's pale, red-rimmed eyes held a glossy sheen. "You're tellin' me true, boy? You know where my girl is?"

"Yes, sir." The heat in Noah's chest rose into his face, burning his eyes. "We have two strong and healthy children."

The man shook Noah by the shoulders and released a big laugh. "Two more grandyoung'uns." He turned back toward the house where an older woman, about his mother's age, came forward in a simple dress and apron. Her golden hair, seasoned with small hints of gray, was twisted tight against her head in a bun with a few locks falling free around her face.

There was no mistaking the resemblance. The fine features and high cheekbones. The eyes.

Other younger women and the children he'd seen on the porch followed behind her, all looking from Noah to Mr. McAdams as if somebody was going mad.

"Caroline." Mr. McAdams laughed again. "This boy, he's married to our Kizzie. She's alive."

Mrs. McAdams paused in her steps, and the color drained from her face as she stared first at Mr. McAdams and then focused on Noah, as if the words took some time to make it to understanding. She stumbled a step forward.

"Did he just say Kizzie is married?" This from the woman he presumed was Laurel. She released a laugh of her own and burst forward, taking her father's place to hug Noah. "And you're her husband?"

"Y–yes. Happily so."

Her eyes lit with her grin, and she squeezed his shoulders. "Well, I'm your sister-in-law, Laurel Taylor, and I'm pleased as punch to meet you, Noah Lewis."

Taylor? Noah's attention flipped from Jonathan back to Mrs. McAdams, who'd moved closer to him, her watery indigo eyes searching his face. So Jonathan was married to Kizzie's older sister.

Then, as if Mrs. McAdams finally believed him, her smile bloomed, and she dipped her head. "I reckon you're tired and hungry from your travelin', Noah. Why don't you come on into Jeb's house and we'll have you rest up a little."

"And you can tell us about our Kizzie," Mr. McAdams added, patting Noah on the back. "And to family, I'm Sam."

"It's a pleasure to meet you all." Noah's face stretched with his grin, and he nodded toward the man, continuing to fight his own emotions for control. "A real pleasure, Sam. A real pleasure."

Kizzie finished cleaning up the front of the store as Charlie taught Julia how to place cans on a little shelf she'd assigned to him. And then, with

Julia's help, he removed the cans and replaced them, over and over again, each time giving Julia different directions.

He called it his "work," and Kizzie chuckled at his delight in finding all sorts of things to put on the shelf along with the cans. A ball. One of his wooden animals. Julia's shoe. A dust bunny.

Her life bloomed with joys of the measureless sort, and the fact that Noah was returning home today just made the day a little brighter. She shouldn't feel so attached to her darling husband, she supposed, but it was the first time they'd been apart since marrying, and she loved him something fierce.

Crazy fierce.

Real love flowed from him every day. Toward her and the children. To others around them as they ran the little store together. Even to the ladies in the boardinghouse, who they were training to employ in the hotel they were building on Noah's inherited property right outside of town.

Noah offered an example to them of how a good man treated women, because most of them were a lot like Kizzie used to be.

Not knowing what real love looked like.

And that knowledge changed everything.

She'd just sent Molly to the back of the shop to restock the fabric section when the doorbell jingled. Kizzie turned to welcome the shopper and halted.

Every bit of heat drained from her body right out the bottom of her boots.

Standing in the doorway in their Sunday best stood her mama...and Daddy. She shook her head, trying to clear her vision, but each time she blinked, there they stood, staring at her like she was at them.

"Mama?" The word scratched from her and broke the frozen moment.

Mama rushed forward, arms wide, and wrapped Kizzie and baby Julia in her arms. The peppermint scent of her mama smelled real. Her arms felt real. But...how?

Kizzie pulled back and looked at her mama's face, waiting for it to disappear. "How?"

Mama laughed, her familiar eyes swimming with unshed tears. "Your man, Noah, he came to find us."

"Noah?" Kizzie glanced toward the door where her daddy still stood, his big shoulders bent a little and his eyes red-rimmed, but not from alcohol.

No.

From tears.

She laughed out a sob. "Daddy?"

His smile wobbled wide, and in three steps he held her in his arms along with her mama. The scent of pipe and honeysuckle and woodstove mingled together with a rush of home and memories, and she pressed into her daddy's massive shoulder, her body shaking with her sobs.

How could this be?

The doorbell jingled again, and she wanted to yell to the patron to come back in an hour, but when she raised her gaze to the door, a whole new set of familiar, teary-eyed, smiling faces greeted her.

Jeb stood beside a curly-haired woman, and he was holding a baby girl in his arms. Laurel pushed forward, holding the hand of a blond-haired stranger dressed so nice he even boasted a bow tie. Maggie waited beside Laurel, her shoulders shaking from crying, and Isom stared wide-eyed around the store. Even little Suzie, who wasn't a baby anymore, stood holding the curly-haired woman's hand on one side and a little twin, James or Jon, on the other.

Her family.

The bell rang again, and this time, her husband entered, hatless. His hair waved in all directions, he had a little dirt smudge on his cheek, and he was easily the handsomest man Kizzie had ever laid eyes on.

His gaze found hers among the suddenly crowded store, and he grinned.

No, *now* her family was all here.

"I'm sorry, girl." Her daddy's rough whisper caressed her ear. "I'm so sorry."

And the crying and hugging started all over again, then the introductions of new faces. Like Laurel's husband, Jonathan. And Jeb's wife, Cora. Then Jeb and Cora's baby girl, Faith.

"How long can you stay?" Kizzie finally asked, as Noah made his way to her side, his smile as big as all the others.

"We reckoned a few days so we could get a good look at your store," Daddy answered, his chin still wobbling a bit.

"And your young'uns," Mama added, wiping at her eyes.

"And Noah mentioned y'all were building a hotel." This from Jeb.

"He also mentioned we'd have a place to stay for free." Laurel tossed out the sentence, brows high in humored anticipation.

"Did he?" Kizzie looked over at her husband, tears still streaming down her cheeks.

Noah slipped an arm around her waist. "I made sure the boarding-house had a few vacancies for the next week."

Kizzie laughed and leaned into him, resting her head against his shoulder before staring back at faces she thought she'd never see again.

"You have a place to stay for as long as you want." She chuckled through another sob.

Noah pressed a kiss to her head before releasing her to introduce Charlie and Julia to her family.

Too wonderful?

Yes, but she was beginning to understand more and more every day that she was loved by a God who celebrated the wonderful and good and hopeful.

And His love bloomed in the most unlikely places. . .and made them beautiful.

Author Note

This book was difficult to write.

I think when you take the skeleton of a family history story and try to give it fictional flesh and bones, while still hoping to remain true to the original heart of the story, it's easy to feel overwhelmed and underqualified. That's certainly been true while writing this book.

My Granny Spencer told me this story from the time I was a little girl—the amazing redemption of my great, great, great granny Kizzie. The fictionalized version is different than the true story because I only know pieces of the true story and, when writing a novel, you're working within a certain book timeline.

So, what was true? Or at least from family history true?

Kizzie left her mountain family when she was 15 years old and went to work in a rich landowner's house. The landowner had recently died, and his widow and only son managed the property for crops and tenants. The son's name was Charles. Not long after Kizzie started working there, she caught Charles's eye. They began a relationship, and she became pregnant. (From what my great aunt said, Charles was considerably older than Kizzie.) Encouraged to return home, she went back to her family only to have her father cast her out. (Granny said that Kizzie's last memory was looking back at the house where her family stood on the porch and seeing her mama crying.) With nowhere else to go, Kizzie returned to Charles, but Charles told her he couldn't marry her or he'd lose his inheritance. (His mother, purportedly, did the same thing as Mrs. Morgan does in the book, threatens Charles's livelihood if he married Kizzie). So Charles builds Kizzie a house on his land so that he can keep her and the baby near. Kizzie's first child was a boy whom she named Charlie, after his daddy. The following year, she had a daughter, and the next year another son. It was at some point after the third child that Kizzie became a Christian and left Charles to move to Mount Airy, North Carolina. (Based on the end of this story, it's pretty evident Charles didn't want her to leave.) While in Mount Airy, Kizzie started working in a mill and kept the children with her while she worked. The owner or overseer of the mill (we're not sure which) noticed Kizzie's faithful work and joyful spirit and pursued her. From what I understand, Kizzie wasn't looking for romance (or didn't imagine a man wanting her), but Lewis (Noah's real name) continued his pursuit and won her heart. They married and he raised the children as his own. Lewis and Kizzie left the mill and opened a mercantile together in Mount Airy.

Sadly, I have no knowledge that Kizzie ever saw her parents and siblings again.

Now, here's the crazy part (as if it's not crazy already): Several years later, when one of Kizzie's boys (we think Charlie) was involved in a knife fight in Mount Airy, Charlie killed his assailant and was charged with murder. News about the trial made it all over the place and court costs mounted. During the trial, Kizzie showed up at the courthouse to find all the court costs had been paid and. . .Charles had found her. He'd seen Charlie's name in the papers (Charlie still carried his mama's maiden name) and came to find Kizzie and the children. His mother had finally died, and he'd inherited a large amount of money and property. Here's how my Granny told it.

Charles: Are you married?

Kizzie: I am.

Charles: Is he good to you?

Kizzie: He is. Real good to me and the children.

Charles: I'm glad. (Clearly not super happy about her being taken, I'm guessing)

Charles: I am a rich man and I've never married. Your children are the only children I have. When I die, I'd like to leave all that is mine to them.

Kizzie (likely pausing to think): I can't let you do that, Charles. You weren't willing to sacrifice to be their daddy when they needed you most, and I ain't gonna shame their daddy now by taking your money.

Charles left and within the next few weeks two stories emerged about two different men. Charlie (Kizzie's son) was found not guilty due to self-defense. Charles (the father) was found hanged in his own barn and all his money went to the state. (The end always takes my breath a little bit!)

But I don't want to end there. Let me finish Kizzie's story with something sweet.

When I asked my Granny if she remembered anything about her great Granny Kizzie, Granny answered:

"Well, here's what I remember and what was most known about her. She always had cookies ready for us young'uns to eat. She kept a messy house. And she was filled with joy."

Life is hard. Sometimes our sin leads us to break our own hearts and sometimes the sin of others breaks it. And sometimes, it's just the hardships of life and loss.

But God. . .

His love wraps us in a hold that doesn't let go and never will. He calls us by name. We are his.

When you know whose you are, what He calls you, it changes everything.

"But now thus says the LORD,
he who created you, O Jacob,
   he who formed you, O Israel:
"Fear not, for I have redeemed you;
   I have called you by name, you are mine.
2 When you pass through the waters, I will be with you;
   and through the rivers, they shall not overwhelm you;
when you walk through fire you shall not be burned,
   and the flame shall not consume you.
3 For I am the LORD your God,
   the Holy One of Israel, your Savior.
I give Egypt as your ransom,
   Cush and Seba in exchange for you.
4 Because you are precious in my eyes,
   and honored, and I love you."
Isaiah 43: 1-4a (ESV)

Pepper Basham is an award-winning author who writes romance peppered with grace and humor. She is a native of the Blue Ridge Mountains where her family have lived for generations. She's the mom of five kids, speech-language pathologist to about fifty more, lover of chocolate, jazz, and Jesus, and proud AlleyCat over at the award-winning Writer's Alley blog. Her debut historical romance novel, *The Thorn Bearer*, released in April 2015, and the second in February 2016. Her first contemporary romance debuted in April 2016.

You can connect with Pepper on her website at www.pepperdbasham.com, Facebook at https://www.facebook.com/pepperbasham, or Twitter at https://twitter.com/pepperbasham.

OTHER APPALACHIA BOOKS
BY PEPPER BASHAM

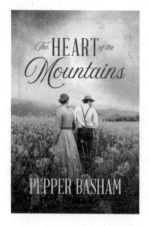

The Heart of the Mountains

To escape marriage, Cora Taylor runs away from her home in England to join her brother in the Blue Ridge Mountains of North Carolina, but not even her time as a nurse in the Great War prepares her for the hard landscape and even harder lives of the mountain people. With the help of Jeb McAdams, a quiet woodcarver, who carries his own battle scars, she fashions a place for herself among these unique people. But the past refuses to let go, and with dangers from within and without, can hearts bruised by war find healing within the wilds of the mountains?

Paperback / 978-1-63609-325-3

The Red Ribbon

Ava Burcham tends to court trouble, but when her curiosity leads her into a feud between an Appalachian clan and the local authorities, her amateur sleuthing propels her into a world of criminal cover-ups, political rivalries, and a battle of wills. The end result? The Hillsville Courthouse Massacre of 1912.

Paperback / 978-1-64352-649-2